DRAMATIC
STORIES T[...]
THE HEART[...]

"THE ABORTION" by Alice Walker, about the choices and unpredictable consequences of pregnancy

"ACCOMPLISHED DESIRES" by Joyce Carol Oates, about an academic couple . . . and the coed who chillingly becomes the "other woman"

"VERMONT" by Ann Beattie, about what happens when the new lover is hers, not his

"THE STORY OF AN HOUR" by Kate Chopin, probing the complex shock of bereavement

"SOMETHING THAT HAPPENED" by Jayne Anne Phillips, about a woman's slow awakening to her deepest needs

And twenty-five more great short stories about—

AMERICAN WIVES

BARBARA H. SOLOMON, chairperson of the Department of English at Iona College, is the editor of four other anthologies available in Mentor editions: *The Awakening and Selected Stories of Kate Chopin*, *The Short Fiction of Sarah Orne Jewett and Mary Wilkins Freeman*, *The Experience of the American Woman*, and *A Mary Wollstonecraft Reader*.

American Wives

30 Short Stories by Women

Edited by
Barbara H. Solomon

A MENTOR BOOK

NEW AMERICAN LIBRARY

NEW YORK AND SCARBOROUGH, ONTARIO

Library of Congress Catalog Card Number: 86-62307

ACKNOWLEDGMENTS

"Making a Change" by Charlotte Perkins Gilman. Originally published in
THE FORERUNNER (1911); Reprinted in THE CHARLOTTE PERKINS
GILMAN READER, edited by Ann J. Lane, Pantheon Books, a Divison
of Random House Inc.
"Sweat" by Zora Neale Hurston. Copyright © 1926 by the Estate of Zora
Neale Hurston. Originally published by J.B. Lippincott.
"Rope" by Katherine Anne Porter. Copyright © 1930, 1958 by Katherine Anne
Porter. Reprinted from FLOWERING JUDAS AND OTHER STORIES by
permission Harcourt Brace Jovanovich, Inc.
"The Pelican's Shadow" by Marjorie Kinnan Rawlings. Copyright © 1940 by
Marjorie Kinnan Rawlings. Copyright renewed © 1968 by Marjorie Kinnan
Rawlings. Reprinted by permission of Brandt & Brandt Literary Agents,
Inc. This story first appeared in *The New Yorker*.
"The Valley Between" by Paule Marshall. Copyright © 1954 by Paule
Marshall. Reprinted by permission of the author.
"Day of Success" by Sylvia Plath. Copyright © 1960 by Ted Hughes.
Reprinted from JOHNNY PANIC AND THE BIBLE OF DREAMS by
permission of Harper & Row, Publishers, Inc.
"Accomplished Desires" by Joyce Carol Oates. Copyright © 1970, 1969,
1968, 1967, 1966, 1965 by Joyce Carol Oates. Reprinted from THE
WHEEL OF LOVE by permission of Vanguard Press, Inc.
"The Absence" by Elizabeth Spencer. Copyright © 1966 by Elizabeth Spencer.
Reprinted from THE STORIES OF ELIZABETH SPENCER by permission
of Doubleday & Company, Inc. This story first appeared in *The New
Yorker*.
"The Good Humor Man" by Rebecca Morris. Copyright © 1967 by Rebecca
Morris. Reprinted by permission of Curtis Brown, Ltd. This story first
appeared in *The New Yorker*.
"A Woman's Story" by Marilyn Krysl. Copyright © 1971 by Marilyn Krysl.
This story first appeared in *Seneca Review*.
"A New Life" by Sallie Bingham. Copyright © 1970, 1971, 1972 by Sallie
Bingham. Reprinted from THE WAY IT IS NOW by permission of Viking
Penguin, Inc.
"To the Members of the D.A.R." by Joanne Greenberg. Copyright © 1966,
1967, 1969, 1971, 1972 by Joanne Greenberg. Reprinted from RITES OF
PASSAGE by permission of Holt, Rinehart and Winston, Publishers.
"Vermont" by Ann Beattie. Copyright © 1975 by *The New Yorker* Magazine,
Inc. Reprinted from DISTORTIONS by Ann Beattie by permission of
Doubleday & Company, Inc. This story first appeared in *The New Yorker*.

(The following page constitutes an extension of this copyright page.)

MENTOR TRADEMARK REG. U.S. PAT. OFF. AND FOREIGN COUNTRIES

REGISTERED TRADEMARK—MARCA REGISTRADA

HECHO EN CHICAGO, U.S.A.

SIGNET, SIGNET CLASSIC, MENTOR, ONYX, PLUME, MERIDIAN and NAL BOOKS are published *in the United States* by NAL PENGUIN INC., 1633 Broadway, New York, New York 10019, *in Canada* by The New American Library of Canada Limited, 81 Mack Avenue, Scarborough, Ontario M1L 1M8

First Printing, December, 1986

2   3   4   5   6   7   8   9   10

PRINTED IN THE UNITED STATES OF AMERICA

This book is affectionately dedicated to my mother-in-law and father-in-law, Lee and Dave Solomon.

ACKNOWLEDGMENTS

I would like to express my appreciation to Professors Carole Weaver and Cedric Winslow for their helpful analyses of the cultural framework of American wifehood as well as to Gary F. Kriss of *The New York Times*. At Iona College, a great deal of assistance was offered by Mary Bruno and the staff of the Secretarial Services Center: Nancy Girardi, Adrianna DiLello, Marie Mariani, Theresa Martin, Antonia Piria, and Patti Besen as well as by the Department of English Student Assistants: Lisa Bonafoux, Rose Emanuele, and Gittel Steinberg. I am indebted to Iona College for a Faculty Enrichment Grant for the fall of 1985.

Contents

Introduction

One of the most surprising results of feminist criticism of recent decades has been the discovery of the extent to which women characters in literature are merely conventional stereotypes rather than individuals. Among the readily identifiable stereotypical images which have regularly appeared are "The Sex Object," "The Goddess on the Pedestal," "The Old Maid," "The Maiden," "The Lady," "The Mother," and two images of wives: "The Wife As Angel in the House" or "The Wife As Shrew." In twentieth-century literature, the latter stereotype has been extended with a particularly powerful American addition, that of "The Wife as Bitch."

As Joanna Russ has noted in "What Can A Heroine Do? Or Why Women Can't Write," the women in American literature often

> exist only in relation to the protagonist (who is male). Moreover, look at them carefully and you will see that they do not really exist at all—at their best they are depictions of the social roles women are supposed to play and often do play, but they are the public roles and not the private women; at their worst they are . . . fantasies about what men want, or hate, or fear.*

*Images of Women in Fiction: Feminist Perspectives, ed. Susan Koppelman Cornillon (Bowling Green: Bowling Green University Popular Press, 1972), p. 5.

Three classic American stories spanning over one hundred years are especially apt examples of the typical pattern. The only significance of the women characters is the relationship which each has to the central male character whose thoughts, decisions, and actions are at the crux of the story. Further-more, each of these stories—Washington Irving's "Rip Van Winkle" (1819), Nathaniel Hawthorne's "The Birthmark" (1843), and Ernest Hemingway's "The Short Happy Life of Francis Macomber" (1936)— portrays a woman who reflects a major category of the stereotypical wife.

In "Rip Van Winkle," Rip's wife is the commonly depicted shrew. She is a nagging wife whose "simple, good-natured" husband is "obedient" and "hen-pecked." When Rip returns home after spending twenty years asleep in the mountains, which had seemed to be only one night to him, he learns, among other pieces of news, that Dame Van Winkle had recently died. We are told that "there was a drop of comfort, at least, in this intelligence." Irving completes the portrait of Rip's comfortable and widowed old age with a description of the idle Rip: "he took his place once more on the bench at the inn door, and was reverenced as one of the patriarchs of the village. . . ." With his wife gone, Rip will be cared for by a pleasant young woman, his daughter, and granted a peaceful old age free of any responsibility.

In "The Birthmark," an allegory about the quest for per-fection, Hawthorne depicts a "Wife as the Angel in the House." She is so beautiful and virtuous that only a small birthmark on her cheek prevents her from being the incarna-tion of heavenly perfection on earth. The submissive wife, Georgiana, will consent to be the subject of the experiment proposed by Aylmer, her scientist husband, because her only goal is to be completely pleasing to him. Georgiana would prefer to die in an attempt to remove the birthmark rather than to offend and shock her husband who has discovered, only after their marriage, that he is obsessed by the small crimson hand on his wife's cheek, a mark which becomes more prominent when she is pale. In dramatizing the destructive effect of Aylmer's demand for complete perfection, Hawthorne requires the acceptance by the reader of the stereotypical Georgiana, who does not value her life if she is not pleasing to her husband and who fervently prays that "for a single moment, she might satisfy his highest and deepest conception" of her. Her death, as a result of the experiment, comes as no surprise to the reader, and the emphasis of the story's conclusion is on the inevitable tragedy of misguided idealism; Georgiana's death provides a lesson for a man who overestimated his powers as a scientist and refused to accept the limitations of the human condition.

The third stereotype, "The Wife As Bitch," is exemplified by the character of Margot in Hemingway's "The Short Happy Life of Francis Macomber." Seemingly disgusted with her wealthy but ineffectual husband, Francis, Margot is portrayed as both beautiful and vicious. The Macombers are on their first safari in Africa, guided by Wilson, an authoritative white hunter. Mrs. Macomber has watched Francis Macomber run away in a wild panic while Wilson stood his ground and finished off an attacking wounded lion. Later that evening, she leaves the tent she shares with her husband to go to Wilson, flaunting her infidelity before the powerless Macomber, who reminds her that she had promised "there wasn't going to be any of that." In thinking about Margot earlier, Wilson had summarized her traits—those of American bitches: "They are, he thought, the hardest in the world; the cruelest, the most predatory and the most attractive and their men have softened or gone to pieces nervously as they have hardened. Or is it that they pick men they can handle?" By the conclusion of the story, Margot has killed her husband in a hunting accident which Wilson does not consider an accident at all. The American bitch in this story, and in numerous other fictional incarnations, is not a joking matter. But even more striking is her incomprehensible behavior. The main concern of the authors who use the bitch stereotype is the effect she has on her male victim and his struggle to overcome her influence. Her motivation is generally obscure.

When we turn to serious and realistic fiction about wifehood in America that is not stereotypical, we find numerous works which depict problems and themes about married life that are slighted or entirely omitted when wives are portrayed as stereotyped figures. Fiction by American women has always been a source of valuable insights about women, especially in matters of courtship and married life, frequently anticipating later sociological studies and statistical data. The stories in this volume vividly dramatize the responsibilities, ideals, and feelings of American wives during the last century and a half.

Significantly, many feminist issues appear as themes in the works of important early writers. For example, a number of stories in this volume depict women experiencing conflict when they attempt to be supportive wives and nurturing mothers as well as fulfilled and independent adults. In Elizabeth Stuart Phelps's "The Angel Over the Right Shoulder" (1852), Mrs. James wishes she could have two hours each day for her personal educational goal. But when she attempts, with her husband's enthusiastic prompting, to reserve a time for herself—a time when she would be unavailable to her husband and when a servant would care for her three young children—she discovers that it is virtually impossible to withdraw from family responsibilities for even a limited respite. Other stories in this collection which embody similar conflicts are "The Story of an Hour" (1894) by Kate Chopin, "Making a Change" (1911) by Charlotte Perkins Gilman, and "The Valley Between" (1954) by Paule Marshall.

Insecurity is a second common problem of wives in this volume. Both the young British wife in "Day of Success" (1960)—a story set in England but clearly informed by Sylvia Plath's American background—and the older wife in Mary Hedin's Plastic Edge to Plastic Edge" (1980) fear that a younger or more attractive rival will win her husband's love because the routine of married life does not supply the opportunity for change and excitement which their husbands might have expected. These wives fear that the domestic comfort they have worked so hard to create may not satisfy their mates. And when in Joyce Carol Oates's "Accomplished Desires" (1965) Mark Arber brings home a young college student ostensibly to be a live-in babysitter, but obviously to be his live-in mistress, his demoralized and desperate wife accepts the situation. As the infatuated student, Dorie, begins to participate in the straightening and cleaning of the house, Barbara Arber, the insecure wife, turns to her husband for assurances about the way she had been keeping house. " 'But I didn't think we lived in such a mess. I didn't think it was so bad,' Barbara would say to Mark in a quiet, hurt voice, and he would pat her hand and say, 'It isn't a mess, she [Dorie] just likes to fool around. *I* don't think it's a mess.' "

"Accomplished Desires" is one of several stories which portray the lives of women married to destructive or vicious husbands. Two other stories—"The Pelican's Shadow" (1940) by Marjorie Kinnan Rawlings and "Sweat" (1926) by Zora Neale Hurston—depict husbands who are threats to their wives in very different ways. In Rawlings' story, Elsa Tifton has married a distinguished scientist and writer who had informed her during their courtship that "his wife must be young and therefore malleable." What she had not realized was that he was also a perfectionist who would hold her responsible for the exact flavor and texture of every dish on his dinner table, who would demand constant adulation, and who would weigh every gesture and remark she makes, criticizing any which fall short of his expectation.

In Hurston's story, the threat to the wife is a physical one, since Sykes Jones has abused his wife almost from the beginning of their fifteen years of marriage. During those years, Delia Jones, his hardworking and religious wife, has supported both of them by taking in washing. Sykes has bullied and beaten his wife so often that a neighbor observes: "He done beat huh' nough tuh kill three women. . . ."

The far less dramatic—but nonetheless serious—problem of the dependent wife appears in Elizabeth Spencer's "The Absence" (1966) and Nancy Huddleston Packer's "The Women Who Walk" (1980). Bonnie Richards, a contented wife, gains some disquieting insights about herself when her husband goes away for a long visit to his ailing parents. She gives up reading mystery books because they are too frightening now that she is alone in the house. Abstract thoughts about the nature of matter and space begin to disturb her, and when she walks the dog at night, she avoids looking at the sky. Without the presence of her husband at the center of her existence, Bonnie formulates a strange wish:

> She wished to be a person, a being, who appeared and disappeared. She should have liked, conveniently, to have the power to disappear even from herself, to put herself away like something folded in a drawer, or simply not to be when there was nothing to be for.

Lacking the vitality and control that Bonnie attributes to her husband, she finds any incident which is out of the ordinary to have a traumatic effect on her.

In "The Women Who Walk" Marian's husband will not be returning. After fifteen years of marriage, Malcolm has abandoned his wife and two children for another woman and demands a divorce. Marian cannot bring herself to tell the children the truth and pretends that their father is away at a conference. After a few weeks, she admits to Malcolm her inability to tell them, and he then handles the responsibility for explaining the situation. Even when he tells her to get a lawyer so that the divorce can proceed, she asks him who to hire.

In a series of painful epiphanies, Marian learns how dependent she has become on her husband's identity and how little of her own pre-marital independence she has retained. Packer uses a series of encounters between Marian and other women who look vaguely familiar to her to suggest that Marian's desperate situation is not an unusual or individual one. Lacking self-esteem, dependent on her ex-husband's judgment, jealous of the new relationship he has formed with a younger woman, Marian finds no freedom in her release from a destructive marriage—only loneliness, emptiness, and regret.

Among the stories in this collection are several which dramatize the daily existence of divorced women with children: "Vermont" (1975) by Ann Beattie, "Bunny Says It's the Death Watch" (1981) by Stephanie Gunn, and "All the

Days of Our Lives'' (1983) by Lee Smith. Rebecca Morris's "The Good Humor Man" (1980) also analyzes the painful experience of a wife being divorced against her will but with very different effects from those in Packer's story.

Finally, a considerable number of stories in this collection dramatize the range of marital conflicts or crises experienced by wives. In some situations the women must respond to pressures from without, as in Joanne Greenberg's "To the Members of the D.A.R." (1972), in which Julia is subjected to the unreasonable and debilitating criticism of her marriage by her parents, or in Toni Cade Bambara's "The Organizer's Wife" (1977), in which Virginia must make a commitment not only to her husband but to the fight for social and economic reforms to which he has dedicated his life. In others, such as Mary Wilkins Freeman's "The Revolt of 'Mother' " (1890) and Mary Peterson's "Travelling" (1985), wives and husbands must cope with the inevitable conflicts which arise when individuals with different needs are a family. Although the conflicts portrayed in these four stories stem from very different situations or character traits, all depict marriages that enrich the lives of both wife and husband as they gain insights into their behavior and grow in understanding and commitment.

—BARBARA H. SOLOMON
Iona College
New Rochelle, New York

The Angel Over the Right Shoulder

ELIZABETH STUART PHELPS

"There! a woman's work is never done," said Mrs. James; "I thought, for once, I was through; but just look at that lamp, now! it will not burn, and I must go and spend half an hour over it."

"Don't you wish you had never been married?" said Mr. James, with a good-natured laugh.

"Yes"—rose to her lips, but was checked by a glance at the group upon the floor, where her husband was stretched out, and two little urchins with sparkling eyes and glowing cheeks, were climbing and tumbling over him as if they found in this play the very essence of fun.

She did say, "I should like the good, without the evil, if I could have it."

"You have no evils to endure," replied her husband.

"That is just all you gentlemen know about it. What would you think, if you could not get an uninterrupted half hour to yourself, from morning till night? I believe you would give up trying to do anything."

"There is no need of that; all you want is *system*. If you arranged your work systematically, you would find that you could command your time."

"Well," was the reply, "all I wish is that you could just follow me around for one day, and see what I have to do. If

8

you could reduce it all to system, I think you would show yourself a genius.''

When the lamp was trimmed, the conversation was resumed. Mr. James had employed the ''half hour'' in meditating on this subject.

''Wife,'' said he, as she came in, ''I have a plan to propose to you, and I wish you to promise me beforehand, that you will accede to it. It is to be an experiment, I acknowledge, but I wish it to have a fair trial. Now to please me, will you promise?''

Mrs. James hesitated. She felt almost sure that his plan would be quite impracticable, for what does a man know of a woman's work? yet she promised.

''Now I wish you,'' said he, ''to set apart two hours every day for your own private use. Make a point of going to your room and locking yourself in; and also make up your mind to let the work which is not done, go undone, if it must. Spend this time on just those things which will be most profitable to yourself. I shall bind you to your promise for one month—then, if it has proved a total failure, we will devise something else.''

''When shall I begin?''

''To-morrow.''

The morrow came. Mrs. James had chosen the two hours before dinner as being, on the whole, the most convenient and the least liable to interruption. They dined at one o'clock. She wished to finish her morning work, get dressed for the day, and enter her room at eleven.

Hearty as were her efforts to accomplish this, the hour of eleven found her with her work but half done; yet, true to her promise, she left all, retired to her room and locked the door.

With some interest and hope, she immediately marked out a course of reading and study for these two precious hours; then, arranging her table, her books, pen and paper, she commenced a schedule of her work with much enthusiasm. Scarcely had she dipped her pen in ink, when she heard the tramping of little feet along the hall, and then a pounding at her door.

"Mamma! mamma! I cannot find my mittens, and Hannah is going to slide without me."

"Go to Amy, my dear; mamma is busy."

"So Amy busy too; she say she can't leave baby."

The child began to cry, still standing close to the fastened door. Mrs. James knew the easiest, and indeed the only way of settling the trouble, was to go herself and hunt up the missing mittens. Then a parley must be held with Frank, to induce him to wait for his sister, and the child's tears must be not dried, and little hearts must be all set right before the children went out to play; and so favorable an opportunity must not be suffered to slip, without impressing on young minds the importance of having a "place for everything and everything in its place;" this took time; and when Mrs. James returned to her study, her watch told her that *half* her portion had gone. Quietly resuming her work, she was endeavoring to mend her broken train of thought, when heavier steps were heard in the hall, and the fastened door was once more besieged. Now, Mr. James must be admitted.

"Mary," said he, "cannot you come and sew a string on for me? I do believe there is not a bosom in my drawer in order, and I am in a great hurry. I ought to have been down town an hour ago."

The schedule was thrown aside, the work-basket taken, and Mrs. James followed him. She soon sewed on the tape, but then a button needed fastening—and at last a rip in his glove was to be mended. As Mrs. James stitched away on the glove, a smile lurked in the corners of her mouth, which her husband observed.

"What are you laughing at?" asked he.

"To think how famously your plan works."

"I declare!" said he, "is this your study hour? I am sorry, but what can a man do? He cannot go down town without a shirt-bosom!"

"Certainly not," said his wife, quietly.

When her liege lord was fairly equipped and off, Mrs. James returned to her room. A half an hour yet remained to her, and of this she determined to make the most. But scarcely had she resumed her pen, when there was another disturbance in the entry. Amy had returned from walking out with the baby, and she entered the nursery with him, that she might get him to sleep. Now it happened that the only room in the house which Mrs. James could have to herself with a fire, was the one adjoining the nursery. She had become so accustomed to the ordinary noise of the children, that it did not disturb her; but the very extraordinary noise which master Charley sometimes felt called upon to make, when he was fairly on his back in the cradle, did disturb the unity of her thoughts. The words which she was reading rose and fell with the screams and lulls of the child, and she felt obliged to close her book, until the storm was over. When quiet was restored in the cradle, the children came in from sliding, crying with cold fingers—and just as she was going to them, the dinner-bell rang.

"How did your new plan work this morning?" inquired Mr. James.

"Famously," was the reply, "I read about seventy pages of German, and as many more in French."

"I am sure *I* did not hinder you long."

"No—yours was only one of a dozen interruptions."

"O, well! you must not get discouraged. Nothing succeeds well the first time. Persist in your arrangement, and by and by the family will learn that if they want anything of you, they must wait until after dinner."

"But what can a man do?" replied his wife; "he cannot go down town without a shirt-bosom."

"I was in a bad case," replied Mr. James, "it may not happen again. I am anxious to have you try the month out faithfully, and then we will see what has come of it."

The second day of trial was a stormy one. As the morning was dark, Bridget over-slept, and consequently breakfast was too late by an hour. This lost hour Mrs. James could not recover. When the clock struck eleven, she seemed but to have commenced her morning's work, so much remained to be done. With mind disturbed and spirits depressed, she left her household matters "in the suds," as they were, and punctually retired to her study. She soon found, however, that she could not fix her attention upon any intellectual pursuit. Neglected duties haunted her, like ghosts around the guilty conscience. Perceiving that she was doing nothing with her books, and not wishing to lose the morning wholly, she commenced writing a letter. Bridget interrupted her before she had proceeded far on the first page.

"What, ma'am, shall we have for dinner? No marketing ha'n't come."

"Have some steaks, then."

"We ha'n't got none, ma'am."

"I will send out for some, directly."

Now there was no one to send but Amy, and Mrs. James knew it. With a sigh, she put down her letter and went into the nursery.

"Amy, Mr. James has forgotten our marketing. I should like to have you run over to the provision store, and order some beef-steaks. I will stay with the baby."

Amy was not much pleased to be sent out on this errand. She remarked, that "she must change her dress first."

"Be as quick as possible," said Mrs. James, "for I am particularly engaged at this hour."

Amy neither obeyed, nor disobeyed, but managed to take her own time, without any very deliberate intention to do so. Mrs. James, hoping to get along with a sentence or two, took her German book into the nursery. But this arrangement was not to master Charley's mind. A fig did he care for German, but "the kitties," he must have, whether or no—and kitties he would find in that particular book—so he turned its leaves over in great haste. Half of the time on the second day of trial had gone, when Amy returned and Mrs. James with a sigh, left her nursery. Before one o'clock, she was twice called into the kitchen to superintend some important dinner arrangement, and thus it turned out that she did not finish one page of her letter.

On the third morning the sun shone, and Mrs. James rose early, made every provision which she deemed necessary for dinner, and for the comfort of her family; and then, elated

by her success, in good spirits, and with good courage, she
entered her study precisely at eleven o'clock, and locked her
door. Her books were opened, and the challenge given to a
hard German lesson. Scarcely had she made the first onset,
when the doorbell was heard to ring, and soon Bridget coming nearer and nearer—then tapping at the door.

"Somebodies wants to see you in the parlor, ma'am."

"Tell them I am engaged, Bridget."

"I told 'em you were to-home, ma'am, and they sent up
their names, but I ha'n't got 'em, jist."

There was no help for it—Mrs. James must go down to
receive her callers. She had to smile when she felt little like
it—to be sociable when her thoughts were busy with her task.
Her friends made a long call—they had nothing else to do
with their time; and when they went, others came. In very
unsatisfactory chit-chat, her morning slipped away.

On the next day, Mr. James invited company to tea, and
her morning was devoted to preparing for it; she did not
enter her study. On the day following, a sick-head-ache confined
her to her bed, and on Saturday the care of the baby devolved
upon her, as Amy had extra work to do. Thus passed the first
week.

True to her promise, Mrs. James patiently persevered for a
month, in her efforts to secure for herself this little fragment
of her broken time, but with what success, the first week's
history can tell. With its close, closed the month of December.

On the last day of the old year, she was so much occupied
in her preparations for the morrow's festival, that the last
hour of the day was approaching, before she made her good
night's call in the nursery. She first went to the crib and
looked at the baby. There he lay in his innocence and beauty,
fast asleep. She softly stroked his golden hair—she kissed
gently his rosy cheek—she pressed the little dimpled hand in
hers, and then, carefully drawing the coverlet over it, tucked
it in, and stealing yet another kiss—she left him to his
peaceful dreams and sat down on her daughter's bed. She
also slept sweetly, with her dolly hugged to her bosom. At
this her mother smiled, but soon grave thoughts entered her

mind, and these deepened into sad ones. She thought of her disappointment and the failure of her plans. To her, not only the past month but the whole past year, seemed to have been one of fruitless effort—all broken and disjointed—even her hours of religious duty had been encroached upon, and disturbed. She had accomplished nothing, that she could see, but to keep her house and family in order, and even this, to her saddened mind, seemed to have been but indifferently done. She was conscious of yearnings for a more earnest life than this. Unsatisfied longings for something which she had not attained, often clouded what, otherwise, would have been a bright day to her; and yet the causes of these feelings seemed to lie in a dim and misty region, which her eye could not penetrate.

What then did she need? To see some *results* from her life's work? To know that a golden cord bound her life-threads together into *unity* of purpose—notwithstanding they seemed, so often, single and broken?

She was quite sure that she felt no desire to shrink from duty, however humble, but she sighed for some comforting assurance of what *was duty*. Her employments, conflicting as they did with her tastes, seemed to her frivolous and useless. It seemed to her that there was some better way of living, which she, from deficiency in energy of character, or of principle, had failed to discover. As she leaned over her child, her tears fell fast upon its young brow.

Most earnestly did she wish, that she could shield that child from the disappointments and mistakes and self-reproach from which the mother was then suffering; that the little one might take up life where she could give it to her—all mended by her own experience. It would have been a comfort to have felt, that in fighting the battle, she had fought for both; yet she knew that so it could not be—that for ourselves must we all learn what are those things which "make for our peace."

The tears were in her eyes, as she gave the good-night to her sleeping daughter—then with soft steps she entered an adjoining room, and there fairly kissed out the old year on another chubby cheek, which nestled among the pillows. At length she sought her own rest.

Soon she found herself in a singular place. She was traversing a vast plain. No trees were visible, save those which skirted the distant horizon, and on their broad tops rested wreaths of golden clouds. Before her was a female, who was journeying towards that region of light. Little children were about her, now in her arms, now running by her side, and as they travelled, she occupied herself in caring for them. She taught them how to place their little feet—she gave them timely warnings of the pit-falls—she gently lifted them over the stumbling-blocks. When they were weary, she soothed them by singing of that brighter land, which she kept ever in view, and towards which she seemed hastening with her little flock. But what was most remarkable was, that, all unknown to her, she was constantly watched by two angels, who reposed on two golden clouds which floated above her. Before each was a golden book, and a pen of gold. One angel, with mild and loving eyes, peered constantly over her right shoulder—another kept as strict watch over her left. Not a deed, not a word, not a look, escaped their notice. When a good deed, word, look, went from her, the angel over the right shoulder with a glad smile, wrote it down in his book; when an evil, however trivial, the angel over the left shoulder recorded it in his book—then with sorrowful eyes followed the pilgrim until he observed penitence for the wrong, upon which he dropped a tear on the record, and blotted it out, and both angels rejoiced.

To the looker-on, it seemed that the traveller did nothing which was worthy of such careful record. Sometimes she did but bathe the weary feet of her little children, but the angel over the *right shoulder*—wrote it down. Sometimes she did but patiently wait to lure back a little truant who had turned his face away from the distant light, but the angel over the *right shoulder*—wrote it down. Sometimes she did but soothe an angry feeling or raise a drooping eye-lid, or kiss away a little grief; but the angel over the right shoulder—*wrote it down*.

Sometimes, her eye was fixed so intently on that golden horizon, and she became so eager to make progress thither, that the little ones, missing her care, did languish or stray. Then it was that the angel over the *left shoulder* lifted his golden pen, and made the entry, and followed her with sorrowful eyes, until he could blot it out. Sometimes she seemed to advance rapidly, but in her haste the little ones had fallen back, and it was the sorrowing angel who recorded her progress. Sometimes so intent was she to gird up her loins and have her lamp trimmed and burning, that the little children wandered away quite into forbidden paths, and it was the angel over the *left shoulder* who recorded her diligence.

Now the observer as she looked, felt that this was a faithful and true record, and was to be kept to that journey's end. The strong clasps of gold on those golden books, also impressed her with the conviction that, when they were closed, it would only be for a future opening.

Her sympathies were warmly enlisted for the gentle traveller, and with a beating heart she quickened her steps that she might overtake her. She wished to tell her of the angels keeping watch above her—to entreat her to be faithful and patient to the end—for her life's work was all written down—every item of it— and the *results* would be known when those golden books should be unclasped. She wished to beg of her to think no duty trivial which must be done, for over her right shoulder and over her left were recording angels, who would surely take note of all!

Eager to warn the traveller of what she had seen, she touched her. The traveller turned, and she recognized or seemed to recognize *herself*. Startled and alarmed she awoke in tears. The gray light of morning struggled through the half-open shutter, the door was ajar and merry faces were peeping in.

"Wish you a happy new year, mamma,"—"Wish you a *Happy new Year*,"—"a happy noo ear."

She returned the merry greeting most heartily. It seemed to her as if she had entered upon a new existence. She had found her way through the thicket in which she had been entangled, and a light was now about her path. The *Angel Over the Right Shoulder* whom she had seen in her dream, would bind up in his golden book her life's work, if it were but well done. He required of her no great deeds, but faithfulness and patience to the end of the race which was set before her. Now she could see plainly enough, that though it was right and important for her to cultivate her own mind and heart, it was equally right and equally important, to meet and perform faithfully all those little household cares and duties on which the comfort and virtue of her family depended; for into these things the angels carefully looked—and these duties and cares acquired a dignity from the strokes of that golden pen—they could not be neglected without danger.

Sad thoughts and sadder misgivings—undefined yearnings and ungratified longings seemed to have taken their flight with the Old Year, and it was with fresh resolution and cheerful hope, and a happy heart, she welcomed the *Glad New Year*. The *Angel Over the Right Shoulder* would go with her, and if she were found faithful, would strengthen and comfort her to its close.

Mrs. Gay's Prescription

LOUISA MAY ALCOTT

Bang, bang when the front door, as Mr. Bennet and the boys hurried off to store and school, leaving Mrs. Bennet to collect her wits and draw a long breath after the usual morning flurry.

The poor little woman looked as if she needed rest but was not likely to get it; for the room was in a chaotic state, the breakfast table presented the appearance of having been devastated by a swarm of locusts, the baby began to fret, little Polly set up her usual whine of "I want sumpin to do," and a pile of work loomed in the corner waiting to be done.

"I don't see how I ever shall get through it all," sighed the despondent matron as she hastily drank a last cup of tea, while two great tears rolled down her cheeks, as she looked from one puny child to the other, and felt the weariness of her own tired soul and body more oppressive than ever.

"A good cry" was impending, when there came a brisk ring at the door, a step in the hall, and a large, rosy woman came bustling in, saying in a cheery voice as she set a flower-pot down upon the table, "Good morning! Nice day, isn't it? Came in early on business and brought you one of my Lady Washingtons, you are so fond of flowers."

"Oh, it's lovely! How kind you are. Do sit down if you can find a chair; we are all behind hand to-day, for I was up half the night with poor baby, and haven't energy enough to go to work yet," answered Mrs. Bennet, with a sudden smile that changed her whole face, while baby stopped fretting to stare at the rosy clusters, and Polly found employment in exploring the pocket of the new comer, as if she knew her way there.

"Let me put the pot on your stand first, girls are so careless, and I'm proud of this. It will be an ornament to your parlor for a week," and opening a door Mrs. Gay carried the plant to a sunny bay window where many others were blooming beautifully.

Mrs. Bennet and the children followed to talk and admire, while the servant leisurely cleared the table.

"Now give me that baby, put yourself in the easy chair, and tell me all about your worries," said Mrs. Gay, in the brisk, commanding way which few people could resist.

"I'm sure I don't know where to begin," sighed Mrs. Bennet, dropping into the comfortable seat while baby changed bearers with great composure.

"I met your husband and he said the doctor had ordered you and these chicks off to Florida for the winter. John said he didn't know how he should manage it, but he meant to try."

"Isn't it dreadful? He can't leave his business to go with me, and we shall have to get Aunt Miranda to come and see to him and the boys while I'm gone, and the boys can't bear her strict, old-fashioned ways, and I've got to go that long journey all alone and stay among strangers, and these heaps of fall work to do first, and it will cost an immense sum to send us, and I don't know what is to become of me."

Here Mrs. Bennet stopped for breath, and Mrs. Gay asked briskly, "What is the matter with you and the children?"

"Well, baby is having a hard time with his teeth and is croupy, Polly doesn't get over scarlet fever well, and I'm used up; no strength or appetite, pain in my side and low spirits. Entire change of scene, milder climate, and less work for me, is what we want, the doctor says. John is very anxious about us, and I feel regularly discouraged."

"I'll spend the day and cheer you up a bit. You just rest and get ready for a new start to-morrow; it is a saving of time to stop short now and then and see where to begin next. Bring me the most pressing job of work, I can sew and see to this little rascal at the same time."

As she spoke off went Mrs. Gay's bonnet, and by the time her hostess returned with the over-flowing work-basket, the energetic lady had put a match to the ready-laid fire on the hearth, rolled up a couch, table, and easy chair, planted baby on the rug with a bunch of keys to play with, and sat blooming and smiling herself, as if work, worry and November weather were not in existence.

"Tot's frocks and Polly's aprons are the things I'm most hurried about; they need so many and I do like my children to look nice among strangers," began Mrs. Bennet, unrolling yards upon yards of ruffling, for the white frocks and pinafores, with a glance of despair at the sewing machine whose click had grown detestable to her ear.

"Make 'em plain if you are in a hurry; children don't need trimming up, they are prettiest in simple clothes. I can finish off that batch of aprons before dinner, if you will put that ruffling away. Come now do, it will be a load off your mind and Polly won't know the difference."

"I always do trim them, and every one does," began Mrs. Bennet who was wedded to her idols.

"When I was in London I saw a duke's children dressed in plain brown linen pinafores, and I thought I'd never seen such splendid babies. Try it, and if people make remarks, bring in the English aristocracy, and it will be all right."

There was a twinkle in Mrs. Gay's eyes that made her friend ashamed to argue, so she laughed and gave up the point, acknowledging with a sigh that it was a relief.

"It is this mania for trimming every thing which is wearing out so many women. Necessary sewing is enough, then drop your needle and read, rest, walk or play with the children, and see how much you have lost heretofore by this everlasting stitching. You'd soon get rid of that pain in your side if you'd let the machine stand idle while you went out for an hour every day.''

"Perhaps I should, but I can't leave the children, Biddy is so careless.''

"Take them with you. Roll baby up and down that nice, dry side-walk and let Polly run before, and you'd be a different set of people in a month.''

"Do you really think so?''

"Not only that, but if you'd change your way of living, I don't believe you'd need to think of going to Florida at all.''

"Why, Mary Gay, what do you mean?'' demanded Mrs. Bennet, sitting erect upon the couch in her surprise at this unexpected remark.

"I have often wanted to say this before, and now I will, though you will think I'm an interfering woman if I do. Never mind, if I can only save you further worry and expense and suffering I won't mind, if you are offended for a time. In the first place, you must move,'' and Mrs. Gay gave such a decided nod that the other lady could only ejaculate, "Why? where? when?''

"Because you want more sun and space, into this room because you will find both, and to-day because I'm here to help you.''

Mrs. Bennet gave a little gasp and looked about her in dismay at the bare idea of living in her cherished best parlor.

"But the back room does very well,'' she protested. "It is warm and small and handy to the kitchen and we always live there.''

"*No*, my dear, it does *not* do very well, for those very reasons. It is *too* warm, and small and near the kitchen to make it a fit place to live in, especially for little children. Why don't you put your plants there if it is such a nice place?'' asked Mrs. Gay, bent on making a clean sweep of her friend's delusions and prejudices.

"Why, they need more sun and air and room, so I keep them in here.''

"Exactly! and your babies need sun and air and room more than your roses, geraniums, and callas. The plants would soon die in that close, hot, dark north room; do you wonder your babies are pale, and fretful and weak? Bring them in here and see how soon they will bloom if you give them a chance.''

"I never thought of that. I'm sure I would do anything to see them well and hearty, but it does seem a pity to spoil my nice parlor. Wouldn't the best chamber overhead do as well?''

"I want that too for your bed-room, and the little one at the side for the children. You use the back chamber now, and have the cribs there also, don't you?''

"Yes. My patience! Mary, would you have me turn my house upside down just for a little more sun?''

"Do you love your best rooms better than your children? Hadn't you rather see them spoilt by daily use than empty and neat, because the little busy feet were gone never to come back? I'm in earnest, Lizzie, and I know you will agree with me when you think it over. My own dear little boy was killed by my ignorance, and I have learned by sad experience that we mothers should make it the study of our lives to keep home healthy and happy for our boys and girls, no matter how much we sacrifice show and fashion. Come now, try it for a month, and see if you don't all feel the better for enjoying the best and sunniest side of life.''

Mrs. Bennet's eye wandered round the pretty room, and went from Polly singing to herself as she sat looking out of the pleasant window, to baby contentedly playing bo-peep through the bars of the fender with the yellow flames, which were his delight, then came back to her friend's kind, earnest face, and seemed to wake with sudden energy and life and resolution.

"I'll try it!'' she said, feeling that it was a heroic thing to give up all her cherished ideas and put her Sunday-best things into every-day wear. But Mrs. Gay's words touched and startled her, and with a self-reproachful pang she resolved that it should never be said she loved her plants more than her children, or that her house should ever miss the sweet clamor of baby voices if she had the power to keep that music there.

"Good! I knew you would, and I'm going to show you

how easy it will be to change the climate you live in as well as the scene, and lighten your work, and benefit your health without going far away,'' cried Mrs. Gay, delighted with her success, and eager to see her reform well carried out.

"What *will* John say?" and Mrs. Bennet felt inclined to laugh and to cry at thought of the coming revolution.

"He will approve; men always like to have things bright and roomy and nice about them. I've been through it and I know, for when we kept in two rooms we got careless and narrow and low-spirited. Now we live all over the house and keep everything as bright and pretty, and nice as we can. George does not shut himself up in his untidy den, but stays with me, and people drop in, and we have a social, happy time of it, all enjoying our good things freely together, and feeling the worth of them."

"How do we begin?" asked Mrs. Bennet, fired with the spirit of emulation now that the first shock was over, for John did shut himself up because the dining-room was so full of an evening with two tumultuous boys, and the little woman wanted to see her husband during the only leisure hour she had out of the twenty-four.

"I should just move all the delicate things into the little library there out of the way of the children. That room is rather bare, and they will make it more attractive. Leave the pictures, they are safe, and it is good to have pretty objects for young eyes to rest upon. Put the covers on to your furniture, a large drugget over your carpet, and take that other bay window for Polly and baby's play corner. It is sunny and snug, and looking out always amuses them; and at night you can just drop the curtains before the recess and hide their little clutter without disturbing it. In the other window there is room for your table and chair, and close by the machine. There you can sit as in a bower with your flowers about you, a pleasant view outside, and everything cheerful, wholesome and pretty, three very important things to a woman. Keep up the open fire, it is worth a dozen furnaces, and have a thermometer to be sure you don't get too warm, that takes all the strength out of you and makes taking cold easy."

"It wouldn't take long to make the change. John isn't coming home to dinner, so we can be all ready by night, if you really can stop and see me through the job. I declare I feel better already, for I *am* tired to death of that back room and don't wonder Polly is always teasing to "go in parlor." The boys will dance for joy to get full swing here, they never are allowed it, except Sundays, and then they behave nicely and seem to enjoy the piano and pretty things, and so does John. Yes, I'll do it right away," and up jumped Mrs. Bennet, finding her most powerful impetus in the thought of pleasing "father and the boys."

Working and talking busily together the friends soon made the necessary changes below, to the great delight of Polly and the entire bewilderment of baby, who fell asleep on the best sofa, as if bound to make the most of his comforts while they lasted.

A hasty lunch, and then, with Biddy to lug heavy articles, they rearranged the chambers, making a splendid nursery of the large one and a nice sleeping room of the smaller for the two children.

"Now you see you can undress them by this pleasant grate, and then put them away in a cool, quiet place to sleep undisturbed by you older people. Only be sure the little mattresses and bed clothes get a good airing and sunning every day. You can shut the door, and let them lie for hours as you couldn't in the back room, and that is a great advantage," said Mrs. Gay, who was in high spirits at carrying everything before her in this fine style.

"It is lucky we seldom have guests to sleep in winter, for that north room isn't at all my ideal of a best chamber, though we have put some of my pretty things there. I feel like company myself in here, and John won't know what to do with so much space, I've kept him cramped so long. It does seem a shame to shut up this big room and not enjoy it. Mary, I have been a goose, and I'm glad you came and told me so."

Contented with that confession, Mrs. Gay kissed her convert, and leaving Biddy to finish off, she took her departure, with many last injunctions about "air, oatmeal, brown living and sunshine."

When Mr. Bennet and the boys, who had been enjoying a holiday, came home to tea, amazement fell upon them at the sight of Mamma and the babies waiting in the new sitting-room with the announcement that there was not going to be any best parlor any more.

When the events of the day had been explained and discussed, a sort of jubilee ensued; for all felt that a pleasant change in the domestic atmosphere had taken place, and all enjoyed it immensely. Mr. Bennet played and the boys and Polly danced and Papa frolicked with baby, who forgot his teeth and crowed gleefully till bed-time.

Of course Mr. Bennet had his joke about women's notions, and his doubts as to the success of the plan, but anything that cheered up his wife pleased him, for his heart sank at the thought of home without her, and Florida was a most distasteful idea to him. He expressed much satisfaction at his improved quarters, however, and that repaid Mrs. Bennet for the sacrifice she had made, though he, being a man, could never know how great a one it was.

It took some time to get fairly settled, but the sunny side of things grew more and more delightful, as the change of scene and better influences did their quiet work. The children soon showed the effects of the daily sunshine, the well aired chambers, simpler food, and cheerful play-place allotted to them, for these little creatures show as quickly as flowers their susceptibility to natural laws. Polly was never tired of looking out of the window at the varying phases of street life, and her observations thereupon gave her mother many a hearty laugh.

Baby throve like a dandelion in spring, though infantile ills occasionally vexed his happy soul; for the mistaken training of months could not be rectified all at once, or teething made easy.

Mrs. Bennet had her moments of regret as she saw the marks of little fingers on her paint and furniture, watched the fading of her carpet, and labored vainly to impress upon the boys that whittling, ball and marbles had better be confined to the dining room. But the big, pleasant parlor was so inviting with the open fire, the comfortable chairs, flowers, babies, work and play, that no one could resist the charm, and tired Papa found it so attractive that he deserted the library set apart for him, and spent his evenings in the bosom of his family, to his wife's great delight.

People got into the way of dropping in, not for a formal call in the prim best parlor, but a social visit with gossip and games, music, or whatever was going on, and soon it was generally agreed that the Bennets' house was the pleasantest in the neighborhood.

The Doctor's standing joke was, "Well, ma'am, are you ready for Florida?" and the answer with ever increasing decision was, "I guess we can get on a little while longer without it."

It certainly seemed as if the chief invalid could, and now that the sewing machine had long rests, and the ducal linen aprons needed only a bit of braid to finish them off, Mrs. Bennet found many a half hour to practice, read, walk with the children, and help the boys with lessons or play. In the evening it soon came to be a habit to clear up the parlor, get the babies cosily to bed, make herself neat and pretty, and be ready to show Papa a cheerful face when he came home. For, being no longer worn out with unnecessary stitching, languid for want of exercise, and nervous for the need of something to break the monotony of a busy house-mother's life, she had spirits to enjoy a social hour, and found it very sweet to be the center of a happy little circle who looked to her for the sunshine of home.

"Some of us *must* go to Florida to get well, but a great many people might save their time and money, and make a land of flowers for themselves out of the simplest materials if they only knew how," said Mrs. Gay when the Bennets thanked her for the advice which did so much good, and every one agreed with her.

The Revolt of "Mother"

MARY WILKINS FREEMAN

"Father!"

"What is it?"

"What are them men diggin' over there in the field for?"

There was a sudden dropping and enlarging of the lower part of the old man's face, as if some heavy weight had settled therein; he shut his mouth tight, and went on harnessing the great bay mare. He hustled the collar on to her neck with a jerk.

"Father!"

The old man slapped the saddle upon the mare's back.

"Look here, father, I want to know what them men are diggin' over in the field for, an' I'm goin' to know."

"I wish you'd go into the house, mother, an' 'tend to your own affairs," the old man said then. He ran his words together, and his speech was almost as inarticulate as a growl.

But the woman understood; it was her most native tongue. "I ain't goin' into the house till you tell me what them men are doin' over there in the field," said she.

Then she stood waiting. She was a small woman, short and straight-waisted like a child in her brown cotton gown. Her forehead was mild and benevolent between the smooth curves of gray hair; there were meek downward lines about her nose and mouth; but her eyes, fixed upon the old man, looked as if the meekness had been the result of her own will, never of the will of another.

They were in the barn, standing before the wide open doors. The spring air, full of the smell of growing grass and unseen blossoms, came in their faces. The deep yard in front was littered with farm wagons and piles of wood; on the edges, close to the fence and the house, the grass was a vivid green, and there were some dandelions.

The old man glanced doggedly at his wife as he tightened the last buckles on the harness. She looked as immovable to him as one of the rocks in his pasture-land, bound to the earth with generations of blackberry vines. He slapped the reins over the horse, and started forth from the barn.

"Father!" said she.

The old man pulled up. "What is it?"

"I want to know what them men are diggin' over there in that field for."

"They're digging a cellar, I s'pose, if you've got to know."

"A cellar for what?"

"A barn."

"A barn? You ain't goin' to build a barn over there where we was goin' to have a house, father?"

The old man said not another word. He hurried the horse into the farm wagon, and clattered out of the yard, jouncing as sturdily on his seat as a boy.

The woman stood a moment looking after him, then she went out of the barn across a corner of the yard to the house. The house, standing at right angles with the great barn and a long reach of sheds and out-buildings, was infinitesimal compared with them. It was scarcely as commodious for people as the little boxes under the barn eaves were for doves.

A pretty girl's face, pink and delicate as a flower, was looking out of one of the house windows. She was watching three men who were digging over in the field which bounded the yard near the road line. She turned quietly when the woman entered.

"What are they digging for, mother?" said she. "Did he tell you?"

"They're diggin' for—a cellar for a new barn."

"Oh, mother, he ain't going to build another barn?"

"That's what he says."

A boy stood before the kitchen glass combing his hair. He combed slowly and painstakingly, arranging his brown hair in a smooth hillock over his forehead. He did not seem to pay any attention to the conversation.

"Sammy, did you know father was going to build a new barn?" asked the girl.

The boy combed assiduously.

"Sammy!"

He turned, and showed a face like his father's under his smooth crest of hair. "Yes, I s'pose I did," he said, reluctantly.

"How long have you known it?" asked his mother.

" 'Bout three months, I guess."

"Why didn't you tell of it?"

"Didn't think 'twould do no good."

"I don't see what father wants another barn for," said the girl, in her sweet, slow voice. She turned again to the window, and stared out at the digging men in the field. Her tender, sweet face was full of a gentle distress. Her forehead was as bald and innocent as a baby's, with the light hair strained back from it in a row of curl-papers. She was quite large, but her soft curves did not look as if they covered muscles.

Her mother looked sternly at the boy. "Is he goin' to buy more cows?" said she.

The boy did not reply; he was tying his shoes.

"Sammy, I want you to tell me if he's goin' to buy more cows."

"I s'pose he is."

"How many?"

"Four, I guess."

His mother said nothing more. She went into the pantry, and there was a clatter of dishes. The boy got his cap from a nail behind the door, took an old arithmetic from the shelf, and started for school. He was lightly built, but clumsy. He went out of the yard with a curious spring in the hips, that made his loose home-made jacket tilt up in the rear.

The girl went to the sink, and began to wash the dishes that were piled up there. Her mother came promptly out of the pantry, and shoved her aside. "You wipe 'em," said she; "I'll wash. There's a good many this mornin'."

The mother plunged her hands vigorously into the water, the girl wiped the plates slowly and dreamily. "Mother," said she, "don't you think it's too bad father's going to build that new barn, much as we need a decent house to live in?"

Her mother scrubbed a dish fiercely. "You ain't found out yet we're women-folks, Nanny Penn," said she. "You ain't seen enough of men-folks yet to. One of these days you'll find it out, an' then you'll know that we know only what men-folks think we do, so far as any use of it goes, an' how we'd ought to reckon men-folks in with Providence, an' not complain of what they do any more than we do of the weather."

"I don't care; I don't believe George is anything like that, anyhow," said Nanny. Her delicate face flushed pink, her lips pouted softly, as if she were going to cry.

"You wait an' see. I guess George Eastman ain't no better than other men. You hadn't ought to judge father, though. He can't help it, 'cause he don't look at things jest the way we do. An' we've been pretty comfortable here, after all. The roof don't leak—ain't never but once—that's one thing. Father's kept it shingled right up."

"I do wish we had a parlor."

"I guess it won't hurt George Eastman any to come to see you in a nice clean kitchen. I guess a good many girls don't have as good a place as this. Nobody's ever heard me complain."

"I ain't complained either, mother."

"Well, I don't think you'd better, a good father an' a good home as you've got. S'pose your father made you go out an' work for your livin'? Lots of girls have to that ain't no stronger an' better able to than you be."

Sarah Penn washed the frying-pan with a conclusive air.

She scrubbed the outside of it as faithfully as the inside. She was a masterly keeper of her box of a house. Her one living-room never seemed to have in it any of the dust which the friction of life with inanimate matter produces. She swept, and there seemed to be no dirt to go before the broom; she cleaned, and one could see no difference. She was like an artist so perfect that he has apparently no art. To-day she got out a mixing bowl and a board, and rolled some pies, and there was no more flour upon her than upon her daughter who was doing finer work. Nanny was to be married in the fall, and she was sewing on some white cambric and embroidery. She sewed industriously while her mother cooked, her soft milk-white hands and wrists showed whiter than her delicate work.

"We must have the stove moved out in the shed before long," said Mrs. Penn. "Talk about not havin' things, it's been a real blessin' to be able to put a stove up in that shed in hot weather. Father did one good thing when he fixed that stove-pipe out there."

Sarah Penn's face as she rolled her pies had that expression of meek vigor which might have characterized one of the New Testament saints. She was making mince-pies. Her husband, Adoniram Penn, like them better than any other kind. She baked twice a week. Adoniram often liked a piece of pie between meals. She hurried this morning. It had been later than usual when she began, and she wanted to have a pie baked for dinner. However deep a resentment she might be forced to hold against her husband, she would never fail in sedulous attention to his wants.

Nobility of character manifests itself at loop-holes when it is not provided with large doors. Sarah Penn's showed itself to-day in flaky dishes of pastry. So she made the pies faithfully, while across the table she could see, when she glanced up from her work, the sight that rankled in her patient and steadfast soul—the digging of the cellar of the new barn in the place where Adoniram forty years ago had promised her their new house should stand.

The pies were done for dinner. Adoniram and Sammy were home a few minutes after twelve o'clock. The dinner was eaten with serious haste. There was never much conversation at the table in the Penn family. Adoniram asked a blessing, and they ate promptly, then rose up and went about their work.

Sammy went back to school, taking soft sly lopes out of the yard like a rabbit. He wanted a game of marbles before school, and feared his father would give him some chores to do. Adoniram hastened to the door and called after him, but he was out of sight.

"I don't see what you let him go for, mother," said he. "I wanted him to help me unload that wood."

Adoniram went to work out in the yard unloading wood from the wagon. Sarah put away the dinner dishes, while Nanny took down her curl-papers and changed her dress. She was going down to the store to buy some more embroidery and thread.

When Nanny was gone, Mrs. Penn went to the door. "Father!" she called.

"Well, what is it!"

"I want to see you jest a minute, father."

"I can't leave this wood nohow. I've got to git it unloaded an' go for a load of gravel afore two o'clock. Sammy had ought to helped me. You hadn't ought to let him go to school so early."

"I want to see you jest a minute."

"I tell ye I can't, nohow, mother."

"Father, you come here." Sarah Penn stood in the door like a queen; she held her head as if it bore a crown; there was that patience which makes authority royal in her voice. Adoniram went.

Mrs. Penn led the way into the kitchen, and pointed to a chair. "Sit down, father," said she; "I've got somethin' I want to say to you."

He sat down heavily; his face was quite stolid, but he looked at her with restive eyes. "Well, what is it, mother?"

"I want to know what you're buildin' that new barn for, father?"

"I ain't got nothin' to say about it."

"It can't be you think you need another barn?"

"I tell ye I ain't got nothin' to say about it, mother; an' I ain't goin' to say nothin'."

"Be you goin' to buy more cows?"

Adoniram did not reply; he shut his mouth tight.

"I know you be, as well as I want to. Now, father, look here"—Sarah Penn had not sat down; she stood before her husband in the humble fashion of a Scripture woman—"I'm goin' to talk real plain to you; I never have sence I married you, but I'm goin' to now. I ain't never complained, an' I ain't goin' to complain now, but I'm goin' to talk plain. You see this room here, father; you look at it well. You see there ain't no carpet on the floor, an' you see the paper is all dirty, an' droppin' off the walls. We ain't had no new paper on it for ten year, an' then I put it on myself, an' it didn't cost but a ninepence a roll. You see this room, father; it's all the one I've had to work in an' eat in an' sit in sence we was married. There ain't another woman in the whole town whose husband ain't got half the means you have but what's got better. It's all the room Nanny's got to have her company in; an' there ain't one of her mates but what's got better, an' their fathers not so able as hers is. It's all the room she'll have to be married in. What would you have thought, father, if we had had our weddin' in a room no better than this? I was married in my mother's parlor, with a carpet on the floor, an' stuffed furniture, an' a mahogany card-table. An' this is all the room my daughter will have to be married in. Look here, father!"

Sarah Penn went across the room as though it were a tragic stage. She flung open a door and disclosed a tiny bedroom, only large enough for a bed and bureau, with a path between. "There, father," said she—"there's all the room I've had to sleep in forty year. All my children were born there—the two that died, an' the two that's livin'. I was sick with a fever there."

She stepped to another door and opened it. It led into the small, ill-lighted pantry. "Here," said she, "is all the buttery I've got—every place I've got for my dishes, to set away my victuals in, an' to keep my milk-pans in. Father, I've been takin' care of the milk of six cows in this place, an' now you're goin' to build a new barn, an' keep more cows, an' give me more to do in it."

She threw open another door. A narrow crooked flight of stairs wound upward from it. "There, father," said she, "I want you to look at the stairs that go up to them two unfinished chambers that are all the places our son an' daughter have had to sleep in all their lives. There ain't a prettier girl in town nor a more ladylike one than Nanny, an' that's the place she has to sleep in. It ain't so good as your horse's stall; it ain't so warm an' tight."

Sarah Penn went back and stood before her husband. "Now, father," said she, "I want to know if you think you're doin' right an' accordin' to what you profess. Here, when we was married, forty year ago, you promised me faithful that we should have a new house built in that lot over in the field before the year was out. You said you had money enough, an' you wouldn't ask me to live in no such place as this. It is forty year now, an' you've been makin' more money, an' I've been savin' of it for you ever since, an' you ain't built no house yet. You've built sheds an' cow-houses an' one new barn, an' now you're goin' to build another. Father, I want to know if you think it's right. You're lodgin' your dumb beasts better than you are your own flesh an' blood. I want to know if you think it's right."

"I ain't got nothin' to say."

"You can't say nothin' without ownin' it ain't right, father. An' there's another thing—I ain't complained; I've got along forty year, an' I s'pose I should forty more, if it wa'n't for that—if we don't have another house. Nanny she can't live with us after she's married. She'll have to go somewheres else to live away from us, an' it don't seem as if I could have it so, noways, father. She wa'n't ever strong. She's got considerable color, but there wa'n't never any backbone to her. I've always took the heft of everything off her, an' she ain't fit to keep house an' do everything herself. She'll be all worn out inside of a year. Think of her doin' all the washin' an' ironin' an' bakin' with them soft white hands an' arms, an' sweepin'! I can't have it so, noways, father."

Mrs. Penn's face was burning; her mild eyes gleamed. She had pleaded her little cause like a Webster; she had ranged from severity to pathos; but her opponent employed that obstinate silence which makes eloquence futile with mocking echoes. Adoniram arose clumsily.

"Father, ain't you got nothin' to say?" said Mrs. Penn.

"I've got to go off after that load of gravel. I can't stan' here talkin' all day."

"Father, won't you think it over, an' have a house built there instead of a barn?"

"I ain't got nothin' to say."

Adoniram shuffled out. Mrs. Penn went into her bedroom. When she came out, her eyes were red. She had a roll of unbleached cotton cloth. She spread it out on the kitchen table, and began cutting out some shirts for her husband. The men over in the field had a team to help them this afternoon; she could hear their halloos. She had a scanty pattern for the shirts; she had to plan and piece the sleeves.

Nanny came home with her embroidery, and sat down with her needlework. She had taken down her curl-papers, and there was a soft roll of fair hair like an aureole over her forehead; her face was as delicately fine and clear as porcelain. Suddenly she looked up, and the tender red flamed all over her face and neck. "Mother," said she.

"What say?"

"I've been thinking—I don't see how we're goin' to have any—wedding in this room. I'd be ashamed to have his folks come if we didn't have anybody else."

"Mebbe we can have some new paper before then; I can put it on. I guess you won't have no call to be ashamed of your belongin's."

"We might have the wedding in the new barn," said Nanny, with gentle pettishness. "Why, mother, what makes you look so?"

Mrs. Penn had started, and was staring at her with a

curious expression. She turned again to her work, and spread out a pattern carefully on the cloth. "Nothin'," said she.

Presently Adoniram clattered out of the yard in his two-wheeled dump cart, standing as proudly upright as a Roman charioteer. Mrs. Penn opened the door and stood there a minute looking out; the halloos of the men sounded louder.

It seemed to her all through the spring months that she heard nothing but the halloos and the noises of saws and hammers. The new barn grew fast. It was a fine edifice for this little village. Men came on pleasant Sundays, in their meeting suits and clean shirt bosoms, and stood around it admiringly. Mrs. Penn did not speak of it, and Adoniram did not mention it to her, although sometimes, upon a return from inspecting it, he bore himself with injured dignity.

"It's a strange thing how your mother feels about the new barn," he said, confidentially, to Sammy one day.

Sammy only grunted after an odd fashion for a boy; he had learned it from his father.

The barn was all completed ready for use by the third week in July. Adoniram had planned to move his stock in on Wednesday, on Tuesday he received a letter which changed his plans. He came in with it early in the morning. "Sammy's been to the post-office," said he, "an' I've got a letter from Hiram." Hiram was Mrs. Penn's brother, who lived in Vermont.

"Well," said Mrs. Penn, "what does he say about the folks?"

"I guess they're all right. He says he thinks if I come up country right off there's a chance to buy jest the kind of a horse I want." He stared reflectively out of the window at the new barn.

Mrs. Penn was making pies. She went on clapping the rolling-pin into the crust, although she was very pale, and her heart beat loudly.

"I dun' know but what I'd better go," said Adoniram. "I hate to go off jest now, right in the midst of hayin', but the ten-acre lot's cut, an' I guess Rufus an' the others can git along without me three or four days. I can't get a horse round here to suit me, nohow, an' I've got to have another for all that wood-haulin' in the fall. I told Hiram to watch out, an' if he got wind of a good horse to let me know. I guess I'd better go.''

''I'll get your clean shirt an' collar,'' said Mrs. Penn calmly.

She laid out Adoniram's Sunday suit and his clean clothes on the bed in the little bedroom. She got his shaving-water and razor ready. At last she buttoned on his collar and fastened his black cravat.

Adoniram never wore his collar and cravat except on extra occasions. He held his head high, with a rasped dignity. When he was all ready, with his coat and·hat brushed, and a lunch of pie and cheese in a paper bag, he hesitated on the threshold of the door. He looked at his wife, and his manner was defiantly apologetic. ''*If* them cows come to-day, Sammy can drive 'em into the new barn,'' said he; ''an' when they bring the hay up, they can pitch it in there.''

''Well,'' replied Mrs. Penn.

Adoniram set his shaven face ahead and started. When he had cleared the door-step, he turned and looked back with a kind of nervous solemnity. ''I shall be back by Saturday if nothin' happens,'' said he.

''Do be careful, father,'' returned his wife.

She stood at the door with Nanny at her elbow and watched him out of sight. Her eyes had a strange, doubtful expression in them; her peaceful forehead was contracted. She went in, and about her baking again. Nanny sat sewing. Her wedding-day was drawing nearer, and she was getting pale and thin with her steady sewing. Her mother kept glancing at her.

''Have you got that pain in your side this mornin'?'' she asked.

''A little.''

Mrs. Penn's face, as she worked, changed, her perplexed forehead smoothed, her eyes were steady, her lips firmly set. She formed a maxim for herself, although incoherently with her unlettered thoughts. ''Unsolicited opportunities are the guide-posts of the Lord to the new roads of life,'' she repeated in effect, and she made up her mind to her course of action.

"S'posin' I *had* wrote to Hiram," she muttered once, when she was in the pantry—"s'posin' I had wrote, an' asked him if he knew of any horse? But I didn't, an' father's goin' wa'n't none of my doin'. It looks like a providence." Her voice rang out quite loud at the last.

"What you talkin' about, mother?" called Nanny.

"Nothin'."

Mrs. Penn hurried her baking; at eleven o'clock it was all done. The load of hay from the west field came slowly down the cart track, and drew up at the new barn. Mrs. Penn ran out. "Stop!" she screamed—"stop!"

The men stopped and looked; Sammy upreared from the top of the load, and stared at his mother.

"Stop!" she cried out again. "Don't you put the hay in that barn; put it in the old one."

"Why, he said to put it in here," returned one of the haymakers, wonderingly. He was a young man, a neighbor's son, whom Adoniram hired by the year to help on the farm.

"Don't you put the hay in the new barn; there's room enough in the old one, ain't there?" said Mrs. Penn.

"Room enough," returned the hired man, in his thick, rustic tones. "Didn't need the new barn, nohow, far as room's concerned. Well, I s'pose he changed his mind." He took hold of the horses' bridles.

Mrs. Penn went back to the house. Soon the kitchen windows were darkened, and a fragrance like warm honey came into the room.

Nanny laid down her work. "I thought father wanted them to put the hay into the new barn?" she said, wonderingly.

"It's all right," replied her mother.

Sammy slid down from the load of hay, and came in to see if dinner was ready.

"I ain't goin' to get a regular dinner to-day, as long as father's gone," said his mother. "I've let the fire go out. You can have some bread an' milk an' pie. I thought we could get along." She set out some bowls of milk, some bread, and a pie on the kitchen table. "You'd better eat your dinner now," said she. "You might jest as well get through with it. I want you to help me afterward."

Nanny and Sammy stared at each other. There was something strange in their mother's manner. Mrs. Penn did not eat anything herself. She went into the pantry, and they heard her moving dishes while they ate. Presently she came out with a pile of plates. She got the clothes-basket out of the shed, and packed them in it. Nanny and Sammy watched. She brought out cups and saucers, and put them in with the plates.

"What you goin' to do, mother?" inquired Nanny, in a timid voice. A sense of something unusual made her tremble, as if it were a ghost. Sammy rolled his eyes over his pie.

"You'll see what I'm goin' to do," replied Mrs. Penn. "If you're through, Nanny, I want you to go up-stairs an' pack up your things; an' I want you, Sammy, to help me take down the bed in the bedroom."

"Oh, mother, what for?" gasped Nanny.

"You'll see."

During the next few hours a feat was performed by this simple, pious New England mother which was equal in its way to Wolfe's storming of the Heights of Abraham. It took no more genius and audacity of bravery for Wolfe to cheer his wondering soldiers up those steep precipices, under the sleeping eyes of the enemy, than for Sarah Penn, at the head of her children, tc move all their little household goods into the new barn while her husband was away.

Nanny and Sammy followed their mother's instructions without a murmur; indeed, they were overawed. There is a certain uncanny and superhuman quality about all such purely original undertakings as their mother's was to them. Nanny went back and forth with her light loads, and Sammy tugged with sober energy.

At five o'clock in the afternoon the little house in which the Penns had lived for forty years had emptied itself into the new barn.

Every builder builds somewhat for unknown purposes, and is in a measure a prophet. The architect of Adoniram Penn's barn, while he designed it for the comfort of four-footed animals, had planned better than he knew for the comfort of humans. Sarah Penn saw at a glance its possibilities. Those great box-stalls, with quilts hung before them, would make better bedrooms than the one she had occupied for forty years, and there was a tight carriage-room. The harness-room, with its chimney and shelves, would make a kitchen of her dreams. The great middle space would make a parlor, by-and-by, fit for a palace. Up stairs there was as much room as down. With partitions and windows, what a house would there be! Sarah looked at the row of stanchions before the allotted space for cows, and reflected that she would have her front entry there.

At six o'clock the stove was up in the harness-room, the kettle was boiling, and the table set for tea. It looked almost as home-like as the abandoned house across the yard had ever done. The young hired man milked, and Sarah directed him calmly to bring the milk to the new barn. He came gaping, dropping little blots of foam from the brimming pails on the grass. Before the next morning he had spread the story of Adoniram Penn's wife moving into the new barn all over the little village. Men assembled in the store and talked it over, women with shawls over their heads scuttled into each other's houses before their work was done. Any deviation from the ordinary course of life in this quiet town was enough to stop all progress in it. Everybody paused to look at the staid, independent figure on the side track. There was a difference of opinion with regard to her. Some held her to be insane; some, of a lawless and rebellious spirit.

Friday the minister went to see her. It was in the forenoon, and she was at the barn door shelling pease for dinner. She looked up and returned his salutation with dignity, then she went on with her work. She did not invite him in. The saintly expression of her face remained fixed, but there was an angry flush over it.

The minister stood awkwardly before her, and talked. She handled the pease as if they were bullets. At last she looked up, and her eyes showed the spirit that her meek front had covered for a lifetime.

"There ain't no use talkin', Mr. Hersey," said she. "I've thought it all over an' over, an' I believe I'm doin' what's right. I've made it the subject of prayer, an' it's betwixt me an' the Lord an' Adoniram. There ain't no call for nobody else to worry about it."

"Well, of course, if you have brought it to the Lord in prayer, and feel satisfied that you are doing right, Mrs. Penn," said the minister, helplessly. His thin gray-bearded face was pathetic. He was a sickly man; his youthful confidence had cooled; he had to scourge himself up to some of his pastoral duties as relentlessly as a Catholic ascetic, and then he was prostrated by the smart.

"I think it's right jest as much as I think it was right for our forefathers to come over from the old country 'cause they didn't have what belonged to 'em," said Mrs. Penn. She arose. The barn threshold might have been Plymouth Rock from her bearing. "I don't doubt you mean well, Mr. Hersey," said she, "but there are things people hadn't ought to interfere with. I've been a member of the church for over forty year. I've got my own mind an' my own feet, an' I'm going to think my own thoughts an' go my own ways, an' nobody but the Lord is goin' to dictate to me unless I've a mind to have him. Won't you come in an' set down? How is Mis' Hersey?"

"She is well, I thank you," replied the minister. He added some more perplexed apologetic remarks; then he retreated.

He could expound the intricacies of every character study in the Scriptures, he was competent to grasp the Pilgrim Fathers and all historical innovators, but Sarah Penn was beyond him. He could deal with primal cases, but parallel ones worsted him. But, after all, although it was aside from his province, he wondered more how Adoniram Penn would deal with his wife than how the Lord would. Everybody shared the wonder. When Adoniram's four new cows arrived, Sarah ordered three to be put in the old barn, the other in the house shed where the cooking-stove had stood. That added to the excitement. It was whispered that all four cows were domiciled in the house.

Towards sunset on Saturday, when Adoniram was expected home, there was a knot of men in the road near the new barn. The hired man had milked, but he still hung around the premises. Sarah Penn had supper all ready. There were brown-bread and baked beans and a custard pie; it was the supper that Adoniram loved on a Saturday night. She had on a clean calico, and she bore herself imperturbably. Nanny and Sammy kept close at her heels. Their eyes were large, and Nanny was full of nervous tremors. Still there was to them more pleasant excitement than anything else. An inborn confidence in their mother over their father asserted itself.

Sammy looked out of the harness-room window. "There he is," he announced, in an awed whisper. He and Nanny peeped around the casing. Mrs. Penn kept on about her work. The children watched Adoniram leave the new horse standing in the drive while he went to the house door. It was fastened. Then he went around to the shed. That door was seldom locked, even when the family was away. The thought how her father would be confronted by the cow flashed upon Nanny. There was a hysterical sob in her throat. Adoniram emerged from the shed and stood looking about in a dazed fashion. His lips moved; he was saying something, but they could not hear what it was. The hired man was peeping around a corner of the old barn, but nobody saw him.

Adoniram took the new horse by the bridle and led him across the yard to the new barn. Nanny and Sammy slunk close to their mother. The barn doors rolled back, and there stood Adoniram, with the long mild face of the great Canadian farm horse looking over his shoulder.

Nanny kept behind her mother, but Sammy stepped suddenly forward, and stood in front of her.

Adoniram stared at the group. "What on airth you all down here for?" said he. "What's the matter over to the house?"

"We've come here to live, father," said Sammy. His shrill voice quavered out bravely.

"What?"—Adoniram sniffed—"what is it smells like cooking?" said he. He stepped forward and looked in the open door of the harness-room. Then he turned to his wife. His old bristling face was pale and frightened. "What on airth does this mean, mother?" he gasped.

"You come in here, father," said Sarah. She led the way into the harness-room and shut the door. "Now, father," said she, "you needn't be scared. I ain't crazy. There ain't nothin' to be upset over. But we've come here to live, an' we're goin' to live here. We've got jest as good a right here as new horses an' cows. The house wa'n't fit for us to live in any longer, an' I made up my mind I wa'n't goin' to stay there. I've done my duty by you forty year, an' I'm goin' to do it now; but I'm goin' to live here. You've got to put in some windows and partitions; an' you'll have to buy some furniture."

"Why, mother!" the old man gasped.

"You'd better take your coat off an' get washed—there's the wash-basin—an' then we'll have supper."

"Why, mother!"

Sammy went past the window, leading the new horse to the old barn. The old man saw him, and shook his head speechlessly. He tried to take off his coat, but his arms seemed to lack the power. His wife helped him. She poured some water into the tin basin, and put in a piece of soap. She got the comb and brush, and smoothed his thin gray hair after he had washed. Then she put the beans, hot bread, and tea on the table. Sammy came in, and the family drew up. Adoniram sat looking dazedly at his plate, and they waited.

"Ain't you goin' to ask a blessin', father?" said Sarah.

And the old man bent his head and mumbled.

All through the meal he stopped eating at intervals, and stared furtively at his wife; but he ate well. The home food tasted good to him, and his old frame was too sturdily healthy to be affected by his mind. But after supper he went out, and sat down on the step of the smaller door at the right of the barn, through which he had meant his Jerseys to pass in stately file, but which Sarah designed for her front house door, and he leaned his head on his hands.

After the supper dishes were cleared away and the milk-pans washed, Sarah went out to him. The twilight was deepening. There was a clear green glow in the sky. Before them stretched the smooth level of field; in the distance was a cluster of hay-stacks like the huts of a village; the air was very cool and calm and sweet. The landscape might have been an ideal one of peace.

Sarah bent over and touched her husband on one of his thin, sinewy shoulders. "Father!"

The old man's shoulders heaved: he was weeping.

"Why, don't do so, father," said Sarah.

"I'll—put up the—partitions, an'—everything you—want, mother."

Sarah put her apron up to her face; she was overcome by her own triumph.

Adoniram was like a fortress whose walls had no active resistance, and went down the instant the right besieging tools were used. "Why, mother," he said, hoarsely, "I hadn't no idee you was so set on't as all this comes to."

The Story of an Hour

KATE CHOPIN

Knowing that Mrs. Mallard was afflicted with a heart trouble, great care was taken to break to her as gently as possible the news of her husband's death.

It was her sister Josephine who told her, in broken sentences; veiled hints that revealed in half concealing. Her husband's friend Richards was there, too, near her. It was he who had been in the newspaper office when intelligence of the railroad disaster was received, with Brently Mallard's name leading the list of "killed." He had only taken the time to assure himself of its truth by a second telegram, and had hastened to forestall any less careful, less tender friend in bearing the sad message.

She did not hear the story as many women have heard the same, with a paralyzed inability to accept its significance. She wept at once, with sudden, wild abandonment, in her sister's arms. When the storm of grief had spent itself she went away to her room alone. She would have no one follow her.

There stood, facing the open window, a comfortable, roomy armchair. Into this she sank, pressed down by a physical exhaustion that haunted her body and seemed to reach into her soul.

She could see in the open square before her house the tops

of trees that were all aquiver with the new spring life. The delicious breath of rain was in the air. In the street below a peddler was crying his wares. The notes of a distant song which some one was singing reached her faintly, and countless sparrows were twittering in the eaves.

There were patches of blue sky showing here and there through the clouds that had met and piled one above the other in the west facing her window.

She sat with her head thrown back upon the cushion of the chair, quite motionless, except when a sob came up into her throat and shook her, as a child who has cried itself to sleep continues to sob in its dreams.

She was young, with a fair, calm face, whose lines bespoke repression and even a certain strength. But now there was a dull stare in her eyes, whose gaze was fixed away off yonder on one of those patches of blue sky. It was not a glance of reflection, but rather indicated a suspension of intelligent thought.

There was something coming to her and she was waiting for it, fearfully. What was it? She did not know; it was too subtle and elusive to name. But she felt it, creeping out of the sky, reaching toward her through the sounds, the scents, the color that filled the air.

Now her bosom rose and fell tumultuously. She was beginning to recognize this thing that was approaching to possess her, and she was striving to beat it back with her will—as powerless as her two white slender hands would have been.

When she abandoned herself a little whispered word escaped her slightly parted lips. She said it over and over under her breath: "free, free, free!" The vacant stare and the look of terror that had followed it went from her eyes. They stayed keen and bright. Her pulses beat fast, and the coursing blood warmed and relaxed every inch of her body.

She did not stop to ask if it were or were not a monstrous joy that held her. A clear and exalted perception enabled her to dismiss the suggestion as trivial.

She knew that she would weep again when she saw the

kind, tender hands folded in death; the face that had never looked save with love upon her, fixed and gray and dead. But she saw beyond that bitter moment a long procession of years to come that would belong to her absolutely. And she opened and spread her arms out to them in welcome.

There would be no one to live for her during those coming years; she would live for herself. There would be no powerful will bending hers in that blind persistence with which men and women believe they have a right to impose a private will upon a fellow-creature. A kind intention or a cruel intention made the act seem no less a crime as she looked upon it in that brief moment of illumination.

And yet she had loved him—sometimes. Often she had not. What did it matter! What could love, the unsolved mystery, count for in face of this possession of self-assertion which she suddenly recognized as the strongest impulse of her being!

"Free! Body and soul free!" she kept whispering.

Josephine was kneeling before the closed door with her lips to the keyhole, imploring for admission. "Louise, open the door! I beg; open the door—you will make yourself ill. What are you doing, Louise? For heaven's sake open the door."

"Go away. I am not making myself ill." No; she was drinking in a very elixir of life through that open window.

Her fancy was running riot along those days ahead of her. Spring days, and summer days, and all sorts of days that would be her own. She breathed a quick prayer that life might be long. It was only yesterday she had thought with a shudder that life might be long.

She arose at length and opened the door to her sister's importunities. There was a feverish triumph in her eyes, and she carried herself unwittingly like a goddess of Victory. She clasped her sister's waist, and together they descended the stairs. Richards stood waiting for them at the bottom.

Some one was opening the front door with a latchkey. It was Brently Mallard who entered, a little travel-stained, composedly carrying his grip-sack and umbrella. He had been far from the scene of the accident, and did not even know there had been one. He stood amazed at Josephine's piercing cry; at Richards' quick motion to screen him from the view of his wife.

But Richards was too late.

When the doctors came they said she had died of heart disease—of joy that kills.

Making a Change

CHARLOTTE PERKINS GILMAN

"Wa-a-a-a-a! Waa-a-a-aaa!"

Frank Gordins set down his coffee cup so hard that it spilled over into the saucer.

"Is there no way to stop that child crying?" he demanded.

"I do not know of any," said his wife, so definitely and politely that the words seemed cut off by machinery.

"I *do*," said his mother with even more definiteness, but less politeness.

Young Mrs. Gordins looked at her mother-in-law from under her delicate level brows, and said nothing. But the weary lines about her eyes deepened; she had been kept awake nearly all night, and for many nights.

So had he. So, as matter of fact, had his mother. She had not the care of the baby—but lay awake wishing she had.

"There's no use talking about it," said Julia. "If Frank is not satisfied with the child's mother, he must say so—perhaps we can make a change."

This was ominously gentle. Julia's nerves were at the breaking point. Upon her tired ears, her sensitive mother's heart, the grating wail from the next room fell like a lash—burnt in like fire. Her ears were hypersensitive, always. She had been an ardent musician before her marriage, and had taught quite successfully on both piano and violin. To any

49

mother a child's cry is painful; to a musical mother it is torment.

But if her ears were sensitive, so was her conscience. If her nerves were weak, her pride was strong. The child was her child, it was her duty to take care of it, and take care of it she would. She spent her days in unremitting devotion to its needs and to the care of her neat flat; and her nights had long since ceased to refresh her.

Again the weary cry rose to a wail.

"It does seem to be time for a change of treatment," suggested the older woman acidly.

"Or a change of residence," offered the younger, in a deadly quiet voice.

"Well, by Jupiter! There'll be a change of some kind, and p. d. q.!" said the son and husband, rising to his feet.

His mother rose also, and left the room, holding her head high and refusing to show any effects of that last thrust.

Frank Gordins glared at his wife. His nerves were raw, too. It does not benefit anyone in health or character to be continuously deprived of sleep. Some enlightened persons use that deprivation as a form of torture.

She stirred her coffee with mechanical calm, her eyes sullenly bent on her plate.

"I will not stand having Mother spoken to like that," he stated with decision.

"I will not stand having her interfere with my methods of bringing up children."

"Your methods! Why, Julia, my mother knows more about taking care of babies than you'll ever learn! She has the real love of it—and the practical experience. Why can't you *let* her take care of the kid—and we'll all have some peace!"

She lifted her eyes and looked at him; deep inscrutable wells of angry light. He had not the faintest appreciation of her state of mind. When people say they are "nearly crazy" from weariness, they state a practical fact. The old phrase which describes reason as "tottering on her throne" is also a clear one.

Julia was more near the verge of complete disaster than the

family dreamed. The conditions were so simple, so usual, so inevitable.

Here was Frank Gordins, well brought up, the only son of a very capable and idolatrously affectionate mother. He had fallen deeply and desperately in love with the exalted beauty and fine mind of the young music teacher, and his mother had approved. She too loved music and admired beauty.

Her tiny store in the savings bank did not allow of a separate home, and Julia had cordially welcomed her to share in their household.

Here was affection, propriety, and peace. Here was a noble devotion on the part of the young wife, who so worshipped her husband that she used to wish she had been the greatest musician on earth—that she might give it up for him! She had given up her music, perforce, for many months, and missed it more than she knew.

She bent her mind to the decoration and artistic management of their little apartment, finding her standards difficult to maintain by the ever-changing inefficiency of her help. The musical temperament does not always include patience, nor, necessarily, the power of management.

When the baby came, her heart overflowed with utter devotion and thankfulness; she was his wife—the mother of his child. Her happiness lifted and pushed within till she longed more than ever for her music, for the free-pouring current of expression, to give forth her love and pride and happiness. She had not the gift of words.

So now she looked at her husband, dumbly, while wild visions of separation, of secret flight—even of self-destruction— swung dizzily across her mental vision. All she said was, "All right, Frank. We'll make a change. And you shall have— some peace."

"Thank goodness for that, Jule! You do look tired, girlie— let Mother see to His Nibs, and try to get a nap, can't you?"

"Yes," she said. "Yes . . . I think I will." Her voice had a peculiar note in it. If Frank had been an alienist, or even a general physician, he would have noticed it. But his work lay in electric coils, in dynamos and copper wiring—not in women's nerves—and he did not notice it.

He kissed her and went out, throwing back his shoulders and drawing a long breath of relief as he left the house behind him and entered his own world.

"This being married—and bringing up children—is not what it's cracked up to be." That was the feeling in the back of his mind. But it did not find full admission, much less expression.

When a friend asked him, "All well at home?" he said, "Yes, thank you—pretty fair. Kid cries a good deal—but that's natural, I suppose."

He dismissed the whole matter from his mind and bent his faculties to a man's task—how he can earn enough to support a wife, a mother, and a son.

At home his mother sat in her small room, looking out of the window at the ground-glass one just across the "well," and thinking hard.

By the disorderly little breakfast table his wife remained motionless, her chin in her hands, her big eyes staring at nothing, trying to formulate in her weary mind some reliable reason why she should not do what she was thinking of doing. But her mind was too exhausted to serve her properly.

Sleep—sleep—sleep—that was the one thing she wanted. Then his mother could take care of the baby all she wanted to, and Frank could have some peace. . . . Oh, dear! It was time for the child's bath.

She gave it to him mechanically. On the stroke of the hour, she prepared the sterilized milk and arranged the little one comfortably with his bottle. He snuggled down, enjoying it, while she stood watching him.

She emptied the tub, put the bath apron to dry, picked up all the towels and sponges and varied appurtenances of the elaborate performance of bathing the first-born, and then sat staring straight before her, more weary than ever, but growing inwardly determined.

Greta had cleared the table, with heavy heels and hands, and was now rattling dishes in the kitchen. At every slam, the young mother winced, and when the girl's high voice began a sort of doleful chant over her work, young Mrs. Gordins rose to her feet with a shiver and made her decision.

She carefully picked up the child and his bottle, and carried him to his grandmother's room.

"Would you mind looking after Albert?" she asked in a flat, quiet voice. "I think I'll try to get some sleep."

"Oh, I shall be delighted," replied her mother-in-law. She said it in a tone of cold politeness, but Julia did not notice. She laid the child on the bed and stood looking at him in the same dull way for a little while, then went out without another word.

Mrs. Gordins, senior, sat watching the baby for some long moments. "He's a perfectly lovely child!" she said softly, gloating over his rosy beauty. "There's not a *thing* the matter with him! It's just her absurd ideas. She's so irregular with him! To think of letting that child cry for an hour! He is nervous because she is. And of course she couldn't feed him till after his bath—of course not!"

She continued in these sarcastic meditations for some time, taking the empty bottle away from the small wet mouth, that sucked on for a few moments aimlessly and then was quiet in sleep.

"I could take care of him so that he'd *never* cry!" she continued to herself, rocking slowly back and forth. "And I could take care of twenty like him—and enjoy it! I believe I'll go off somewhere and do it. Give Julia a rest. Change of residence, indeed!"

She rocked and planned, pleased to have her grandson with her, even while asleep.

Greta had gone out on some errand of her own. The rooms were very quiet. Suddenly the old lady held up her head and sniffed. She rose swiftly to her feet and sprang to the gas jet—no, it was shut off tightly. She went back to the dining-room—all right there.

"That foolish girl has left the range going and it's blown out!" she thought, and went to the kitchen. No, the little room was fresh and clean, every burner turned off.

"Funny! It must come in from the hall." She opened the door. No, the hall gave only its usual odor of diffused basement. Then the parlor—nothing there. The little alcove called by the renting agent "the music room," where Julia's closed piano and violin case stood dumb and dusty—nothing there.

"It's in her room—and she's asleep!" said Mrs. Gordins, senior; and she tried to open the door. It was locked. She knocked—there was no answer; knocked louder—shook it—rattled the knob. No answer.

Then Mrs. Gordins thought quickly. "It may be an accident, and nobody must know. Frank mustn't know. I'm glad Greta's out. I *must* get in somehow!" She looked at the transom, and the stout rod Frank had himself put up for the portieres Julia loved.

"I believe I can do it, at a pinch."

She was a remarkably active woman of her years, but no memory of earlier gymnastic feats could quite cover the exercise. She hastily brought the step-ladder. From its top she could see in, and what she saw made her determine recklessly.

Grabbing the pole with small strong hands, she thrust her light frame bravely through the opening, turning clumsily but successfully, and dropping breathlessly and somewhat bruised to the floor, she flew to open the windows and doors.

When Julia opened her eyes she found loving arms around her, and wise, tender words to soothe and reassure.

"Don't say a thing, dearie—I understand. I *understand,* I tell you! Oh, my dear girl—my precious daughter! We haven't been half good enough to you, Frank and I! But cheer up now—I've got the *loveliest* plan to tell you about! We *are* going to make a change! Listen now!"

And while the pale young mother lay quiet, petted and waited on to her heart's content, great plans were discussed and decided on.

Frank Gordins was pleased when the baby "outgrew his crying spells." He spoke of it to his wife.

"Yes," she said sweetly. "He has better care."

"I knew you'd learn," said he, proudly.

"I have!" she agreed. "I've learned—ever so much!"

He was pleased, too, vastly pleased, to have her health improve rapidly and steadily, the delicate pink come back to her cheeks, the soft light to her eyes; and when she made music for him in the evening, soft music, with shut doors—not to waken Albert—he felt as if his days of courtship had come again.

Greta the hammer-footed had gone, and an amazing French matron who came in by the day had taken her place. He asked no questions as to this person's peculiarities, and did not know that she did the purchasing and planned the meals, meals of such new delicacy and careful variance as gave him much delight. Neither did he know that her wages were greater than her predecessor's. He turned over the same sum weekly, and did not pursue details.

He was pleased also that his mother seemed to have taken a new lease on life. She was so cheerful and brisk, so full of little jokes and stories—as he had known in his boyhood; and above all she was so free and affectionate with Julia, that he was more than pleased.

"I tell you what it is!" he said to a bachelor friend. "You fellows don't know what you're missing!" And he brought one of them home to dinner—just to show him.

"Do you do all that on thirty-five a week?" his friend demanded.

"That's about it," he answered proudly.

"Well, your wife's a wonderful manager—that's all I can say. And you've got the best cook I ever saw, or heard of, or ate of—I suppose I might say—for five dollars."

Mrs. Gordins was pleased and proud. But he was neither pleased nor proud when someone said to him, with displeasing frankness, "I shouldn't think you'd want your wife to be giving music lessons, Frank!"

He did not show surprise or anger to his friend, but saved it for his wife. So surprised and so angry was he that he did a most unusual thing—he left his business and went home early in the afternoon. He opened the door of his flat. There was no one in it. He went through every room. No wife; no child; no mother; no servant.

The elevator boy heard him banging about, opening and shutting doors, and grinned happily. When Mr. Gordins came out, Charles volunteered some information.

"Young Mrs. Gordins is out, sir; but old Mrs. Gordins and the baby—they're upstairs. On the roof, I think."

Mr. Gordins went to the roof. There he found his mother, a smiling, cheerful nursemaid, and fifteen happy babies.

Mrs. Gordins, senior, rose to the occasion promptly.

"Welcome to my baby-garden, Frank," she said cheerfully. "I'm so glad you could get off in time to see it."

She took his arm and led him about, proudly, exhibiting her sunny roof-garden, her sand-pile and big, shallow, zinc-lined pool, her flowers and vines, her seesaws, swings, and floor mattresses.

"You see how happy they are," she said. "Celia can manage very well for a few moments." And then she exhibited to him the whole upper flat, turned into a convenient place for many little ones to take their naps or to play in if the weather was bad.

"Where's Julia?" he demanded first.

"Julia will be in presently," she told him, "by five o'clock anyway. And the mothers come for the babies by then, too. I have them from nine or ten to five."

He was silent, both angry and hurt.

"We didn't tell you at first, my dear boy, because we knew you wouldn't like it, and we wanted to make sure it would go well. I rent the upper flat, you see—it is forty dollars a month, same as ours—and pay Celia five dollars a week, and pay Dr. Holbrook downstairs the same for looking over my little ones every day. She helped me to get them, too. The mothers pay me three dollars a week each, and don't have to keep a nursemaid. And I pay ten dollars a week board to Julia, and still have about ten of my own."

"And she gives music lessons?"

"Yes, she gives music lessons, just as she used to. She loves it, you know. You must have noticed how happy and well she is now—haven't you? And so am I. And so is Albert. You can't feel very badly about a thing that makes us all happy, can you?"

Just then Julia came in, radiant from a brisk walk, fresh and cheery, a big bunch of violets at her breast.

"Oh, Mother," she cried, "I've got tickets and we'll all go to hear Melba—if we can get Celia to come in for the evening."

She saw her husband, and a guilty flush rose to her brow as she met his reproachful eyes.

"Oh, Frank!" she begged, her arms around his neck. "Please don't mind! Please get used to it! Please be proud of us! Just think, we're all so happy, and we earn about a hundred dollars a week—all of us together. You see, I have Mother's ten to add to the house money, and twenty or more of my own!"

They had a long talk together that evening, just the two of them. She told him, at last, what a danger had hung over them—how near it came.

"And Mother showed me the way out, Frank. The way to have my mind again—and not lose you! She is a different woman herself now that she has her heart and hands full of babies. Albert does enjoy it so! And *you've* enjoyed it—till you found it out!

"And dear—my own love—I don't mind it now at all! I love my home, I love my work, I love my mother, I love you. And as to children—I wish I had six!"

He looked at her flushed, eager, lovely face, and drew her close to him.

"If it makes all of you as happy as that," he said, "I guess I can stand it."

And in after years he was heard to remark, "This being married and bringing up children is as easy as can be—when you learn how!"

Sweat

ZORA NEALE HURSTON

It was eleven o'clock of a Spring night in Florida. It was
Sunday. Any other night, Delia Jones would have been in bed
for two hours by this time. But she was a washwoman, and
Monday morning meant a great deal to her. So she collected
the soiled clothes on Saturday when she returned the clean
things. Sunday night after church, she sorted them and put the
white things to soak. It saved her almost a half day's start. A
great hamper in the bedroom held the clothes that she brought
home. It was so much neater than a number of bundles lying
around.

She squatted in the kitchen floor beside the great pile of
clothes, sorting them into small heaps according to color, and
humming a song in a mournful key, but wondering through it
all where Sykes, her husband, had gone with her horse and
buckboard.

Just then something long, round, limp and black fell upon
her shoulders and slithered to the floor beside her. A great
terror took hold of her. It softened her knees and dried her
mouth so that it was a full minute before she could cry out or
move. Then she saw that it was the big bull whip her
husband liked to carry when he drove.

She lifted her eyes to the door and saw him standing there
bent over with laughter at her fright. She screamed at him.

"Sykes, what you throw dat whip on me like dat? You know it would skeer me—looks like a snake, an' you knows how skeered Ah is of snakes."

"Course Ah knowed it! That's how come Ah done it." He slapped his leg with his hand and almost rolled on the ground in his mirth. "If you such a big fool dat you got to have a fit over a earth worm or a string, Ah don't keer how bad Ah skeer you."

"You aint got no business doing it. Gawd knows it's a sin. Some day Ah'm gointuh drop dead from some of yo' foolishness. 'Nother thing, where you been wid mah rig? Ah feeds dat pony. He aint fuh you to be drivin' wid no bull whip."

"You sho is one aggravatin' nigger woman!" he declared and stepped into the room. She resumed her work and did not answer him at once. "Ah done tole you time and again to keep them white folks' clothes outa dis house."

He picked up the whip and glared down at her. Delia went on with her work. She went out into the yard and returned with a galvanized tub and set it on the washbench. She saw that Sykes had kicked all of the clothes together again, and now stood in her way truculently, his whole manner hoping, *praying*, for an argument. But she walked calmly around him and commenced to re-sort the things.

"Next time, Ah'm gointer kick 'em outdoors," he threatened as he struck a match along the leg of his corduroy breeches.

Delia never looked up from her work, and her thin, stooped shoulders sagged further.

"Ah aint for no fuss t'night, Sykes. Ah just come from taking sacrament at the church house."

He snorted scornfully. "Yeah, you just come from de church house on a Sunday night, but heah you is gone to work on them clothes. You aint nothing but a hypocrite. One of them amen-corner Christians—sing, whoop, and shout, then come home and wash white folks' clothes on the Sabbath."

He stepped roughly upon the whitest pile of things, kicking them helter-skelter as he crossed the room. His wife gave a little scream of dismay, and quickly gathered them together again.

"Sykes, you quit grindin' dirt into these clothes! How can Ah git through by Sat'day if Ah don't start on Sunday?"

"Ah don't keer if you never git through. Anyhow, Ah done promised Gawd and a couple of other men, Ah aint gointer have it in mah house. Don't gimme no lip neither, else Ah'll throw 'em out and put mah fist up side yo' head to boot."

Delia's habitual meekness seemed to slip from her shoulders like a blown scarf. She was on her feet; her poor little body, her bare knuckly hands bravely defying the strapping hulk before her.

"Looka heah, Sykes, you done gone too fur. Ah been married to you fur fifteen years, and Ah been takin' in washin' fur fifteen years, Sweat, sweat, sweat! Work and sweat, cry and sweat, pray and sweat!"

"What's that got to do with me?" he asked brutally.

"What's it got to do with you, Sykes? Mah tub of suds is filled yo' belly with vittles more times than yo' hands is filled it. Mah sweat is done paid for this house and Ah reckon Ah kin keep on sweatin' in i⁺."

She seized the iron skillet from the stove and struck a defensive pose, which act surprised him greatly, coming from her. It cowed him and he did not strike her as he usually did.

"Naw you won't," she panted, "that ole snaggle-toothed black woman you runnin' with aint comin' heah to pile up on *mah* sweat and blood. You aint paid for nothin' on this place, and Ah'm gointer stay right heah till Ah'm toted out foot foremost."

"Well, you better quit gittin' me riled up, else they'll be totin' you out sooner than you expect. Ah'm so tired of you Ah don't know whut to do. Gawd! how Ah hates skinny wimmen!"

A little awed by his new Delia, he sidled out of the door and slammed the back gate after him. He did not say where he had gone, but she knew too well. She knew very well that he would not return until nearly daybreak also. Her work over, she went on to bed but not to sleep at once. Things had come to a pretty pass!

She lay awake, gazing upon the debris that cluttered their matrimonial trail. Not an image left standing along the way. Anything like flowers had long ago been drowned in the salty stream that had been pressed from her heart. Her tears, her sweat, her blood. She had brought love to the union and he had brought a longing after the flesh. Two months after the wedding, he had given her the first brutal beating. She had the memory of his numerous trips to Orlando with all of his wages when he had returned to her penniless, even before the first year had passed. She was young and soft then, but now she thought of her knotty, muscled limbs, her harsh knuckly hands, and drew herself up into an unhappy little ball in the middle of the big feather bed. Too late now to hope for love, even if it were not Bertha it would be someone else. This case differed from the others only in that she was bolder than the others. Too late for everything except her little home. She had built it for her old days, and planted one by one the trees and flowers there. It was lovely to her, lovely.

Somehow, before sleep came, she found herself saying aloud: "Oh well, whatever goes over the Devil's back, is got to come under his belly. Sometime or ruther, Sykes, like everybody else, is gointer reap his sowing." After that she was able to build a spiritual earthworks against her husband. His shells could no longer reach her. *Amen.* She went to sleep and slept until he announced his presence by kicking her feet and rudely snatching the covers away.

"Gimme some kivah heah, an' git yo' damn foots over on yo' own side! Ah oughter mash you in yo' mouf fuh drawing dat skillet on me."

Delia went clear to the rail without answering him. A triumphant indifference to all that he was or did.

The week was full of work for Delia as all other weeks, and Saturday found her behind her little pony, collecting and delivering clothes.

It was a hot, hot day near the end of July. The village men on Joe Clarke's porch even chewed cane listlessly. They did not hurl the caneknots as usual. They let them dribble over the edge of the porch. Even conversation had collapsed under the heat.

"Heah come Delia Jones," Jim Merchant said, as the shaggy pony came 'round the bend of the road toward them. The rusty buckboard was heaped with baskets of crisp, clean laundry.

"Yep," Joe Lindsay agreed. "Hot or col', rain or shine, jes ez reg'lar ez de weeks roll roun' Delia carries 'em an' fetches 'em on Sat'day."

"She better if she wanter eat," said Moss. "Syke Jones aint wuth de shot an' powder hit would tek tuh kill 'em. Not to *huh* he aint."

"He sho' aint," Walter Thomas chimed in. "It's too bad, too, cause she wuz a right pritty lil trick when he got huh. Ah'd uh mah'ied huh mahseff if he hadnter beat me to it."

Delia nodded briefly at the men as she drove past.

"Too much knockin' will ruin *any* 'oman. He done beat huh 'nough tuh kill three women, let 'lone change they looks," said Elijah Moseley. "How Syke kin stommuck dat big black greasy Mogul he's layin' roun' wid, gits me. Ah swear dat eight-rock couldn't kiss a sardine can Ah done thowed out de back do' 'way las' yeah."

"Aw, she's fat, thass how come. He's allus been crazy 'bout fat women," put in Merchant. "He'd a' been tied up wid one long time ago if he could a' found one tuh have him. Did Ah tell yuh 'bout him come sidlin' in' roun' *mah* wife—bringin' her a basket uh peecans outa his yard fuh a present? Yessir, mah wife! She tol' him tuh take em right straight back home, cause Delia works so hard ovah dat wash tub she reckon everything on de place taste lak sweat an' soapsuds. Ah jus' wisht Ah'd a caught 'im 'roun' dere! Ah'd a' made his hips ketch on fiah down dat shell road."

"Ah know he done it, too. Ah sees 'im grinnin' at every 'oman dat passes," Walter Thomas said. "But even so, he useter eat some mighty big hunks uh humble pie tuh git dat lil' 'oman he got. She wuz ez pritty ez a speckled pup! Dat wuz fifteen yeahs ago. He useter be so skeered uh losin' huh, she could make him do some parts of a husband's duty. Dey never wuz de same in de mind."

"There oughter be a law about him," said Lindsay. "He aint fit tuh carry guts tuh a bear."

Clarke spoke for the first time. "Taint no law on earth dat kin make a man be decent if it aint in 'im. There's plenty men dat takes a wife lak dey do a joint uh sugar-cane. It's round, juicy an' sweet when dey gits it. But dey squeeze an' grind, squeeze an' grind an' wring tell dey wring every drop uh pleasure dat's in 'em out. When dey's satisfied dat dey is wrung dry, dey treats 'em jes lak dey do a cane-chew. Dey throws 'em away. Dey knows whut dey is doin' while dey is at it, an' hates theirselves fuh it but they keeps on hangin' after huh tell she's empty. Den dey hates huh fuh bein' a cane-chew an' in de way."

"We oughter take Syke an' dat stray 'oman uh his'n down in Lake Howell swamp an' lay on de rawhide till they cain't say Lawd a' mussy.' He allus wuz uh ovahbearin' niggah, but since dat white 'oman from up north done teached 'im how to run a automobile, he done got too biggety to live—an' we oughter kill 'im." Old man Anderson advised.

A grunt of approval went around the porch. But the heat was melting their civic virtue and Elijah Moseley began to bait Joe Clarke.

"Come on, Joe, git a melon outa dere an' slice it up for yo' customers. We'se all sufferin' wid de heat. De bear's done got *me*!"

"Thass right, Joe, a watermelon is jes' whut Ah needs tuh cure de eppizudicks," Walter Thomas joined forces with Moseley. "Come on dere, Joe. We all is steady customers an' you aint set us up in a long time. Ah chooses dat long, bowlegged Floridy favorite."

"A god, an' be dough. You all gimme twenty cents and slice way." Clarke retorted. "Ah needs a col' slice m'self. Heah, everybody chip in. Ah'll lend y'll mah meat knife."

The money was quickly subscribed and the huge melon

brought forth. At that moment, Sykes and Bertha arrived. A determined silence fell on the porch and the melon was put away again.

Merchant snapped down the blade of his jackknife and moved toward the store door.

"Come on in, Joe, an' gimme a slab uh sow belly an' uh pound uh coffee—almost fuhgot 'twas Sat'day. Got to git on home." Most of the men left also.

Just then Delia drove past on her way home, as Sykes was ordering magnificently for Bertha. It pleased him for Delia to see.

"Git whutsoever yo' heart desires, Honey. Wait a minute, Joe. Give huh two bottles uh strawberry soda-water, uh quart uh parched ground-peas, an' a block uh chewin' gum."

With all this they left the store, with Sykes reminding Bertha that this was his town and she could have it if she wanted it.

The men returned soon after they left, and held their watermelon feast.

"Where did Syke Jones git da 'oman from nohow?" Lindsay asked.

"Ovah Apopka. Guess dey musta been cleanin' out de town when she lef'. She don't look lak a thing but a hunk uh liver wid hair on it."

"Well, she sho' kin squall," Dave Carter contributed. "When she gits ready tuh laff, she jes' opens huh mouf an' latches it back tuh de las' notch. No ole grandpa alligator down in Lake Bell aint got nothin' on huh."

Bertha had been in town three months now. Sykes was still paying her room rent at Della Lewis'—the only house in town that would have taken her in. Sykes took her frequently to Winter Park to "stomps." He still assured her that he was the swellest man in the state.

"Sho' you kin have dat lil' ole house soon's Ah kin git dat 'oman outa dere. Everything b'longs tuh me an' you sho' kin have it. Ah sho' 'bominates uh skinny 'oman. Lawdy, you sho' is got one portly shape on you! You kin git *anything* you wants. Dis is *mah* town an' you sho' kin have it.''

Delia's work-worn knees crawled over the earth in Gethesemane and up the rocks of Calvary many, many times during these months. She avoided the villagers and meeting places in her efforts to be blind and deaf. But Bertha nullified this to a degree, by coming to Delia's house to call Sykes out to her at the gate.

Delia and Sykes fought all the time now with no peaceful interludes. They slept and ate in silence. Two or three times Delia had attempted a timid friendliness, but she was repulsed each time. It was plain that the breaches must remain agape.

The sun had burned July to August. The heat streamed down like a million hot arrows, smiting all things living upon the earth. Grass withered, leaves browned, snakes went blind in shedding and men and dogs went mad. Dog days!

Delia came home one day and found Sykes there before her. She wondered, but started to go on into the house without speaking, even though he was standing in the kitchen door and she must either stoop under his arm or ask him to move. He made no room for her. She noticed a soap box beside the steps, but paid no particular attention to it, knowing that he must have brought it there. As she was stooping to pass under his outstretched arm, he suddenly pushed her backward, laughingly.

"Look in de box dere Delia, Ah done brung yuh somethin'!"

She nearly fell upon the box in her stumbling, and when she saw what it held, she all but fainted outright.

"Syke! Syke, mah Gawd! You take dat rattlesnake 'way from heah! You *gottuh*. Oh, Jesus, have mussy!"

"Ah aint gut tuh do nuthin' uh de kin'—fact is Ah aint got tuh do nothin' but die. Taint no use uh you puttin' on airs makin' out lak you skeered uh dat snake—he's gointer stay right heah tell he die. He wouldn't bite me cause Ah knows how tuh handle 'im. Nohow he wouldn't risk breakin' out his fangs 'gin *yo'* skinny laigs.''

"Naw, now Syke, don't keep dat thing 'roun' heah tuh skeer me tuh death. You knows Ah'm even feared uh earth worms. Thass de biggest snake Ah evah did see. Kill 'im Syke, please.''

"Doan ast me tuh do nothin' fuh yuh. Goin' 'roun' tryin' tuh be so damn asterperious. Naw, Ah aint gonna kill it. Ah think uh damn sight mo' uh him dan you! Dat's a nice snake an' anybody doan lak 'im kin jes' hit de grit.''

The village soon heard that Sykes had the snake, and came to see and ask questions.

"How de hen-fire did you ketch dat six-foot rattler, Syke?'' Thomas asked.

"He's full uh frogs so he caint hardly move, thass how Ah eased up on 'm. But Ah'm a snake charmer an' knows how tuh handle 'em. Shux, dat aint nothin'. Ah could ketch one eve'y day if Ah so wanted tuh.''

"Whut he needs is a heavy hick'ry club leaned real heavy on his head. Dat's de bes' way tuh charm a rattlesnake.''

"Naw, Walt, y'll jes' don't understand dese diamon' backs lak Ah do,'' said Sykes in a superior tone of voice.

The village agreed with Walter, but the snake stayed on. His box remained by the kitchen door with its screen wire covering. Two or three days later it had digested its meal of frogs and literally came to life. It rattled at every movement in the kitchen or the yard. One day as Delia came down the kitchen steps she saw his chalky-white fangs curved like scimitars hung in the wire meshes. This time she did not run away with averted eyes as usual. She stood for a long time in the doorway in a red fury that grew bloodier for every second that she regarded the creature that was her torment.

That night she broached the subject as soon as Sykes sat down to the table.

"Syke, Ah wants you tuh take dat snake 'way fum heah. You done starved me an' Ah put up widcher, you done beat me an Ah took dat, but you done kilt all mah insides bringin' dat varmint heah.''

Sykes poured out a saucer full of coffee and drank it deliberately before he answered her.

"A whole lot Ah keer 'bout how you feels inside uh out. Dat snake aint goin' no damn wheah till Ah gits ready fuh 'im tuh go. So fur as beatin' is concerned, yuh aint took near all dat you gointer take ef yuh stay 'roun' *me*."

Delia pushed back her plate and got up from the table. "Ah hates you, Sykes," she said calmly. "Ah hates you tuh de same degree dat Ah useter love yuh. Ah done took an' took till mah belly is full up tuh mah neck. Dat's de reason Ah got mah letter fum de church an' moved mah membership tuh Woodbridge—so Ah don't haftuh take no sacrament wid yuh. Ah don't wantuh see yuh 'roun' me atall. Lay 'roun' wid dat 'oman all yuh wants tuh, but gwan 'way fum me an' mah house. Ah hates yuh lak uh suck-egg dog."

Sykes almost let the huge wad of corn bread and collard greens he was chewing fall out of his mouth in amazement. He had a hard time whipping himself up to the proper fury to try to answer Delia.

"Well, Ah'm glad you does hate me. Ah'm sho' tiahed uh you hangin' ontuh me. Ah don't want yuh. Look at yuh stringey ole neck! Yo' rawbony laigs an' arms is enough tuh cut uh man tuh death. You looks jes' lak de devvul's doll-baby tuh *me*. You cain't hate me no worse dan Ah hates you. Ah been hatin' *you* fuh years."

"Yo' ole black hide don't look lak nothin' tuh me, but uh passle uh wrinkled up rubber, wid yo' big ole yeahs flappin' on each side lak uh paih uh buzzard wings. Don't think Ah'm gointuh be run 'way fum mah house neither. Ah'm goin' tuh de white folks bout *you*, mah young man, de very nex' time you lay yo' han's on me. Mah cup is done run ovah."

Delia said this with no signs of fear and Sykes departed from the house, threatening her, but made not the slightest move to carry out any of them.

That night he did not return at all, and the next day being Sunday, Delia was glad she did not have to quarrel before she hitched up her pony and drove the four miles to Woodbridge.

She stayed to the night service—"love feast"—which was very warm and full of spirit. In the emotional winds her domestic trials were borne far and wide so that she sang as she drove homeward,

"Jurden water, black an' col'
Chills de body, not de soul
An' Ah wantah cross Jurden in uh calm time."

She came from the barn to the kitchen door and stopped.

"Whut's de mattah, ol' satan, you aint kickin' up yo' racket?" She addressed the snake's box. Complete silence. She went on into the house with a new hope in its birth struggles. Perhaps her threat to go to the white folks had frightened Sykes! Perhaps he was sorry! Fifteen years of misery and suppression had brought Delia to the place where she would hope *anything* that looked towards a way over or through her wall of inhibitions.

She felt in the match safe behind the stove at once for a match. There was only one there.

"Dat niggah wouldn't fetch nothin' heah tuh save his rotten neck, but he kin run thew whut Ah brings quick enough. Now he done toted off nigh on tuh haff uh box uh matches. He done had dat 'oman heah in mah house too."

Nobody but a woman could tell how she knew this even before she struck the match. But she did and it put her into a new fury.

Presently she brought in the tubs to put the white things to soak. This time she decided she need not bring the hamper out of the bedroom: she would go in there and do the sorting. She picked up the pot-bellied lamp and went in. The room was small and the hamper stood hard by the foot of the white iron bed. She could sit and reach through the bedposts—resting as she worked.

"Ah wantah cross Jurden in uh calm time." She was singing again. The mood of the "love feast" had returned. She threw back the lid of the basket almost gaily. Then, moved by both horror and terror, she sprang back toward the door. *There lay the snake in the basket!* He moved sluggishly at first, but even as she turned round and round, jumped up and down in an insanity of fear, he began to stir vigorously. She saw him pouring his awful beauty from the basket upon the bed, then she seized the lamp and ran as fast as she could to the kitchen. The wind from the open door blew out the light and the darkness added to her terror. She sped to the darkness of the yard, slamming the door after her before she thought to set down the lamp. She did not feel safe even on the ground, so she climbed up in the hay barn.

There for an hour or more she lay sprawled upon the hay a gibbering wreck.

Finally she grew quiet, and after that, coherent thought. With this, stalked through her a cold, bloody rage. Hours of this. A period of introspection, a space of retrospection, then a mixture of both. Out of this an awful calm.

"Well, Ah done de bes' Ah could. If things aint right, Gawd knows taint mah fault."

She went to sleep—a twitch sleep—and woke up to a faint gray sky. There was a loud hollow sound below. She peered out. Sykes was at the wood-pile, demolishing a wire-covered box.

He hurried to the kitchen door, but hung outside there some minutes before he entered, and stood some minutes more inside before he closed it after him.

The gray in the sky was spreading. Delia descended without fear now, and crouched beneath the low bedroom window. The drawn shade shut out the dawn, shut in the night. But the thin walls held back no sound.

"Dat ol' scratch is woke up now!" She mused at the tremendous whirr inside, which every woodsman knows, is one of the sound illusions. The rattler is a ventriloquist. His whirr sounds to the right, to the left, straight ahead, behind, close under foot—everywhere but where it is. Woe to him who guesses wrong unless he is prepared to hold up his end of the argument! Sometimes he strikes without rattling at all.

Inside, Sykes heard nothing until he knocked a pot lid off the stove while trying to reach the match safe in the dark. He had emptied his pockets at Bertha's.

The snake seemed to wake up under the stove and Sykes made a quick leap into the bedroom. In spite of the gin he had had, his head was clearing now.

"Mah Gawd!" he chattered, "ef Ah could on'y strack uh light!"

The rattling ceased for a moment as he stood paralyzed. He waited. It seemed that the snake waited also.

"Oh, fuh de light! Ah thought he'd be too sick"—Sykes was muttering to himself when the whirr began again, closer, right underfoot this time. Long before this, Sykes' ability to think had been flattened down to primitive instinct and he leaped—onto the bed.

Outside Delia heard a cry that might have come from a maddened chimpanzee, a stricken gorilla. All the terror, all the horror, all the rage that man possibly could express, without a recognizable human sound.

A tremendous stir inside there, another series of animal screams, the intermittent whirr of the reptile. The shade torn violently down from the window, letting in the red dawn, a huge brown hand seizing the window stick, great dull blows upon the wooden floor punctuating the gibberish of sound long after the rattle of the snake had abruptly subsided. All this Delia could see and hear from her place beneath the window, and it made her ill. She crept over to the four-o'clocks and stretched herself on the cool earth to recover.

She lay there. "Delia, Delia!" She could hear Sykes calling in a most despairing tone as one who expected no answer. The sun crept on up, and he called. Delia could not move— her legs were gone flabby. She never moved, he called, and the sun kept rising.

"Mah Gawd!" She heard him moan, "Mah Gawd fum Heben!" She heard him stumbling about and got up from her flower-bed. The sun was growing warm. As she approached the door she heard him call out hopefully, "Delia, is dat you Ah heah?"

She saw him on his hands and knees as soon as she reached the door. He crept an inch or two toward her—all that he was able, and she saw his horribly swollen neck and his one open eye shining with hope. A surge of pity too strong to support bore her away from that eye that must, could not, fail to see the tubs. He would see the lamp. Orlando with its doctors was too far. She could scarcely reach the Chinaberry tree, where she waited in the growing heat while inside she knew the cold river was creeping up and up to extinguish that eye which must know by now that she knew.

Rope

KATHERINE ANNE PORTER

On the third day after they moved to the country he came walking back from the village carrying a basket of groceries and a twenty-four-yard coil of rope. She came out to meet him, wiping her hands on her green smock. Her hair was tumbled, her nose was scarlet with sunburn; he told her that already she looked like a born country woman. His gray flannel shirt stuck to him, his heavy shoes were dusty. She assured him he looked like a rural character in a play.

Had he brought the coffee? She had been waiting all day long for coffee. They had forgot it when they ordered at the store the first day.

Gosh, no, he hadn't. Lord, now he'd have to go back. Yes, he would if it killed him. He thought, though, he had everything else. She reminded him it was only because he didn't drink coffee himself. If he did he would remember it quick enough. Suppose they ran out of cigarettes? Then she saw the rope. What was that for? Well, he thought it might do to hang clothes on, or something. Naturally she asked him if he thought they were going to run a laundry? They already had a fifty-foot line hanging right before his eyes? Why, hadn't he noticed it really? It was a blot on the landscape to her.

He thought there were a lot of things a rope might come in

handy for. She wanted to know what, for instance. He thought a few seconds, but nothing occurred. They could wait and see, couldn't they? You need all sorts of strange odds and ends around a place in the country. She said, yes, that was so; but she thought just at that time when every penny counted, it seemed funny to buy more rope. That was all. She hadn't meant anything else. She hadn't just seen, not at first, why he felt it was necessary.

Well, thunder, he had bought it because he wanted to, and that was all there was to it. She thought that was reason enough, and couldn't understand why he hadn't said so, at first. Undoubtedly it would be useful, twenty-four yards of rope, there were hundreds of things, she couldn't think of any at the moment, but it would come in. Of course. As he had said, things always did in the country.

But she was a little disappointed about the coffee, and oh, look, look, look at the eggs! Oh, my, they're all running! What had he put on top of them? Hadn't he known eggs mustn't be squeezed? Squeezed, who had squeezed them, he wanted to know. What a silly thing to say. He had simply brought them along in the basket with the other things. If they got broke it was the grocer's fault. He should know better than to put heavy things on top of eggs.

She believed it was the rope. That was the heaviest thing in the pack, she saw him plainly when he came in from the road, the rope was a big package on top of everything. He desired the whole wide world to witness that this was not a fact. He had carried the rope in one hand and the basket in the other, and what was the use of her having eyes if that was the best they could do for her?

Well, anyhow, she could see one thing plain: no eggs for breakfast. They'd have to scramble them now, for supper. It was too damned bad. She had planned to have steak for supper. No ice, meat wouldn't keep. He wanted to know why she couldn't finish breaking the eggs in a bowl and set them in a cool place.

Cool place! if he could find one for her, she'd be glad to set them there. Well, then, it seemed to him they might very well cook the meat at the same time they cooked the eggs and then warm up the meat for tomorrow. The idea simply choked her. Warmed-over meat, when they might as well have had it fresh. Second best and scraps and makeshifts, even to the meat! He rubbed her shoulder a little. It doesn't really matter so much, does it, darling? Sometimes when they were playful, he would rub her shoulder and she would arch and purr. This time she hissed and almost clawed. He was getting ready to say that they could surely manage somehow when she turned on him and said, if he told her they could manage somehow she would certainly slap his face.

He swallowed the words red hot, his face burned. He picked up the rope and started to put it on the top shelf. She would not have it on the top shelf, the jars and tins belonged there; positively she would not have the top shelf cluttered up with a lot of rope. She had borne all the clutter she meant to bear in the flat in town, there was space here at least and she meant to keep things in order.

Well, in that case, he wanted to know what the hammer and nails were doing up there? And why had she put them there when she knew very well he needed that hammer and those nails upstairs to fix the window sashes? She simply slowed down everything and made double work on the place with her insane habit of changing things around and hiding them.

She was sure she begged his pardon, and if she had had any reason to believe he was going to fix the sashes this summer she would have left the hammer and nails right where he put them; in the middle of the bedroom floor where they could step on them in the dark. And now if he didn't clear the whole mess out of there she would throw them down the well.

Oh, all right, all right—could he put them in the closet? Naturally not, there were brooms and mops and dustpans in the closet, and why couldn't he find a place for his rope outside her kitchen? Had he stopped to consider there were seven God-forsaken rooms in the house, and only one kitchen?

He wanted to know what of it? And did she realize she was

making a complete fool of herself? And what did she take him for, a three-year-old idiot? The whole trouble with her was she needed something weaker than she was to heckle and tyrannize over. He wished to God now they had a couple of children she could take it out on. Maybe he'd get some rest.

Her face changed at this, she reminded him he had forgot the coffee and had bought a worthless piece of rope. And when she thought of all the things they actually needed to make the place even decently fit to live in, well, she could cry, that was all. She looked so forlorn, so lost and despairing he couldn't believe it was only a piece of rope that was causing all the racket. What *was* the matter, for God's sake?

Oh, would he please hush and go away, and *stay* away, if he could, for five minutes? By all means, yes, he would. He'd stay away indefinitely if she wished. Lord, yes, there was nothing he'd like better than to clear out and never come back. She couldn't for the life of her see what was holding him, then. It was a swell time. Here she was, stuck, miles from a railroad, with a half-empty house on her hands, and not a penny in her pocket, and everything on earth to do; it seemed the God-sent moment for him to get out from under. She was surprised he hadn't stayed in town as it was until she had come out and done the work and got things straightened out. It was his usual trick.

It appeared to him that this was going a little far. Just a touch out of bounds, if she didn't mind his saying so. Why the hell had he stayed in town the summer before? To do a half-dozen extra jobs to get the money he had sent her. That was it. She knew perfectly well they couldn't have done it otherwise. She had agreed with him at the time. And that was the only time so help him he had ever left her to do anything by herself.

Oh, he could tell that to his great-grandmother. She had her notion of what had kept him in town. Considerably more than a notion, if he wanted to know. So, she was going to bring all that up again, was she? Well, she could just think what she pleased. He was tired of explaining. It may have looked funny but he had simply got hooked in, and what could he do? It was impossible to believe that she was going to take it seriously. Yes, yes, she knew how it was with a man: if he was left by himself a minute, some woman was certain to kidnap him. And naturally he couldn't hurt her feelings by refusing!

Well, what was she raving about? Did she forget she had told him those two weeks alone in the country were the happiest she had known for four years? And how long had they been married when she said that? All right, shut up! If she thought that hadn't stuck in his craw.

She hadn't meant she was happy because she was away from him. She meant she was happy getting the devilish house nice and ready for him. That was what she had meant, and now look! Bringing up something she had said a year ago simply to justify himself for forgetting her coffee and breaking the eggs and buying a wretched piece of rope they couldn't afford. She really thought it was time to drop the subject, and now she wanted only two things in the world. She wanted him to get that rope from underfoot, and go back to the village and get her coffee, and if he could remember it, he might bring a metal mitt for the skillets, and two more curtain rods, and if there were any rubber gloves in the village, her hands were simply raw, and a bottle of milk of magnesia from the drugstore.

He looked out at the dark blue afternoon sweltering on the slopes, and mopped his forehead and sighed heavily and said, if only she could wait a minute for *anything,* he was going back. He had said so, hadn't he, the very instant they found he had overlooked it?

Oh, yes, well . . . run along. She was going to wash windows. The country was so beautiful! She doubted they'd have a moment to enjoy it. He meant to go, but he could not until he had said that if she wasn't such a hopeless melancholiac she might see that this was only for a few days. Couldn't she remember anything pleasant about the other summers? Hadn't they ever had any fun? She hadn't time to talk about it, and now would he please not leave that rope lying around for her to trip on? He picked it up, somehow it had toppled off the table, and walked out with it under his arm.

Was he going this minute? He certainly was. She thought so. Sometimes it seemed to her he had second sight about the precisely perfect moment to leave her ditched. She had meant to put the mattresses out to sun, if they put them out this minute they would get at least three hours, he must have heard her say that morning she meant to put them out. So of course he would walk off and leave her to it. She supposed he thought the exercise would do her good.

Well, he was merely going to get her coffee. A four-mile walk for two pounds of coffee was ridiculous, but he was perfectly willing to do it. The habit was making a wreck of her, but if she wanted to wreck herself there was nothing he could do about it. If he thought it was coffee that was making a wreck of her, she congratulated him: he must have a damned easy conscience.

Conscience or no conscience, he didn't see why the mattresses couldn't very well wait until tomorrow. And anyhow, for God's sake, were they living *in* the house, or were they going to let the house ride them to death? She paled at this, her face grew livid about the mouth, she looked quite dangerous, and reminded him that housekeeping was no more her work than it was his: she had other work to do as well, and when did he think she was going to find time to do it at this rate?

Was she going to start on that again? She knew as well as he did that his work brought in the regular money, hers was only occasional, if they depended on what *she* made—and she might as well get straight on this question once for all!

That was positively not the point. The question was, when both of them were working on their own time, was there going to be a division of the housework, or wasn't there? She merely wanted to know, she had to make her plans. Why, he thought that was all arranged. It was understood that he was to help. Hadn't he always, in summers?

Hadn't he, though? Oh, just hadn't he? And when, and where, and doing what? Lord, what an uproarious joke!

It was such a very uproarious joke that her face turned slightly purple, and she screamed with laughter. She laughed so hard she had to sit down, and finally a rush of tears spurted from her eyes and poured down into the lifted corners of her mouth. He dashed towards her and dragged her up to her feet and tried to pour water on her head. The dipper hung by a string on a nail and he broke it loose. Then he tried to pump water with one hand while she struggled in the other. So he gave it up and shook her instead.

She wrenched away, crying out for him to take his rope and go to hell, she had simply given him up: and ran. He heard her high-heeled bedroom slippers clattering and stumbling on the stairs.

He went out around the house and into the lane; he suddenly realized he had a blister on his heel and his shirt felt as if it were on fire. Things broke so suddenly you didn't know where you were. She could work herself into a fury about simply nothing. She was terrible, damn it: not an ounce of reason. You might as well talk to a sieve as that woman when she got going. Damned if he'd spend his life humoring her! Well, what to do now? He would take back the rope and exchange it for something else. Things accumulated, things were mountainous, you couldn't move them or sort them out or get rid of them. They just lay and rotted around. He'd take it back. Hell, why should he? He wanted it. What was it anyhow? A piece of rope. Imagine anybody caring more about a piece of rope than about a man's feelings. What earthly right had she to say a word about it? He remembered all the useless, meaningless things she bought for herself: Why? because I wanted it, that's why! He stopped and selected a large stone by the road. He would put the rope behind it. He would put it in the tool-box when he got back. He'd heard enough about it to last him a life-time.

When he came back she was leaning against the post box beside the road waiting. It was pretty late, the smell of broiled steak floated nose high in the cooling air. Her face was young and smooth and fresh-looking. Her unmanageable funny black hair was all on end. She waved to him from a distance, and he speeded up. She called out that supper was ready and waiting, was he starved?

You bet he was starved. Here was the coffee. He waved it at her. She looked at his other hand. What was that he had there?

Well, it was the rope again. He stopped short. He had meant to exchange it but forgot. She wanted to know why he should exchange it, if it was something he really wanted. Wasn't the air sweet now, and wasn't it fine to be here?

She walked beside him with one hand hooked into his leather belt. She pulled and jostled him a little as he walked, and leaned against him. He put his arm clear around her and patted her stomach. They exchanged wary smiles. Coffee, coffee for the Ootsum-Wootsums! He felt as if he were bringing her a beautiful present.

He was a love, she firmly believed, and if she had had her coffee in the morning, she wouldn't have behaved so funny . . . There was a whippoorwill still coming back, imagine, clear out of season, sitting in the crab-apple tree calling all by himself. Maybe his girl stood him up. Maybe she did. She hoped to hear him once more, she loved whippoorwills . . . He knew how she was, didn't he?

Sure, he knew how she was.

The Pelican's Shadow

MARJORIE KINNAN RAWLINGS

The lemon-colored awning over the terrace swelled in the southeasterly breeze from the ocean. Dr. Tifton had chosen lemon so that when the hungry Florida sun had fed on the canvas the color would still be approximately the same.

"Being practical on one's honeymoon," he had said to Elsa, "stabilizes one's future."

At the moment she had thought it would have been nicer to say "our" honeymoon and "our" future, but she had dismissed it as another indication of her gift for critical analysis, which her husband considered unfortunate.

"I am the scientist of the family, my mouse," he said often. "Let me do the analyzing. I want you to develop all your latent femininity."

Being called "my mouse" was probably part of the development. It had seemed quite sweet at the beginning, but repetition had made the mouse feel somehow as though the fur were being worn off in patches.

Elsa leaned back in the long beach chair and let the magazine containing her husband's new article drop to the rough coquina paving of the terrace. Howard did express himself with an exquisite precision. The article was a gem, just scientific enough, just humorous, just human enough to give the impression of a choice mind back of it. It was his semi-scientific writings that had brought them together.

Fresh from college, she had tumbled, butter side up, into a job as assistant to the feature editor of *Home Life*. Because of her enthusiasm for the Tifton series of articles, she had been allowed to handle the magazine's correspondence with him. He had written her, on her letter of acceptance of "Algae and Their Human Brothers":

> MY DEAR MISS WHITTINGTON:
>   Fancy a woman's editor being appealed to by my algae! Will you have tea with me, so that my eyes, accustomed to the microscope, may feast themselves on a *femme du monde* who recognizes not only that science is important but that in the proper hands it may be made important even to those little fire-lit circles of domesticity for which your publication is the *raison d'être*!

She had had tea with him, and he had proved as distinguished as his articles. He was not handsome. He was, in fact, definitely tubby. His hair was steel-gray and he wore gray tweed suits, so that, for all his squattiness, the effect was smoothly sharp. His age, forty-odd, was a part of his distinction. He had marriage, it appeared, in the back of his mind. He informed her with engaging frankness that his wife must be young and therefore malleable. His charm, his prestige, were irresistible. The "union," as he called it, had followed quickly, and of course she had dropped her meaningless career to give a feminine backing to his endeavors, scientific and literary.

"It was not enough," he said, "to be a scientist. One must also be articulate."

He was immensely articulate. No problem, from the simple ones of a fresh matrimony to the involved matters of his studies and his writings, found him without an expression.

"Howard intellectualizes about everything," she wrote her former editor, May Morrow, from her honeymoon. She felt a vague disloyalty as she wrote it, for it did not convey his terrific humanity.

"A man is a man first," he said, "and *then* a scientist."

His science took care of itself, in his capable hands. It was his manhood that occupied her energies. Not his male potency—which again took care of itself, with no particular concern for her own needs—but all the elaborate mechanism that, to him, made up the substance of a man's life. Hollandaise sauce, for instance. He had a passion for hollandaise, and like his microscopic studies, like his essays, it must be perfect. She looked at her wristwatch. It was his wedding gift. She would have liked something delicate and diamond-studded and feminine, something suitable for "the mouse," but he had chosen a large, plain-faced gold Hamilton of railroad accuracy. It was six o'clock. It was not time for the hollandaise, but it was time to check up on Jones, the manservant and cook. Jones had a trick of boiling the vegetables too early, so that they lay limply under the hollandaise instead of standing up firm and decisive. She stirred in the beach chair and picked up the magazine. It would seem as though she were careless, indifferent to his achievements, if he found it sprawled on the coquina instead of arranged on top of the copies of *Fortune* on the red velvet fire seat.

She gave a start. A shadow passed between the terrace and the ocean. It flapped along on the sand with a reality greater than whatever cast the shadow. She looked out from under the awning. One of those obnoxious pelicans was flapping slowly down the coast. She felt an unreasonable irritation at sight of the thick, hunched shoulders, the out-of-proportion wings, the peculiar contour of the head, lifting at the back to something of a peak. She could not understand why she so disliked the birds. They were hungry, they searched out their food, they moved and mated like every living thing. They were basically drab, like most human beings, but all that was no reason for giving a slight shudder when one passed over the lemon-colored awning and winged its self-satisfied way down the Florida coastline.

She rose from the beach chair, controlling her annoyance.

Howard was not sensitive to her moods, for which she was grateful, but she had found that the inexplicable crossness which sometimes seized her made her unduly sensitive to his. As she feared, Jones had started the cauliflower ahead of time. It was only just in the boiling water, so she snatched it out and plunged it in ice water.

"Put the cauliflower in the boiling water at exactly six-thirty," she said to Jones.

As Howard so wisely pointed out, most of the trouble with servants lay in not giving exact orders.

"If servants knew as much as you do," he said, "they would not be working for you. Their minds are vague. That is why they are servants."

Whenever she caught herself being vague, she had a moment's unhappy feeling that she should probably have been a lady's maid. It would at least have been a preparation for matrimony. Turning now from the cauliflower, she wondered if marriage always laid these necessities for exactness on a woman. Perhaps all men were not concerned with domestic precision. She shook off the thought, with the sense of disloyalty that always stabbed her when she was critical. As Howard said, a household either ran smoothly, with the mechanism hidden, or it clanked and jangled. No one wanted clanking and jangling.

She went to her room to comb her hair and powder her face and freshen her lipstick. Howard liked her careful grooming. He was himself immaculate. His gray hair smoothed back over his scientist's head that lifted to a little peak in the back, his gray suits, even his gray pajamas were incredibly neat, as smooth and trim as feathers.

She heard the car on the shell drive and went to meet him. He had brought the mail from the adjacent city, where he had the use of a laboratory.

"A ghost from the past," he said sententiously, and handed her a letter from *Home Life*.

He kissed her with a longer clinging than usual, so that she checked the .te in her mind. Two weeks ago—yes, this was his evening to make love to her. Their months of marriage

were marked off into two-week periods as definitely as
though the / line on the typewriter cut through them. He drew
off from her with disapproval if she showed fondness between a / and a /. She went to the living room to read her
letter from May Morrow.

DEAR ELSA:

Your beach house sounds altogether too idyllic. What
prévious incarnated suffering has licenced you to drop into
an idyll? And so young in life. Well, maybe I'll get mine
next time.

As you can imagine, there have been a hundred people
after your job. The Collins girl that I rushed into it tempo-
rarily didn't work out at all, and I was beginning to despair
when Jane Maxe, from *Woman's Outlook,* gave me a ring
and said she was fed up with their politics and would come
to us if the job was permanent. I assured her that it was
hers until she had to be carried out on her shield. You see,
I know your young type. You've burned your bridges and
set out to be A Good Wife, and hell will freeze before you
quit anything you tackle.

Glad the Distinguished Spouse proves as clever in daily
conversation as in print. Have you had time to notice that
trick writers have of saying something neat, recognizing it
at once as a precious nut to be stored, then bringing it out
later in the long hard winter of literary composition? You
will. Drop me a line. I wonder about things sometimes.

MAY

She wanted to sit down at the portable at once, but Dr.
Tifton came into the room.

"I'll have my shower later," he said, and rolled his round
gray eyes with meaning.

His mouth, she noticed, made a long, thin line that gave
the impression of a perpetual half-smile. She mixed the Martinis and he sipped his with appreciation. He had a smug
expectancy that she recognized from her brief dealings with

established authors. He was waiting for her favorable comment on his article.

"Your article was grand," she said. "If I were still an editor, I'd have grabbed it."

He lifted his eyebrows. "Of course," he said, "editors were grabbing my articles before I knew you." He added complacently, "And after."

"I mean," she said uncomfortably, "that an editor can only judge things by her own acceptance."

"An editor?" He looked sideways at her. His eye seemed to have the ability to focus backward. "And what does a wife think of my article?"

She laughed. "Oh, a wife thinks that anything you do is perfect." She added, "Isn't that what wives are for?"

She regretted the comment immediately, but he was bland.

"I really think I gave the effect I wanted," he said. "Science is of no use to the layman unless it's humanized."

They sipped the Martinis.

"I'd like to have you read it aloud," he said, studying his glass casually. "One learns things from another's reading."

She pickled up the magazine gratefully. The reading would fill nicely the time between cocktails and dinner.

"It really gives the effect, doesn't it?" he said when she had finished. "I think anyone would get the connection, of which I am always conscious, between the lower forms of life and the human."

"It's a swell job," she said.

Dinner began successfully. The donac broth was strong enough. She had gone out in her bathing suit to gather the tiny clams just before high tide. The broiled pompano was delicately brown and flaky. The cauliflower was all right, after all. The hollandaise, unfortunately, was thin. She had so frightened Jones about the heinousness of cooking it too long that he had taken it off the fire before it had quite thickened.

"My dear," Dr. Tifton said, laying down his fork, "surely it is not too much to ask of an intelligent woman to teach a servant to make a simple sauce."

She felt a little hysterical. "Maybe I'm not intelligent," she said.

"Of course you are," he said soothingly. "Don't misunderstand me. I am not questioning your intelligence. You just do not realize the importance of being exact with an inferior."

He took a large mouthful of the cauliflower and hollandaise. The flavor was beyond reproach, and he weakened.

"I know," he said, swallowing and scooping generously again, "I know that I am a perfectionist. It's a bit of a bother sometimes, but of course it is the quality that makes me a scientist. A literary—shall I say literate?—no, articulate scientist."

He helped himself to a large pat of curled butter for his roll. The salad, the pineapple mousse, the after-dinner coffee and liqueur went off acceptably. He smacked his lips ever so faintly.

"Excuse me for a moment, my mouse," he said. His digestion was rapid and perfect.

Now that he was in the bathroom, it had evidently occurred to him to take his shower and get into his dressing gown. She heard the water running and the satisfied humming he emitted when all was well. She would have time, for he was meticulous with his fortnightly special toilet, to begin a letter to May Morrow. She took the portable typewriter out to a glass-covered table on the terrace. The setting sun reached benignly under the awning. She drew a deep breath. It was a little difficult to begin. May had almost sounded as though she did not put full credence in the idyll. She wanted to write enthusiastically but judiciously, so May would understand that she, Elsa, was indeed a fortunate young woman, wed irrevocably, by her own deliberate, intelligent choice, to a brilliant man—a real man, second only in scientific and literary rating to Dr. Beebe.

DEAR MAY:

It was grand to hear from you. I'm thrilled about Jane Maxe. What a scoop! I could almost be jealous of both of you if my lines hadn't fallen into such gloriously pleasant places.

I am, of course, supremely happy—

She leaned back. She was writing gushily. Married women had the damnedest way, she had always noticed, of gushing. Perhaps the true feminine nature was sloppy, after all. She deleted "gloriously," crossed out "supremely," and inserted "tremendously." She would have to copy the letter.

A shadow passed between the terrace and the ocean. She looked up. One of those beastly pelicans was flapping down the coast over the sand dunes. He had already fed, or he would be flapping, in that same sure way of finding what he wanted, over the surf. It was ridiculous to be disturbed by him. Yet somewhere she suspected there must be an association of thoughts that had its base in an unrecognized antipathy. Something about the pelican's shadow, darkening her heart and mind with that absurd desperation, must be connected with some profound and secret dread, but she could not seem to put her finger on it.

She looked out from under the lemon-colored awning. The pelican had turned and was flapping back again. She had a good look at him. He was neatly gray, objectionably neat for a creature with such greedy habits. His round head; lifted to a peak, was sunk against his heavy shoulders. His round gray eye looked down below him, a little behind him, with a cold, pleased, superior expression. His long, thin mouth was unbearably smug, with the expression of a partial smile.

"Oh, go on about your business!" she shouted at him.

The Valley Between

PAULE MARSHALL

Cassie tasted the milk, lowered the gas under the pot, and continued to stir slowly. Her short, rather slim body was bent slightly forward at the waist, her eyes focused on nothing. It was pleasurable not to have to think—at least not yet—to be aware only of the warm, sustaining feeling of the brightly lighted kitchen and of the fine rain which blurred the window over the sink. Ellen's voice sounded small and faraway as she began her usual morning sing song:

"Mommy—milk. Mommy—milk."

Cassie poured the warm milk into the chipped pink and white cup marked "Baby." She fingered the relief figures of the dancing boy and girl on its side; the touch brought the image clearly to her mind: she saw their round dimpled faces and the innocent, unwavering smile on their lips, and her first thought was that she had not smiled—really smiled for a long time. On her way to the nursery she took Ellen's juice from the refrigerator and laid Abe's stewed prunes on the table and plugged in her percolator, glancing nervously at the clock.

In the half-light of the nursery, Ellen was sitting in her crib, busily beating on the toy drum which Abe had brought home for her last night and which already had a rent in the skin of the upper part. Ellen had managed to put on her shirt and shorts. Cassie smiled to herself with pride at Ellen's smooth, firm legs and the cherubic curve of her small child's arms.

"Okay, Ellen, time to drink your juice and milk."

Cassie moved her slim fingers over her daughter's soft, brown hair, pushing it back from the forehead, smoothing it gently over her head letting her fingers linger on the delicately formed neck. Ellen moved blissfully under the caress, her eyes wide and grey-blue over the rim of the cup. Cassie wondered if Ellen would ever remember these mornings when they stood so close in their silent caress. It was unfair that none of the peaceful moments of childhood ever returned to comfort and to make you forget. . . .

"Mommy, what you gonna learn in school today?"

Cassie laughed.

"I'll tell you all about it when I come home. And then you can show me how well you learned your A B C's, all right?"

"I'd much rather go out and play."

"Not today, Ellie, it's raining outside, and you've got a little cold already. Promise me you won't nag Grandma about going out. Just sit in the chair and learn your lesson and play with your dolls."

The sound of the coffee whistle broke across Cassie's voice, startling her.

"Oh, there goes Daddy's coffee—go make him get up. His coffee's boiling."

Cassie went back into the kitchen and pulled out the plug. With quick, jerky movements she hastily placed bread and butter on the table and set two eggs to boil. As she passed through the tastefully furnished living room, she picked up one of Ellen's stray dolls. Almost timidly, she opened the bedroom door; Abe was sitting on the edge of the bed, his feet thrust into a pair of large, loose slippers, sleepily scratching his tousled head and pulling off his rumpled pyjamas.

"Oh, you're up—" Cassie said hesitantly.

"Yeah, that whistle did it. What time?"

"Just seven."

"God, that early? . . . What you doing up so soon?"

Cassie fidgeted with the doll, trying unconsciously to fix its broken head back into the socket of the neck.

"I've got an early class this morning."

Abe didn't bother answering and Cassie began to put away the night-clothes scattered on the chairs. She watched Abe furtively, fearful that if their eyes met they would have to say something decisive and final to each other. She noted vaguely as he moved toward the bathroom in his slow, heavy manner that he was beginning to put on weight.

The water soon ran hoarsely in the basin, then the buzz of the electric razor.

"Is Ellen up?"

She discerned his form, dark and shapeless behind the shut glass door of the bathroom.

"Yes, she's already had her milk. You know she's already mutilated the new drum. Just been having a jam session with herself this morning. Where does she get the energy from? . . ." Cassie stopped, her voice tapering into silence as the shower rasped on, for she knew he couldn't hear her—knew that he hadn't even been listening after the second word.

She went to the kitchen and sat down while Abe said good-morning to Ellen. She noticed now how dreary the day really was and that the white of the kitchen, which had seemed so bright and warm awhile ago, was just a worn, faded yellow. Ellen's shrieks of laughter filled the small apartment, and Cassie smiled—how effortlessly those two loved each other. . . .

Abe came into the kitchen, holding up the tattered drum and laughing.

"That kid is a terror."

He flung it on the table, noticing that there was only one place set.

"Say, aren't you eating?"

"I've eaten already. I told you, Wednesday's my early day."

"What do you do with yourself if you get there late?" Abe asked, his face turned away from her.

"Oh," she almost laughed with relief, "stand outside the

locked door a few minutes and utter a few curses. Then maybe I'll go to the library and read.''

"It beats me to figure out why you're killing yourself." Abe sighed heavily, his eyes still averted, "Getting up at all ungodly hours of the morning, running around in all kinds of weather. What for? If we didn't have Ellen, okay, but this nonsense. . . . Look, in the town I come from, a girl gets married and she settles down to take care of her house and kids; she's satisfied with that. Sure, she's got her bridge parties and all that. But not you. What's your rush? Afraid you'll die without having your degrees!''

"I'm not killing myself," Cassie said evenly, trying to keep the anger and scorn from her voice. "There's nothing wrong with my finishing school even if I do have Ellen. Your ideas are a century behind the times. If I could only explain. . . . I have only two more years; I want to finish them. It's something I have to do that's important to me. Mother doesn't mind keeping Ellen. You're the only one that's making a problem out of it.''

"But why aren't you satisfied? You got everything. What's the point of knocking yourself out, leaving Ellen, and trotting off to school like you were a kid, too. I didn't marry no school girl. . . .''

"You couldn't understand if I told you," Cassie flung at him contemptuously. "What's the use. And it's vicious of you to even imply that I neglect Ellen.''

"Well, then what about me? Okay, so you take care of Ellen. But what about me? Am I supposed to moon around here by myself evenings while you bury yourself in books? I gotta take Ellen to the park on Saturdays and the museums so you can have quiet—to study. You always got your nose buried in a book even when you're eating. God, you're a woman of twenty-four. Aren't you tired of school? Didn't you give up all that when we got married? What am I supposed to do—sit home and hold hands with myself?''

Abe stabbed viciously at the prunes, splattering the dark, heavy syrup on the white plastic tablecloth.

"Please stop yelling! Oh, Abe can't you see that two years

is such a little bit of time." And her voice was low and wistful. "I thought this would have been such a good idea. Both of us would have had something new in our lives. But it's so different now that I'm scared. I'm afraid it's not just my going to school but something much bigger, we're so far apart. . . ."

She couldn't tell him that the past few months had been like a slow dying for her—for both of them, perhaps; that there was a wide, untraceable valley between them and that they were the two proud mountains, unwilling to even look at each other, incapable of coming together. No, she couldn't tell him this.

"No more, let's not bother talking about it any more." She felt beaten and worn; her voice was empty and bitter. "To-night when we're both calmer, maybe." And she began to walk unsteadily toward the nursery. Abe yelled after her, "Well, make up your mind once and for all. I've taken my fill of it." The kitchen door closed on his voice.

"Is Daddy shouting again?"

"It's nothing, Ellen. Come, let me put on your dress and shoes." She turned her face away and swiftly finished dressing her, finding comfort in the soft, warm body as if this were the only friendly thing left in the world. Ellen ran before her into the hall and began climbing the stairs, leaning over to kiss Cassie, and then ran up. Cassie watched until she disappeared into her mother's apartment. Then she hastily pulled on a short coat over her slacks and white turtle-neck sweater. A beret covered her short dark curls and her eyes were very grey and tired as they met in the mirror.

Outside, the day had fully broken, sullen and grey. The delicately hued autumn leaves capered in the wind and the light rain, and clung damply to the sidewalks and porches. The wind moaned softly over the low roofs and Cassie thought of the many times she had walked past these same small, comfortable houses—of how her lifetime was being spent in one compressed, limited place. She took off her beret and let the short, damp gusts blow through her hair.

As she passed Mrs. Lewitt's house, she noticed that the

grass was still bright and summer-like; its color greener and sharper because of the beads of moisture shining on the slim, green stalks, clear and jewel-like. She remembered how, on rainy days, she would take this same path to the library—just a girl in a worn rain coat and rubbers which were always too big for her. The library had been her sanctuary, not only against the rainy world, but against all that was incomprehensible and ugly in life. Each day she had found a new world before her. And along with the joy of reading had come, with the years, the desire to learn—to have all the muddled ideas made clear, defined in words and images, and thus made a part of her. It was a never-ending search, giving sustained pleasure, making her life, for that moment at least, meaningful.

Abe, too, in those days which seemed so long ago and dead, had given meaning to her life. She saw him again in his tight sailor suit, slim and graceful, his hair like an Apollo's against the white cap. He was always talking in his queer mid-western twang, and he used to hold her hand as if it were fragile china. Somehow, books weren't important then. . . . How happy and carefree they had been in those early days! And Ellen was their love merged into something tangible and alive, their idea defined in flesh.

And when had it started again—at what point had she begun to feel depressed, aware that something basic to herself was missing? Aware (and the thought for the first time crystallized within her) that the girl in the worn rain coat and the oversized boots was dying, without having been realized and somehow fulfilled. It was then that she had begun to feel bored, realizing that her life was routined, secured and warm. Yes, warm, that was the word. It was the suffocating warmth of the afternoons in the park, having to listen to the unceasing gossip of the other mothers. It was the ritual of seven o'clock dinners and having the same people over to play cards. In desperation, she had suggested that she would like to return to school, and Abe's laughter had resounded through the house, hurting her more than all his present open defiance, making her realize that this was no longer the laughing sailor. There was a blind spot within him, with which she couldn't reason. . . .

Cassie walked like a somnambulist toward the bus stop. The thoughts which she had tried to shut out in the early morning surged around her like mad Furies, making her oblivious to the bustling early morning crowd on the bus. Automatically, she got off at the college and began walking slowly across the campus. The chimes of the library bell broke through her thoughts, heralding the entrance to her ever-changing world of ideas—a world whose academic purity had no place for Abe's harsh words or her own angry answers. And with profound relief she joined the other jostling students.

"Cassie, Cassie!"

"Yes, mother. I didn't mean to stay so late. Send Ellen down." Cassie flung her coat on the hook. "Has she been a . . ."

Her mother opened the upstairs door, her small, bent figure blocking out the light behind her.

"Cassie, why are you so late? I tried to get in touch with you. Now don't get excited, but Ellen sneaked out . . . in all that rain without a coat. . . ."

Cassie didn't hear much more, and with some part of her which was still rational and aware she whispered, "I stopped, had coffee with some of the girls. . . ." Then, as if she suddenly realized what her mother was saying, she asked, "Ellen, where's Ellen?"

Her mother's voice trailed after her as she ran to the darkened nursery. Ellen's eyes were slightly open; her cheeks were very warm to Cassie's touch.

"I called the doctor right away," her mother continued. "He left some pills for the fever. She'll be all right in a few days."

Cassie said quietly, her hands still on Ellen's face, "I should have been here."

"Now, Cassie, it's not my fault. She could have done the same thing if you had been home with her."

"No, mother, I don't mean that. It's just that now he's won because he'll say it's my fault. He's won . . ." she murmured.

Her mother moved her worn hand over Cassie's hair.

"Stay here and rest. She's sleeping now. I'll cook dinner for you upstairs."

Cassie heard the soft, whispery steps of her mother as she climbed the stairs and the quiet slam of the upstairs door. The sounds came to her as from a great distance—a distance that could not be measured in time or space. The only thing that occupied space was the huddled figure of her child, breathing heavily; time was the fragile second between each breath. Cassie bent over, pulling up the covers around her neck. If she had only come straight home instead of going with them to the restaurant! But it had been so good to talk to someone without being tense. Her head sank on the bar of the crib.

She glanced at the clock, noticing that it was seven just as Abe's key sounded in the lock. She remained there motionless, her lips moving silently.

"Don't let him shout, please, don't let him shout!"

When he came into the kitchen, she was standing in front of Ellen's door, holding the knob behind her.

"What's wrong with you? Where's Ellen? She's sleeping so early?"

"Well, Abe," Cassie started, her voice pleading and tense, her fingers tightening around the knob, "don't get excited but Ellen went out today in the rain and caught a slight cold— nothing serious—just a little temperature. The doctor came and said she'll be all right in a few days. Anyway," she said with a short, nervous laugh, "the rest will do her good."

Abe had whirled around, his eyes staring at her in disbelief as she spoke. He pushed her roughly out of the way, but she clung to his sleeve determinedly.

"Don't go in and wake her. It's not that serious. And I won't let you wake her. I'm going to stay home a few days and take care of her."

"You're damn right you'll stay home and take care of her. Either that or you can leave us alone altogether and go live in your precious school and get lost among your thick books, for all I care!"

Abe sank down in his chair, flinging his head back against the wall, his eyes wild and unseeing.

"Christ, what next?" he moaned.

"I'm sorry. I knew you would take it this way. You can't even see that this isn't my fault. . . ."

"It wouldn't have happened if the kid had been where she belonged." Abe's anger silenced her. "Your mother's too old to take care of a young, mischievous kid. She tries her best because she doesn't want to refuse you. It's unfair for you to impose upon her—but then you're selfish, anyway. I never knew when I married you that you could be so self-centered. Nobody matters but Cassie."

Cassie sat quietly opposite him; her voice, strangely, was strong and steady as if his words had had no effect on her.

"Yes, I'm selfish and self-centered, just as you are bull-headed and blind. It's not so much school or even Ellen—it's just us—two people who should never have met each other. You would have been much better off with some girl from your home town. And I—well, that doesn't matter—I should have just finished up one phase of my life before starting another. I wasn't ready for the kind of life you have to offer me, and I couldn't give you very much."

Abe averted his eyes, his face wary and guarded.

"Just make up your mind, that's all. I'm through arguing. This," he said, waving in the direction of the nursery, "decides it." Then, shaking his head dully, "I don't know what's gotten into you, you were so different before. . . ."

"And so were you different," she flung at him, a new, hard anger welling up within. "We were both different strangers putting on our best fronts for each other, and we're still strangers now in a worse way, though."

An uneasy stillness fell between them. Abe's eyes still stared at the dark rainy night beyond the window behind Cassie; her gaze bent unwaveringly on him. The minutes fled by. She heard the sounds of the house as the water flowed down a pipe and her mother's footsteps on the floor above. Only when she heard Ellen's slight cough did she speak.

"There's nothing for me to decide. You've done that for me. I'm in the corner now. You'll have your way." Her voice was barely audible, for she was no longer speaking to him. "It's strange, the strong always win somehow. All the cards fall their way—they're the victors even though they're wrong. . . ."

She rose, moved wearily to the sink.

Abe's voice was hesitant and almost soft for the first time in months.

"I didn't mean to brow-beat you, Cassie. I don't want to hurt my own wife. But this way is the best—maybe we can work out something else later on. I'm not a heel."

Cassie cut across him, without turning around. "Stop trying to say that I hate you—I only pity both of us for having lost so much simply because you want me to be happy on your terms. I haven't got the strength to defy you anymore—you and your male strength! Let's not talk."

"Look," he said eagerly, "it'd be like the old days again, you watch! The three of us together all the time. . . ."

He reached for her hand, holding it tentatively. Cassie turned to look at him with vacant, hopeless eyes. She slipped her hand from his, shaking her head sadly, and said very gently,

"Your supper's ready by now, Abe."

Day of Success

SYLVIA PLATH

Ellen was on her way to the bedroom with an armload of freshly folded diapers when the phone rang, splintering the stillness of the crisp autumn morning. For a moment she froze on the threshold, taking in the peaceful scene as if she might never see it again— the delicate rose-patterned wall-paper, the forest-green cord drapes she'd hemmed by hand while waiting for the baby to come, the old-fashioned four-poster inherited from a loving but moneyless aunt, and, in the corner, the pale pink crib holding sound-asleep six-month-old Jill, the center of it all.

Please don't let it change, she begged of whatever fates might be listening. *Let the three of us stay happy as this forever.*

Then the shrill, demanding bell roused her, and she stowed the pile of clean diapers on the big bed and went to pick up the receiver reluctantly, as if it were some small, black instrument of doom.

"Is Jacob Ross there?" inquired a cool, clean feminine voice. "Denise Kay speaking." Ellen's heart sank as she pictured the elegantly groomed red-headed woman at the other end of the wire. She and Jacob had been to lunch with the brilliant young television producer only a month before to discuss the progress of the play Jacob was working on—his first. Even at that early date, Ellen had secretly hoped Denise would be struck by lightning or spirited to Australia rather than have her thrown together with Jacob in the crowded, intimate days of rehearsal—author and producer collaborating on the birth of something wonderful, uniquely theirs.

"No, Jacob's not home at the moment." It occurred to Ellen, a bit guiltily, how easy it would be to call Jacob down from Mrs. Frankfort's flat for such an obviously important message. His finished script had been in Denise Kay's office for almost two weeks now, and she knew by the way he ran down the three flights of stairs each morning to meet the postman how eager he was to hear the verdict. Still, hadn't she promised to behave like a model secretary and leave his hours of writing time uninterrupted? "This is his wife, Miss Kay," she added, with perhaps unnecessary emphasis. "May I take a message, or have Jacob call you later?"

"Good news," Denise said briskly. "My boss is enthusiastic about the play. A bit odd, he thinks, but beautifully original, so we're buying it. I'm really thrilled to be the producer."

This is it, Ellen thought miserably, unable to see anything for the vision of that smooth-sheened coppery head bent with Jacob's dark one over a thick mimeographed script. *The beginning of the end.*

"That's wonderful, Miss Kay. I . . . I know Jacob will be delighted."

"Fine. I'd like to see him for lunch today, if I may, to talk about casting. We'll be wanting some name actors, I think. Could you possibly ask him to pick me up in my office about noon?"

"Of course . . ."

"Righto. Goodbye, then." And the receiver descended with a businesslike click.

Bewildered by an alien and powerful emotion, Ellen stood at the window, the confident, musical voice that could offer success casually as a bunch of hothouse grapes echoing in her ears. As her gaze lingered on the green square below, its patch-barked plane trees thrusting into the luminous blue sky above the shabby housefronts, a leaf, dull gold as a three-penny bit, let go and waltzed slowly to the pavement. Later in the day, the square would be loud with motorbikes and the shouts of children. One summer afternoon Ellen had counted twenty-five youngsters within view of her bench under the plane trees: untidy, boisterous, laughing—a miniature United Nations milling about the geranium-planted plot of grass and up the narrow, cat-populated alleys.

How often she and Jacob had promised themselves the legendary cottage by the sea, far from the city's petrol fumes and smoky railroad yards—a garden, a hill, a cove for Jill to explore, an unhurried, deeply savored peace!

"Just one play sale, darling," Jacob had said earnestly. "Then I'll know I can do it, and we'll take the risk." The risk, of course, was moving away from this busy center of jobs—odd jobs, part-time jobs, jobs Jacob could manage with relative ease while writing every spare minute—and depending solely on his chancy income from stories, plays and poems. Poems! Ellen smiled in spite of herself, remembering the gloomy, bill-harassed day before Jill's birth, just after they'd moved into the new flat.

She'd been down on her knees, laboriously slapping light gray lino paint on the depressing, chewed-up, hundred-year-old floorboards when the postman rang. "I'll go." Jacob laid down the saw he was using to cut bookshelf lengths. "You want to save yourself stairs, love." Ever since Jacob had begun sending manuscripts to magazines the postman, in his blue uniform, was a sort of possible magic godfather. Any day, instead of the disheartening fat manila envelopes and the impersonal printed rejection slips, there might be an encouraging letter from an editor or even . . .

"Ellen! Ellen!" Jacob took the steps two at a time, waving the opened airmail envelope. "I've done it! Isn't it beautiful!" And he dropped into her lap the pale blue, yellow-bordered check with the amazing amount of dollars in black and the cents in red. The glossy American weekly she'd addressed an envelope to a month before was delighted with Jacob's contribution. They paid a pound a line and Jacob's poem was long enough to buy—what? After giggling over the possibility of theater tickets, dinner in Soho, pink champagne, the cloud of common sense began to settle.

"You decide." Jacob bowed, handing her the check, frail and gay as a rare butterfly. "What does your heart desire?"

Ellen didn't need to think twice. "A pram," she said softly. "A great big beautiful pram with room enough for twins!"

Ellen toyed with the idea of saving Denise's message until Jacob came loping downstairs for lunch—too late to meet the attractive producer at her office—but immediately felt profoundly ashamed of herself. Any other wife would have called her husband to the phone excitedly, breaking all writing-schedule rules for this exceptional news, or at least rushed to him the minute she hung up, proud to be the bearer of such good tidings. *I'm jealous,* Ellen told herself dully. *I'm a regular jet-propelled, twentieth-century model for the jealous wife, small-minded and spiteful. Like Nancy Regan.* This thought pulled her up short, and she headed purposefully into the kitchen to brew herself a cup of coffee.

I'm just stalling, she realized wryly, putting the pot on the stove. Still, as long as Jacob remained unaware of Denise Kay's news, she felt, half-superstitiously, she would be safe—safe from Nancy's fate.

Jacob and Keith Regan had been schoolmates, served in Africa together, and come back to postwar London determined to avoid the subtle pitfalls of full-time bowler-hat jobs which would distract them from the one thing that mattered: writing. Now waiting for the water to boil, Ellen recalled those down-at-heel yet challenging months she and Nancy Regan had swapped budget recipes and the secret woes and worries of all wives whose husbands are unsalaried idealists, patching body and soul together by nightwatching, gardening, any odd job that happened to turn up.

Keith made the grade first. A play staged in an out-of-the-way theater catapulted through the hoop of please-see-it! reviews into the West End and kept going like some beautiful, lucky-star guided missile to land smack in the middle of Broadway. That's all it took. And as at the wave of a wand, the beaming Regans were whisked from an unheated, cold-water flat and a diet of spaghetti and potato soup into the luxuriant green pastures of Kensington with a backdrop of vintage wines, sports cars, chic furs and, ultimately, the more somber decor of the divorce courts. Nancy simply couldn't compete—in looks, money, talent, oh, in anything that counted—with the charming blond leading lady who added such luster to Keith's play on its debut in the West End. From the wide-eyed adoring wife of Keith's lean years, she had lapsed gradually into a restless, sharp-tongued, cynical woman-about-town, with all the alimony she could want, but little else. Keith, of course, had soared out of their orbit. Still, whether out of pity or a sort of weatherproof affection, Ellen kept in touch with Nancy, who seemed to derive a certain pleasure from their meetings, as if through the Ross's happy, child-gifted marriage she could somehow recapture the best days of her own past.

Ellen set out a cup and saucer on the counter and was about to pour herself a large dose of scalding coffee when she laughed, ruefully, and reached for a second cup. *I'm not a deserted wife yet!* She arranged the cheap tin tray with care—table napkin, sugar bowl, cream pitcher, a sprig of gilded autumn leaves beside the steaming cups—and started up the steeply angled steps to Mrs. Frankfort's top-floor flat.

Touched by Jacob's thoughtfulness in lugging her coal buckets, emptying her trash bins and watering her plants when she visited her sister, the middle-aged widow had offered him the use of her flat during the day while she was at work. "Two rooms won't hold a writer, his wife and a bouncing baby! Let me contribute my mite to the future of world literature." So Ellen could let baby Jill creep and crow loud as she liked downstairs without fear of disturbing Jacob.

Mrs. Frankfort's door swung open at a touch of her fingetips, framing Jacob's back, his dark head and broad shoulders in the shaggy fisherman's sweater whose elbows she had mended more times than she liked to remember, bent over the spindly table littered with scrawled papers. As she poised there, holding her breath, Jacob raked his fingers absent-mindedly through his hair and creaked round in his chair. When he saw her, his face lit up, and she came forward smiling, to break the good news.

After seeing Jacob off, freshly shaven, combed and handsome in his well-brushed suit—his only suit—Ellen felt strangely let down. Jill woke from her morning nap, cooing and bright-eyed. "Dadada," she prattled, while Ellen deftly changed the damp diaper, omitting the customary game of peekaboo, her mind elsewhere, and put her to play in the pen.

It won't happen right away, Ellen mused, mashing cooked carrots for Jill's lunch. *Breakups seldom do. It will unfold slowly, one little telltale symptom after another like some awful, hellish flower.*

Propping Jill against the pillows on the big bed for her noon feed, Ellen caught sight of the tiny cut-glass vial of French perfume on the bureau, almost lost in the wilderness of baby-powder cans, cod-liver-oil bottles and jars of cotton wool. The few remaining drops of costly amber liquid seemed to wink at her mockingly—Jacob's one extravagance with the poem money left over from the pram. Why had she never indulged wholeheartedly in the perfume, instead of rationing it so cautiously, drop by drop, like some perishable elixir of life? A woman like Denise Kay must have a sizeable part of her salary earmarked: Delectable Scents.

Ellen was broodily spooning mashed carrot into Jill's mouth when the doorbell rang. *Darn!* She dumped Jill unceremoniously in her crib and made for the stairs. *It never fails.*

An unfamiliar, immaculately dressed man stood on the doorstep beside the clouded battalion of uncollected milk bottles. "Is Jacob Ross in? I'm Karl Goodman, editor of *Impact*."

Ellen recognized, with awe, the name of the distinguished monthly which only a few days ago had accepted three of Jacob's poems. Uncomfortably aware of her carrot-spattered blouse and bedraggled apron, Ellen murmured that Jacob wasn't at home. "You took some poems of his!" she said shyly, then. "We were delighted."

Karl Goodman smiled. "Perhaps I should tell you what I've come for. I live nearby and happened to be home for lunch, so I thought I'd come round in person . . ."

Denise Kay had phoned *Impact* that morning to see if they couldn't arrange to publish part or all of Jacob's play in time to coincide with the performance. "I just wanted to make sure your husband wasn't committed to some other magazine first," Karl Goodman finished.

"No, I don't think he is." Ellen tried to sound calm. "In fact I know he's not. I'm sure he'd be happy to have you consider the play. There's a copy upstairs. May I get it for you. . . ?"

"That would be very kind."

As Ellen hurried into the flat, Jill's outraged wails met her. *Just a minute, love,* she promised. Snatching up the impressively fat manuscript she had typed from Jacob's dictation through so many hopeful teatimes, she started downstairs again.

"Thank you, Mrs. Ross." Abashed, Ellen felt Karl Goodman's shrewd eyes assess her, from the coronet of brown braids to the scuffed though polished tips of her flat walking shoes. "If we accept this, as I'm almost sure we shall, I'll have the check sent to you in advance."

Ellen flushed, thinking: *We're not that desperate. Not quite.* "That would be fine," she said.

Slowly she trudged upstairs to the shrill tune of Jill's cries. *Already I don't fit. I'm homespun, obsolete as last year's hemline. If I were Nancy, I'd grab that check the minute it dropped through the mail slot and be off to a fancy hairdresser's and top off the beauty treatment by cruising Regent Street in a cab loaded with loot. But I'm not Nancy,* she reminded herself firmly, and mustering a motherly smile, went in to finish feeding Jill. Thumbing through the smart fashion magazines in the doctor's office that afternoon, waiting for Jill's regular checkup, Ellen mused darkly on the gulf separating her from the self-possessed fur-, feather- and jewel-bedecked models who gazed back at her from the pages with astounding large, limpid eyes.

Do they ever start the day on the wrong foot? she wondered. *With a headache . . . or a heartache?* And she tried to imagine the fairytale world where these women woke dewy-eyed and pink-cheeked, yawning daintily as a cat does, their hair, even at daybreak, a miraculously intact turret of gold, russet, blue-black or perhaps lavender-tinted silver. They would rise, supple as ballerinas, to prepare an exotic breakfast for the man-of-their-heart—mushrooms and creamy scrambled eggs, say, or crabmeat on toast—trailing about a sparkling American kitchen in a foamy negligee, satin ribbons fluttering like triumphal banners . . .

No, Ellen readjusted her picture. They would, of course, have breakfast brought to them in bed, like proper princesses, on a sumptuous tray: crisp toast, the milky luster of frail china, water just off the boil for the orange-flower tea . . . And into the middle of this fabulous papier-mâché world the upsetting vision of Denise Kay insinuated itself. Indeed, she seemed perfectly at home there, her dark brown, almost black eyes profound under a ravishing cascade of coppery hair. *If only she were superficial, empty-headed.* Ellen was momentarily swamped by speculations unworthy of a resourceful wife. *If only . . .*

"Mrs. Ross?" The receptionist touched her shoulder, and Ellen snapped out of her daydream. *If only Jacob's home when I get back,* she changed her tack hopefully, *his feet up on the sofa, ready for tea, the same as ever . . .* And, hoisting Jill, she followed the efficient, white-uniformed woman into the doctor's consulting room.

Ellen unlatched the door with deliberate cheerfulness. Yet even as she crossed the threshold, Jill drowsing in her arms, she felt a wave of dismay. *He's not here . . .*

Mechanically she bedded Jill for her afternoon nap and started, with small heart, to cut out the pattern of a baby's nightgown she planned to run up on a neighbor's hand-wind sewing machine that evening. The clear blue morning had betrayed its promise, she noticed. Looming clouds let their soiled parachute silks sag low above the small square, making the houses and sparse-leaved trees seem drabber than ever.

I love it here. Ellen attacked the warm red flannel with defiant snips. *Pouf to Mayfair, pouf to Knightsbridge, pouf to Hampstead* . . . She was snuffing out the silver spheres of luxury like so many pale dandelion clocks when the phone rang.

Red cloth, pins, tissue pattern pieces and scissors flew helter-skelter onto the rug as she scrambled to her feet. Jacob always called if he was held up somewhere, so she wouldn't worry. And at this particular moment, some token of his thoughtfulness, however small, would be more welcome than cool water to a waif in the desert.

"Hallo, darling!" Nancy Regan's cocky, theatrical voice vibrated across the wire. "How are things?"

"Fine," Ellen fibbed. "Just fine." She sat down on the edge of the chintz-covered trunk that doubled as a wardrobe and telephone table to steady herself. No use hiding the news. "Jacob's just had his first play accepted."

"I know, I know."

"But how. . . ?" *How does she manage to pick up the least glitter of gossip? Like a professional magpie, a bird of ill-omen* . . .

"It was easy, darling. I ran across Jacob in the Rainbow Room tête-à-tête with Denise Kay. You know me. I couldn't resist finding out why the celebration. I didn't know Jacob went in for martinis, darling. Let alone redheads . . ."

A crawling prickle of misery, rather like gooseflesh, made Ellen go hot, then cold. In the light of Nancy's suggestive tone, even her worst dreads seemed naïve. "Oh, Jacob needs a change of scenery after all the work he's been doing." She tried to sound casual. "Most men take the weekend off, at least, but Jacob . . ."

Nancy's brittle laugh rang out. "Don't tell me! I'm the expert to end all experts when it comes to newly discovered playwrights. Are you going to have a party?"

"Party?" Then Ellen remembered the spectacular fatted calf the Regans had served up by way of commemorating their first really big check—friends, neighbors and strangers cramming the small, smoke-filled rooms, singing, drinking, dancing till night blued and the dawn sky showed pale as watered silk above the cockeyed chimney pots. If bottles with awe-inspiring labels and dozens of Fortnum and Mason chicken pies and imported cheeses and a soup plate of caviar were any measure of success, the Regans had cornered a lion's share. "No, no party, I think, Nancy. We'll be glad enough to have the gas and electric bills paid a bit in advance, and the baby's outgrowing her layette so fast . . ."

"Ellen!" Nancy moaned. "Where's your imagination?"

"I guess," Ellen confessed, "I just haven't got any."

"Excuse an old busybody, but you sound really blue, Ellen! Why don't you invite me round for tea? Then we can have one of our chats and you'll perk up in no time."

Ellen smiled wanly. Nancy was irrepressible, you had to say that for her. No one could accuse *her* of moping or wallowing in self-pity. "Consider yourself invited."

"Give me twenty minutes, darling."

"Now what you really should do, Ellen . . ." Stylish if a bit plump, in the dressy suit and fur toque, Nancy dropped her voice to a conspiratorial whisper and reached for her third cupcake. "Mmm," she murmured, "better than Lyons'. What you really should do," she repeated, "if you'll pardon me for being frank, is assert yourself." And she sat back with a triumphant expression.

"I don't quite see what you mean." Ellen bent over Jill, admiring the baby's clear gray eyes as she sipped her orange juice. It was getting on toward five, and still no word from Jacob. "What have I got to assert?"

"Your inner woman, of course!" Nancy exclaimed impatiently. "You need to take a good, long look at yourself in the mirror. The way I should have, before it was too late," she added grimly. "Men won't admit it, but they do want a

woman to look *right*, really *fatale*. The right hat, the right
hair color . . . Now's your chance, Ellen. Don't miss it!''

"I've never been able to afford a hairdresser," Ellen said
lamely. *Jacob likes my hair long,* a small, secret voice protested. *He said so, when was it? Last week, last month . . .*

"Of course not," Nancy crooned. "You've been sacrific-
ing all the expensive little feminine tricks for Jacob's career.
But now he's arrived. You can go wild, darling. Simply
wild."

Ellen entertained a brief vision of herself leaning seduc-
tively with priceless hunks of jewelry, green eye shadow
heavy enough to astound Cleopatra, one of the new pale lip
colors, a coquettish feather cut complete with kiss curls . . .
But she wasn't deceived—at least not for more than a few
seconds. "I'm not the type."

"Oh, rubbish!" Nancy waved a ring-winking, vermilion-
tipped hand that resembled, Ellen thought, a bright, predatory
claw. "That's your trouble, Ellen. You've no self-confidence."

"You're wrong there, Nancy," Ellen returned with some
spirit. "I've about two bobs' worth."

Nancy dumped a heaping spoon of sugar into her fresh cup
of tea. "Shouldn't," she chided herself, and then rattled on
without looking at Ellen, "I don't wonder if you're a tiny bit
worried about Denise. She's a legend, one of those professional home wreckers. She specializes in family men."

Ellen felt her stomach lurch, as if she were on a boat in a
gale. "Is she married?" she heard herself say. She didn't
want to know. She wanted nothing more than to put her
hands to her ears and flee into the comforting rose-patterned
bedroom and find some outlet for the tears that were gathering to a hard lump in her throat.

"Married?" Nancy gave a dry little laugh. "She wears a
ring, and that's covered a good deal. The current one—her
third, I think—has a wife and three children. The wife won't
hear of a divorce. Oh, Denise is a real career girl—she always
manages to land a man with complications, so she never ends
up drying dishes or wiping a baby's nose." Nancy's bright
chatter slowed and began to run down, like a record, into an

abyss of silence. "Pet!" she exclaimed, catching sight of Ellen's face. "You're as white as paper! I didn't mean to upset you—honestly, Ellen. I just figured you ought to know what you're up against. I mean, I was the last to know about Keith. In those days," and Nancy's wry smile didn't succeed in hiding the tremor in her voice, "I thought everybody had a heart of gold, everything was open and aboveboard."

"Oh, Nan!" Ellen laid an impulsive hand on her friend's arm. "We did have good times, didn't we!" But in her heart a new refrain sang itself over and over: *Jacob's not like Keith, Jacob's not like Keith* . . .

" 'The days of auld lang syne.' Huh!" With a delicate snort Nancy dismissed the past and began to draw on her admirably classic mauve gloves.

The moment the door closed on Nancy, Ellen started to behave in a curious and completely uncharacteristic fashion. Instead of putting on her apron and bustling about in the kitchen to prepare supper, she stowed Jill in her pen with a rusk and her favorite toys and disappeared into the bedroom to rummage through the bureau drawers with sporadic mutterings, rather like a female Sherlock Holmes on the scent of a crucial clue.

Why don't I do this every night? she was asking herself half an hour later as, flushed and freshly bathed, she slipped into the royal blue silk Japanese jacket she had been sent several Christmases ago by a footloose school friend circling the globe on a plump legacy, but never worn—an exquisite whispery, sapphire-sheened piece of finery that seemed to have no business whatsoever in her commonsensical world. Then she undid her coronet of braids and swept her hair up into a quite dashing impromptu topknot which she anchored precariously with a few pins. With a couple of tentative waltz steps she accustomed herself to her holiday pair of steep black heels and, as a final touch, doused herself thoroughly with the last drops of the French perfume. During this ritual, Ellen resolutely kept her eyes from lingering on the round

moon face of the clock, which had already inched its short
black hand past six. *Now all I have to do is wait . . .*

Breezing into the living room, she felt a sudden pang. *I've
forgotten Jill!* The baby was sprawled sound asleep in the
corner of her playpen, thumb in mouth. Gently Ellen picked
up the warm little form and carried her into the bedroom.

They had a wonderful bathtime. Jill laughed and kicked
until water flew all over the room, but Ellen hardly noticed,
thinking how the baby's dark hair and serene gray eyes
mirrored Jacob's own. Even when Jill knocked the cup of
porridge out of her hand and onto her best black skirt she
couldn't get really angry. She was spooning stewed plums
into Jill's mouth when she heard the click of a key in the
front door lock and froze. The day's fears and frustrations,
momentarily brushed aside, swept back over her in a rush.

"Now that's what I like to see when I come home after a
hard day!" Jacob leaned against the doorjamb, lit by a mysterious glow that didn't, somehow, seem to stem from martinis
or redheads. "Wife and daughter waiting by the fireside to
welcome the lord of the house . . ." Jill was, in fact, treating
her father to a spectacular blue ear-to-ear smile, composed
largely of stewed plums. Ellen giggled, and her desperate
silent prayer of that morning appeared close to being granted
when Jacob crossed the room in two strides and enveloped
her, sticky plum dish and all, in a hearty bear hug.

"Mmm, darling, you smell good!" Ellen waited demurely
for some mention of the French perfume. "A sort of marvelous homemade blend of Farex and cod liver oil. A new
bedjacket too!" He held her tenderly at arm's length. "You
look fresh from the tub with your hair up like that."

"Oooh!" Ellen shook herself free. "Men!" But her tone
gave her away—Jacob obviously saw her as the wife and
mother type, and she couldn't be better pleased.

"Seriously, love, I've a surprise."

"Isn't the play enough for one day?" Ellen asked dreamily, tilting her head to Jacob's shoulder and wondering why
she didn't feel in the least like making a scene about his

luncheon with Denise or his unexplained absence all the tedious, worrisome afternoon.

"I've been on the phone to the estate agent."

"Estate agent?"

"Remember that funny out-of-the-way little office we stopped at for a lark on our holiday in Cornwall, just before Jill came. . . ?"

"Ye-es." Ellen didn't dare let herself jump to conclusions.

Well, he still has that place for sale . . . that cottage we rented overlooking the inlet. Want it?"

"*Want* it!" Ellen almost shouted.

"I sort of hoped you did, after the way you raved about the place last spring," Jacob said modestly. "Because I've arranged to make the down payment with the check Denise handed me at lunch."

For a second, the merest snag of foreboding caught at Ellen's heart. "Won't you have to stay around London for the play. . . ?"

Jacob laughed. "Not on your life! That Denise Kay is a career woman with a mind of her own—a regular diesel engine. Catch me crossing her path! Why, she's so high-powered she even fueled up on the martini she'd ordered for me when I told her I never touch the stuff on weekdays."

The phone, curiously muted, almost musical, interrupted him. Ellen bundled Jill into his arms for her goodnight lullaby and tucking-in and floated into the living room to answer.

"Ellen, darling." Nancy Regan's voice sounded giddy and thin as tinsel over a raucous background of jazz and laughter. "I've been racking my brain for what I could do to pep you up, and I've made you an appointment with my Roderigo for Saturday at eleven. It's amazing how an utterly new hairdo can raise your morale . . ."

"Sorry, Nan," Ellen said gently, "but I think you'd better cancel my appointment. I've news for you."

"News?"

"Braids are back in style this season, love—the latest thing for the country wife!"

Accomplished Desires

JOYCE CAROL OATES

There was a man she loved with a violent love, and she spent much of her time thinking about his wife.

No shame to it, she actually followed the wife. She followed her to Peabody's Market, which was a small, dark, crowded store, and she stood in silence on the pavement as the woman appeared again and got into her station wagon and drove off. The girl, Dorie, would stand as if paralyzed, and even her long fine blond hair seemed paralyzed with thought— her heart pounded as if it too was thinking, planning—and then she would turn abruptly as if executing one of the steps in her modern dance class and cross through Peabody's alley and out to the Elks' Club parking lot and so up toward the campus, where the station wagon was bound.

Hardly had the station wagon pulled into the driveway when Dorie, out of breath, appeared a few houses down and watched. How that woman got out of a car!—you could see the flabby expanse of her upper leg, white flesh that should never be exposed, and then she turned and leaned in, probably with a grunt, to get shopping bags out of the back seat. Two of her children ran out to meet her, without coats or jackets. They had nervous, darting bodies—Dorie felt sorry for them—and their mother rose, straightening, a stout woman in a colorless coat, either scolding them or teasing them, one

112

bag in either muscular arm—and so—so the mother and chldren went into the house and Dorie stood with nothing to stare at except the battered station wagon, and the small snowy wilderness that was the Arbers' front yard, and the house itself. It was a large, ugly, peeling Victorian home in a block of similar homes, most of which had been fixed up by the faculty members who rented them. Dorie, who had something of her own mother's shrewd eye for hopeless, cast-off things, believed that the house could be remodeled and made presentable—but as long as he remained married to *that woman* it would be slovenly and peeling and ugly.

She loved that woman's husband with a fierce love that was itself a little ugly. Always a rather stealthy girl, thought to be simply quiet, she had entered his life by no accident— had not appeared in his class by accident—but every step of her career, like every outfit she wore and every expression on her face, was planned and shrewd and desperate. Before her twenties she had not thought much about herself; now she thought about herself continuously. She was leggy, long-armed, slender, and had a startled look—but the look was stylized now, and attractive. Her face was denuded of make-up and across her soft skin a galaxy of freckles glowed with health. She looked like a girl about to bound onto the tennis courts—and she did play tennis, though awkwardly. She played tennis with *him*. But so confused with love was she that the game of tennis, the relentless slamming of the ball back and forth, had seemed to her a disguise for something else, the way everything in poetry or literature was a disguise for something else—for love?—and surely he must know, or didn't he know? Didn't he guess? There were many other girls he played tennis with, so that was nothing special, and her mind worked and worked while she should have slept, planning with the desperation of youth that has never actually been young—planning how to get him, how to get him, for it seemed to her that she would never be able to overcome her desire for this man.

The wife was as formidable as the husband. She wrote narrow volumes of poetry Dorie could not understand and he, the famous husband, wrote novels and critical pieces. The wife was a big, energetic, high-colored woman; the husband, Mark Arber, was about her size though not so high-colored— his complexion was rather putty-colored, rather melancholy. Dorie thought about the two of them all the time, awake or asleep, and she could feel the terrible sensation of blood flowing through her body, a flowing of desire that was not just for the man but somehow for the woman as well, a desire for her accomplishments, her fame, her children, her ugly house, her ugly body, her very life. She had light, frank blue eyes and people whispered that she drank; Dorie never spoke of her.

The college was a girls' college, exclusive and expensive, and every girl who remained there for more than a year understood a peculiar, even freakish kinship with the place—as if she had always been there and the other girls, so like herself with their sleepy unmade-up faces, the skis in winter and the bicycles in good weather, the excellent expensive professors, and the excellent air—everything, everything had always been there, had existed for centuries. They were stylish and liberal in their cashmere sweaters with soiled necks; their fingers were stained with ballpoint ink; and like them, Dorie understood that most of the world was wretched and would never come to this college, never, would be kept back from it by armies of helmeted men. She, Dorie Weinheimer, was not wretched but supremely fortunate, and she must be grateful always for her good luck, for there was no justification for her existence any more than there was any justification for the wretched lots of the world's poor. And there would flash to her mind's eye a confused picture of dark-faced starving mobs, or emaciated faces out of an old-fashioned Auschwitz photograph, or something—some dreary horror from the *New York Times'* one hundred neediest cases in the Christmas issue— She had, in the girls' soft, persistent manner, an idealism-turned-pragmatism under the influence of the college faculty, who had all been idealists at Harvard and Yale as undergraduates but who were now in their forties, and as impatient with normative values as they were with their students' occasional lockets-shaped-into-crosses; Mark Arber was the most disillusioned and the most eloquent of the Harvard men.

In class he sat at the head of the seminar table, leaning back in his leather-covered chair. He was a rather stout man. He had played football once in a past Dorie could not quite imagine, though she wanted to imagine it, and he had been in the war—one of the wars—she believed it to be World War II. He had an ugly, arrogant face and discolored teeth. He read poetry in a raspy, hissing, angry voice. "Like Marx, I believe that poetry has had enough of love; the hell with it. Poetry should now cultivate the whip," he would say grimly, and Dorie would stare at him to see if he was serious. There were four senior girls in this class and they sometimes asked him questions or made observations of their own, but there was no consistency in his reaction. Sometimes he seemed not to hear, sometimes he nodded enthusiastically and indifferently, sometimes he opened his eyes and looked at them, not distinguishing among them, and said: "A remark like that is quite characteristic." So she sat and stared at him and her heart seemed to turn to stone, wanting him, hating his wife and envying her violently, and the being that had been Dorie Weinheimer for twenty-one years changed gradually through the winter into another being, obsessed with jealousy. She did not know what she wanted most, this man or the victory over his wife.

She was always bringing poems to him in his office. She borrowed books from him and puzzled over every annotation of his. As he talked to her he picked at his fingernails, settled back in his chair, and he talked on in his rushed, veering, sloppy manner, as if Dorie did not exist or were a crowd, or a few intimate friends, it hardly mattered, as he raved about frauds in contemporary poetry, naming names, "that bastard with his sonnets," "that cow with her daughter-poems," and getting so angry that Dorie wanted to protest, no, no, why are you angry? Be gentle. Love me and be gentle.

When he failed to come to class six or seven times that

winter the girls were all understanding. "Do you think he really is a genius?" they asked. His look of disintegrating, decomposing recklessness, his shiny suit and bizarre loafer shoes, his flights of language made him so different from their own fathers that it was probable he was a genius; these were girls who believed seriously in the existence of geniuses. They had been trained by their highly paid, verbose professors to be vaguely ashamed of themselves, to be silent about any I.Q. rated under 160, to be uncertain about their talents within the school and quite confident of them outside it—and Dorie, who had no talent and only adequate intelligence, was always silent about herself. Her talent perhaps lay in her faithfulness to an obsession, her cunning patience, her smile, her bared teeth that were a child's teeth and yet quite sharp. . . .

One day Dorie had been waiting in Dr. Arber's office for an hour with some new poems for him. He was late but he strode into the office as if he had been hurrying all along, sitting heavily in the creaking swivel chair, panting; he looked a little mad. He was the author of many reviews in New York magazines and papers and in particular the author of three short, frightening novels, and now he had a burned-out, bleached-out look. Like any of the girls at this college, Dorie would have sat politely if one of her professors set fire to himself, and so she ignored his peculiar stare and began her rehearsed speech about—but what did it matter what it was about? The poems of Emily Dickinson or the terrible yearning of Shelley or her own terrible lust, what did it matter?

He let his hand fall onto hers by accident. She stared at the hand, which was like a piece of meat—and she stared at him and was quite still. She was pert and long-haired, in the chair facing him, an anonymous student and a minor famous man, and every wrinkle of his sagging, impatient face was bared to her in the winter sunlight from the window—and every thread of blood in his eyes—and quite calmly and politely she said, "I guess I should tell you, Dr. Arber, that I'm in love with you. I've felt that way for some time."

"You what, you're what?" he said. He gripped her feeble

hand as if clasping it in a handshake. "What did you say?" He spoke with an amazed, slightly irritated urgency, and so it began.

II

His wife wrote her poetry under an earlier name, Barbara Scott. Many years before she had had a third name, a maiden name— Barbara Cameron—but it belonged to another era about which she never thought except under examination from her analyst. She had a place cleared in the dirty attic of her house and she liked to sit up there, away from the children, and look out the small octagon of a window and think. People she saw from her attic window looked bizarre and helpless to her. She herself was a hefty, perspiring woman, and all her dresses—especially her expensive ones— were stained under the arms with great lemon-colored half-moons no dry cleaner could remove. Because she was so large a woman, she was quick to see imperfections in others, as if she used a magnifying glass. Walking by her window on an ordinary morning were an aged tottering woman, an enormous Negro woman—probably someone's cleaning lady—and a girl from the college on aluminum crutches, poor brave thing, and the white-blond child from up the street who was precocious and demonic. Her own children were precocious and only slightly troublesome. Now two of them were safe in school and the youngest, the three-year-old, was asleep somewhere.

Barbara Scott had won the Pulitzer Prize not long before with an intricate sonnet series that dealt with the "voices" of many people; her energetic, coy line was much imitated. This morning she began a poem that her agent was to sell, after Barbara's death, to the *New Yorker:*

> *What awful wrath*
> *what terrible betrayal*
> *and these aluminum crutches, rubber-tipped. . . .*

She had such a natural talent that she let words take her anywhere. Her decade of psychoanalysis had trained her to hold nothing back; even when she had nothing to say, the very authority of her technique carried her on. So she sat that morning at her big, nicked desk—over the years the children had marred it with sharp toys—and stared out the window and waited for more inspiration. She felt the most intense kind of sympathy when she saw someone deformed—she was anxious, in a way, to see deformed people because it released such charity in her. But apart from the girl on the crutches she saw nothing much. Hours passed and she realized that her husband had not come home; already school was out and her two boys were running across the lawn.

When she descended the two flights of stairs to the kitchen, she saw that the three-year-old, Geoffrey, had opened a white plastic bottle of ammonia and had spilled it on the floor and on himself; the stench was sickening. The two older boys bounded in the back door as if spurred on by the argument that raged between them, and Barbara whirled upon them and began screaming. The ammonia had spilled onto her slacks. The boys ran into the front room and she remained in the kitchen, screaming. She sat down heavily on one of the kitchen chairs. After half an hour she came to herself and tried to analyze the situation. Did she hate these children, or did she hate herself? Did she hate Mark? Or was her hysteria a form of love, or was it both love and hate together . . . ? She put the ammonia away and made herself a drink.

When she went into the front room she saw that the boys were playing with their mechanical inventors' toys and had forgotten about her. Good. They were self-reliant. Slight, cunning children, all of them dark like Mark and prematurely aged, as if by the burden of their prodigious intelligences, they were not always predictable: they forgot things, lost things, lied about things, broke things, tripped over themselves and each other, mimicked classmates, teachers, and their parents, and often broke down into pointless tears. And yet sometimes they did not break down into tears when Barbara punished them, as if to challenge her. She did not always know what she had given birth to: they were so remote, even in their struggles and assaults, they were so fictional, as if she had imagined them herself. It had been she who'd imagined them, not Mark. Their father had no time. He was always in a hurry, he had three aged typewriters in his study and paper in each one, an article or a review or even a novel in progress in each of the machines, and he had no time for the children except to nod grimly at them or tell them to be quiet. He had been so precocious himself, Mark Arber, that after his first, successful novel at the age of twenty-four he had had to whip from place to place, from typewriter to typewriter, in a frantic attempt to keep up with—he called it keeping up with his "other self," his "real self," evidently a kind of alter ego who was always typing and creating, unlike the real Mark Arber. The real Mark Arber was now forty-five and he had made the transition from "promising" to "established" without anything in between, like most middle-aged critics of prominence.

Strachey, the five-year-old, had built a small machine that was both a man and an automobile, operated by the motor that came with the set of toys. "This is a modern centaur," he said wisely, and Barbara filed that away, thinking perhaps it would do well in a poem for a popular, slick magazine. . . . She sat, unbidden, and watched her boys' intense work with the girders and screws and bolts, and sluggishly she thought of making supper, or calling Mark at school to see what had happened . . . that morning he had left the house in a rage and when she went into his study, prim and frowning, she had discovered four or five crumpled papers in his wastebasket. It was all he had accomplished that week.

Mark had never won the Pulitzer Prize for anything. People who knew him spoke of his slump, familiarly and sadly; if they disliked Mark they praised Barbara, and if they disliked Barbara they praised Mark. They were "established" but it did not mean much, younger writers were being discovered all the time who had been born in the mid- or late forties, strangely young, terrifyingly young, and people the Arbers' age were being crowded out, hustled toward the exits. . . .

Being "established" should have pleased them, but instead it
led them to long spiteful bouts of eating and drinking in the
perpetual New England winter.

She made another drink and fell asleep in the chair. Sometime later her children's fighting woke her and she said,
"Shut up," and they obeyed at once. They were playing in
the darkened living room, down at the other end by the big
brick fireplace that was never used. Her head ached. She got
to her feet and went out to make another drink.

Around one o'clock Mark came in the back door. He
stumbled and put the light on. Barbara, in her plaid bathrobe,
was sitting at the kitchen table. She had a smooth, shiny,
bovine face, heavy with fatigue. Mark said, "What the hell
are you doing here?"

She attempted a shrug of her shoulders. Mark stared at her.
"I'm getting you a housekeeper," he said. "You need more
time for yourself, for your work. For your work," he said,
twisting his mouth at the word to show what he thought of it.
"You shouldn't neglect your poetry so we're getting in a
housekeeper, not to do any heavy work, just to sort of watch
things—in other words—a kind of external consciousness.
You should be freed from ordinary considerations."

He was not drunk but he had the appearance of having
been drunk, hours before, and now his words were muddled
and dignified with the air of words spoken too early in the
morning. He wore a dirty tweed overcoat, the same coat he'd
had when they were married, and his necktie had been pulled
off and stuffed somewhere, and his puffy, red face looked
mean. Barbara thought of how reality was too violent for
poetry and how poetry, and the language itself, shimmered
helplessly before the confrontation with living people and
their demands. "The housekeeper is here. She's outside,"
Mark said. "I'll go get her."

He returned with a college girl who looked like a hundred
other college girls. "This is Dorie, this is my wife Barbara,
you've met no doubt at some school event, here you are,"
Mark said. He was carrying a suitcase that must have belonged to the girl. "Dorie has requested room and board with

a faculty family. The Dean of Women arranged it. Dorie will babysit or something—we can put her in the spare room. Let's take her up.''

Barbara had not yet moved. The girl was pale and distraught; she looked about sixteen. Her hair was disheveled. She stared at Barbara and seemed about to speak.

"Let's take her up, you want to sit there all night?'' Mark snarled.

Barbara indicated with a motion of her hand that they should go up without her. Mark, breathing heavily, stomped up the back steps and the girl followed at once. There was no indication of her presence because her footsteps were far too light on the stairs. She said nothing, only a slight change in the odor of the kitchen indicated something new—a scent of cologne, hair scrubbed clean, a scent of panic. Barbara sat listening to her heart thud heavily inside her and she recalled how, several years before, Mark had left her and had turned up at a friend's apartment in Chicago—he'd been beaten up by someone on the street, an accidental event—and how he had blackened her eye once in an argument over the worth of Samuel Richardson, and how—there were many other bitter memories—and of course there had been other women, some secret and some known—and now this—

So she sat thinking with a small smile of how she would have to dismiss this when she reported it to their friends: *Mark has had this terrible block for a year now, with his novel, and so . . .*

She sat for a while running through phrases and explanations, and when she climbed up the stairs to bed she was grimly surprised to see him in their bedroom, asleep, his mouth open and his breath raspy and exhausted. At the back of the house, in a small oddly shaped maid's room, slept the girl; in their big dormer room slept the three boys, or perhaps they only pretended to sleep; and only she, Barbara, stood in the dark and contemplated the bulk of her own body, wondering what to do and knowing that there was nothing she would

do, no way for her to change the process of events any more
than she could change the heavy fact of her body itself. There
was no way to escape what the years had made her.

III

From that time on they lived together like a family. Or it
was as Mark put it: "Think of a babysitter here permanently.
Like the Lunt girl, staying on here permanently to help, only
we won't need that one any more." Barbara made breakfast
for them all, and then Mark and Dorie drove off to school and
returned late, between six and six-thirty, and in the evenings
Mark worked hard at his typewriters, going to sit at one and
then the next and then the next, and the girl, Dorie, helped
Barbara with the dishes and odd chores and went up to her
room, where she studied . . . or did something, she must
have done something.

Of the long afternoons he and the girl were away Mark said
nothing. He was evasive and jaunty; he looked younger. He
explained carefully to Dorie that when he and Mrs. Arber
were invited somewhere she must stay home and watch the
children, that she was not included in these invitations: and
the girl agreed eagerly. She did so want to help around the
house! She had inherited from her background a dislike for
confusion—so the mess of the Arber house upset her and she
worked for hours picking things up, polishing tarnished objects Barbara herself had forgotten were silver, cleaning, arranging, fixing. As soon as the snow melted she was to be
seen outside, raking shyly through the flower beds. How to
explain her to the neighbors? Barbara said nothing.

"But I didn't think we lived in such a mess. I didn't think
it was so bad," Barbara would say to Mark in a quiet, hurt
voice, and he would pat her hand and say, "It isn't a mess,
she just likes to fool around. *I* don't think it's a mess."

It was fascinating to live so close to a young person.
Barbara had never been young in quite the way Dorie was
young. At breakfast—they ate crowded around the table—

everyone could peer into everyone else's face, there were no secrets, stale mouths and bad moods were inexcusable, all the wrinkles of age or distress that showed on Barbara could never be hidden, and not to be hidden was Mark's guilty enthusiasm, his habit of saying, "*We* should go to . . . ," "*We* are invited . . ." and the "we" meant either him and Barbara, or him and Dorie, but never all three; he had developed a new personality. But Dorie was fascinating. She awoke to the slow gray days of spring with a panting, wondrous expectation, her blond hair shining, her freckles clear as dabs of clever paint on her heartbreaking skin, her teeth very, very white and straight, her pert little lips innocent of lipstick and strangely sensual . . . yes, it was heartbreaking. She changed her clothes at least twice a day while Barbara wore the same outfit—baggy black slacks and a black sweater— for weeks straight. Dorie appeared downstairs in cashmere sweater sets that were the color of birds' eggs, or of birds' fragile legs, and white trim blouses that belonged on a genteel hockey field, and bulky pink sweaters big as jackets, and when she was dressed casually she wore stretch slacks that were neatly secured by stirrups about her long, narrow, white feet. Her eyes were frankly and emptily brown, as if giving themselves up to every observer. She was so anxious to help that it was oppressive; "No, I can manage, I've been making breakfast for eight years by myself," Barbara would say angrily, and Dorie, a chastised child, would glance around the table not only at Mark but at the children for sympathy. Mark had a blackboard set up in the kitchen so that he could test the children's progress in languages, and he barked out commands for them—French or Latin or Greek words—and they responded with nervous glee, clacking out letters on the board, showing off for the rapt, admiring girl who seemed not to know if they were right or wrong.

"Oh, how smart they are—how wonderful everything is," Dorie breathed.

Mark had to drive to Boston often because he needed his prescription for tranquillizers refilled constantly, and his doctor would not give him an automatic refill. But though Bar-

bara had always looked forward to these quick trips, he rarely
took her now. He went off with Dorie, now his "secretary,"
who took along a notebook decorated with the college's
insignia to record his impressions in, and since he never gave
his wife warning she could not get ready in time, and it was
such an obvious trick, so crudely cruel, that Barbara stood in
the kitchen and wept as they drove out. . . . She called up
friends in New York but never exactly told them what was
going on. It was so ludicrous, it made her seem such a fool.
Instead she chatted and barked with laughter; her conversations with these people were always so witty that nothing,
nothing seemed very real until she hung up the receiver again;
and then she became herself, in a drafty college-owned house
in New England, locked in this particular body.

She stared out the attic window for hours, not thinking.
She became a state of being, a creature. Downstairs the
children fought, or played peacefully, or rifled through their
father's study, which was forbidden, and after a certain amount
of time something would nudge Barbara to her feet and she
would descend slowly, laboriously, as if returning to the real
world where any ugliness was possible. When she slapped the
boys for being bad, they stood in meek defiance and did not
cry. "Mother, you're out of your mind," they said. "Mother,
you're losing control of yourself."

"It's your father who's out of his mind!" she shouted.

She had the idea that everyone was talking about them,
everyone. Anonymous, worthless people who had never published a line gloated over her predicament; high-school baton
twirlers were better off than Barbara Scott, who had no
dignity. Dorie, riding with Mark Arber on the expressway to
Boston, was at least young and stupid, anonymous though
she was, and probably she too had a slim collection of poems
that Mark would manage to get published . . . and who knew
what would follow, who could tell? Dorie Weinheimer was
like any one of five hundred or five thousand college girls
and was no one, had no personality, and yet Mark Arber had
somehow fallen in love with her, so perhaps everyone would
eventually fall in love with her . . . ? Barbara imagined

with panic the parties she knew nothing about to which Mark
and his new girl went: Mark in his slovenly tweed suits,
looking like his own father in the thirties, and Dorie chic as a
Vogue model in her weightless bones and vacuous face.

"Is Dorie going to stay here long?" the boys kept asking.

"Why, don't you like her?"

"She's nice. She smells nice. Is she going to stay long?"

"Go ask your father that," Barbara said angrily.

The girl was officially boarding with them; it was no lie.
Every year certain faculty families took in a student or two,
out of generosity or charity, or because they themselves
needed the money, and the Arbers themselves had always
looked down upon such hearty liberalism. But now they had
Dorie, and in Peabody's Market Barbara had to rush up and
down the aisles with her shopping cart, trying to avoid the
wives of other professors who were sure to ask her about the
new boarder; and she had to buy special things for the girl,
spinach and beets and artichokes, while Barbara and Mark
liked starches and sweets and fat, foods that clogged up the
blood vessels and strained the heart and puffed out the
stomach. While Barbara ate and drank hungrily, Dorie sat
chaste with her tiny forkfuls of food, and Barbara could eat
three platefuls to Dorie's one; her appetite increased savagely
just in the presence of the girl. (The girl was always asking
politely, "Is it the boys who get the bathroom all dirty?" or
"Could I take the vacuum cleaner down to have it fixed?"
and these questions, polite as they were, made Barbara's
appetite increase savagely.)

In April, after Dorie had been boarding with them three
and a half months, Barbara was up at her desk when there
was a rap on the plywood door. Unused to visitors, Barbara
turned clumsily and looked at Mark over the top of her
glasses. "Can I come in?" he said. "What are you working on?"

There was no paper in her typewriter. "Nothing," she
said.

"You haven't shown me any poems lately. What's wrong?"

He sat on the window ledge and lit a cigarette. Barbara felt a spiteful satisfaction to see how old he looked—he hadn't her fine, fleshed-out skin, the smooth complexion of an overweight woman; he had instead the bunched, baggy complexion of an overweight man whose weight keeps shifting up and down. Good. Even his fingers shook as he lit the cigarette.

"This is the best place in the house," he said.

"Do you want me to give it up to Dorie?"

He stared at her. "Give it up—why? Of course not."

"I thought you might be testing my generosity."

He shook his head, puzzled. Barbara wondered if she hated this man or if she felt a writer's interest in him. Perhaps he was insane. Or perhaps he had been drinking again; he had not gone out to his classes this morning, and she'd heard him arguing with Dorie. "Barbara, how old are you?" he said.

"Forty-three. You know that."

He looked around at the boxes and other clutter as if coming to an important decision. "Well, we have a little problem here."

Barbara stared at her blunt fingernails and waited.

"She got herself pregnant. It seems on purpose."

"She what?"

"Well," Mark said uncomfortably, "she did it on purpose."

They remained silent. After a while, in a different voice he said, "She claims she loves children. She loves our children and wants some of her own. It's a valid point, I can't deny her her rights . . . but . . . I thought you should know about it in case you agree to help."

"What do you mean?"

"Well, I have something arranged in Boston," he said, not looking at her, "and Dorie has agreed to it . . . though reluctantly . . . and unfortunately I don't think I can drive her myself . . . you know I have to go to Chicago. . . ."

Barbara did not look at him.

"I'm on this panel at the University of Chicago, with John

Ciardi. You know, it's been set up for a year, it's on the state of contemporary poetry—you know—I can't possibly withdraw from it now—''

"And so?"

"If you could drive Dorie in—"

"If I could drive her in?"

"I don't see what alternative we have," he said slowly.

"Would you like a divorce so you can marry her?"

"I have never mentioned that," he said.

"Well, would you?"

"I don't know."

"Look at me. Do you want to marry her?"

A nerve began to twitch in his eye. It was a familiar twitch—it had been with him for two decades. "No, I don't think so. I don't know—you know how I feel about disruption."

"Don't you have any courage?"

"Courage?"

"If you want to marry her, go ahead. I won't stop you."

"Do you want a divorce yourself?"

"I'm asking you. It's up to you. Then Dorie can have her baby and fulfill herself," Barbara said with a deathly smile. "She can assert her rights as a woman twenty years younger than I. She can become the third Mrs. Arber and become automatically envied. Don't you have the courage for it?"

"I had thought," Mark said with dignity, "that you and I had an admirable marriage. It was different from the marriages of other people we know—part of it is that we don't work in the same area, yes, but the most important part lay in our understanding of each other. It has taken a tremendous generosity on your part, Barbara, over the last three months and I appreciate it," he said, nodding slowly, "I appreciate it and I can't help asking myself whether . . . whether I would have had the strength to do what you did, in your place. I mean, if you had brought in—"

"I know what you mean."

"It's been an extraordinary marriage. I don't want it to end on an impulse, anything reckless or emotional," he said vaguely. She thought that he did look a little mad, but quietly mad; his ears were very red. For the first time she began to feel pity for the girl who was, after all, nobody, and who had no personality, and who was waiting in the ugly maid's room for her fate to be decided.

"All right, I'll drive her to Boston," Barbara said.

IV

Mark had to leave the next morning for Chicago. He would be gone, he explained, about a week—there was not only the speaking appearance, but other things as well. The three of them had a kind of farewell party the night before. Dorie sat with her frail hand on her flat, child's stomach and drank listlessly, while Barbara and Mark argued about the comparative merits of two English novelists—their literary arguments were always witty, superficial, rapid, and very enjoyable. At two o'clock Mark woke Dorie to say good-by and Barbara, thinking herself admirably discreet, went upstairs alone.

She drove Dorie to Boston the next day. Dorie was a mother's child, the kind of girl mothers admire—clean, bright, passive—and it was a shame for her to be so frightened. Barbara said roughly, "I've known lots of women who've had abortions. They lived."

"Did you ever have one?"

"No."

Dorie turned away as if in reproach.

"I've had children and that's harder, maybe. It's thought to be harder," Barbara said, as if offering the girl something.

"I would like children, maybe three of them," Dorie said.

"Three is a good number, yes."

"But I'd be afraid . . . I wouldn't know what to do. . . . I don't know what to do now. . . ."

She was just a child herself, Barbara thought with a rush of sympathy; of all of them it was Dorie who was most trapped.

The girl sat with a scarf around her careless hair, staring out the window. She wore a camel's hair coat like all the girls and her fingernails were colorless and uneven, as if she had been chewing them.

"Stop thinking about it. Sit still."

"Yes," the girl said listlessly.

They drove on. Something began to weigh at Barbara's heart, as if her flesh were aging moment by moment. She had never liked her body. Dorie's body was so much more prim and chaste and stylish, and her own body belonged to another age, a hearty nineteenth century where fat had been a kind of virtue. Barbara thought of her poetry, which was light and sometimes quite clever, the poetry of a girl, glimmering with half-seen visions and echoing with peculiar off-rhymes—and truly it ought to have been Dorie's poetry and not hers. She was not equal to her own writing. And, on the highway like this, speeding toward some tawdry destination, she had the sudden terrible conviction that language itself did not matter and that nothing mattered ultimately except the body, the human body and the bodies of other creatures and objects: what else existed?

"Her own body was the only real fact about her. Dorie, huddled over in her corner, was another real fact and they were going to do something about it, defeat it. She thought of Mark already in Chicago, at a cocktail party, the words growing like weeds in his brain and his wit moving so rapidly through the brains of others that it was, itself, a kind of lie. It seemed strange to her that the two of them should move against Dorie, who suffered because she was totally real and helpless and gave up nothing of herself to words.

They arrived in Boston and began looking for the street. Barbara felt clumsy and guilty and did not dare to glance over at the girl. She muttered aloud as they drove for half an hour, without luck. Then she found the address. It was a small private hospital with a blank gray front. Barbara drove past it and circled the block and approached it again. "Come on, get hold of yourself," she said to Dorie's stiff profile, "this is no picnic for me either."

She stopped the car and she and Dorie stared out at the hospital, which looked deserted. The neighborhood itself seemed deserted. Finally Barbara said, with a heaviness she did not yet understand, "Let's find a place to stay tonight first. Let's get that settled." She took the silent girl to a motel on a boulevard and told her to wait in the room, she'd be back shortly. Dorie stared in a drugged silence at Barbara, who could have been her mother—there flashed between them the kind of camaraderie possible only between mother and daughter—and then Barbara left the room. Dorie remained sitting in a very light chair of imitation wood and leather. She sat so that she was staring at the edge of the bureau; occasionally her eye was attracted by the framed picture over the bed, of a woman in a red evening gown and a man in a tuxedo observing a waterfall by moonlight. She sat like this for quite a while, in her coat. A nerve kept twitching in her thigh but it did not bother her; it was a most energetic, thumping twitch, as if her very flesh were doing a dance. But it did not bother her. She remained there for a while, waking to the morning light, and it took her several panicked moments to remember where she was and who had brought her here. She had the immediate thought that she must be safe—if it was morning she must be safe—and someone had taken care of her, had seen what was best for her and had carried it out.

V

And so she became the third Mrs. Arber, a month after the second one's death. Barbara had been found dead in an elegant motel across the city, the Paradise Inn, which Mark thought was a brave, cynical joke; he took Barbara's death with an alarming, rhetorical melodrama, an alcoholic melancholy Dorie did not like. Barbara's "infinite courage" made Dorie resentful. The second Mrs. Arber had taken a large dose of sleeping pills and had died easily, because of the strain her body had made upon her heart; so that was that. But somehow it wasn't—because Mark kept talking about it, speculating on it, wondering: "She did it for the baby, to preserve life. It's astonishing, it's exactly like something in a novel," he said. He spoke with a perpetual guilty astonishment.

She married him and became Mrs. Arber, which surprised everyone. It surprised even Mark. Dorie herself was not very surprised, because a daydreamer is prepared for most things and in a way she had planned even this, though she had not guessed how it would come about. Surely she had rehearsed the second Mrs. Arber's suicide and funeral already a year before, when she'd known nothing, could have guessed nothing, and it did not really surprise her. Events lost their jagged edges and became hard and opaque and routine, drawing her into them. She was still a daydreamer, though she was Mrs. Arber. She sat at the old desk up in the attic and leaned forward on her bony elbows to stare out the window, contemplating the hopeless front yard and the people who strolled by, some of them who—she thought—glanced toward the house with a kind of amused contempt, as if aware of her inside. She was almost always home.

The new baby was a girl, Carolyn. Dorie took care of her endlessly and she took care of the boys; she hadn't been able to finish school. In the evening when all the children were at last asleep Mark would come out of his study and read to her in his rapid, impatient voice snatches of his new novel, or occasionally poems of his late wife's, and Dorie would stare at him and try to understand. She was transfixed with love for him and yet—and yet she was unable to locate this love in this particular man, unable to comprehend it. Mark was invited everywhere that spring; he flew all the way out to California to take part in a highly publicized symposium with George Steiner and James Baldwin, and Dorie stayed home. Geoffrey was seeing a psychiatrist in Boston and she had to drive him in every other day, and there was her own baby, and Mark's frequent visitors who arrived often without notice and stayed a week—sleeping late, staying up late, drinking, eating, arguing—it was exactly the kind of life she had known would be hers, and yet she could not adjust to it. Her baby was somehow mixed up in her mind with the other wife, as if it had been that woman's and only left to her, Dorie, for safekeeping. She was grateful that her baby was a girl because wasn't there always a kind of pact or understanding between women?

In June two men arrived at the house to spend a week, and Dorie had to cook for them. They were long, lean gray-haired young men who were undefinable, sometimes very fussy, sometimes reckless and hysterical with wit, always rather insulting in a light, veiled manner Dorie could not catch. They were both vegetarians and could not tolerate anyone eating meat in their presence. One evening at a late dinner Dorie began to cry and had to leave the room, and the two guests and Mark and even the children were displeased with her. She went up to the attic and sat mechanically at the desk. It did no good to read Barbara Scott's poetry because she did not understand it. Her understanding had dropped to tending the baby and the boys, fixing meals, cleaning up and shopping, and taking the station wagon to the garage perpetually . . . and she had no time to go with the others to the tennis courts, or to accompany Mark to New York . . . and around her were human beings whose lives consisted of language, the grace of language, and she could no longer understand them. She felt strangely cheated, a part of her murdered, as if the abortion had taken place that day after all and something had been cut permanently out of her.

In a while Mark climbed the stairs to her. She heard him coming, she heard his labored breathing. "Here you are," he said, and slid his big beefy arms around her and breathed his liquory love into her face, calling her his darling, his beauty. After all, he did love her, it was real and his arms were real, and she still loved him although she had lost the meaning of that word. "Now will you come downstairs and apologize, please?'' he said gently. "You've disturbed them and it can't be left like this. You know how I hate disruption."

She began weeping again, helplessly, to think that she had disturbed anyone, that she was this girl sitting at a battered desk in someone's attic, and no one else, no other person who might confidently take upon herself the meaning of this man's words—she was herself and that was a fact, a final fact she would never overcome.

The Absence

ELIZABETH SPENCER

Her husband having gone away on his long visit, Bonnie Richards settled down to a stack of books. They were all about science, about which she knew little, and designed for the popular reader. She was alone in the house except for the dog, who took to looking at her curiously. She thought he only missed his master and wanted to ask about him, but nonetheless his large, beseeching eyes could be disquieting. She read the science books at night and became more disquieted than ever. Matter was made of atoms, as she already knew, but the behavior and organization of these small active objects were extremely uncertain. No one knew just what matter was. No instrument was delicate enough to observe atoms without making a grave impact, which altered their habits. They thus enjoyed an unbreakable privacy. Some scientists had seriously conjectured that particles within atoms were not compelled to behave as they did but could choose what they felt like doing. All conclusions seemed open to doubt.

Space she had to quit reading about, early on. It was unthinkably gigantic, yet finite, was exploding outward, had already burst at points. There was no up or down; we were like creatures placed on the round surface of an expanding balloon, and all she had remembered from high school geometry, which had to do with flat surfaces, was no use, because nothing was flat. The moon used to be so near the earth that tides three miles high were shooting up to meet it, out in the Pacific. It was difficult not to see this awesome spectacle, in the mind's eye. When she took the dog walking in the evening, she avoided looking at the sky. Mystery books were out, for the ones she liked always unfolded in creaky old houses where dogs started barking for no reason. Her house was not old, but occasionally it creaked at night.

Bonnie was not a visitor of neighbors; most of the Richards' friends were scattered out. They had her come to dinner or for drinks, and once she drank too much and skinned her knee on the front steps when she came home. The hall light had burned out and the dog was asleep under the bed in the guest room. There was a peculiar smell in the basement, like an oil leak, but no oil was visible.

Days, she went to the grocery, and once she went to the ballet, standing at intermission in the thickly carpeted foyer, feeling elegant and somewhat mysterious in her black pumps and gray silk. Another afternoon, she went to the movies in the rain, where, wearing her old raincoat, flat heels, and a scarf, she began to feel as she had back in college. She got the house painter to come and redecorate the living room, and had such a fine time with him over coffee that she stayed in love with him for two days. He was aware of this, it was obvious, when he came the next time. She was trying to reason her way either out of it or into it, when his ladder slipped (he had grown somewhat nervous) and he broke a large window. By the time the details of repairing it were ironed out, she was simply impatient with him. He was ignorant, and when they went to the hardware store to have new glass cut, he tried to explain to her, on observing some bad reproductions of modern painting, that there was really nothing to Picasso.

The weather grew warmer, and she took out her dissatisfaction on the flower beds, planting salvia and portulaca, lobelia and marigolds, weeding the day lilies and wrecking her hands. Her husband wrote that he was having a splendid time and that his parents' health had improved since his arrival. She went to the library on quite a warm day—the warmest so far—and read for a time before large windows opening on a small park, where red cannas, freshly set out, were beginning to unscroll. Birds splashed in a rough ornamental crater filled with water. Sometimes, when they tilted up for their steep ascent, water fell from their serrated wing tips in splashes bright as mercury. She did not know what she was reading.

It was coming over her gradually what she wished to be— something she had never consciously thought of before. She wished to be a person, a being, who appeared and disappeared. She should have liked, conveniently, to have the power to disappear even from herself, to put herself away like something folded in a drawer, or simply not to be when there was nothing to be for. If not in a drawer, then better still to go outward as a color, soft and pleasing, or to be a bird's wing, or the water that the bird splashed in. She might even arrange to exist, to be in the regard, the very glance, of her husband or of those dear to her when they most or least looked for her—emerging into rooms or from around corners, coming toward them with a piece of news or a cup of coffee. The conception had started, she now realized, some time ago, back in the winter, when, coming in out of a sub-zero night, she had drawn herself close against her husband in bed and shivered for such a long time he said she should turn back into a rib, which was what wives had come from originally. She had rather fancied the idea, for her husband had a fine, practical way of carrying his body—shoulders, head, skin, bones, and all—in a manner rapid yet controlled, with a good deal of vitality and the definite promise of good things unfolding before him as he went along. He was invariably warm. She couldn't be better disposed of than in this fashion.

The next day, the dog ran off but was eventually brought back home by a small girl named Doris, whose family had been living three doors down, in an apartment in one wing of a widow's house. Bonnie invited Doris in and gave her some cookies as a reward. Doris sat down quite amiably and talked away, eating cookies. She expressed a liking for "Batman" and "The Man from U.N.C.L.E.," and said she wanted to become a dancer in shows and night clubs. It seemed unlikely at the moment that she was very promising material for this career, being mousy and rather fat, but she said it so matter-of-factly that Bonnie was persuaded she would go straight to the goal, even becoming lithe and blond and beautiful at the appropriate moment. Every day thereafter, Doris came to look at TV, since her family did not have a set. One day, her mother came for her. She said it was time for Doris to come to dinner, and asked Bonnie as a special favor if she would cash a check for ten dollars, because she had to run to the grocery, and the grocer was notoriously reluctant to cash checks. Bonnie had one of her moments of definitely appearing, and gave the money quite happily. She heard herself already telling her husband, "They are not especially nice people, but I let the girl come to pass the time. I'll just say I'm busy or something if she begins to make it a habit."

Two days later, she went by the bank to cash the check. She then learned that Doris's family had moved away in the night, having given a number of worthless checks like her own before departing. The child herself had distributed some of them, though whether or not aware of what she was doing was not known. Nobody knew where they had gone.

That night, Bonnie did not sleep at all. Nothing has happened, she kept telling herself. What's ten dollars? Why is a bird's wing waterproof? What is an atom up to? How did the moon get as high as it is? What is the dog trying to say? If the smell in the basement is not oil, then what is it? What do I myself think of Batman? The dog whimpered, and jumped on the bed and lay close to her, and though she had never allowed this before, she let him stay.

Her husband materialized exactly on schedule, through the doors into the waiting room at the airport, which sprang open magically, even royally, when he approached them.

"Is everything O.K.?" she asked.

"Fine, fine, everything's fine. Nobody was seriously sick

after all. You should have come. Why are you pale, why are you crying? Come on, let's get a drink.''

He was walking rapidly, bag in one hand, hustling her along. He looked brown and happy. All her reasons for things came back. They sat down together in the airport bar. It was bright and friendly, the music familiar and gay.

''The neighbor's child writes checks that bounce,'' she told him, which was not quite true. She was laughing. ''Oh, it's a long story. I'll tell you about it.'' And she told him.

''I don't see anything so long about it,'' he said. ''And anyway, what's ten dollars?''

''I wondered that, too,'' she said.

The Good Humor Man

REBECCA MORRIS

All through that hot, slow summer, I lived alone, on ice-cream sandwiches and gin, in a one-room apartment on Carmine Street, waiting while James divorced me. In June he sent a letter saying, "Dear Anne, I have gone West to get the divorce." I was not sure where he meant by "West" and I did not believe he could just do that, without me, until I noticed that he had used the definite article. James was an English instructor at Columbia, and his grammar was always precise. So I knew that he could. The letter arrived two days before graduation. I remember taking it from the mailbox as I left the apartment, stopping just inside the shadow of the doorway to open it. Outside, the sun glanced off Carmine Street and rose in waves of heat, assaulting the unemptied garbage cans by the stoop. For the past week I had been planning to go to graduation. I wanted to see James walk in the academic procession as a member of the faculty, wearing a cap and gown. When the pain struck, I also felt a childish chagrin at having been disappointed.

For the past year, everything had gone badly with us, and James had wanted a separation. He had met someone else. I didn't want him to leave, and for months I alternated between anger and tears. With each new outburst, he became more determined. I never meant to throw his copy of Milton out the

139

window. Finally, just after Christmas, James left, packing his share of our belongings. I didn't know where he had moved to; he wouldn't tell me. I put the rest—one half of everything—in storage and sublet a small walkup in the South Village. I still wanted to see James, though I knew there was someone else, and I began to search for him. He did not want to encounter me; he hated scenes. That winter and spring, I pursued James through the cold, crowded streets of New York like an incompetent sleuth. What I remember of those sad months merges into one speeded-up sequence, as silent and jumpy as an old movie.

It started one January afternoon, chilly and gray. I was wearing a trenchcoat and scarf. Rain blew in on me where I stood, in the doorway of the Chinese laundry on Amsterdam Avenue. My bangs were dripping down onto my dark glasses, so that I could scarcely see who got off the No. 11 bus opposite Columbia. I was coming down with a damn cold. Inside, the Chinaman could be seen talking rapidly to his wife. He pointed repeatedly to me and then to his watch.

In February, I spotted James leaving Butler Library. He glanced nervously over his shoulder. Four girls in scarves and trenchcoats were approaching him from various directions of the campus; they were converging on the library. His cheek twitched and he pulled his coat collar high up around his neck.

March, and I sat on a stool looking out the window of the Chock Full O'Nuts at 116th Street and Broadway, watching the subway entrance. The sun burned through the plate glass, and the four cups of coffee I had already drunk were making me so hot that the subway entrance seemed to swim. I ordered an orange drink.

April. James started down the steps of the New York Public Library. Forty-second Street was jammed with marchers. It was a peace demonstration and they were walking—carrying signs, carrying babies—to the U.N. Some were singing. On the other side of Fifth Avenue, a girl in dark glasses and a trenchcoat jumped up and down, apparently waving to him. He ducked his head and slipped in among the

New Jersey contingent, whose signs proclaimed that they had walked from New Brunswick. Someone handed him a sign. He held it in front of his face and crossed Fifth Avenue. The girl in dark glasses greeted her friend, a woman in tweeds, and they walked off toward Peck & Peck. I stepped out from behind the south lion and joined the march.

And then May. I was baby-sitting for another faculty wife, who supplied me with an infant in yellow overalls and a large aluminum stroller. Under new leaves, cinematically green, we traveled slowly back and forth, bumping over the bricks of Campus Walk, courting sunstroke. It was my most effective disguise. I concentrated my attention on Hamilton Hall, trying to see in the windows. Suddenly there was a rending howl from the stroller. I went rigid with shock: I had forgotten about the baby. James, disguised as a Ph.D., left by a side entrance.

June. Once again I was in that doorway on Carmine Street. I was always standing in that doorway. I was about to cry, and then I walked down the street unable to stop crying. I didn't know where I was going.

And so I lived in the one room I had sublet all that summer. I can still see it. There was a couch, a grand piano, and a window that looked out onto a tree and the back of Our Lady of Pompeii School. (The first morning, I was abruptly awakened by a loudspeaker ordering me to wear my hat tomorrow to mass. I was confused; I didn't think I had a hat.) The couch, the piano, and I were the three largest objects in the apartment, and we felt a kinship. It was very quiet when the school term ended. I slept on the couch and set my orange-juice glass on the grand piano. The one or two people whom I knew in New York seemed to have left for the summer. They were faculty people anyway—more James's friends than mine. The part-time job I had in a branch of the Public Library was over; they had gone on summer hours.

I see it so clearly—the window, the couch, the glass on the piano. It is as if I am still there and that endless summer is just beginning. I pour a little more gin in my orange juice. I am drinking orange juice because it has vitamin C, and I don't like gin straight. Gin is for sleep; it is infallible. I sit on the couch facing the piano and switch the light off behind me. Through the leaves of the tree I can see the lighted back windows of Leroy Street. The dark air coming in my open window is sweet, smelling of night, garbage, and cats. Sounds hover just outside, hesitating to cross the sill. I lean to hear them, and sit in the window, placing my orange juice on the fire escape. Down through the black iron slats I can dimly make out . . . two, three neighborhood cats stalking each other, brushing through the high weeds, converging toward some lusty surprise. On the top of the piano there is a metronome. I reach over and release its armature. The pendulum swings free—*tock*-over, *tock*-over. I sit looking out across the night. *Tock* in the heavy, slow darkness. *Tock*-over. People framed in the Leroy Street windows are eating at tables, talking soundlessly, passing back and forth. Yellow light filters down in shadows, through the leaves and onto the court, darkly outlining the high wild grass, the rusted cans and gray bottles. I reach over and slide the weight all the way down. The pendulum springs away from my hand, ticking wildly, gathering velocity. Accelerando! In the dark below, the cats dance.

When I awake the next morning, it is already hot and my head hurts. I carefully circle the piano and fill the bathroom basin with cold water. I plunge my face into it, staring down through the cold at the pockmarked porcelain, the gray rubber stopper, until my lungs hurt. After a few minutes, I leave the apartment, bangs dripping, walk through the dark hallway, down a flight of stairs, and out onto the burning pavement of Carmine Street. Pushing against the heat, I cross to the luncheonette on Father Demo Square. This is where I buy my morning ice-cream sandwich. The ice cream is for protein, its cold for my head; the two chocolate-cookie layers merely make it manageable. The sun dries my wet bangs into stiff points over my throbbing forehead. I squint and wish I had my dark glasses. Standing by the corner of Bleecker and Sixth Avenue is a glaring white metal pushcart. A squat man in white pants and rolled shirt sleeves leans a hairy arm on its handle and with the other wipes his brow beneath his white cap. Along the side of the cart, brown letters on a yellow background announce CHOCOLATE MALT GOOD HUMOR. I walk toward the sign, drawn slowly across Bleecker Street. On the sidewalk chairs at Provenzano's Fish Market two old Italians are slipping clams down their throats, sipping juice from the shells. Dead fish, plumped in barrels of ice, eye me, baleful but cool. The air smells of fish and lemon. I confront the Good Humor man and we squint at each other. "Chocolate Malt Good Humor," I say.

The next week, the Good Humor flavor changes. As I cross Carmine Street, dry-mouthed and stunned in the sunny morning, I read STRAWBERRY SHORTCAKE GOOD HUMOR. The letters, red against pink, vibrate in the glare. Behind the Good Humor cart, Bleecker Street is in motion. Provenzano's has strung black-and-silver eels in the window. The shop awnings are unrolled, and the canopied vegetable carts form an arcade up toward Seventh Avenue. Italian housewives in black are arguing with the vendors, ruffling lettuces, squeezing the hot flesh of tomatoes, fondling gross purple eggplants. Ice melts and runs from the fish barrels. I tear the wrapper of my Good Humor—frozen cake crumbs over strawberry-rippled vanilla ice cream—and, tasting its cold, proceed up this noisy *galleria*. My sandals leak, and I hold my breath passing the clam bar. Loose cabbage leaves scush under my soles, and strawberry sherbet runs down the stick onto my fingers. It is another hot day. At one o'clock, the Department of Parks outdoor swimming pool on the corner of Carmine, where Seventh Avenue becomes Varick Street, is going to open. I have discovered that for thirty-five cents I can stay there until seven in the evening, swimming endless lengths, pastorally shielded from Seventh Avenue by the bathhouse and the two-story Hudson Park branch public library. There my neighbors and I lie and tan on the hot city cement, shivering when the late-afternoon shadow of the building creeps over the pale water and turns it dark green. I stay there late every day, until all warmth is gone and evening falls. I no longer cry. I merely wait.

In the last week of June (Coconut Good Humor—a shaggy all-white confection of shredded coconut frozen on vanilla ice cream), I receive a letter from a Fifth Avenue lawyer telling me that he represents James and that I must consult him in his offices. I find his address formidable. It reminds me that I have not left my safe, low neighborhood for weeks. When I arrive, the lawyer is all smiles and amiability. I sit tensely, feeling strange in white gloves and high heels, while he tells me that James is in Reno, establishing a residence. He asks me if I have a lawyer of my own. I shake my head; I do not want a lawyer. This seems to surprise and annoy him. He shows me a paper that I may sign delegating some Nevada lawyer to represent me. It is only a form, but it is necessary. When it is all over, he says I may have some money, a fair and equable share of our joint assets—if I sign the paper. He offers me a cigarette while I think about it, but I am wearing gloves and I refuse. I do not want to take them off, as if this gesture will somehow make me vulnerable. My gloved hands in my lap look strange, too white below my brown arms. I stare at them and wish I were back on Carmine Street. The lawyer's office is very elegant, with green velvet curtains and an Oriental rug. There is a slim-legged sofa and a low marble-topped coffee table. All of the walls are paneled in dark oak, and there is a fireplace. I wonder who he is trying to kid. The lawyer pretends to reasonableness. I only want to see James. I do not want to sign anything. I shake my head; I will wait. He looks pained. He does not say so, but he manages to indicate that I am being foolish and unreasonable. I nod yes, and sit mute. I want to tell this man that when James comes home I am going to be perfect. I wish someone could tell James now that I have stopped crying. The lawyer sighs and takes out a summons, explaining that he is serving me now, if that is all right with me, because he would only have to send someone to serve me with it later. This is saving us both trouble. I nod and hold my hands in my lap. I wonder what would happen if I suddenly jumped up and hid behind the sofa. He extends the paper over his desk, and I watch it come nearer, until it wavers in front of my chest. I reach out and take it. The summons orders me to answer James's complaint in Nevada within twenty days and give reason why I should not be divorced, or be judged by default. I fold the summons in half and put it in my straw handbag. The lawyer smiles, still talking as he walks me to the elevator and shakes my hand. I am glad I am wearing gloves. He is not my friend.

On the Fourth of July, the Good Humor company exceeds itself and, in a burst of confectionery patriotism, produces Yankee Doodle Dandy Good Humor. I admire it as I turn it around on its stick. Frozen red, white, and blue coconut on a thin coating of white encasing strawberry-striped vanilla ice cream. I salute the Good Humor man as he hands me my change.

I spend most of my time at the pool now. On hot days, the whole neighborhood lines Seventh Avenue, waiting to get in. We stand outside the brick bathhouse in the sun, smelling chlorine on the city air and eating ice cream to keep cool—children, housewives with babies, retired men, office workers taking their vacations at home. Inside the bathhouse—women's locker room to the left, men's to the right—we hurry into our bathing suits, stuffing our clothes into green metal lockers. The air is steamy from the showers. Children shriek and splash, running through the icy footbath that leads to the pool. Out in the sunlight, we greet the water with shouts, embracing the cold shock, opening our eyes beneath the silent green chill to see distorted legs of swimmers and then breaking the sun-glazed surface again, into the noise and splashing. I wear my old black racing suit from college and slather white cream over my nose. Around the pool edge, four teen-age lifeguards in orange Department of Parks suits rove the cement or take turns sitting astride the high painted iron guard chair. They are neighborhood heroes and accept admiration from small boys with rough graciousness. The pool cop rolls up his blue shirtsleeves and sits with his cap in the doorway of the first-aid room, drinking Coca-Cola. We greet each other and exchange views on the heat. He looks wistfully at the pale aqua water, but he is on duty. I line up behind the crowd at the diving board. I am working on my one-and-a-half this week, pounding the yellow plank, trying to get some spring out of the stiff wood. My form is good, and the board conceals what I lack in daring. Sometimes Ray Palumbo, Paul Anthony, and Rocky (I never did learn his last name), three of the guards, practice with me. We criticize each other and take turns holding a bamboo pole out in front of the board, high above the water, for the others to dive over and try to enter the water neatly. I am teaching Ray's little sister, Ellen, to back-dive, and her shoulders are rosy from forgetting to arch. We all stand around the board, dripping in the sun, and talk about swimming. The boys are shy with me and respectful of my age, but with their friends they are great wits; they patrol the pool, chests out for the benefit of the teen-age girls, swinging their whistles before them like censers.

I have begun to know the other regular swimmers, too. Only the very young and the very old are as free as I am. There is Paul's grandfather, who is retired; he swims a stately breast stroke the length of the pool, smiling, with his white head held high. And Mama Vincenzio, a dignified sixty, who arrives each evening resplendent in a black dressmaker suit three feet wide. She waits her turn with us at the four-foot board, wobbles to its end, and drops off, *ka-plunk*. She does this over and over, never sinking more than a foot or two below the surface before she bobs up again; *pasta*. I am not sure that she can swim, but, on the other hand, she doesn't sink, and she propels herself to the ladder as if she were sweeping floors. We smile shyly at each other for two weeks. When I finally ask her why she comes so late, she tells me she cooks supper for ten people each evening. I also recognize Mr. Provenzano, who closes the store at four-thirty in the summer and comes swimming. I have taught him to scull feet first, and now when I pass his store in the mornings he offers me a peeled shrimp or—I hold my breath and swallow—a raw clam. I sit in the sun, dangling my feet in the water, and think of James. I try imagining him around a roulette wheel or on a dude ranch, but it doesn't work. My idea of Reno is limited. I know he should be studying, and I am sure there can't be a good library there. I wonder what he is doing, but I cannot visualize a thing. When I try, his face begins to look like a photograph I have of him, but I know he never looked like that photograph. This frightens me, so I don't think at all. I swim, and in the evenings I drink.

The thirty-first of July is my birthday. I am twenty-five years old. It is also the day of our trial. I will not know this, however, until the twenty-seventh of August, when the divorce decree arrives in the mail. In the morning's mail I receive a funny card from my mother and one from my aunt. My mother encloses a small check "to buy something you need." I buy a bottle of Gordon's gin. When I announce my birthday to the Good Humor man, he presents me with a Hawaiian Pineapple Good Humor, gratis. It looks like a good day.

My regular friends are already at the pool when I arrive, and we wave to each other. From the two-foot board, Ellen Palumbo shouts for me to watch. She has lost her rubber band, and long black hair streams over her shoulders. Still waving, she turns carefully backward, balancing on her toes, and then, arching perfectly, as I have taught her, falls *splat* on her shoulders in the water. I wince and smile encouragingly as she surfaces. Rocky is in the water doing laps of flutter kick, holding on to a red Styrofoam kickboard. I get another board from the first-aid room and join him. We race through the green water, maneuvering around small boys playing water tag; our feet churn spray. Suddenly my shoulder is grabbed and I am ducked from behind by Rocky's ten-year-old brother, Tony. My kickboard bobs away, and Rocky and I go after Tony, who is swimming quickly to the deep end. He escapes up the ladder and races to the diving board. Thumbing his nose, he executes a comic dive in jackknife position, one leg extended, ending in a high, satisfying splash. It is the signal for follow-the-leader. With shouts, children arrive from all sides of the pool, throwing themselves off the yellow board in imitation.

On the deck, Paul's grandfather is sunning himself, eyes closed, smiling upward toward heaven. I pull myself out of the water and join him. He squints and grins toothlessly, delighted to have someone to talk to. The night before, he has been to see a free outdoor Shakespeare performance. A mobile theatre unit is performing in our neighborhood this week, in Walker Park playground. We sit together in puddles on the cement, leaning against the bathhouse wall, and he tells me the story of *King Lear*. He has been going to the free Shakespeare performances every summer since they began and has seen each play two or three times, except for *Richard II*; he saw that one six times. We watch the boys diving, and he proudly lists all the plays he has seen. When I admit that I never have seen one of the open-air performances, he says I must. He thinks for a minute, then shyly offers to escort me. He will wait in the ticket line at Walker Park this evening and save me a place. I protest, but he says he has nothing at all to do in the evening and he probably will go again. I tell him it is my birthday. He smiles; July is a good month to be born. See?—he holds up his wrinkled, brown hands and turns them over in the sun; on the second of July he was seventy.

When I arrive at the playground that evening, the line seems endless. It stretches along Hudson Street, and I pass whole families seated on the cement, eating supper out of paper bags, reading books, playing cards. Ice-cream vendors wheel carts up and down. I recognize my Good Humor man, and we wave to each other. He is selling sherbet sticks to two girls. Frost steams up from the cold depths when he opens his cart. Mr. Anthony is at the front of the line; he must have been waiting for hours. He is wearing a good black wool suit, of an old-fashioned cut. It is a little too big, as if he has shrunk within it. I suspect that it is the suit he wears to weddings and funerals, and I am glad that I have put on my green linen dress, even if it will go limp in the heat. I have braided my wet hair and wound it round my head in a damp coronet. I look like a lady. We smile shyly, proud of our finery.

At eight, the line begins moving into the playground, where the Parks Department has put up wooden bleachers. They form a semicircle around the mobile stage; folding chairs are ranged in rows in front of the bleachers. We surge through the entrance with the crowd and find seats quite close to the apron. Behind the gray scaffolding of the stage I can see the wall of the handball court and the trees on Leroy Street; to the south, the old Food and Maritime Trades High School. Trumpets and recorded Elizabethan music herald our arrival. The crowd fills the playground, and the sky gradually darkens. Floodlights dim, and light falls upon the scaffolding. Onstage, Lear summons his three daughters; the play begins. Mr. Anthony and I lean forward from our folding chairs drawn into the court of Britain. Under the calm, blinking stars, Lear runs mad, contending with the far-off rumble of traffic on Hudson Street. High above, an airplane passes.

During intermission, I tell Mr. Anthony all I can remember about the Elizabethan stage, of the theatre that was a wooden O. We eat ice cream out of Dixie cups with miniature wooden paddles, and he compliments me. I would be a good teacher; in this city they need teachers. Later, as the final act closes, we sit and weep, on our folding chairs, for Lear, for Cordelia, for ourselves. "Never, never, never, never, never." Floodlights open over the playground; it is over. We crowd out with a thousand others onto Clarkson Street, past the dark swimming pool that is reflecting the street lights, to Seventh Avenue. On the way home, Mr. Anthony buys me a glass of red wine at Emilio's to celebrate. We walk by the dark steps of Our Lady of Pompeii, and on my doorstep we smile at each other and shake hands.

On August 27, the decree arrives—four pieces of typed paper stapled to heavy blue backing, with two gold seals. It

looks like a diploma. I read it in the doorway, then walk back
upstairs and drop in inside the lid of the grand piano. It is all
over, but just now I am late. I eat my toasted almond Good
Humor hurriedly, on the way to the pool. The Parks Department has been giving free swimming lessons to beginners,
from ten o'clock to twelve o'clock in the mornings, and I
help teach. When I get there, there are at least thirty children
waiting for me around the pool edge, kicking their feet in the
water.

That summer, Labor Day weekend comes early. Few people in my neighborhood are leaving town, and the pool is
crowded; everyone goes swimming. The pool will be closing
soon. It is my last swim. Tomorrow I begin at P.S. 84 as a
substitute teacher; I want to find out if Mr. Anthony is right.
The day is hot, making the water icy by contrast. My bathing
suit has bleached to a sooty gray now, and my wet hair drips
in a long braid down my back. Children shout and splash,
and the tarred seams on the pool bottom leap and break in
refracted patterns on the moving water. At the far end, in the
playground, old men throw boccie. My dark glasses begin
sliding down the white cream on my nose. I push them up
and join my friends sunning beyond the diving boards. The
Good Humor man has parked his truck in the street, just
beyond the wire fence. Children range the fence, handing
dimes and nickels through, carefully drawing ice-cream sticks
in. Mama Vincenzio has come early today, and she buys this
week's special, Seven Layer Cake Super Humor, for her two
noisy grandchildren and me. We eat them carefully, backs to
the sun, counting to make sure we get seven different layers
of ice cream and alternating chocolate. The children's faces
smear with melted chocolate, and ice cream runs down my
arm to the elbow. I toss my stick in the trash can and dive
into the water. The green chill slides over me, and I move in
long strokes toward the bottom, cool and weightless. Ellen
Palumbo passes me and we bubble faces at each other. When
my air runs out, I pick up a stray bobby pin as my civic duty
(it would leave a rust mark on the bottom) and, flexing, push
to the surface. Oooh.

From the guard chair, Ray beckons to me, and I swim over. For weeks, Rocky and Ray have been working on flips, somersaulting in tucked position. They have reached a point where they have perfected a double flip—two of them, arms linked, somersaulting in unison. All of the younger boys have been imitating them, working variations—forward, backward, spinning in twos above the green water. We have had one broken leg. Now Ray thinks that a triple flip can be done. No one has tried it yet, but if they can do a double— why not? It will be dangerous, of course. If anyone is off,' everyone may get hurt. You have to have reliable buddies. He and Rocky wonder if I will try it with them. I'm not as daring as their friends, but my form is better. I won't open at the wrong time. They tell me that I always keep my head. I swallow, standing there in the sun, and wonder if they have ever seen me weeping up a fit over on the Gansevoort Pier, crying into the Hudson as I angrily skip stones. I nod and promise not to crack us up. I am apprehensive.

Rocky grins and chases everyone off the board. Children stand around, dripping puddles, watching us as we carefully pace to the end. The sun burns our shoulders, and the board wavers and dips as our combined weight passes the fulcrum. Above, the sky is bright blue. We link upper arms tightly to make a pivot of our shoulders, and at Rocky's signal we begin flexing for spring, playing the board. "Now!" We are lifted and thrown upward, tucking into the air. The pool turns upside down, sky spins over our knees, the bathhouse revolves. We turn, holding together like monkeys, high above the glazed water. I have a snapshot Mr. Provenzano took of that historic moment. In it, we hang, crouched against the sky, backsides to heaven; one second later we will cut the water together, perfectly straight, to shouts and cheering. We break apart underwater and surface separately, mouths open, to the applause of our small pupils, who rim the deep end and now flop into the water like seals. On the deck, we congratulate each other, shaking hands. Then Rocky climbs the playground wall and high-dives, just missing the cement, into the ' deep end. It is the traditional signal to close the pool. He surfaces, puts on his orange Department of Parks poncho, and the guards begin blowing their whistles; everybody out of the pool. Summer is over.

When I leave the bathhouse, the sun is slanting. Walking up Carmine Street, I buy myself a Chocolate Eclair Good Humor as a reward. The long summer is over at last. Summer is over, and I have kept my head.

A Woman's Story

MARILYN KRYSL

I

It is night. We are alone in our house, these rooms, quiet, warm. The good, glowing objects we live with, chairs of gold wood, brick of the hearth, baskets, books, clean envelopes, pillows, light, glass, space. We live here, and outside the glass is dark, and in this dark we live together.

Now we will sleep. I will lie as close to you as I can. It is night.

II

I am reading. "Without a thought, then, I walked around that desert, and held my screams in check." A chill; cloud over the sun. Remembering my own past, that I lived through a time, through time, without love, of any kind. Remembering it, some distant trip to a foreign country, not here, not now. Now in my kitchen there are lovely things, red onions, potatoes, cruets of vinegar, salt. The cats are asleep in the doorway, in the sun. In me our child is quietly growing. You will come home.

III

Nausea. I go outside, get the shovel and my gloves and begin to move the irises from the north bed to the south, near the hedge. It's better, in the air, in the sun. But this presence in my body is insistent, pulling me down below surface into deep water, warm earth water. Aware of my body. This present stays with me always, quietly. I move in a dream of the presence, the earth of my body. Pregnant a month, two months. A long time. So now I find out what time is. The day comes around me like a coat. The sun is time.

And this is my life, good days after good days. In the refrigerator there is a cabbage, and milk. And sometimes in the eggs, a blue egg. And you are here, present in this house.

IV

You are sullen. You suspect me of some indiscretion? Or you've found evidence of some negligence. And damn it, it's going to rain. Saturday, we're going to stay inside listening to sad music on the stereo. And I'm going to let a couple of pots boil over, a scene, a mess. Or break plates. Stupid! Because in fact I like it here, I won't live like this. Oh come out of yourself! I won't tiptoe around. I want our serenity back.

You're flipping through *Time*. Yesterday I washed the windows with vinegar and water. Now I see the storm coming from the southwest, tossing the lilacs, and it rains, torrents, spilling over the Antones' gutter, the sound everywhere, like ringing in the ears. Then: a surprise: I'm happpy, and the rain. A private joke: do men know what storms are? Pulled down into earth water, on the bench by the window, the cat on my lap, babe in my belly. Steam. Breath fog on the glass.

V

3:00 a.m. Rain. I get up and sit at the foot of the bed and watch it rain, hard, battering the pavement, wind in the cedars, in the walnut tree. Later it slacks to a slow, steady rain, and I get back in bed, listening until birds begin to sing inside the sound of gentle rain, and then I sleep.

VI

We go to a lecture, molecular biology. The double helix. At first I listen closely. The information becomes more and more detailed, minute; still, it is clear, thoughtfully presented, and I understand. But then: what does it matter that I understand—the information, what he says, how the DNA code is carried, always A and T together, C and G together—what do I know when I know that? Nothing I can use in my life, *nothing I can touch.*

You are excited, tense in your chair to the end. You ask the lecturer a question. There are other questions, discussion. How different the information you need, the information I need.

I am not here. This woman sitting beside you is not me. I am down the street in that pool of mud. I am in the park looking for a really good coffee. I am in the closet sewing all the coats open. I am blowing in the wind outside this auditorium. Don't lose me. Don't let me float away.

VII

A bath together. Our baby is still invisible, quiet. We lie in the steam, laughing, talking and not talking. The heat saps our muscles, we relax, drift. Steam rises, making its small sound. Through the fog your face, close, touch, laugh, we are laughing in a circle of water. You wash me with your hands, with lavender soap. I wash you with my hands, I look at you and always it seems that I see for the first time: you have entered my life.

VIII

We are walking in the park, past the swings and slide, tables where families are eating, children jumping and shouting. You are talking. You are telling me about work, something about work; excited, agitated, the importance of an incident, the coincidental circumstances, what was said. You are there, inside that event. You do not see the park; you don't know what day it is, what time of day; gesturing, the words coming fast, intense.

Walking beside you here, I know I am in this day, this time, evening, the families, the children laughing and scrambling, the cool new oak leaves above us. I try, but I cannot come into your words, that place far away, not here, not now. Which moment is the right one to be in? Do I fail you, here, walking among black trunks of pines, sword ferns, over years' accumulation of needles, through new growth of the present? Do you fail me?

I only know where I am. I take your hand, not to be completely lost.

IX

Always, opportunities for infidelity. Strangers. Looking at me straight, saying, "This is what I want—will you?" Sometimes that makes me sad, those furtive passes. And sometimes I feel rage. On a Greyhound bus, when I was fifteen, the man beside me turned and put his hand on my breast. I don't remember him; I remember frightening depression. I wished at that moment I did not exist.

But today I thumb my nose at them, high on a private joke

they couldn't understand: I love you. And I am waiting for you, beautifully prepared, the folds of my mind soft as a skirt around me.

X

I lie down on the couch, a dark afternoon. Rain. You have built a fire and I am warm, drowsy, I sleep. Later you come into the room and I wake, just a little, just enough to know you are in the room. You stoke the fire, quietly, and then you come to me and carefully replace the blanket I have twisted off, tuck it around me. I sleep again.

XI

You say something thoughtless, cruel. You probably don't even know that it hurt me. I pretend to be looking at the peonies, feeling the earth beneath me the only kindness. In fact I do notice the peonies, sepals drawn tight, stretched thin over the packed buds, swelling, expanding.

It is almost dark. After a while I stop thinking about what you said. Wind sways the cherry branches, the dark is cool on my skin. The telephone rings, I go inside.

XII

I like magnolia when the petals fade, drop. In their state of perfect bloom I don't trust them. How can perfection exist? Afterward they begin to slip, they make mistakes, faltering, brown wrinkled stains, a waste, scattered.

I understand that, and want all of it, not just the blossom cut, in a vase for a day, then tossed out, out of sight. Only all of it is real, the whole story. I know what it means, it does not make me sad.

But peacocks in winter: not that one. In February at Carolyn's, wrapped in the dark overcast, a hot cup in my hand, lulled by heavy, continuous rain. Standing at the window, and noticing the cock, in July so confident, brazen, rattling his fan, now crouched on the fence. Feeling a quick awakening of dread and recognition, all the nerve ends in me instantly alert.

Not that love bird, all plumage gone, huddled in the rain, the iridescent eyes gone flat. Carolyn saying something and I don't hear, or don't hear the meaning of the words, just a voice, as I think: it's like everything else, a view of ourselves. Some beautiful things go ridiculous, as milk goes bad.

XIII

I am beating egg whites. It is late, and dark. A lock of hair falls, hangs near the corner of my eye. The egg whites turn snowy, drift. The beaters carve ridges, destroy them, carve them again.

You come behind me, put your hands on my shoulders, whisper. I can't hear you. Your words are lost. They will not come back. The whirr of the beaters is my life at this moment.

XIV

Today, pulling crabgrass from the iris bed, I doubt us. On my knees in the dirt, in the morning sunlight, doubt comes over me quietly, fog, a wave of nausea, from nowhere.

Why? There is no sign, no ill omen. The stream moves smoothly, the day comes on at its usual pace. Wind rustles the blades of iris leaves, the budded stalks, and I doubt us. I doubt our living, suspect us of slipping away, scarcely noticing we slip, falling away from the center.

Here inside this morning, at this moment, I am not strong. Where are you? Why do I have no trust? I went inside, lay on the sofa and put my hand on my womb, felt the hard, expanding muscle of uterus. I lay, stunned by reality; and thought, it is time, the sun in my belly. We can't last.

XV

Out of milk and sugar this morning. Driving back from the supermarket I pass a Volkswagen. The boy, driving, leans over, kisses the girl on the cheek, and I remember that I'm loved, and I love.

I am warm, I am safe, I am well. You will be home when I get there. The baby inside me. The trees, new green over the street, the houses, the people living inside them, the world, everything everywhere.

I roll down the window, breathe the cold air. *We live here. Now.*

XVI

The sun burns in the sky. Its fuel is time, our lives. This morning I bought silk to line a dress, and bone buttons. Stopped at a restaurant just off the main street for coffee. Alone, I sat at the counter, poured cream into the hot black cup, watched the white disappear, down, in the center, then rise, clouding the sides.

A man sat down beside me, spoke. I answered. It happened that we both knew Marcia; his secretary and Marcia were in the same league chapter, he had sold her liability insurance. Clatter of cups and saucers. Bright sun. I thought "lackadaisical." I thought of the silk, wanted to reach into the sack and touch it, feel its smoothness, coolness.

He invited me to lunch. The jukebox began "Don't Pass Me By." I thought "lackadaisical, sun, the clock ticks, the hands move, a length of silk on the counter." I declined. We smiled, said goodby, walked in opposite directions. *Terra infidel? Terra infidel.*

I only have time for one life, can only imagine one, the one I am in now, the one I try to be good to, the one that is good to me. I step off the curb, understand everything.

XVII

Early morning. We are leaving on a trip. You are checking the oil level, or something in the engine. I wander into your workshop. Still, all the tools and materials in their place, quiet, motionless. Drill, bits, plane, sand papers, coils of electric cord, level, square, hammer. And glue and three-in-one oil; pieces of glass; sawdust, scraps of wood.

I pick up a piece of cedar from the floor, blow off the dust. It is smooth and aromatic. On a shelf over the table saw is a can of lemon wax. I take some on the tip of my finger and rub it into the cedar. The cedar glows.

From the driveway you call me. Nails glitter in a shaft of light. Jagged mirror flashes from a corner. This is your place, your things. You must care for them as much as I care for mine. It's good here, in your place, and I want a talisman of you to remember this by. Something to hold in my pocket while talking to strangers. You call me again. The piece of cedar is small, and I drop it into my purse and go out, carefully closing the door.

XVIII

Friends for dinner. You are with them in the living room. Laughter, talk, delicate clink of glasses. The window above the kitchen sink damp, opaque with steam. I wipe a pane with the palm of my hand, see the maidenhair ferns on the mossy, north side of the Antones' house, opening, relaxing their tight curls. From the living room gay voices. Candles on the table. Warm, among friends, in our home, a rich expanding life abundant around us.

Grapefruit, avocados, figs. The perishables have a special loveliness. Watch them, take good care of them now, their brief existence. I would take such good care of our life together.

A New Life

SALLIE BINGHAM

On the third day after the baby was born, the air conditioner in Mina's hospital room began to sing. "Over the seas," it sang in a rich female voice. "Over the seas, over the seas to Ireland." Frightened, Mina stared at the thing, clamped between the jaws of the plate-glass window. Then she got up to look at herself in the mirror and was shocked to see how ugly she had become; her face peered out like a starved tiger's from the tangles of her reddish hair. Do something about yourself, the fierce lecture began. Don't just lie there! Have them come and cut your hair or brush it yourself, at least. The voice was her mother's, but her mother had never spoken to her so savagely; gentle, a little timid, she had seldom done more than glance, weightily, over the barrier between the front and back seats when they were being driven interminably somewhere. "Over the seas," the air conditioner droned like a bee engrossed in a flower. Mina doubted that the song existed, but she knew she was responsible for it because it had aroused the other voice, the voice of the lecturer, and that had always been hers.

She had waked early that morning, before the street lamps were turned off outside her window. Raising the shade, she had looked out at the green shoulders of the park trees, which she had passed so often, blindly. A million small new leaves

162

were fluttering in the morning breeze, and she had felt surrounded by lightly clapping hands. A little later, she had heard her baby cry as he was wheeled to her down the hall, and the new milk had tingled in her breasts, spilling out in two small cloudy drops. For the first time, there were no choices: the baby was hungry and she was there to feed him. She had spent most of her life picking and sorting, trying in anguish to decide what was important, what was at least worth while. She had always been told that the serious things, the work, must be put first, yet she had felt that she was losing everything in the process. With the baby, work was play, the searching, deadly play of his mouth on her nipple. There had been no need to sort and pick, and she had dozed while he fed. The air conditioner's song died down and she heard the voice strike through. Sleeping night and day, it said. Seems to me you've done nothing here but sleep.

That's not true, she answered. I didn't sleep at all. I wouldn't even let them give me Pentothal.

Arguing with the voice never got any further than that: a statement, and an answer. Her conviction wilted in the silence that followed. She was not sorry to find herself fading into agreement. After all, she had grown up with the voice; they had lived together in more or less perfect harmony while the slow scenery of her childhood passed. On the silence of the country house, on the silence that lay between her parents, the voice had struck blow after blow, forging maxims which had seemed both discreet and comforting: Work, learn, be honorable, watch your weight, avoid the fond whims of the flesh; scorn the vicious purple lipstick and the low ideals of the people you find around you. When she went away to college, she had heard, for the first time, the strange clang of it; people there spoke to each other while she spoke in asides, against the clatter in her head. Fortunately, she had met Stephen that first fall and they had spent most of their evenings and all of their weekends together. She had not needed to tell him about the voice because he too had the shining look of someone who is directed from within. Looking back, Mina saw them straight as a pair of candles in the midst of the jungling confusion, the dirt and disorder of their friends. A week after graduation, they had married.

For a while then, Mina had lived in a peaceful gabble of lists and compliments. Eventually that chorus had died down and she had heard her old voice again, ranting on a sharper note. When Stephen came home at night, he would find her standing with something in her hand, a potholder or a book, as though he had interrupted her; she had not dared to tell him that sometimes she had been standing like that for half an hour, listening to the lecturer. She had been afraid that he would be disappointed with her, for, like her parents, he loved her liveliness and efficiency.

When she had become pregnant—passing on, by plan, to the next important task—the voice had taken on a new tone, conspiratorial and wary, as though to guide her through a perilous swamp. She had felt the danger too: she had been nearly overwhelmed by appetite and energy. Once she had sat down in front of a loaf of bread and eaten it, slice by slice, from one end to the other, and all the time, the baby had lunged in her stomach as though it rejoiced. Afterward she had rushed to the scale, but it had failed to register the pound of pleasure. At that moment it had seemed unlikely that she would ever be thin or well disciplined again.

As the baby was born, she had seen the top of his head, dark and wet, in the mirror over the delivery table. "I'm glad!" she had said, or nearly shouted; she had seen her words splash on the white masks around her. Shameless, she had turned back the sheet to admire her body. Stark again, it had retained the look of the labor it had accomplished, like a tractor parked beside a plowed field. She had been so proud that she had not even noticed the sullen silence inside her head. "Seas, seas," the air conditioner crooned, and she leaned forward to listen and heard instead the other: Everyone feels this way, everyone. It's called post partum . . . The tune rose, sliding over the rest.

Determined to avoid another harangue, she got out of bed and went to the door of her room. She had never opened it before, and she was surprised to find that it was very heavy. She crept out and looked up and down. There was no one in sight, and so she began to walk, following the arrows to the nursery and keeping close to the rank of closed doors.

The broad glass windows of the nursery flashed with light and she hesitated, wondering who might look out at her from behind the babies. At last she crept forward and looked in. Their boxes stood in a row against the window, each topped with a card of typed facts; she read those before looking at the babies. Two had been born on the same day as her own and she was amazed by that, as though she might share something with those women—a lifelong link, buried in the flesh.

Her own baby lay propped on his side, one mittened fist beating the air. She hated those mittens; when he was brought to nurse, she fingered them tentatively, feeling his fingers inside. Her own mittens had been canvas, tied on at night with stout pink laces; years after she had stopped sucking her thumb, she had seen them hanging from a hook in her closet, like a pair of small chained hands. The baby's mittens were made of flannel, close and soft.

As she watched, he began to cry, his mouth shaping sounds she could not hear. She pressed closer to the glass. A nurse sat on the other side, marking sheets of paper, and for a wild moment, Mina imagined rapping on the glass. Then she noticed that most of the babies were crying while the others lay asleep among them, undisturbed. It seemed the order of things that some should sleep and some should cry while the nurse sat marking her papers. Mina's concern withered and she went back to her room. Closing the door, she was startled by the silence. The air conditioner had stopped its song.

She sat on the edge of her bed, waiting for the voice to start; she expected it to take advantage of the silence. After a while, she began to wonder if the voice and the song had fused so that one could not break out without the other. Leaning back, she heard, for the first time, the dim scurry of traffic outside her window, and then the lunch cart rattling down the hall. All around her, women were sitting up in bed, smiling, pushing back their hair.

When the nurse brought her tray, Mina thanked her pro-fusely and saw a glint of recognition, a submerged smile, in the woman's eyes. Immediately, Mina was ashamed of her misplaced emotion. She ate a leaf of lettuce and two slices of tomato, cold and grained with salt. After a while, the quiet dark-eyed nurse, her favorite, came to take the tray away, and Mina closed her eyes so that she would not have to talk.

As soon as the nurse had gone, the air conditioner picked up its song, quickly, in the middle of a line: "To Ireland." Under it, the other voice marched; hysterical, hysterical, it said. Mina put her fingers in her ears and heard the voice, without the song, plodding in her brain.

She snatched her fingers out. The tune ran over the voice, melting its ferocity. She fixed her attention on the tune; it was essential to find or forge a permanent connection. Ireland. She had been there once on a summer jaunt with her parents; the memory was vague. It had been only one of many carefully planned trips. She did remember that the hotel in Dublin had been something of a fraud, for in spite of its grandeur, it was built over the railroad station. No one had remarked on the constant noise of trains, and Mina had not opened her bedroom curtains to see what lay outside. Finally one night, feeling stifled, she had snatched the curtains back. An iron network of tracks spread below her, leading away as though she were the lode; a long arrangement, precise yet ecstatic where the double lines dissected, curved, and shot off. A small engine was marching there. She had dropped the curtain quickly, feeling the coal soot fret her hand. The next afternoon, in a tea room, she had disagreed with her parents over whether they should order scones or save the calories for dinner and suddenly, passionately, she had declared that she wanted to go home. Her father had ordered the scones as she had wished and her mother had reached across the table to pat her fiery hand. They had seemed to understand why she was so angry, but she had not understood at all. Afterward, she had not been able to mention the scene in order to apologize because the anger stuck in her throat like a splinter of glass.

Obviously, she had not made the right connection with the

song: the air conditioner dozed off into silence and she was left alone for the rest of the afternoon. At five, a nurse brought in a large bunch of pink roses, and tears came suddenly into Mina's eyes. She had not been expecting flowers, and she begged the nurse to take them away: "They'll just make a mess for you, shedding their petals in here." But the nurse told her that good money had been spent on the roses. "And what if your friends come and don't see them!" Mina could not remember the faces of the couple who had sent the roses, and she was ashamed of her vagueness and ingratitude. She got up to wash her face and comb her hair before the baby was brought. She did not want him to find her slovenly.

He took the breast eagerly, without opening his eyes. Mina lay waiting for him to finish. Her nipples were sore, and his strong tug hurt her; she looked down at his avid face and did not relent. He was male, whole and complete, and he would use her for one thing or another for the rest of her life. He was wearing his mittens, and the sight of his blind hand flapping against her arm made her weep. When the nurse came to take him away, Mina asked for a sedative and saw for the second time a gleam of recognition, a shaming understanding in the woman's eyes.

The pill came in a little plastic cup; she licked it up surreptitiously. Then it was time to prepare herself for Stephen. She dreaded visiting hours; then all the doors were open and male voices disrupted the silence of the hall. The men sounded fierce and excitable as they wove their ways between their wives' rooms and the nursery. They came bearing books, flowers, fresh nightgowns, all inessential, yet after they had left, Mina could feel the depression, thick as wax, which sealed the women in their separate rooms.

Stephen burst in exactly at seven, tired, smiling, trailing the hot smells of the city day. He whirled toward her with kisses, the newspaper—white hopes extended. She was ready for him. "Don't you think it's warm in here?"

"A little. I'll turn this thing up." He went toward the air conditioner.

"Yes, please." She waited while he turned the knob; the rush of air increased but the song did not begin. "It's been singing at me all day," she told him gaily.

"What does it sing?" He was used to her whimsy.

"Oh, some foolishness." She was suddenly unwilling to tell him. "Over the seas to Ireland, something like that."

"Did you ask the nurse to give you something?"

"Yes, and she gave me a pill as though she expected it." She was overcome by disparagement and began to cry.

He came and held her solemnly, aware, she thought, of the increased weight of his responsibilities. She wondered if he had felt chained and weighted when he stood beside her in the labor room. "Did you want all this to happen?" she asked.

"Of course!"

"But doesn't it occur to you, even if we didn't want it, even if we changed our minds . . . I can't remember when I wanted it!"

"Don't you remember, in Vermont?"

"I remember we walked to the top of a hill, through an old orchard. That time in Dublin I wanted to jump out my window and get on a train and go anywhere."

"Alone?"

"I guess that was the point."

"This room is too cut off."

"But it's worse," she said, "when someone is here."

At that the song began, with a shout. She looked at Stephen sharply.

"I brought you the mail—a magazine, and three letters." He turned away, opening his brief case. "Also your beer." When he brought them, she touched his hand.

"You can't hear anything, can you? I know you can't."

"I'm going to turn that damned thing off."

She snatched his arm. "No, don't. It's not the song I mind, it's the voice underneath and that's stopped now."

He smiled at her. "I always thought one voice was enough."

"Oh no! You've got to have two, to count. The talking one keeps saying I'm no good." She made a face like a sad clown and they both laughed.

At nine o'clock, the speaker over Mina's bed announced that visiting hours were over, and Stephen stood up and uncapped a bottle of beer. "For night sadness," he said, and patted her and kissed her and left. Mina drank all the beer as quickly as she could and then lay back in the curve of her pillows. After a while, she began to feel flushed and easy, and she feasted on something Stephen had said: "You make such a pretty mother." He had said it quickly, embarrassed by such obviousness. She wished she had forced him back to repeat and elaborate, to examine her face, her breasts, her thin slack body and tell her that she was all pretty, and well equipped for the task. How surprised he would have been, surprised and, she imagined, a little disappointed; he would have stared at her, seeing the mauve ribbons in her bed jacket and the mauve ribbon in her hair.

The baby was brought at ten o'clock and fastened to her breast by a brisk nurse with red iron hands. Mina's nipples were still sore and the baby drew and drew in a frenzy; he did not seem to get a drop. Mina knew that if she asked, they would give him a bottle, and felt beforehand her guilt and despair. Cruel failures lay on all sides and her successes were as thin as ribbons. The baby would be brought again at two and there was nothing she could do to prevent it except give up, abandon the whole thing. The tight silence of the room pressed against her, molding itself to her body, and she longed for the song of the air conditioner. It purred instead, mechanically tranquil. At last the baby was taken away and she turned out the light and lay, gripped in silence, waiting for two o'clock. It seemed to her that she was being eaten alive.

The nurse who came in at two snapped on the light and dropped the baby like a small bomb on Mina's bed. "Just ten minutes, each side," she warned. "I'll be back for him." This time, the baby's eyes were open and he was not crying. He looked up at Mina calmly, his hands, in the flannel mittens, folded on his chest. She looked at him for a while, aware of the way they were enclosed in the yellow bell of light from the standing lamp. She began to feel, against all reason, that the baby knew her; he looked up at her so confidently, waiting for her to begin. Cautiously, she took his left hand and peeled back the mitten.

She had not seen his hands since the night he was born and for a moment, she was afraid. Then she peeled back the other mitten and held his hands closely, as though to prevent him from doing some harm. Finally, she let them go. His left arm lifted and the hand unfurled slowly, like a leaf. His fingers were thicker than she had expected, with a flake of skin at the corner of each nail to remind her of the way he had grown, week by week, inside her eagerness. Then the air conditioner began to sing. She groaned and caught his hands again, waiting for the voice to start. After a while, she heard it, far off, chanting venomously. Anybody can. Anybody can. Anybody can have a baby. Suddenly the air conditioner's song rose, drowning the voice, which went down with a shriek of vengefulness. "Over the seas!" the air conditioner shouted.

Mina put the baby to her breast and lay back in the pillows. He sucked and sucked and then, for the first time, he began to swallow. She heard his long hard gulps and saw a bubble of milk forming at the corner of his mouth. His bare hand waved as though to set the beat for his delight, and his face, suffused, was the color of a candle flame. She looked at him with amazement. At the same time, she noticed something new, a creamy warmth at the front of her body. Something feels good, she told herself cautiously. She did not want to examine the feeling too closely, and for a while, she thought it was the baby's warm head, pressing against her arm. Finally she realized it was his mouth on her healing nipple.

She was ashamed for a moment, and she heard something whine at the back of her mind. Then the air conditioner's song rose a little, peacefully droning. "Seas, seas." She fell asleep before the baby had finished.

She woke when he was lifted out of her arms. Opening her eyes, she saw the nurse pulling the mitten back over his hand.

A small rage gripped her and she sat up. "I'd like those mittens left off, please."

The nurse glanced at her and smiled. She started to pull on

the second mitten, propping the sleeping baby against her hip.

"I want those things left off," Mina said, and this time her light voice rose.

The nurse looked at her.

"He should be able to suck his fingers if he wants to." She was beginning to tremble with rage.

"Don't you know he can't get his hand to his mouth?" the nurse asked kindly. "You want something to help you get back to sleep?"

"No!" Mina shouted. "I want those things off!" A great blush of delight spread over her face.

Sighing, the nurse uncovered the baby's right hand. Mina watched, tigerish, while she freed the other. The sleeping hands curved up like little cups. "Now he'll scratch his pretty face for sure," the nurse said, sighing.

Mina was so surprised that she laughed. It had never occurred to her that there was another reason. "Never mind," she gasped when the nurse looked at her uneasily. Throbbing with laughter, she watched the baby go and remembered that in two more days, she would take him home.

After that she lay awake for a long time, listening to the air conditioner croon its beautiful song. She knew that sooner or later the old voice would break in but she was not afraid: the song and the voice were finally braided together. Among the strands, she thought that she would be able to find her own light voice, but magnified, intense and brilliant as a streak of blood.

To the Members of the D.A.R.

JOANNE GREENBERG

There were letters: *To the Members of the D.A.R.*, *To the American Camera Club*, *To the International Brotherhood of Trainmen*, *To the alumni of the Eastman School of Music*. When they all met at Heron Landing at three o'clock on the sixteenth of May, as per instruction, all bright-flowered dresses and bandoliered with cameras (ready for the Convention, the Tryouts, the Concert), they looked, each of them, for one of his own kind.

She looked for choral singers, and wondered who the other people could be. The social distinctions drawn from preference are unmistakable, "... and this is not an a capella crowd," she told her husband.

He looked at the milling, waiting group, bright against the gray, ramshackled landing, and had to agree.

She turned to the woman beside her. "I'm looking forward to Lassus and Byrd," she said, testing.

The woman, testing, smiled. "Are you a Daughter?"

Then they both said, "I beg your pardon?"

He, to a man: "Eastman Singers?"

The man, to him: "Eastman Kodak Camera club."

Their bright clothes began to boil: turning, submerging and rising again, moving to ask, to answer, to ask. Then someone shouted from the center of the turning, "We've been

172

*tricked, fooled, brought out to this godforsaken place! It's
some kind of trick!"* Then the crowd turned outward from
itself to seek the reason there. It was too late. They were
surrounded by the stolid, uniformed men and the simple,
unequivocal horror of the guns. . . .

She screamed.

"What is it?" Martin cried, shocked from sleep.

"What is it?" the two old people cried, running along the
hall to their daughter's room.

"She's had a nightmare, that's all." Martin took his wife
in his arms and comforted her, and the two old people looked
away, unconvinced of his power to comfort and saddened by
their own helplessness. They went back to their room unconvinced and tried to sleep again.

"It was awful," Julia said. "It was weird, but something
made it seem so real. . . ."

He smoothed the covers over her and got into bed. "It's all
right," he said. "It was just a dream."

In the morning there were all the calls to make to relatives,
and new apologies to Julia's parents for having left the kids at
home this time. Her parents didn't seem to be moved by the
relentlessness of the apologies; they didn't realize how relentless their questions were. Julia was inside on the phone and
Martin could hear her answering the same questions with the
same apologies.

"Does Julia always have such horrible dreams?" Mrs.
Spiro asked.

Martin found himself defensive and said "Of course not,"
which made it seem as if they or their house were at fault,
and so he had to exculpate everyone again: It was the trip, the
excitement, and so on, and so on. . . . They didn't believe
him; he could see it. Their Nicholas had married and gone
away with his vulgar wife and never came to visit unless he
was called. Their George had gone away with his stupid wife
and never came to them unless he was called, and this one
had taken their Julia a thousand miles away and they came in
only once a year and hurried back as from a plague.

Martin remembered that in the vacation atmosphere of the plane he had planned to do something worthwhile along with their visit to Julia's parents. There were some fine Speech Therapy Departments in this city. He had thought he might stop by some of them to talk shop and see if any special work was being done. He knew now that he would have to stay with Julia, who was tied to the house, the phone, apologies, and excuses. He had to defend her every minute, and in the end, to defend himself.

"They are our grandchildren," Mr. Spiro complained, as the evening echoed the morning, "yet if we saw them on the street, we wouldn't recognize them."

"Oh, I don't think——"

"Yet, I suppose you have reasons——"

Martin was feeling raw and sensitive after his day of defending. "We've never had much time to ourselves. My work is demanding, and Julia is always home with the kids."

"I suppose when people are young" Mr. Spiro said, gliding past the answer as if it had been inaudible, "they think less of duty and more of pleasure."

Martin held that description up against his life and failed to see any similarity between it and the old house he and his family lived in, money problems, the kids' mumps and measles, his patients, and Julia's tired evening face. There was from that world, however, nothing to declare.

Mr. Spiro began to sound on another tightened string. "These insane people you work with—you say it is demanding work—"

"My patients aren't mentally ill," Martin explained, as he had explained on each yearly visit for all the seven years of his marriage. "Some of them are stroke victims; some have brain damage which gives them aphasia. They have to learn to speak again. I help them learn."

"You have explained this before," Mr. Spiro said a little peevishly. "I did not understand it then. I do not understand it now. What sort of work is this for a man to do?"

Martin felt the spring snapping. The man didn't know

aphasia from Eurasia, but he knew where the fret on that string was and how to give it the breaking twist. It was an amazing, clear vision, a gift with him, a talent. He couldn't *know* that most speech therapists were women, and that the pay of a speech therapist was woman's pay. The part that hurt, of course, had to do with the way he felt about keeping Julia in a house she hated. It was an old house, but it was all they could afford. It meant poverty to her, a feeling that nothing could really help them, that they were defeated by the job Martin loved. She hadn't complained about it lately, but now, in his father-in-law's house, he was reminded of it. He began talking about an interesting case. He talked to keep from thinking until Julia and her mother finished the dishes.

They rode in small motor skiffs through labyrinthine swamps festooned with moss and vines and rank with living things and dead. Snakes peered at them with clinical eyes and undulated away to wait in tussocks of coarse grass. Crocodiles rose and sank with deliberate silence. Bubbles and oily scum glazed the fermenting water, and the prisoners gasped for breath. Terror had changed all of them. Their ruddy faces were already sallow, their bright clothes already gray. She stood close to him in the boat, but she felt alone, ashamed of him for being helpless, of herself for having been the cause of it. In the middle of a pond of gray water the boats stopped, and while the guards stared impassively, one boatman poled over to a large dead tree sticking out of the water. He opened some sort of door cut into the tree and reached inside. There was a buzzing sound and a huge grid lifted out of the water. The boats started up again and the grid fell back after them. "Electrified," the guard said; "five thousand volts. . . . Won't be long now—we're almost there."

When they reached the Island, it was almost dark. They were marched to rows of barracks—the men to one, women to another, children to a third. No one went out. Some slept out their exhaustion and dreamed; some stayed awake and wept with fear or rage.

"First few nights," the guards said. *"After that, they don't have the strength."*

"Julia!" Martin turned on the light. "I heard you moaning. . . . Are you all right?"

"Dream . . ." she said, and struggled to free the swamp from her eyes and hair.

"Are you all right?"

She looked around the room for any shreds of the mossy trees that might still be hanging from the wall, or for an empty alligator skin draped over the chair like a discarded costume.

"Julia . . . ?"

"Just a bad dream," she said. "I'm okay now. Turn the light out. We don't want to disturb them." Her eyes turned to where her parents lay beyond the wall. She was sure that Martin wanted to ask her if it was the same one she had had last night. "It wasn't the same; it sort of continued from the one yesterday, but I still don't really know what it was about——"

"How can you not know? Didn't it have any logic to it?"

"It's lurid and unreal, but it's like reading on in a story, and now it's just a crazy fragment that I can't even explain." She pulled the sheet up taut and smoothed the blanket. "Turn out the light," she whispered. "I'm okay."

There was a stirring from the other room and Martin hastily hid them in the darkness.

"I called Nicholas and George this morning," Mr. Spiro said. "You are with us so seldom that your brothers should be eager to come in to see you."

Martin bit his lip. That one was double-bladed. He fought back a response.

"But they don't have to come in to see us," Julia said. "It was one of the reasons we didn't bring the kids this time. It would be so much easier for us to go to see them instead of asking them in for us. . . ."

Her father had a habit of summoning people, and the

summoned didn't like it. Julia knew that her brothers were different here, sitting stiffly beside their wives and their stiff, clean children. She had managed to take Martin twice to see them. The visits had been with loved, familiar brothers and generous, proud sisters-in-law.

At home, Nicholas was a quiet, gentle man whose wife, Natalie, brought a vivacity and color to his life. Summoned, he was mute as furniture, and Natalie, a loud, exaggerated puppet, talking to fill her lungs with air so that she might be saved from drowning.

At home George was witty in a rather caustic way; his attempt to cover the fact of his amazement at being loved wildly, passionately, and totally by a jolly, maternal wife and five spirited children. Summoned, he became venomous toward everyone, wife and children included, and Grace countered by subsiding into a cowlike acquiescence that heightened the sense of his cruelty while seeming to make it deserved. The family meetings made different people of them all.

Without speaking of it to each other, Julia and Martin each wondered what it made of them. Martin saw himself as being reduced to endless explanation, defense, and apology. He saw Julia, whom he loved and trusted, becoming subtly disloyal and taking her parents' side against him. Julia thought of herself as harried and besieged, at the mercy of one faction and then another. She was shocked that Martin, strong and patient at home, was capricious and unstable here.

"What sacrifice do I ask?" Mr. Spiro demanded. "Not to cut their throats—just to come and see their parents and their sister."

Martin made a last try. "I've been looking forward to visiting separately with Nick and Natalie, and then with George and Grace. I don't know them really well enough, and there's more time to get to talk with each one that way. . . ."

Julia, out of the corner of her eye, caught her mother's shock.

Martin had been talking about getting to know his in-laws, but Mrs. Spiro was hearing only that he wanted to get away from their house, their table—to go anywhere, nowhere, even to the dubious hospitality of Natalie and Grace. Julia had to interrupt him and delicately undercut his point. "Well, we can see them here, of course, and if they do come, we'd be sure of getting together." She knew, guiltily, that Nick and George were always "on call." A visit now would mean that they might not have to come in so soon again and that she and Martin would be here to take on some of the weight of that duty. So much of the daily part of it had been left to Nick and George. . . .

"All right, all right, fine, fine," Martin said. He was helpless and resigned. Julia saw that, too, and wished she could tell him why now. She would explain later. Later he would see all the good reasons.

They dined on the children. "I cook all the delicious Greek food your babies like," the grandmother complained, "but it is too hard and long to bring them to eat it. You once told me you wanted them to know of their heritage from Greece, yet it is too hard to bring them."

"Don't you remember how upset you both were when they came with us last time?" Julia tried to say it without bitterness. "Of course they loved the food, and they think the sun rises and sets on their grandpa and you, but you were upset by their—manners. . . . I just thought we'd all be more relaxed with them at home—until they grow up a bit."

"Julia, if you can't stand a word of criticism, how will you ever learn?"

"It isn't that you criticized them to me; it's what you criticized about. . . ."

She was lost in something she couldn't explain to them, or even to herself. If the boys had misbehaved, whined, broken things or been mulish, she would have been glad of the honesty of the grandparents' irritation. The faults they found, however, were not in what the boys did, but in what they felt, and in what they thought—in a sense, in what they were. ("Why does Timothy seem to have no loyalty? He never defends his little brother. . . . The children have no respect. They speak of their teachers with scorn—of you as if you

were their servants. . . . Why does Mark have no sense of
the fitness of things? There is nothing on which he will give
way.'')

These faults were so basic as to be incurable, qualities
which were woven into the family plaid of opposing personal-
ities and cross-running needs. There was no way she could
tell her parent-judges the difference between criticisms of
faults of behavior and of faults of being, and that to faults of
being they should be allowed no voice. She only sat still.

"Nonsense," Mrs. Spiro was saying. "They are fine little
boys, but they are disloyal to the family; that I told you. They
must be taught respect."

Martin wondered if eating Greek food would teach them
respect. Julia smiled a bit bitterly at her picutre of the boys
throwing carefully stuffed grape leaves at each other. She
sighed and Martin instinctively covered her lapse. "This
Greek cheese is wonderful. What do you call it?"

*A large, barnlike building. They were lined up before it
and went into it one by one. One by one they were stripped
and one by one stood shocked in nakedness before the huge
light. Her turn . . . The light . . . She staggered backward
and heard a quiet voice from beyond the light: "No, no,
don't be frightened, you don't want to spoil your beautiful
skin by being frightened, do you? See, it is all blotched now.
You must never be afraid. You are being made ready for a
great fulfillment."*

*The light was turned off, and when she could see the sides
of the sun-printed after-image in her eyes, there was a small,
scholarly man in a doctor's white coat leaning toward her in
a kindly way. His manner was calming, almost loving, and
after a while she was able to come down from the platform to
him when he gestured to her: "Come, I want to show you, to
convince you by concern, not by violence, that what I plan to
bring to all of you is a benefit, a beauty—the greatest beauty
mankind has ever known." He turned and spoke to a guard,
"Please bring the demonstration lady in."*

*Someone else came to the platform naked. The light. The
Demonstration Lady moaned in it. "That woman—is—is tat-*

tooed!'' Julia said, recoiling because the horrible painting covered every inch of the woman's body except her eyes and mouth—great garish swirls of color forming strange swirls like excrescences modeled on her body.

The doctor chided gently, ''Of course not. Tattooing is a vulgar, ugly way to achieve the adornment of man's beautiful body. Man wasn't meant to wear clothes, to hide himself, to keep secrets. He was meant to be close to truth, to adorn his body without hiding it guiltily in smelly clothes. Here, on my Island, each one is adorned with mementos of the things he values. This lady, for example, is one of the annual baking-contest winners. We have given her a lovely bread-twist design.''

The Demonstration Lady was led away and when the guard took her arm, she screamed.

''Did you see how wonderfully vivid the colors were?'' the doctor asked enthusiastically. ''How can a tattoo match work done on living flesh?''

''What?''

He said quietly, as if it were self-evident, ''We must first remove the skin.''

She lay screaming and trembling until the light went on and Martin gave her his presence and the reality of the room. She could only look through the broken edges of her nightmare to where Martin stood with his futile comfort. Then there were the parents to calm again. Their granite manners had fallen away from them in sleep. They were not the dignified, monumental judges of daytime, whose classic strength Martin still half admired, but simply two old people, confused and a little frightened, standing in their nightclothes at the guest room door like tourists on the brink of a volcano.

Julia looked at them as they were, softened a little by their sleep, and a wave of her childhood's love carried her up in its swift, unreasoning course toward them. She apologized, weeping. It was only a nightmare—too much to eat—because the food had been so delicious. Finally the old people nodded and went back to gather up the fragments of their own night.

Martin sat by her for a while and smoked a cigarette. "Honey, what do you dream about?"

"Not now," she said, and shivered, "not now."

"Julia, this is the third night, and you are obviously dreaming about something horrible. What kind of dream is it? Is it the same one as before?"

"I had a dream, and then another that sort of followed from it, and this one followed from the second. I'm not trying to hide anything from you; it's just that the dreams are so . . . stupid. It's a nightmare out of a horror comic, a tenth-rate mystery show. It's even got a mad scientist in it. I'd feel silly telling it to you, and I don't even know what it's about." He was going to object, but she looked at him and her eyes were wide with disbelief. "Marty, when I'm dreaming—it's all so real and awful."

"Am I the mad scientist?" he asked, only half kidding.

She shook her head.

He got up and tucked her in like a child, kissing her on the cheek. She smiled and he found himself moved by the smile. Back home there was closeness between them. It was there despite their fights and separate wishes, his job, their house, the kids, the world; but here, with her relatives, he felt vulnerable because he couldn't count on any support from her when he needed it. The smile had reminded him of a real Julia, the one he had left at home. "Don't leave me alone," he said. "Don't leave me here all alone."

"I'll tell you about it when I can. As soon as I can."

He wanted to say he had meant she mustn't leave him alone with the people here.

"Good night, try to sleep. . . ." She was already sleeping.

Sunday breakfast, a ritual. The air was full of hierarchal bells. Romans, Orthodox, and Protestants were all loudly and discordantly summoning the city to its separate togetherness. Mrs. Spiro was rather pointedly missing church for the sake of her transcendent duty to family. Mr. Spiro, who was not a churchgoer, was exulting in his leisure.

"Let me say," he began, pontificating with his knife in the

spirit of the bells, "you gave us quite a night. In the Old World dreams were omens. If one had a dream, especially a nightmare, all the old women in the village would be ready to forecast an event. When I came to this country as a boy, my teacher told me that the only thing dreams reflect is too much supper. But since then, I have been reading *The Reader's Digest*, and I see many articles that say how dreams have a meaning."

He looked sharply at Julia. "Have you done something of which you are ashamed?"

"I don't know," she answered and watched his expression cloud with irritation.

"Why is it that you young people can never admit simply what you've done? The bad people say they are sick and the good people say they are really no better than the bad. Either you have obeyed the laws or not; either you have obeyed the moral laws or not."

Julia opened her mouth to speak but thought better of it. Mrs. Spiro had come in with some more hot rolls. "Children, Aunt Thalia called this morning and she wants you to come over to see her. The cousins will be in after church."

Julia and Martin murmured softly about duty rightly done, and ran for their clothes. It would be good to get out, but it would have been unwise to admit loving the scatterbrained, charming old lady and wanting to see her. In the family, duty always seemed to Julia like kissing the whip. If to see someone was a pleasure, it was no duty. If it was no duty, it had no value. In their room they smiled like conspirators.

Aunt Thalia's uncritical lunacy was like the joy of water to tired runners. She could talk and she could listen. She told her own stories and roared with laughter over Julia's which, at a year's remove, had become their family joke.

One day last year the pipes had frozen and burst, Tim was stunned by a falling tree branch, and an animal of some sort had gotten into the house and died somewhere in the heating system. Her calls to the plumber, doctor, and heating man had kept the line busy so that Martin couldn't get through to ask her to bring down a set of case records he had left at home. When he finally got her, too late, he mentioned acidly that she might spend less time gossiping over the phone. This short comment had been greeted with an explosion of bitterness, a recital of his faults, and a flood of tears. Now, the memory was changed. All the facts were the same, only the reality had been altered. It was a joke now, a recital of plagues only the multiplication of which had brought her down. At home, where she was competent, the joke said, such things happened singly all the time, and she foresaw them, fought them, endured them, and cleaned up after them with confident good humor.

Now, as Julia wavered between calling another aunt to prevent jealousy, and checking with her brothers to see if they were coming, she seemed scarcely to believe that the usually level-headed, harassed woman in the story was herself.

Their wonderful Aunt Thalia. . . . When her own children came on *their* summons, she was every bit as demanding and overpowering as Julia's mother, except that her way was petulance and not cold questions. After a few shocked minutes of listening to the eternal complaint—"Where were you last week? Why didn't you call or come to see me? You know I am not well"—Martin began to signal Julia with his eyes. When they were out on the street, he said, "It's bad enough we have to get it in your house—I sure didn't need to hear anybody else getting it."

"That's a terrible thing to say," Julia answered. There was a petulant quality in her voice, perhaps an echo of what they had just been hearing, and it made Martin cringe. She was leaving him alone again.

He sighed, trying to remember that he had to submit only until Thursday. Then they could go home for another year and be happy and sad and a family together in their wretched mistake of a house with old irritations and responsibilities. They seemed very far away and very precious to him.

"Look, honey," he said in a cajoling voice which was irritating even to himself, "why don't we go out together

somewhere, just in the afternoons—to a museum, a hospital,
a show? Every time we come for a visit we are *there*—there
every minute—or else visiting a relative. Let's be mad, reckless, gay. Let's go down to the bank and watch 'em foreclose
on a widow. Let's go fish off the pier, Let's———''

She sighed. "It's not worth the trouble. We'd have to go
without telling them, or they'd be hurt. Aunt Thalia's calling
them now, I bet, or they're calling her. Last time it was
because of the kids and this time because of my nightmares.
Mother thinks I don't look well. If we go, we'll only have to
lie and be questioned. I'm tired; I really haven't had a
peaceful sleep since we got here. You go, Marty, I just don't
have the energy."

When they got back, Mr. and Mrs. Spiro were in the living
room planning the family afternoon with logistics worthy of
the Normandy Invasion. They called Julia and Martin in to
help with choices which they did not state.

"Let Natalie sit in the middle, between Nick and George,"
Mr. Spiro said. "I don't care to hear any more about that
family tree of hers, or her grandfather or her great grandfather. Put her in the middle."

"A woman should be proud of her husband's family,"
Mrs. Spiro said, and pursed her lips. Martin tried to keep his
expression blank. Every time he or Julia mentioned *his* parents, the woman acted as if he had gotten himself parents for
the purpose of irritating her.

"She is always talking nonsense, that one," Mr. Spiro
said, "I don't know how Nicholas can put up with it."

"A featherbrain is better than a cow," Mrs. Spiro said.
"When George speaks to his wife, he is speaking to a cow.
She sits in her fat and smiles like an imbecile."

So much for the in-laws' wives. As if they had forgotten
the presence of Julia and the in-law husband, outlaw usurper
of her time and duty. Mr. Spiro took a breath and opened his
mouth to speak, then perhaps remembered that the flawed
creature who had taken his daughter into foreign bondage was
present, and he stopped and exhaled. To Martin their recital

of complaints seemed to have been habitual, almost formal. He tried to feel that their scorn was general and so should not affect him. In this he failed. He had admired the straight lean strength of Julia's father and the dignity and pride of her mother for so long that their scorn still hurt him. They seemed to have no understanding of why or how he was being given pain if he did not, in fact, deserve it.

"Don't let it happen to your boys, what has happened to Nicholas' children. If Nicholas does not stop that wife of his from ruining them, they will end on the gallows. She's a tramp. She brags about her fine family, but—yes, Julia, she is a tramp!"

Julia had turned away, murmuring "Please" against the relentlessly judging faces before her. Now, Mr. Spiro took up the burden: "You were at college, Julia, a young woman, and nobody wished to tell you such things. He met her in a saloon. She slept with him like a whore for months before they were married. His mother had to wash his underclothes that had her—her body on them."

"At least the Cow waited for a wedding ring——"

"*Mother,*" Julia shouted, desperately and too loud, "Aunt Thalia looked very well today, and we saw Stavros and Maria. Margharita came later, too."

"Yes," Mrs. Spiro countered as a move back to the ground of her target, "Stavros is doing very well."

Martin leapt eagerly behind the change of subject: "I've often wanted to talk to Stavros. Neurology is close to my field, and with new work being done every day in——"

The parents were looking at him in surprise.

"He is a doctor," Mr. Spiro said.

"A Specialist," Mrs. Spiro completed.

They stood together in the bedroom and Julia wrung her hands and kneaded them into one another. "I didn't want to hear things like that about Nick and Natalie— I don't want their secrets—to think about them in a way that's—not my business." Martin wondered why she hadn't chosen to defend *him* against the obvious slur about his being too insignificant

to speak to Stavros Who Was A Doctor, A Specialist. But he
was too tired to bring it up and it would have been useless
anyway. . . .

They tried an extra pillow under Julia's head, hoping it
would help, but she was afraid to sleep. She stayed awake for
hours, tossing on her bed and staring into the darkness.

*The prisoners were silent, but they moaned softly when the
wind blew. One could trace the tides of the wind as it came
across their raw bodies. They cringed from the heat of the
sun, from rain, water, wind. Beds were agony, the rubbing of
a sheet, torture. They learned not to touch one another. They
were naked. Even if the doctor hadn't been so convinced of
the body's decorated beauty, no one was brave enough to
endure the touch of clothing. Pain without ease and the
feeling of having been distorted and made victims loosened
the prisoners' tenuous holds on all the civilizing emotions. No
one prayed; no one tried forgetting with art or music, teaching or learning. They drifted out of the sun, the rain, away
from sitting or lying down, away from one another, away
from themselves. The only happiness that some of the prisoners had was the happiness that they had not brought their
children and so were free of their agonies. After the age of
nine the children too were "scraped" and decorated with dots or
stripes or garish flowers, but sometimes the doctor left them
undecorated so that their veins, pulsing and branched and
visible in the raw flesh made patterns of their own.*

*Martin came one afternoon to where she was standing out
of the sun. She remembered having loved him, having built a
family with him, but now she was annoyed because he would
break into the daydream she was having.*

"I can't take this any more," he said.

She didn't answer.

*"I know the general direction of the Landing. There are
three of us—we're going as a team. One is eleven, one is
thirteen, one is grown."*

*She was still in her daydream, scarcely listening to him.
"Part of us will be killed, but if one gets through, he will be*

*able to tell——" He spoke without moving his face or lips, in a
dead voice, the habit on the Island, to save the muscles of the
stripped face.*

*"Good-bye," she said. She was relieved that he had not
asked her to go. She had no more strength for pain. She went
back to the daydream.*

"Julia!"

Again. . . . She sat up in bed. "Did I scream?"

"You were moaning. My god, what's happening? I want
to help you, to share it at least, and I can't——"

"Nobody can help me," she said. "Nobody helps anybody
else, and after a while, they stop wanting to."

She sounded resigned and a little self-pitying, and while
he knew that she was talking about the dream, he couldn't
help his own bitterness.

"You're the one who stops helping," he said. "Your
father involves us in things we don't want, and when I need you
to stand against them, you fade away on me and I'm felt as
the big Destroyer, the Outlander Who Doesn't Know What
Family Means."

"They come with so many *reasons*, she said. "I can't fight
them with nothing."

"Your reasons should be that I don't *want* them. One—I
don't want a family party. Two—I don't want to sit and smile
and let them pick me apart. Three—I don't want to spend
every single day of my vacation doing these things. . . . I
just don't want to and when I say so, Julia, I want you to
defend me."

"But I *can't*. Don't you see? I know why they are criticizing you, and that it doesn't even involve you personally.
They may love us, Marty, but they're afraid."

They were sitting up in bed. It was still dark, but only
gray-dark. They had this hour or two of private time before
the day began . . . and the party. Ordinarily, they might have
made love, but they both found it hard to do with Julia's
parents sleeping in the next room. There was also the change
in each of them that made them strange to each other.

She tried to tell him about the summoning and the denials.
A Greek family, she said, is supposed to be *one*. The parents
had both grown up with that, and for many years, poverty
and strangeness had made it so. They huddled together in close
family businesses, made "good" marriages for the family,
formed no friendships that might rival the unity they needed
to survive. This was the dream, the picture, the hope—a huge
family, all together, all one.

"The ideal would be a kind of family world. You're
sick—you go to Stavros; you're in trouble—you call Nicholas, the lawyer. You want clothes—George has a store. America is a big place; it's got too many choices. A world is
frightening if it is bigger than a small Greek village. But see
what happened—Stavros decided to specialize in something
nobody ever got sick from; Nicholas moved away *because* he
didn't want to be a lawyer, but an engineer. Who needs
engineers in a small Greek village? When George found that
getting his own business meant that everyone depended on
deliveries, free, any time, any place, he moved out too. They
raised us to fit in the picture, but we didn't want it and we
destroyed it."

". . . And you married a speech therapist who works with
aphasics and wants to live in a small town."

All right, he thought. Now they both knew the reasons for
the picking and poking and criticism, but understanding had
taken the fight out of Julia and would probably blunt his own
will to resist. The very choice that frightened the parents had
given strength to the children. The family parties then, were
partly funerals, with little cakes and speeches about the virtues
of the dead. Unfortunately, the dead were very much alive,
living in the enemy world—thriving in it. Angry funerals.
The present children had murdered the children who were
supposed to be there, close, self-nourishing, ideal.

He saw why Julia couldn't defend him—she was fighting
shadows. He leaned back and looked at her. He could make
out her features now. It was almost day; the night of bad
dreams was being pried up from the rim of the world. It was
quiet; they were alone, stealing peace. But the day they were

facing was one he dreaded. His wife had horrible dreams from which she woke screaming; her family had dreams from which they could not wake at all; and he, too, felt his will dissolving as the days passed. Yet he had nothing with which to engage. He sighed and turned to her. "It looks like a nice day. Why don't we go for a walk?"

"I wish I could," she said listlessly, "but Mother will be cooking and baking for the big get-together this afternoon and she hates to do that alone. You know what the pattern is—the women for their men . . ."

"The pattern, the pattern . . . I know."

The relatives came to the house almost on tiptoe. They greeted Julia and Martin as though something not to be admitted had kept them away for so long. Julia was puzzled by the almost sacerdotal stillness until she realized that it must be because of the dreams—four nights of screaming, whimpering, and moaning, cut off by commands of the inde-cent, secret-keeping husband. It must have been made public knowledge: one with Natalie's manias and morals, and Grace's bovine calm. Everyone knew, but not in the comfortable Greek way of omens of the imponderable future. Her parents were not the only students of *Reader's Digest* which spoke of present guilt and past shame and Julia, in her misery, hoped that Martin didn't understand the reason for the soft voices and the clumsy, well-meant concern. She had never, until this day, considered herself possessed by the dreams instead of being their possessor. Now, with the fact of her nightmares the property of everyone, she began to wonder at her mind's power to conceive of them. Night after night, she had gone back to circle over that man and woman as they walked stripped bare, all the defining, protecting skin peeled away, suffering agony for the whim of a madman. Yet suddenly, in the middle of her relatives' muted gentling, she had come to see the horror of it, and herself not as Julia, but as Someone Who Dreamed, whose dreams hung over her in shock like the sky after lightning.

Their compassion frightened her, and the more she felt them soothing and agreeing, the more frightened she was.

From across the room Martin looked at her in puzzlement, and when he could break away, he came over and whispered, "What is it, honey? You look all flushed?"

"It's nothing."

"What's it all about? Everyone is acting as if there'd been a death in the family and they're trying hard not to mention it."

A death! She shuddered.

"Honey"—he took her arm gently as if to try to convince her of something (Aunt Thalia looked and then looked away. Stavros looked and then looked away.)—"Why don't you sneak out and lie down and rest awhile?"

For a minute she thought of telling him that her parents had chosen to be disloyal to both of them. Brothers and sisters-in-law who hadn't seen her for a year and knew nothing about her life, knew now that she had nightmares and that she screamed her way free of them. She began to tell him, but before two words were out, she had to stop. He was too vulnerable. He would be furious and thwarted. What was there to do or say that wasn't more madness and more bad dreams?

"I can't go," she said. "They'd miss me and this afternoon is supposed to be for us, after all. I'll be all right." She smiled up at him and he let himself be silenced because of the people all around him. He dipped back into his well of duty. Grace, Aunt Tecla, and Aunt Thalia were arguing happily until he came and struck silence. For the tenth time that afternoon, he began, in a mystified way, to weave a conversation with thin air.

Now that Julia knew what had happened, she was free to look around and see how the afternoon was going. They were all acting, talking themselves past her haunted house, and it did them good actually, until her parents spoke to them. Natalie had been a little muted, George was less vitriolic, Stavros and Aunt Thalia acted with good nature, the roles written for them, but whenever The Parents joined a group in conversation, a kind of helpless anguish bloomed in their presence.

At last it was time to serve. There were huge plates of Greek food and glasses of raisin wine and ouzo, for which no one had much appetite, since the meal came between lunch and dinner. The guests seemed almost unwilling to sit close to one another.

There were toasts: To the ones who live so far—may they find with their own people the peace of mind they have lost.

Whose own people? Martin's family hadn't even been invited.

At last everyone had eaten all he could be urged to eat and had begun to signal and mouth words: ". . . the baby sitter . . . . We promised around six . . ." and raise the voice a little for finality: "It certainly was a wonderful afternoon, really."

By six-thirty they had all gone. When the door closed on Aunt Tecla, Martin went limp with the release and Julia's eyes fell into the fixed, glazed look that they had been fighting all day. She was exhausted.

Mr. Spiro was just getting his second wind: "I don't like George's eyes—they were almost yellow. He smokes too much."

His wife nodded him on. "Did you notice? His fingers trembled. He works too hard supporting that fat cow and all those children."

Her husband made no comment, but went on with his own thought: "Nicholas is getting fat. A man should not lose to a woman—to be made like a pet dog."

"Did you notice Stavros?" Mr. Spiro asked. "His eyes are pure, like a saint. Did you see how he always waited for the Mother to speak?" She sighed.

"Stavros will wait to marry."

"Stavros will not marry a streetwalker."

"If only the children had come. I think they are trying to keep the children from us."

"Children are not raised well any more.

"Julia didn't even bring her children—why should the others?"

Julia was thinking that they hadn't brought the children

because one does not bring children to a place where someone is insane.

*One-Is-Eleven, One-Is-Thirteen, One-Is-Grown. They crept
into the path of sunrise's blinding light, murmuring in pain.
They eased into the water, biting pain into the small sticks
they kept in their mouths for it. When they were far enough
away from the Island, they struck out toward the west, swimming through foul water and fresh, watching snakes thread
the water and the slow eyes of swamp creatures following
them.*

*The effort of bending and stretching was great, but they
were away, free. They would have to get to the Landing by
nightfall. Stroke, bite down, rest, stroke. One-Is-Eleven tried
to swim faster because he was the youngest and was guilty
about holding them back. He swam faster and faster and hit
the electrified grid before he knew it. The water boiled up
and then was still. The two others swam dumbly through the
grid which had been shorted out by One-Is-Eleven's body.
They went on, winding through mazes of sawgrass and pools
through which fish swam. The sun was almost at noon now.
Stroke, bite, rest, stroke. They became afraid of swimming
endlessly in circles, dying by minutes until night, and death
by snake or quicksand.*

*One-Is-Thirteen was beginning to lag. He was exhausted.
He saw the alligator settle in the water and glide toward
One-Is-Grown. He began to think wildly of all the moments of
power and love a grown man could have, but not being
grown himself, he missed the quality of those moments and
their weight. He thought of love that bonded families together. Then One-Is-Thirteen saw the man forcing the crocodile's jaws shut. He thought at that moment of the uncertain
quality of family love—too much, too little, love given or
denied at the wrong time. The alligator clawed the man's raw
flesh. One-Is-Thirteen thought desperately of a spring day
when he had gone for a walk with his mother, stopping to
look at each miracle of the new season. The man had his hold
on the alligator's mouth and was holding the creature under*

water to drown it. Then, without being able to stop, One-Is-Thirteen began to see his mother in ambiguous scenes—playing cards, gossiping, irritated at his interruptions, blaming him unfairly. The alligator gave a great roll in the water, freed itself, and turned on One-Is-Grown, breaking his neck and shoulder in its awful jaws. One-Is-Thirteen swam on. He was dimmed with pain and weakness; he noticed nothing, he had no hope or plan. Stroke, bite, rest, stroke. The sun rode low. It began to go behind the great overhung trees. Nocturnal things began to wake and prepare themselves for their hunger. Ahead of him the swamp stopped. It was the Landing. . . .

The naked, red boy appeared like a horrid ghost. The people of the Landing saw him and couldn't believe what they saw. A man came over to where One-Is-Thirteen stood at the very edge of the water, looked at him and went back, nodding in amazement.

"He has no skin." Then the man went up to the boy again, and back. "Look how he is." Again the man came back. "What happened, boy? Tell us what happened."

One-Is-Thirteen opened his mouth to tell them how the sun seethed on the prisoners' bodies and cracked their flesh, about the mild madman and the beautification colors, the electric grid, the alligator, the ones who died, the way the Island moaned when the wind came up, the Decorated Ones. He stood there with his mouth opened, thinking of the Island, wanting to speak, to tell them. The men of the Landing waited and encouraged him. "Come on, son, we're not going to hurt you." But he could not speak. He tried again and again. No sound. Night fell. One by one the people of the Landing turned and went to their houses and the mute boy stood alone and beginning to die, in the empty street.

This time Julia was crying when Martin woke her. She found herself awake in the middle of a wail of sorrow. She cut off the second and looked up at him and then at the door. No one was there, but she knew that the parents were awake, listening in the blind night. "Are you all right?" he whispered.

"Yes. . . ." and she slept again.

*   *   *

At breakfast they were all silent. What evil they must think she had done to be so tormented! Martin wanted her to tell him what the dreams were, but she didn't truly know. In the end they seemed not fearful so much as despairing. One-Is-Thirteen (she had no trouble seeing the three of them as one man at different ages), having come all that way, knowing the horror in his own flesh, could say nothing, and in the end, could do nothing. She kept seeing him as she had left him, a small, lone figure in the small street, dying.

Today was the day Julia had been given to call her old friends, but she didn't call anyone. She was too tired. The dream, now completed, hung between herself and the world, dimming it and blurring her picture of herself in it—the competent, aware person she was at home. Tonight they would begin to pack and tomorrow they would leave. But it wouldn't be the same, even at home. She felt like an invalid being sent away for "rest," and it was nearly true—having been spoken to gently in a dozen phone calls during the morning.

After breakfast she washed some clothes slowly, trying to pull out the time. Then she did her hair and set it . . . slowly . . . slowly. And the clock said 10.05. The day was rising like a tidal wave, vast and impersonal. Her mother talked; her father talked. She answered them automatically, promising everything, agreeing to anything. After a while Martin came in and she answered him automatically, promising and agreeing. "It's your day out, Julia."

"I'm so tired—"

"For godsake! We can't stay cooped up here all day. I've got to get out!"

"Well, why don't you go?" She thought: Why doesn't he go and leave me in peace? Then she stopped, caught something in the past somewhere. Did he say that before? Someone had said that before and she had thought it—no, someone else . . . "Where is there to go?"

"Burma, Mozambique, the park. Come on, will you? Tie something on those martian rollers and let's break out. The guards have been drugged, the watchdogs tied—or is it the other way around? Put on your lipstick and we're over the wall. *Come on!*'' he said. Even in his quips there was a desperation that was disturbing. "Please before they sound the alarm.''

The picture of the electric grid came to her mind. The guard had pressed a place in a tree. It slid up, dripping water. It had been waiting in the water for One-Is-Eleven. Then there was his body tangled in it.

"Julia, please—come on!''

It was too bright outside; the glare burned her eyes. "I want to go home,'' she said.

"I know. We'll be home tomorrow night, and it'll be all right after that.'' He had thought she meant their home and not her parents'. She let him think it.

"Some vacation,'' he went on. "You *dream* and I end up feeling like a cuticle bitten down to the quick. It happens every time. It beats me, this whole business. I get so torn up, I'm nothing but a raw, quivering ego. And next time we'll have to bring the kids.''

She walked another block in silence and then stopped suddenly, almost accusingly in the middle of the sidewalk. "What did you say?''

"I said we'd have to bring—''

"Before that.''

"I didn't mean it maliciously, and I didn't say it to get a rise out of you. It's true. I said I felt like a quivering . . . raw ego.''

She looked at him for a minute and then she began to laugh. He stood by helplessly, wishing he could forget himself in laughter too, while people passed them half ashamed to smile in case she was laughing at him. "Back there you said it was a prison.'' she began to walk again. "You said, 'Let's break out.' ''

"Forget it. I don't want to get into another——''

"No, it was good. You rescued me, in a way. I've been

having these dreams, and what you said was what I was dreaming about.''

"I don't get it.''

"I got it. Technicolor and Panavision, and it's something close to what you said about being a raw ego. I haven't figured it all out yet, but let me tell you what I know. In the beginning, there were letters. To the Members of the D.A.R. and other groups. It gathered them at a small Greek village, exotic to me, and isolated. In the village there was a patriarch and he decided what the villagers should become. But the villagers weren't born there—they came from many places and they came to the village in love. Natalie came, so proud of her illustrious family, and Grace, so proud of her homemaking. Imagine, a baking-contest lady. And you and I came together, in love. The patriarch . . . He wishes he could love us too, but we seem always to be hiding. He strips us of our secrets and weakens us with their loss so we cannot escape. But you escape, Martin; you escape.''

She was shivering in the summer heat. He stepped away from her for a moment because he was frightened by her. She looked as she had when she had broken the night screaming after one of those dreams. Then he moved back, close, to try to comfort her. "Julia——''

"I was so weakened that I betrayed you. You had to go alone—more than alone. Oh, God, you had to go *divided*.''

She looked almost as if she were arguing and people walked around them with a quickened pace so as not to be involved. "Then''—and she half-smiled as more of the pieces fit—"two thirds gone, and the best two thirds you thought, you got to safety, to freedom, to a 'landing,' and what was there to say then?''

"Come on, honey, let's go to the park. Okay? And pick out a bench and sit there and talk like old, old people. You're scared, or maybe angry, and I——''

"Not scared any more,'' she said. "Ashamed. I'm so sorry and so ashamed. Seven years of it, and how I betrayed you. No wonder I felt so lost in the boat—coming to my own deception.''

"But you said the dream had a mad scientist——"

"He's not our problem; I am. The problem is deception. If there's any defense, it is that my secrets and our lives were taken from me against my will. I never meant. . . . I don't know to this minute how I can change things—or if I can change them—but for this minute, right now, I know what I've done to you, and I'm ashamed, and I want to try to *do* something——"

"We're going home early tomorrow. It will be all right."

"No!" she shouted. "It will definitely not be all right. I want to remember the whole, ugly, awful thing. It was why it was so ugly, I guess. You were electrocuted and eaten by a crocodile. In the end, you weren't even able to tell anyone about what had happened."

"Good Lord, girl, I have days like that all the time!"

"But then you come home and I'm there."

"And then *we* eat the crocodile."

"If you'd finished yours yesterday, you wouldn't have to put up with the leftovers."

"I can hardly wait," he said.

Vermont

ANN BEATTIE

Noel is in our living room shaking his head. He refused my offer and then David's offer of a drink, but he has had three glasses of water. It is absurd to wonder at such a time when he will get up to go to the bathroom, but I do. I would like to see Noel move; he seems so rigid that I forget to sympathize, forget that he is a real person. "That's not what I want," he said to David when David began sympathizing. Absurd, at such a time, to ask what he does want. I can't remember how it came about that David started bringing glasses of water.

Noel's wife, Susan, has told him that she's been seeing John Stillerman. We live on the first floor, Noel and Susan on the second, John on the eleventh. Interesting that John, on the eleventh, should steal Susan on the second floor. John proposes that they just rearrange—that Susan moved up to the eleventh, into the apartment John's wife only recently left, that they just . . . John's wife had a mastectomy last fall, and in the elevator she told Susan that if she was losing what she didn't want to lose, she might as well lose what she did want to lose. She lost John—left him the way popcorn flies out of the bag on the roller coaster. She is living somewhere in the city, but John doesn't know where. John is a museum curator, and last month, after John's picture appeared in a newsmagazine, showing him standing in front of an empty space where a stolen canvas had hung, he got a one-word note from his wife: "Good." He showed the note to David in the elevator. "It was tucked in the back of his wallet—the way all my friends used to carry rubbers in high school," David told me.

"Did you guys know?" Noel asks. A difficult one; of course we didn't *know*, but naturally we guessed. Is Noel able to handle such semantics? David answers vaguely. Noel shakes his head vaguely, accepting David's vague answer. What else will he accept? The move upstairs? For now, another glass of water.

David gives Noel a sweater, hoping, no doubt, to stop his shivering. Noel pulls on the sweater over pajamas patterned with small gray fish. David brings him a raincoat, too. A long white scarf hangs from the pocket. Noel swishes it back and forth listlessly. He gets up and goes to the bathroom.

"Why did she have to tell him when he was in his pajamas?" David whispers.

Noel comes back, looks out the window. "I don't know why I didn't know. I can tell you guys knew."

Noel goes to our front door, opens it, and wanders off down the hallway.

"If he had stayed any longer, he would have said, 'Jeepers,' " David says.

David looks at his watch and sighs. Usually he opens Beth's door on his way to bed, and tiptoes in to admire her. Beth is our daughter. She is five. Some nights, David even leaves a note in her slippers, saying that he loves her. But tonight he's depressed. I follow him into the bedroom, undress, and get into bed. David looks at me sadly, lies down next to me, turns off the light. I want to say something but don't know what to say. I could say, "One of us should have gone with Noel. Do you know your socks are still on? You're going to do to me what Susan did to Noel, aren't you?"

"Did you see his poor miserable pajamas?" David whispers finally. He throws back the covers and gets up and goes back to the living room. I follow, half asleep. David sits in the chair, puts his arms on the armrests, presses his neck

against the back of the chair, and moves his feet together.
"Zzzz," he says, and his head falls forward.

Back in bed, I lie awake, remembering a day David and I
spent in the park last August. David was sitting on the swing
next to me, scraping the toes of his tennis shoes in the loose
dirt.

"Don't you want to swing?" I said. We had been playing
tennis. He had beaten me every game. He always beats me at
everything—precision parking, three-dimensional ticktacktoe,
soufflés. His soufflés rise as beautifully curved as the moon.

"I don't know how to swing," he said.

I tried to teach him, but he couldn't get his legs to move
right. He stood the way I told him, with the board against his
behind, gave a little jump to get on, but then he couldn't
synchronize his legs. "Pump!" I called, but it didn't mean
anything. I might as well have said, "Juggle dishes." I still
find it hard to believe there's anything I can do that he can't
do.

He got off the swing. "Why do you act like everything is a
goddamn contest?" he said, and walked away.

"Because we're always having contests and you always
win!" I shouted.

I was still waiting by the swings when he showed up half
an hour later.

"Do you consider it a contest when we go scuba diving?"
he said.

He had me. It was stupid of me last summer to say how he
always snatched the best shells, even when they were closer
to me. That made him laugh. He had chased me into a
corner, then laughed at me.

I lie in bed now, hating him for that. But don't leave me, I
think—don't do what Noel's wife did. I reach across the bed
and gently take hold of a little wrinkle in his pajama top. I
don't know if I want to yank his pajamas—do something
violent—or smooth them. Confused, I take my hand away
and turn on the light. David rolls over, throws his arm over
his face, groans. I stare at him. In a second he will lower his

arm and demand an explanation. Trapped again. I get up and put on my slippers.

"I'm going to get a drink of water," I whisper apologetically.

Later in the month, it happens. I'm sitting on a cushion on the floor, with newspapers spread in front of me, repotting plants. I'm just moving the purple passion plant to a larger pot when David comes in. It is late in the afternoon—late enough to be dark outside. David has been out with Beth. Before the two of them went out, Beth, confused by the sight of soil indoors, crouched down beside me to ask, "Are there ants, Mommy?" I laughed. David never approved of my laughing at her. Later, that will be something he'll mention in court, hoping to get custody: I laugh at her. And when that doesn't work, he'll tell the judge what I said about his snatching all the best seashells.

David comes in, coat still buttoned, blue silk scarf still tied (a Christmas present from Noel, with many apologies for losing the white one), sits on the floor, and says that he's decided to leave. He is speaking very reasonably and quietly. That alarms me. It crosses my mind that he's mad. And Beth isn't with him. He has killed her!

No, no, of course not. I'm mad. Beth is upstairs in her friend's apartment. He ran into Beth's friend and her mother coming into the building. He asked if Beth could stay in their apartment for a few minutes. I'm not convinced: What friend? I'm foolish to feel reassured as soon as he names one— Louisa. I feel nothing but relief. It might be more accurate to say that I feel nothing. I would have felt pain if she were dead, but David says she isn't, so I feel nothing. I reach out and begin stroking the plant's leaves. Soft leaves, sharp points. The plant I'm repotting is a cutting from Noel's big plant that hangs in a silver ice bucket in his window (a wedding gift that he and Susan had never used). I helped him put it in the ice bucket. "What are you going to do with the top?" I asked. He put it on his head and danced around.

"I had an uncle who got drunk and danced with a lampshade

on his head," Noel said. "That's an old joke, but how many people have actually *seen* a man dance with a lampshade on his head? My uncle did it every New Year's Eve."

"What the hell are you smiling about?" David says. "Are you listening to me?"

I nod and start to cry. It will be a long time before I realize that David makes me sad and Noel makes me happy.

Noel sympathizes with me. He tells me that David is a fool; he is better off without Susan, and I will be better off without David. Noel calls or visits me in my new apartment almost every night. Last night he suggested that I get a babysitter for tonight, so he could take me to dinner. He tries very hard to make me happy. He brings expensive wine when we eat in my apartment and offers to buy it in restaurants when we eat out. Beth prefers it when we eat in; that way, she can have both Noel and the toy that Noel inevitably brings. Her favorite toy, so far, is a handsome red tugboat pulling three barges, attached to one another by string. Noel bends over, almost double in half, to move them across the rug, whistling and calling orders to the imaginary crew. He does not just bring gifts to Beth and me. He has bought himself a new car, and pretends that this is for Beth and me. ("Comfortable seats?" he asks me. "That's a nice big window back there to wave out of," he says to Beth.) It is silly to pretend that he got the car for the three of us. And if he did, why was he too cheap to have a radio installed, when he knows I love music? Not only that but he's bowlegged. I am ashamed of myself for thinking bad things about Noel. He tries so hard to keep us cheerful. He can't help the odd angle of his thighs. Feeling sorry for him, I decided that a cheap dinner was good enough for tonight. I said that I wanted to go to a Chinese restaurant.

At the restaurant I eat shrimp in black bean sauce and drink a Heineken's and think that I've never tasted anything so delicious. The waiter brings two fortune cookies. We open them; the fortunes make no sense. Noel summons the waiter for the bill. With it come more fortune cookies—four this time. They are no good, either: talk of travel and money. Noel says, "What bloody rot." He is wearing a gray vest and a white shirt. I peek around the table without his noticing and see that he's wearing gray wool slacks. Lately it has been very important for me to be able to see everything. Whenever Noel pulls the boats out of sight, into another room, I move as quickly as Beth to watch what's going on.

Standing behind Noel at the cash register, I see that it has started to rain—a mixture of rain and snow.

"You know how you can tell a Chinese restaurant from any other?" Noel asks, pushing open the door. "Even when it's raining, the cats still run for the street."

I shake my head in disgust.

Noel stretches the skin at the corners of his eyes. "Sorry for honorable joke," he says.

We run for the car. He grabs the belt of my coat, catches me, and half lifts me with one arm, running along with me dangling at his side, giggling. Our wool coats stink. He opens my car door, runs around, and pulls his open. He's done it again; he has made me laugh.

We start home.

We are in heavy traffic, and Noel drives very slowly, protecting his new car.

"How old are you?" I ask.

"Thirty-six," Noel says.

"I'm twenty-seven," I say.

"So what?" he says. He says it pleasantly.

"I just didn't know how old you were."

"Mentally, I'm neck and neck with Beth," he says.

I'm soaking wet, and I want to get home to put on dry clothes. I look at him inching through traffic, and I remember the way his face looked that night he sat in the living room with David and me.

"Rain always puts you in a bad mood, doesn't it?" he says. He turns the windshield wipers on high. Rubber squeaks against glass.

"I see myself dead in it," I say.

"You see yourself dead in it?"

Noel does not read novels. He reads *Moneysworth,* the *Wall Street Journal, Commentary.* I reprimand myself; there must be fitting ironies in the *Wall Street Journal.*

"Are you kidding?" Noel says. "You seemed to be enjoying yourself at dinner. It was a good dinner, wasn't it?"

"I make you nervous, don't I?" I say.

"No. You don't make me nervous."

Rain splashes under the car, drums on the roof. We ride on for blocks and blocks. It is too quiet; I wish there were a radio. The rain on the roof is monotonous, the collar of my coat is wet and cold. At last we are home. Noel parks the car and comes around to my door and opens it. I get out. Noel pulls me close, squeezes me hard. When I was a little girl, I once squeezed a doll to my chest in an antique shop, and when I took it away the eyes had popped off. An unpleasant memory. With my arms around Noel, I feel the cold rain hitting my hands and wrists.

A man running down the sidewalk with a small dog in his arms and a big black umbrella over him calls, "Your lights are on!"

It is almost a year later—Christmas—and we are visiting Noel's crazy sister, Juliette. After going with Noel for so long, I am considered one of the family. Juliette phones before every occasion, saying, "You're one of the family. Of course you don't need an invitation." I should appreciate it, but she's always drunk when she calls, and usually she starts to cry and says she wishes Christmas and Thanksgiving didn't exist. Jeanette, his other sister, is very nice, but she lives in Colorado. Juliette lives in New Jersey. Here we are in Bayonne, New Jersey, coming in through the front door—Noel holding Beth, me carrying a pumpkin pie. I tried to sniff the pie aroma on the way from Noel's apartment to his sister's house, but it had no smell. Or else I'm getting another cold. I sucked chewable vitamin C tablets in the car, and now I smell of oranges. Noel's mother is in the living room, crocheting. Better, at least, than David's mother, who was always discoursing about Andrew Wyeth. I remember with satisfaction that the last time I saw her I said, "It's a simple fact that Edward Hopper was better."

Juliette: long, whitish-blond hair tucked in back of her pink ears, spike-heel shoes that she orders from Frederick's of Hollywood, dresses that show her cleavage. Noel and I are silently wondering if her husband will be here. At Thanksgiving he showed up just as we were starting dinner, with a black-haired woman who wore a dress with a plunging neckline. Juliette's breasts faced the black-haired woman's breasts across the table (tablecloth crocheted by Noel's mother). Noel doesn't like me to criticize Juliette. He thinks positively. His other sister is a musician. She has a husband and a weimaraner and two rare birds that live in a birdcage built by her husband. They have a lot of money and they ski. They have adopted a Korean boy. Once, they showed us a film of the Korean boy learning to ski. Wham, wham, wham—every few seconds he was groveling in the snow again.

Juliette is such a liberal that she gives us not only the same bedroom but a bedroom with only a single bed in it. Beth sleeps on the couch.

Wedged beside Noel that night, I say, "This is ridiculous."

"She means to be nice," he says. "Where else would we sleep?"

"She could have let us have her double bed and she could sleep in here. After all, he's not coming back, Noel."

"Shh."

"Wouldn't that have been better?"

"What do you care?" Noel says. "You're nuts about me, right?"

He slides up against me and hugs my back.

"I don't know how people talk any more," he says. "I don't know any of the current lingo. What expression do people use for 'nuts about'?"

"I don't know."

"I just did it again! I said 'lingo.' "

"So what? Who do you want to sound like?"

"The way I talk sounds dated—like an old person."

"Why are you always worried about being old?"

He snuggles closer. "You didn't answer before when I said you were nuts about me. That doesn't mean that you don't like me, does it?"

"No."

"You're big on the one-word answers."

"I'm big on going to sleep."

" 'Big on.' See? there must be some expression to replace that now."

I sit in the car, waiting for Beth to come out of the building where the ballet school is. She has been taking lessons, but they haven't helped. She still slouches forward and sticks out her neck when she walks. Noel suggests that this might be analyzed psychologically; she sticks her neck out, you see, not only literally but . . . Noel thinks that Beth is waiting to get it. Beth feels guilty because her mother and father have just been divorced. She thinks that she played some part in it and therefore she deserves to get it. It is worth fifty dollars a month for ballet lessons to disprove Noel's theory. If it will only work.

I spend the day in the park, thinking over Noel's suggestion that I move in with him. We would have more money . . . We are together so much anyway . . . Or he could move in with me, if those big windows in my place are really so important. I always meet reasonable men.

"But I don't love you," I said to Noel. "Don't you want to live with somebody who loves you?"

"Nobody has ever loved me and nobody ever will," Noel said. "What have I got to lose?"

I am in the park to think about what I have to lose. Nothing. So why don't I leave the park, call him at work, say that I have decided it is a very sensible plan?

A chubby little boy wanders by, wearing a short jacket and pants that are slipping down. He is holding a yellow boat. He looks so damned pleased with everything that I think about accosting him and asking, "Should I move in with Noel? Why am I reluctant to do it?" The young have such wisdom—

some of the best and worst thinkers have thought so: Wordsworth, the followers of the Guru Maharaj Ji . . . "Do the meditations, or I will beat you with a stick," the Guru tells his followers. Tell me the answer, kid, or I will take away your boat.

I sink down onto a bench. Next, Noel will ask me to marry him. He is trying to trap me. Worse, he is not trying to trap me but only wants me to move in so we can save money. He doesn't care about me. Since no one has ever loved him, he can't love anybody. Is that even true?

I find a phone booth and stand in front of it, waiting for a woman with a shopping bag to get out. She mouths something I don't understand. She has lips like a fish; they are painted bright orange. I do not have any lipstick on. I have a raincoat, pulled over my nightgown, and sandals and Noel's socks.

"Noel," I say on the phone when I reach him, "were you serious when you said that no one ever loved you?"

"Jesus, it was embarrassing enough just to admit it," he says. "Do you have to question me about it?"

"I have to know."

"Well, I've told you about every woman I ever slept with. Which one do you suspect might have loved me?"

I have ruined his day. I hang up, rest my head against the phone. "Me," I mumble. "I do." I reach in the raincoat pocket. A Kleenex, two pennies, and a pink rubber spider put there by Beth to scare me. No more dimes. I push open the door. A young woman is standing there waiting for me. "Do you have a few moments?" she says.

"Why?"

"Do you have a moment? What do you think of this?" she says. It is a small stick with the texture of salami. In her other hand she holds a clipboard and a pen.

"I don't have time," I say, and walk away. I stop and turn. "What is that, anyway?" I ask.

"Do you have a moment?" she asks.

"No. I just wanted to know what that thing was."

"A dog treat."

She is coming after me, clipboard outstretched.

"I don't have time," I say, and quickly walk away.

Something hits my back. "Take the time to stick it up your ass," she says.

I run for a block before I stop and lean on the park wall to rest. If Noel had been there, she wouldn't have done it. My protector. If I had a dime, I could call back and say, "Oh, Noel, I'll live with you always if you'll stay with me so people won't throw dog treats at me."

I finger the plastic spider. Maybe Beth put it there to cheer me up. Once, she put a picture of a young, beautiful girl in a bikini on my bedroom wall. I misunderstood, seeing the woman as all that I was not. Beth just thought it was a pretty picture. She didn't understand why I was so upset.

"Mommy's just upset because when you put things on the wall with Scotch Tape, the Scotch Tape leaves a mark when you remove it," Noel told her.

Noel is wonderful. I reach in my pocket, hoping a dime will suddenly appear.

Noel and I go to visit his friends Charles and Sol, in Vermont. Noel has taken time off from work; it is a vacation to celebrate our decision to live together. Now, on the third evening there, we are all crowded around the hearth—Noel and Beth and I, Charles and Sol and the women they live with, Lark and Margaret. We are smoking and listening to Sol's stereo. The hearth is a big one. It was laid by Sol, made out of slate he took from the side of a hill and bricks he found dumped by the side of the road. There is a mantel that was made by Charles from a section of an old carousel he picked up when a local amusement park closed down; a gargoyle's head protrudes from one side. Car keys have been draped over the beast's eyebrows. On the top of the mantel there is an L. L. Bean catalogue, Margaret's hat, roaches and a roach clip, a can of peaches, and an incense burner that holds a small cone in a puddle of lavender ashes.

Noel used to work with Charles in the city. Charles quit when he heard about a big house in Vermont that needed to be fixed up. He was told that he could live in it for a hundred dollars a month, except in January and February, when skiers rented it. The skiers turned out to be nice people who didn't want to see anyone displaced. They suggested that the four stay on in the house, and they did, sleeping in a side room that Charles and Sol fixed up. Just now, the rest of the house is empty; it has been raining a lot, ruining the skiing.

Sol has put up some pictures he framed—old advertisements he found in a box in the attic (later Charles repaired the attic stairs). I study the pictures now, in the firelight. The Butter Lady—a healthy coquette with pearly skin and a mildewed bottom lip—extends a hand offering a package of butter. On the wall across from her, a man with oil-slick black hair holds a shoe that is the same color as his hair.

"When you're lost in the rain in Juarez and it's Eastertine, too," Dylan sings.

Margaret says to Beth, "Do you want to come take a bath with me?"

Beth is shy. The first night we were here, she covered her eyes when Sol walked naked from the bathroom to the bedroom.

"I don't have to take a bath while I'm here, do I?" she says to me.

"Where did you get that idea?"

"Why do I have to take a bath?"

But she decides to go with Margaret, and runs after her and grabs on to her wool sash. Margaret blows on the incense stick she has just lit, and fans it in the air, and Beth, enchanted, follows her out of the room. She already feels at ease in the house, and she likes us all and wanders off with anyone gladly, even though she's usually shy. Yesterday, Sol showed her how to punch down the bread before putting it on the baking sheet to rise once more. He let her smear butter over the loaves with her fingers and then sprinkle cornmeal on the top.

Sol teaches at the state university. He is a poet, and he has been hired to teach a course in the modern novel. "Oh, well," he is saying now. "If I weren't a queer and I'd gone into the Army, I guess they would have made me a cook. That's usually what they do, isn't it?''

"Don't ask me," Charles says. "I'm queer, too." This seems to be an old routine.

Noel is admiring the picture frames. "This is such a beautiful place," he says. "I'd love to live here for good."

"Don't be a fool," Sol says. "With a lot of fairies?"

Sol is reading a student's paper. "This student says, 'Humbert is just like a million other Americans,' " he says.

"Humbert?" Noel says.

"You know—that guy who ran against Nixon."

"Come on," Noel says. "I know it's from some novel."

"Lolita," Lark says, all on the intake. She passes the joint to me.

"Why don't you quit that job?" Lark says. "You hate it."

"I can't be unemployed," Sol says. "I'm a faggot and a poet. I've already got two strikes against me." He puffs twice on the roach, lets it slip out of the clip to the hearth. "And a drug abuser," he says. "I'm as good as done for."

"I'm sorry you feel that way, dear," Charles says, putting his hand gently on Sol's shoulder. Sol jumps. Charles and Noel laugh.

It is time for dinner—moussaka, and bread, and wine that Noel brought.

"What's moussaka?" Beth asks. Her skin shines, and her hair has dried in small narrow ridges where Margaret combed it.

"Made with mice," Sol says.

Beth looks at Noel. Lately, she checks things out with him. He shakes his head no. Actually, she is not a dumb child; she probably looked at Noel because she knows it makes him happy.

Beth has her own room—the smallest bedroom, with a fur rug on the floor and a quilt to sleep under. As I talk to Lark after dinner, I hear Noel reading to Beth: *"The Trout Fishing Diary of Alonso Hagen."* Soon Beth is giggling.

I sit in Noel's lap, looking out the window at the fields, white and flat, and the mountains—a blur that I know is mountains. The radiator under the window makes the glass foggy. Noel leans forward to wipe it with a handkerchief. We are in winter now. We were going to leave Vermont after a week—then two, now three. Noel's hair is getting long. Beth has missed a month of school. What will the Board of Education do to me? "What do you think they're going to do?" Noel says. "Come after us with guns?"

Noel has just finished confiding in me another horrendous or mortifying thing he would never, never tell anyone and that I must swear not to repeat. The story is about something that happened when he was eighteen. There was a friend of his mother's whom he threatened to strangle if she didn't let him sleep with her. She let him. As soon as it was over, he was terrified that she would tell someone, and he threatened to strangle her if she did. But he realized that as soon as he left she could talk, and that he could be arrested, and he got so upset that he broke down and ran back to the bed where they had been, pulled the covers over his head, and shook and cried. Later, the woman told his mother that Noel seemed to be studying too hard at Princeton—perhaps he needed some time off. A second story was about how he tried to kill himself when his wife left him. The truth was that he couldn't give David his scarf back because it was stretched from being knotted so many times. But he had been too chicken to hang himself and he had swallowed a bottle of drugstore sleeping pills instead. Then he got frightened and went outside and hailed a cab. Another couple, huddled together in the wind, told him that they had claimed the cab first. The same couple was in the waiting room of the hospital when he came to.

"The poor guy put his card next to my hand on the stretcher," Noel says, shaking his head so hard that his beard scrapes my cheek. "He was a plumber. Eliot Raye. And his wife, Flora."

A warm afternoon. "Noel!" Beth cries, running across the soggy lawn toward him, her hand extended like a fisherman with his catch. But there's nothing in her hand—only a little spot of blood on the palm. Eventually he gets the story out of her: she fell. He will bandage it. He is squatting, his arm folding her close like some giant bird. A heron? An eagle? Will he take my child and fly away? They walk toward the house, his hand pressing Beth's head against his leg.

We are back in the city. Beth is asleep in the room that was once Noel's study. I am curled up in Noel's lap. He has just asked to hear the story of Michael again.

"Why do you want to hear that?" I ask.

Noel is fascinated by Michael, who pushed his furniture into the hall and threw his small possessions out the window into the back yard and then put up four large, connecting tents in his apartment. There was a hot plate in there, cans of Franco-American spaghetti, bottles of good wine, a flashlight for when it got dark . . .

Noel urges me to remember more details. What else was in the tent?

A rug, but that just happened to be on the floor. For some reason, he didn't throw the rug out the window. And there was a sleeping bag . . .

What else?

Comic books. I don't remember which ones. A lemon meringue pie. I remember how disgusting that was after two days, with the sugar oozing out of the meringue. A bottle of Seconal. There was a drinking glass, a container of warm juice . . . I don't remember.

We used to make love in the tent. I'd go over to see him, open the front door, and crawl in. That summer he collapsed the tents, threw them in his car, and left for Maine.

"Go on," Noel says.

I shrug. I've told this story twice before, and this is always my stopping place.

"That's it," I say to Noel.

He continues to wait expectantly, just as he did the two other times he heard the story.

One evening, we get a phone call from Lark. There is a house near them for sale—only thirty thousand dollars. What

Noel can't fix, Charles and Sol can help with. There are ten acres of land, a waterfall. Noel is wild to move there. But what are we going to do for money, I ask him. He says we'll worry about that in a year or so, when we run out. But we haven't even seen the place, I point out. But this is a fabulous find, he says. We'll go see it this weekend. Noel has Beth so excited that she wants to start school in Vermont on Monday, not come back to the city at all. We will just go to the house right this minute and live there forever.

But does he know how to do the wiring? Is he sure it can be wired?

"Don't you have any faith in me?" he says. "David always thought I was a chump, didn't he?"

"I'm only asking whether you can do such complicated things."

My lack of faith in Noel has made him unhappy. He leaves the room without answering. He probably remembers—and knows that I remember—the night he asked David if he could see what was wrong with the socket of his floor lamp. David came back to our apartment laughing. "The plug had come out of the outlet," he said.

In early April, David comes to visit us in Vermont for the weekend with his girlfriend, Patty. She wears blue jeans, and has kohl around her eyes. She is twenty years old. Her clogs echo loudly on the bare floorboards. She seems to feel awkward here. David seems not to feel awkward, although he looked surprised when Beth called him David. She led him through the woods, running ahead of Noel and me, to show him the waterfall. When she got too far ahead, I called her back, afraid, for some reason, that she might die. If I lost sight of her, she might die. I suppose I had always thought that if David and I spent time together again it would be over the hospital bed of our dying daughter—something like that.

Patty has trouble walking in the woods; the clogs flop off her feet in the brush. I tried to give her a pair of my sneakers, but she wears size 8½ and I am a 7. Another thing to make her feel awkward.

David breathes in dramatically. "Quite a change from the high rise we used to live in," he says to Noel.

Calculated to make us feel rotten?

"You used to live in a high rise?" Patty asks.

He must have just met her. She pays careful attention to everything he says, watches with interest when he snaps off a twig and breaks it in little pieces. She is having trouble keeping up. David finally notices her difficulty in keeping up with us, and takes her hand. They're city people; they don't even have hiking boots.

"It seems as if that was in another life," David says. He snaps off a small branch and flicks one end of it against his thumb.

"There's somebody who says that every time we sleep we die; we come back another person, to another life," Patty says.

"Kafka as realist," Noel says.

Noel has been reading all winter. He has read Brautigan, a lot of Borges, and has gone from Dante to García Márquez to Hilma Wolitzer to Kafka. Sometimes I ask him why he is going about it this way. He had me make him a list—this writer before that one, which poems are early, which late, which famous. Well, it doesn't matter. Noel is happy in Vermont. Being in Vermont means that he can do what he wants to do. Freedom, you know. Why should I make fun of it? He loves his books, loves roaming around in the woods outside the house, and he buys more birdseed than all the birds in the North could eat. He took a Polaroid picture of our salt lick for the deer when he put it in, and admired both the salt lick ("They've been here!") and his picture. Inside the house there are Polaroids of the woods, the waterfall, some rabbits—he tacks them up with pride, the way Beth hangs up the pictures she draws in school. "You know," Noel said to me one night, "when Gatsby is talking to Nick Carraway and he says, 'In any case, it was just personal'—what does that mean?"

"When did you read *Gatsby*?" I asked.

"Last night, in the bathtub."

As we turn to walk back, Noel points out the astonishing number of squirrels in the trees around us. By David's expression, he thinks Noel is pathetic.

I look at Noel. He is taller than David but more stooped; thinner than David, but his slouch disguises it. Noel has big hands and feet and a sharp nose. His scarf is gray, with frayed edges. David's is bright red, just bought. Poor Noel. When David called to say he and Patty were coming for a visit, Noel never thought of saying no. And he asked me how he could compete with David. He thought David was coming to his house to win me away. After he reads more literature he'll realize that is too easy. There will have to be complexities. The complexities will protect him forever. Hours after David's call, he said (to himself, really—not to me) that David was bringing a woman with him. Surely that meant he wouldn't try anything.

Charles and Margaret come over just as we are finishing dinner, bringing a mattress we are borrowing for David and Patty to sleep on. They are both stoned, and are dragging the mattress on the ground, which is white with a late snow. They are too stoned to hoist it.

"Eventide," Charles says. A circular black barrette holds his hair out of his face. Margaret lost her hat to Lark some time ago and never got around to borrowing another one. Her hair is dusted with snow. "We have to go," Charles says, weighing her hair in his hands, "before the snow woman melts."

Sitting at the kitchen table late that night, I turn to David. "How are you doing?" I whisper.

"A lot of things haven't been going the way I figured," he whispers.

I nod. We are drinking white wine and eating cheddar-cheese soup. The soup is scalding. Clouds of steam rise from the bowl, and I keep my face away from it, worrying that the steam will make my eyes water, and that David will misinterpret.

"Not really things. People," David whispers, bobbing an ice cube up and down in his wineglass with his index finger.

"What people?"

"It's better not to talk about it. They're not really people you know."

That hurts, and he knew it would hurt. But climbing the stairs to go to bed I realize that, in spite of that, it's a very reasonable approach.

Tonight, as I do most nights, I sleep with long johns under my nightgown. I roll over on top of Noel for more warmth and lie there, as he has said, like a dead man, like a man in the Wild West, gunned down in the dirt. Noel jokes about this. "Pow, pow," he whispers sleepily as I lower myself on him. "Poor critter's deader 'n a doornail." I lie there warming myself. What does he want with me?

"What do you want for your birthday?" I ask.

He recites a little list of things he wants. He whispers: a bookcase, an aquarium, a blender to make milkshakes in.

"That sounds like what a ten-year-old would want," I say.

He is quiet too long; I have hurt his feelings.

"Not the bookcase," he says finally.

I am falling asleep. It's not fair to fall asleep on top of him. He doesn't have the heart to wake me and has to lie there with me sprawled on top of him until I fall off. Move, I tell myself, but I don't.

"Do you remember this afternoon, when Patty and I sat on the rock to wait for you and David and Beth?"

I remember. We were on top of the hill, Beth pulling David by his hand, David not very interested in what she was going to show him, Beth ignoring his lack of interest and pulling him along. I ran to catch up, because she was pulling him so hard, and I caught Beth's free arm and hung on, so that we formed a chain.

"I knew I'd seen that before," Noel says. "I just realized where—when the actor wakes up after the storm and sees Death leading those people across the hilltop in *The Seventh Seal*."

Six years ago. Seven. David and I were in the Village, in the winter, looking in a bookstore window. Tires began to squeal, and we turned around and were staring straight at a car, a ratty old blue car that had lifted a woman from the street into the air. The fall took much too long; she fell the way snow drifts—the big flakes that float down, no hurry at all. By the time she hit, though, David had pushed my face against his coat, and while everyone was screaming—it seemed as if a whole chorus had suddenly assembled to scream—he had his arms around my shoulders, pressing me so close that I could hardly breathe and saying, "If anything happened to you . . . If anything happened to you . . . ."

When they leave, it is a clear, cold day. I give Patty a paper bag with half a bottle of wine, two sandwiches, and some peanuts to eat on the way back. The wine is probably not a good idea; David had three glasses of vodka and orange juice for breakfast. He began telling jokes to Noel—dogs in bars outsmarting their owners, constipated whores, talking fleas. David does not like Noel; Noel does not know what to make of David.

Now David rolls down the car window. Last-minute news. He tells me that his sister has been staying in his apartment. She aborted herself and has been very sick. "Abortions are legal," David says. "Why did she do that?" I ask how long ago it happened. A month ago, he says. His hands drum on the steering wheel. Last week, Beth got a box of wooden whistles carved in the shape of peasants from David's sister. Noel opened the kitchen window and blew softly to some birds on the feeder. They all flew away.

Patty leans across David. "There are so many animals here, even in the winter," she says. "Don't they hibernate any more?"

She is making nervous, polite conversation. She wants to leave. Noel walks away from me to Patty's side of the car, and tells her about the deer who come right up to the house. Beth is sitting on Noel's shoulders. Not wanting to talk to David, I wave at her stupidly. She waves back.

David looks at me out the window. I must look as stiff as one of those wooden whistles, all carved out of one piece, in my old blue ski jacket and blue wool hat pulled down to my eyes and my baggy jeans.

"*Ciao*," David says. "Thanks."

"Yes," Patty says. "It was nice of you to do this." She holds up the bag.

It's a steep driveway, and rocky. David backs down cautiously—the way someone pulls a zipper after it's been caught. We wave, they disappear. That was easy.

The Little Pub

PATRICIA ZELVER

It was January. Night fell abruptly, shrouding the oak-studded hills of Vista Verde in deep shadows. Only a few lights were visible from the picture window where Mrs. Jessup stood having her Happy Hour, her first—he or was it her second?— vodka martini in her hand. She stood at the window in her house on La Floresta Lane, looking at the lights far below. They were the lights, she said to herself, of the Little Pub. The lights of the Little Pub twinkled cheerily in the darkness. Smoke would be curling out of its chimney in tidy loops like the chimney smoke in a child's drawing. Big Bill has lit a fire, she thought. Perhaps I should call Ruff and walk down there. But would we be able to find our way in the dark? There were no sidewalks and no street lights in Vista Verde, very different from Chestnut Hill, where she and Mr. Jessup had lived, before moving here. The lights were visible from the house, but would they be, in the darkness, on the lane? Probably not visible, she decided. Probably we would lose our way. And, anyhow, I have the cards to finish. First things first, she told herself. Sacrifices are always entailed whenever people put first things first, as they must if they want to do things worthwhile.

That morning Mrs. Jessup had driven to the city to attend a Seminar for Executive Wives at the Hyatt Regency, sponsored by Mr. Jessup's corporation. It had been an extremely rewarding session. A Social Anthropologist had spoken to them on "Developing Inner Resources Through Creativity." Or was it a Social Psychologist? She must try to remember to tell Mr. Jessup when he returned. Distinctions of that sort were important to him, and rightly so, though she was not absolutely sure why.

The Social Anthropologist or Social Psychologist had traced the forces which made up the Modern World. The old-fashioned sort of Community Life, which was extolled in magazines and films and on TV, and about which so many people were foolishly nostalgic, was archaic—a thing of the past. It was particularly a thing of the past for dynamic men who set high goals for themselves. The world, not just their tiny community, was their milieu; mobility their Life Style. It was important, he said, to face facts. But this did not mean that their wives need lack fulfillment. It was, he had pointed out, really up to them. There were endless avenues open in which to be creative. He had enumerated some of these open endless avenues—foreign language lessons; decorating and art and gourmet cooking courses; working as a docent in a museum; volunteering to help the handicapped; entertaining graciously; bringing up children; graciously volunteering to entertain graciously; even, and perhaps most important of all, providing a serene and loving atmosphere for the executive husband. They—the executive wives—should think of their jobs as a part of a Team Effort. Sacrifices were, of course, entailed, but sacrifices were always entailed whenever people did things worthwhile. The rewards would be their own personal growth and their husbands' gratitude.

Mrs. Jessup had explored most of these avenues at one time or another, but she had not explored them lately. For the last six months, ever since they had moved into Vista Verde, she had really stopped exploring altogether. Almost the moment she had the furniture arranged and the new curtains up, Mr. Jessup had told her, in his proud, quiet way, that another Transfer was in the air, this time a very important one; the Chairman of the Board was about to retire, and he was in line for this position. It would be—now was—the culmination of his career. She had therefore done nothing in the way of exploring or making new acquaintances, and for this reason she was grateful to the Social Anthropologist-Psychologist for reminding her of what he called her "potential." As the wife of the Chairman of the Board, Inner Resources Through Creativity would be more useful than ever.

After the seminar, she had gone to the city's largest stationery store and searched through the cards, hoping to find a more original one than the ones she had sent so many times before. She had not succeeded, and had to hurry home in order to be there when Mr. Jessup, who was at a conference at the Airport Hilton—or was it the Airport Sheraton?—would phone her. There was three hours' difference, and with three hours' differences he always called at three o'clock to be present at the conference's Happy Hour before dinner. On the way, she had been struck by an idea. Perhaps she could make a card herself? During an art class she had taken once, in a past exploration of avenues, she had learned how to make a block print with a raw potato. Various designs and messages occurred to her. Cartoon figures? An old-fashioned script? Black and white? Colors? She had suggested the idea, somewhat shyly, to Mr. Jessup when he phoned.

"Make one?" said Mr. Jessup. "What did you have in mind?"

"I don't know yet. Something humorous, maybe. I thought it might be fun."

"Oh, let's keep it kosher," Mr. Jessup said.

"You mean, buy a card?"

"It seems to me you have enough to do, just addressing them," he said thoughtfully.

As soon as he hung up, Mrs. Jessup drove down to the Vista Verde Shopping Center, below their house, and bought the simplest card she could find. It was then almost four. She had called Ruff to feed him, but Ruff had crawled out from under the fence again, and was gone.

The nice young Vista Verde patrolman will bring him back, Mrs. Jessup said to herself.

Whenever Mr. Jessup was out of town, the private patrol car stopped by in the early evening, and the nice young man rang her doorbell and asked her if everything was all right. This was something Mr. Jessup insisted upon. Mrs. Jessup didn't mind because she liked the young man. He reminded her, somewhat, of her younger son, an engineer, now married and working in Saudi Arabia. She also liked the nice relationship the young man had with Ruff. He either brought Ruff back from the shopping center, where he liked to go, or, if Ruff came to the door with her, he would pat Ruff's gray fat back, while Ruff wriggled all over in ecstasy.

"I guess you can't be too lonely with old Ruff," the young man would say.

"Ruff is a good companion," Mrs. Jessup would tell the young man. "Of course, if a burglar came, he wouldn't be much help."

"Oh, we all know Ruff. He'd show the burglar around the house," the young man would say.

"Would you care to come in and have a drink?" Mrs. Jessup had said once.

"I'd sure like to, Ma'am, but we're not allowed to, when we're on duty."

"Of course, how silly of me," said Mrs. Jessup.

"Now, you take care of yourself, Ma'am. Just call us if you've any problems."

"Thank you, it's good just to know I can," Mrs. Jessup said.

The view from the picture window was of the wooded hills, now black shadows against the sky. Except for the lights of the Little Pub in the distance, you would never guess there were other homes around. The Vista Verde Neighborhood Association reviewed the plans of each house before it was built to be certain that no one's view was obstructed. The ad for the Jessup house, which was running in the Vista Verde *Crier* now, was similar to the ads the real estate people had run the last six times they had moved:

Spanking new executive mansion in exclusive neighborhood. Secluded, three-acre, wooded retreat. AEK. Pool, three-car garage. Country Club.

Except for the lights of the Little Pub, one might think one was stranded, alone, perhaps the last person alive in the whole world. Mrs. Jessup had once read a book like that; the memory of it still made her feel funny. She mixed herself another cocktail at the wet bar, then she went into the kitchen and opened the oven and looked at the frozen Stouffer cheese soufflé she had put in before her first drink. Then she returned to the living room window. If she did not have the other cards to do, she decided, she would definitely call Ruff and walk down there; they would, somehow, find their way in the dark. How pleasant it would be, if she did not have the cards to do, to sit in her favorite chair beside the Little Pub's fireplace—the old, sprung, cracked leather chair—or was it the old, sprung, chintz chair? It didn't matter. The chair was not the important thing. What was important was the general ambience.

The general ambience of the Little Pub was very agreeable. The credit for this went to Bill. Big Bill, the regulars called him. Mrs. Jessup was a bit too reserved for this; it was not her style. She left off the "Big" and addressed him simply as "Bill." Bill called her "Sugar."

"The usual, Sugar?" Big Bill would say to her, when she had settled herself down in her favorite chair.

She would smile—a bit coquettishly—and nod. With anyone else, she might have been offended, but not with Big Bill. Big Bill, she thought, could call the Duchess of Windsor "Sugar" and get away with it. He had such a nice, easy manner with the ladies, and everyone else, too, for that matter.

"One vodka martini on the rocks for my little Sugar," Big Bill would sing out, as he mixed the drink himself. This was a little joke they had together. He would then bring the drink on a tray to Mrs. Jessup, and present it with a comical flourish. "And what is Ruff's pleasure?" he would say, looking down at Ruff.

Mrs. Jessup would laugh. This was another joke she shared with Big Bill.

Mrs. Jessup sipped her cocktail and thought about the Little Pub. About her chair, the crackling fire, about Big Bill. About the general agreeable ambience.

"I'm leaving, Mr. Jessup is being transferred," she would tell him.

She could imagine Big Bill's regret at hearing this. "He's Chairman of the Board," she would say. "It's quite an honor, of course, but I shall miss the Little Pub."

Big Bill would, undoubtedly, present her with a drink on the house; perhaps he would even toast her and Mr. Jessup's future. Certainly he would ask about Ruff. "What about Ruff?" he would say. "How does he feel about this?"

"I'm afraid Ruff doesn't care much for Transfers," Mrs. Jessup would tell him. "The last one made him so upset I had to give him some of my tranquilizers."

Mrs. Jessup looked at her watch. It was five-thirty, almost time for the patrolman to bring Ruff home. In the meantime, it was pleasant to think about the Little Pub.

At the Little Pub you were surrounded by people of all ages and sexes. People of all sexes, including men. Yes, even though she was no longer nubile, as they said somewhere—perhaps in Japan—though she was of a "certain age," as they said in the Scandinavian countries—or was it France?—or "over the hill," as the common folk saying went, she still enjoyed a room with men, now and then, on a lonely evening during the Happy Hour.

She liked, she thought, the way men looked. The way their jackets scrunched up in back, and their trousers wrinkled at the crotch; the way they talked, sometimes in monosyllables or little grunts. Their laughs—their hearty men chuckles—she liked this, too. There were, of course, men in her life. The check-out clerk at the Vista Verde market, the pharmacist, her doctor, the hardware man, the nice young patrolman; Mr. Tanaguchi, the gardener. She had an especially warm relationship with Mr. Tanaguchi, who possessed an amazing understanding of plants. It would be resourceful—even creative—to go to the phone, right now, and call him up and invite him and Mrs. Tanaguchi over for a cocktail. But what if Mr. Tanaguchi didn't drink? Or, suppose he drank only sake? She had no sake in the house. Or—worst of all—suppose Mrs. Tanaguchi, whom she had never had the pleasure of meeting, misunderstood her warm relationship with Mr. Tanaguchi? No, this particular avenue was not open; she could not be the cause of any embarrassment to Mr. Tanaguchi.

The doorbell rang. Mrs. Jessup went to answer it. The young patrolman was standing on the doorstep. Mrs. Jessup smiled at him. Just seeing him there gave her a nice feeling.

This time the young man did not smile back. His face, she noticed, was serious, actually quite pale. Could he be ill? Mrs. Jessup wondered.

"Ma'am, I have something to tell you," he said. His voice was not as hearty as usual, and he cleared his throat nervously. "Maybe you'd like me to come in, and you can sit down?"

Mrs. Jessup led him into the living room. She sat down, but the young man remained awkwardly standing.

He cleared his throat again. "It's about Ruff, Ma'am. I don't know exactly how to say it, but—we found him this evening. He was run over by a car on the road. I'm afraid there was nothing we could do. He was already—gone."

Mrs. Jessup's first thought was of the young man. How kind he was! How apologetic! But it was not his fault. Silly old Ruff was always digging out from under the fence and roaming around, which was against the Vista Verde leash law. Mrs. Jessup tried very hard to think of something to say to cheer him up.

"Dogs," she said after a moment, "are incapable of sacrifice."

The young man looked at her in an odd way. He seemed almost frightened, the way he stood there, clutching at his cap. Mrs. Jessup was determined to get her point over in order to reassure him.

"Dogs enjoy an old-fashioned community life, they are foolishly nostalgic," she said. "New neighborhoods—new

and unusual odors and noises—fill them with a kind of
frenzy. They forget their house-training, chew things up, dig
under fences—and get run over! They lack inner resources
and are not at all creative!''

''Mrs. Jessup, I have Ruff's body out there in the truck. I
didn't know . . . Do you want us to take care of it, or would
you prefer to?'' He was stammering slightly, backing toward
the door as he spoke.

Mrs. Jessup pretended not to notice his nervousness. Instead, she considered his words carefully. It would be nice,
she thought, to bury Ruff in the back yard, with a little
monument of some sort over his grave. ''Ruff—A Good
Dog.'' Something like that. But she could not expect the
people who bought the house to keep up a grave. ''It would
be very kind of you—to dispose of it,'' she said.

The young man put out his hand, and Mrs. Jessup shook it.
''Take care of yourself, now,'' he said, and left hurriedly.

Mrs. Jessup returned to the picture window. Should she go
down to the Little Pub, she wondered, and tell Big Bill about
Ruff? ''Ruff is dead,'' she would say. It was important to
face facts. It was important, too, to stop thinking about the
Little Pub. There was no Little Pub. This was another fact
that needed to be faced. No Little Pub existed in Vista Verde,
and never would. Imagine the Neighborhood Association per-
mitting such a thing! It would be against the zoning regula-
tions, which did not allow Commercial Uses—only executive-
style houses with proper setbacks and shake roofs on three
acres. Worst of all, a Little Pub would attract Undesirable
Elements. Undesirable Elements, sitting in old squashed
leather—or chintz?—chairs (it did not matter), smiling coquettishly at Big Bill, letting Big Bill call them ''Sugar.''

One could not have that. She finished her drink and went
into the kitchen and took out the soufflé and put it on the
dining room table in its foil container. It was limp and sticky,
but she managed to get most of it down. Then she went into
the den and began, again, upon the cards.

''Helen and Bill,'' she wrote, filling out the blanks, ''are
moving to 4 Old Country Lane, Greenwich, Connecticut.''

There was a drawing of a doormat, and under that it said, "The Welcome Mat is Out."

She finished all of Mr. Jessup's list, which Mr. Jessup's secretary had sent her from his office. Tomorrow, she would begin the list of their friends. It was then ten-thirty. She made herself a nightcap and took it into the bedroom with her and flipped on the TV. She lay in bed, watching the middle of an old movie, sipping the drink, and thinking how surprised and grateful Mr. Jessup would be that she had accomplished so much in his absence.

The Organizer's Wife

TONI CADE BAMBARA

The men from the co-op school were squatting in her
garden. Jake, who taught the day students and hassled the
town school board, was swiping at the bushy greens with his
cap, dislodging slugs, raising dust. The tall gent who ran the
graphics workshop was pulling a penknife open with his
teeth, scraping rust from the rake she hadn't touched in
weeks. Old Man Boone was up and down. Couldn't squat too
long on account of the ankle broken in last spring's demonstration when the tobacco weights showed funny. Jack-in-the-
box up, Boone snatched at a branch or two and stuffed his
pipe—crumblings of dry leaf, bits of twig. Down, he eased
string from the seams of his overalls, up again, thrumbling up
tobacco from the depths of his pockets.

She couldn't hear them. They were silent. The whole
morning stock-still, nothing stirring. The baby quiet too,
drowsing his head back in the crook of her arm as she stepped
out into the sun already up and blistering. The men began to
unbend, shifting weight to one leg then the other, watching
her move about the jumbled yard. But no one spoke.

She bathed the baby with the little dew that had gathered
on what few leaves were left on the branches crackling,
shredding into the empty rain barrels. The baby gurgled,
pinching her arms. Virginia had no energy for a smile or a

228

wince. All energy summoned up at rising was focused tightly on her two errands of the day. She took her time going back in, seeing the men shift around in the heaps of tomatoes, in the snarl of the strawberry runners. Stamped her shoe against each step, carrying the baby back in. Still no one spoke, though clearly, farmers all their lives, they surely had some one thing to say about the disarray of her garden.

The young one, whose voice she well knew from the sound truck, had his mouth open and his arm outstretched as though to speak on the good sense of turning every inch of ground to food, or maybe to rant against the crime of letting it just go. He bent and fingered the brown of the poke salad that bordered the dry cabbages, his mouth closing again. Jake rose suddenly and cleared his throat, but turned away to light Old Man Boone's pipe, lending a shoulder for the old one to hunch against, cupping the bowl and holding the match, taking a long lingering time, his back to her. She sucked her teeth and went in.

When she came out again, banding the baby's carry straps around her waist, she moved quickly, stepping into the radishes, crushing unidentifiable shoots underfoot. Jake stepped back out of the way and caught his cuffs in the rake. Jake was the first in a long line to lose his land to unpaid taxes. The bogus receipts were pinned prominently as always to his jacket pocket. Signed by someone the county said did not exist, but who'd managed nonetheless to buy up Jake's farm at auction and turn it over swiftly to the granite company. She looked from the huge safety pin to the hot, brown eyes that quickly dropped. The other men rose up around her, none taller than she, though all taller than the corn bent now, grit-laden with neglect. Out of the corner of her eye, she saw a white worm work its way into the once-silky tufts turned straw, then disappear.

"Mornin," she said, stretching out her hand.

The men mumbled quickly, clearing their throats again. Boone offering a hand in greeting, then realizing she was extending not her hand but the small, round tobacco tin in it. Graham's red tobacco tin with the boy in shiny green astride an iron horse. It was Graham's habit, when offering a smoke, to spin some tale or other about the boy on the indestructible horse, a tale the smoker would finish. The point always the same—the courage of the youth, the hope of the future. Boone drew his hand back quickly as though the red tin was aflame. She curled her hand closed and went out the gate, slowly, deliberately, fixing her tall, heavy image indelibly on their eyes.

"Good-for-nuthin."

They thought that's what they heard drift back over her shoulder. Them? The tin? The young one thought he saw her pitch it into the clump of tomatoes hanging on by the gate. But no one posed the question.

"Why didn't you say somethin?" Jake demanded of his star pupil, the orator, whose poems and tales and speeches delivered from the sound truck had done more to pull the districts together, the women all said, than all the leaflets the kids cluttered the fields with, than all the posters from the co-op's graphic workshop masking the road signs, than all the meetings which not all the folk could get to.

"Why didn't you speak?" Jake shoved the young one, and for a minute they were all stumbling, dancing nimbly to avoid destroying food that could still be salvaged.

"Watch it, watch it now," Old Boone saying, checking his foot brace and grabbing the young one up, a fistful of sleeve.

"You shoulda said somethin," the tall gent spat.

"Why me?" The young one whined—not in the voice he'd cultivated for the sound truck. "I don't know her no better than yawl do."

"One of the women shoulda come," said the tall gent.

The men looked at each other, then stared down the road. It was clear that no one knew any more how to talk to the bristling girl-woman, if ever any had.

It wasn't a shift in breeze that made the women look up, faces stuck out as if to catch the rain. 'Cause there was no breeze and there'd been no rain. And look like, one of them said, there'd be no bus either. The strained necks had more to do with sound than weather. Someone coming. A quick check said all who worked in town were already gathered at the bus stop. Someone coming could only mean trouble—fire broke out somewhere, riot in town, one of the children hurt, market closed down, or maybe another farm posted. The women standing over their vegetable baskets huddled together for conference, then broke apart to jut their bodies out over the road for a look-see. The women seated atop the bags of rags or uniforms, clustered to question each other, then scattered, some standing tiptoe, others merely leaning up from the rocks to question the market women. And in that brief second, as bodies pulled upward, the rocks blotted up more sun to sear them, sting them, sicken them with. These stones, stacked generations ago to keep the rain from washing the road away, banked higher and broader by the young folk now to keep the baking earth from breaking apart.

Virginia nodded to the women, her earrings tinkling against her neck. The "Mornins" and "How do's" came scraggly across the distance. The bus-stop plot was like an island separated from the mainland road by shimmering sheets of heat, by arid moats and gullies that had once been the drainage system, dried-out craters now misshapen, as though pitted and gouged by war.

One clear voice rising above the scattered sopranos, calling her by name, slowed Virginia down. Frankie Lee Taylor, the lead alto in the choir, was standing on the rocks waving, out of her choir robes and barely recognizable but for that red-and-yellow jumper, the obligatory ugly dress just right for the kitchens in town. "Everything all right?" the woman asked for everyone there. And not waiting for a word once Virginia's face could be read by all, she continued: "Bus comin at all, ever?"

Virginia shrugged and picked up her pace. If the six-thirty bus was this late coming, she thought, she could make the first call and be back on the road in time for the next bus to town. She wouldn't have to borrow the church station wagon after all. She didn't want to have to ask for nothing. When she saw Graham that afternoon she wanted the thing stitched

up, trimmed, neat, finished. Wanted to be able to say she
asked for "nuthin from nobody and didn't nobody offer up
nuthin." It'd be over with. They'd set bail and she'd pay it
with the money withheld from the seed and the fertilizer, the
wages not paid to the two students who used to help in the
garden, the money saved 'cause she was too cranky to eat, to
care. Pay the bail and unhook them both from this place. Let
some other damn fool break his health on this place, the
troubles.

She'd been leaving since the first day coming, the day her
sister came home to cough herself to death and leave her
there with nobody to look out for her 'cept some hinkty
cousins in town and Miz Mama Mae, who shook her head
sadly whenever the girl spoke of this place and these troubles
and these people and one day soon leaving for some other
place. She'd be going now for sure. Virginia was smiling
now and covering a whole lotta ground.

Someone was coming up behind her, churning up the loose
layers of clay, the red-and-yellow jumper a mere blur in the
haze of red dust. Everyone these dry, hot days looked like
they'd been bashed with a giant powder puff of henna. Virginia examined her own hands, pottery-red like the hands of
her cousins seen through the beauty-parlor windows in town,
hands sunk deep in the pots, working up the mud packs for
the white women lounging in the chairs. She looked at her
arms, her clothes, and slowed down. Not even well into the
morning and already her skimpy bath ruined. The lime-boiled
blouse no longer white but pink.

"Here, Gin," the woman was saying. "He a good man,
your man. He share our hardships, we bear his troubles, our
troubles." She was stuffing money in between the carry
straps, patting the chubby legs as the baby lolled in his cloth
carriage. "You tell Graham we don't forget that he came
back. Lots of the others didn't, forgot. You know, Gin, that
you and me and the rest of the women . . ." She was going
to say more but didn't. Was turning with her mouth still
open, already trotting up the road, puffs of red swirling about

her feet and legs, dusting a line in that red-and-yellow jumper the way Miz Mama Mae might do making hems in the shop.

Virginia hoisted the baby higher on her back and rewound the straps, clutching the money tight, flat in her fist. She thought about Miz Mama Mae, pins in her mouth, fussing at her. "What's them hanky-type hems you doin, Gin?" she'd say, leaning over her apprentice. "When ya sew for the white folks you roll them kinda stingy hems. And you use this here oldish thread to insure a quick inheritance. But when you sew for us folks, them things got to last season in and season out and many a go-round exchange. Make some hefty hems, girl, hefty."

And Virginia had come to measure her imprisonment by how many times that same red-and-yellow jumper met her on the road, faded and fading some more, but the fairly bright hem getting wider and wider, the telltale rim recording the seasons past, the owners grown. While she herself kept busting out of her clothes, straining against the good thread, outdistancing the hefty hems. Growing so fast from babe to child to girl to someone, folks were always introducing and reintroducing themselves to her. It seemed at times that the walls wouldn't contain her, the roof wouldn't stop her. Busting out of childhood, busting out her clothes, but never busting out the place.

And now the choir woman had given her the money like that and spoken, trying to attach her all over again, root her, ground her in the place. Just when there was a chance to get free. Virginia clamped her jaws tight and tried to go blank. Tried to blot out all feelings and things—the farms, the co-op sheds, the lone gas pump, a shoe left in the road, the posters promising victory over the troubles. She never wanted these pictures called up on some future hot, dry day in some other place. She squinted, closed her eyes even, 'less the pictures cling to her eyes, store in the brain, to roll out later and crush her future with the weight of this place and its troubles.

Years before when there'd been rain and ways to hold it, she'd trotted along this road not seeing too much, trotting

and daydreaming, delivering parcels to and from Miz Mama
Mae's shop. She could remember that one time, ducking and
dodging the clods of earth chucked up by the horse's hooves.
Clods spinning wet and heavy against her skirts, her legs, as
she followed behind, seeing nothing outside her own pictures
but that horse and rider. Trying to keep up, keep hold of the
parcel slipping all out of shape in the drizzle, trying to piece
together the things she would say to him when he finally
turned round and saw her. She had lived the scene often
enough in bed to know she'd have to speak, say something to
make him hoist her up behind him in the saddle, to make him
gallop her off to the new place. She so busy dreaming, she let
the curve of the road swerve her off toward the edge. Mouth-
ing the things to say and even talking out loud with her hands
and almost losing the slippery bundle, not paying good enough
attention. And a ball of earth shot up and hit her square in the
chest and sent her stumbling over the edge into the gully. The
choir organist's robe asprawl in the current that flushed the
garbage down from the hill where the townies lived, to the
bottom where the folks lived, to the pit where the co-op
brigade made compost heaps for independence, laughing.

Graham had pulled her up and out by the wrists, pulled her
against him and looked right at her. Not at the cabbage leaves
or chicory on her arms, a mango sucked hairy to its pit
clinging to her clothes. But looked at her. And no screen door
between them now. No glass or curtain, or shrub peeked
through.

"You followin me." He grinned. And she felt herself
swimming through the gap in his teeth.

And now she would have to tell him. 'Cause she had lost
three times to the coin flipped on yesterday morning. Had lost
to the icepick pitched in the afternoon in the dare-I-don't-I
boxes her toe had sketched in the yard. Had lost at supper to
the shadow slanting across the tablecloth that reached her
wrist before Miz Mama Mae finished off the corn relish. Had
lost that dawn to the lazy lizard, suddenly quickened in his
journey on the ceiling when the sun came up. Lost against
doing what she'd struggled against doing in order to win one

more day of girlhood before she jumped into her womanstride
and stalked out on the world. I want to come to you. I want
to come to you and be with you. I want to be your woman,
she did not say after all.

"I want to come to the co-op school," she said. "I want to
learn to read better and type and figure and keep accounts so I
can get out of , . ."—this place, she didn't say—"my
situation."

He kept holding her and she kept wanting and not wanting
to ease out of his grip and rescue the choir robe before it
washed away.

"I had five years schooling 'fore I came here," she said,
talking way too loud. "Been two years off and on at the
church school . . . before you came."

"You do most of Miz Mama Mae's cipherin I hear? Heard
you reading the newspapers to folks in the tobacco shed. You
read well."

She tried to pull away then, thinking he was calling her a
liar or poking fun some way. "Cipherin" wasn't how he
talked. But he didn't let go. She expected to see her skin
twisted and puckered when she looked at where he was
holding her. But his grip was soft. Still she could not step
back.

"You been watchin me," he said with the grin again. And
looking into his face, she realized he wasn't at all like she'd
thought. Was older, heavier, taller, smoother somehow. But
then looking close up was not like sneaking a look from the
toolshed as he'd come loping across the fields with his pi-
geon-toed self and in them soft leather boots she kept waiting
to see fall apart from rough wear till she finally decided he
must own pairs and pairs of all the same kind. Yes, she'd
watched him on his rounds, in and out of the houses, the
drying sheds, down at the docks, after fellowship in the
square. Talking, laughing, teaching, always moving. Had
watched him from the trees, through windows as he banged
tables, arguing about deeds, urging, coaxing, pleading, hol-
lering, apologizing, laughing again. In the early mornings,
before Miz Mama Mae called the girls to sew, she had

watched him chinning on the bar he'd slammed between the
portals of the co-op school door. Huffing, puffing, cheeks
like chipmunks. The dark circle of his gut sucking in purple,
panting out blue. Yes, she watched him. But she said none of
this or of the other either. Not then.

"I want to come to night school" was how she put it. "I
don't know yet what kinda work I can do for the co-op. But I
can learn."

"That's the most I ever heard you talk," he was saying,
laughing so hard, he loosened his grip. "In the whole three
years I've been back, that's the most—" He was laughing
again. And he was talking way too loud himself.

She hadn't felt the least bit foolish standing there in the
drizzle, in the garbage, tall up and full out of her clothes
nearly, and Graham laughing at her. Not the least bit foolish
'cause he was talking too loud and laughing too hard. And
she was going to go to his school. And whether he knew it or
not, he was going to take her away from this place.

Wasn't but a piece of room the school, with a shed tacked
on in back for storage and sudden meetings. The furniture
was bandaged but brightly painted. The chemistry equipment
was old but worked well enough. The best thing was the
posters. About the co-op, about Malcolm and Harriet and
Fannie Lou, about Guinea-Bissau and Vietnam. And the
posters done by the children, the pictures cut from magazines, the maps—all slapped up as though to hold the place
together, to give an identity to the building so squat upon the
land. The identity of the place for her was smells. The smell
of mortar vibrating from the walls that were only wood. The
smell of loam that curled up from the sink, mostly rusted
metal. The green-and-brown smell rising up over heads sunk
deep into palms as folks leaned over their papers, bearing
down on stumps of pencil or hunks of charcoal, determined to
get now and to be what they'd been taught was privilege
impossible, what they now knew was their right, their destiny.

"Season after season," Graham was dictating that first
night, leaning up against the maps with the ruler, "we have

pulled gardens out of stones, creating something from nothing—creators."

Sweat beading on a nose to her left, a temple to her right. Now and then a face she knew from fellowship looking up as Graham intoned the statements, tapping the ruler against the table to signal punctuation traps. And she working hard, harder than some, though she never ever did learn to speak her speak as most folks finally did. But grateful just to be there, and up in front, unlike the past when, condemned by her size, she'd been always exiled in the rear with the goldfish tanks or the rabbits that always died, giving her a suspect reputation.

"The first step toward getting the irrigation plant," he continued, crashing the ruler down, "is to organize."

"Amen," said one lady by the window, never looking up from her paper, certain she would finally train herself and be selected secretary of the church board. "That way us folks can keep track of them folks," was how she'd said it when she rose to speak her speak one summer night.

"What can defeat greed, technological superiority, and legal lawlessness," Graham had finished up, "is discipline, consciousness, and unity."

Always three sentences that folks would take home for discussion, for transformation into well-ordered paragraphs that wound up, some of them, in the co-op newsletter or on the posters or in the church's bulletin. Many became primers for the children.

Graham had been wearing the denim suit with the leather buckles the first night in class. Same fancy suit she'd caught sight of through the screen door when he'd come calling on Miz Mama Mae to buy the horse. A denim suit not country-cut at all—in fact, so *not* she was sure he would be leaving. Dudes in well-cut denim'd been coming and leaving since the days she wore but one yard of cloth. It was his would-be-moving-on clothes that had pulled her to him. But then the pull had become too strong to push against once his staying-on became clear.

*　　*　　*

She often fixed him supper in a metal cake tin once used for buttons. And Miz Mama Mae joked with the pin cushion, saying the girl weren't fooling nobody but herself sneaking around silly out there in the pantry with the button box. Telling the bobbins it was time certain folk grew up to match they size. And into the night, treadling away on the machine, the woman addressed the dress form, saying a strong, serious-type schoolteacher man had strong, serious work to do. Cutting out the paper patterns, the woman told the scissors that visiting a man in his rooms at night could mean disaster or jubilee one. And Virginia understood she would not be stopped by the woman. But some felt she was taking up too much of his time, their time. He was no longer where they could find him for homework checks or questions about the law. And Jake and Old Man Boone sullen, nervous that the midnight strategy meetings were too few now and far between. The women of the nearby district would knock and enter with trapped firefly lanterns, would shove these on the table between the couple, and make their point as Graham nodded and Virginia giggled or was silent, one.

His quilt, Graham explained, leaving the earrings on the table for her to find, was made from patches from his daddy's overalls, and scraps from Boone's wedding cutaway, white remnants from his mother's shroud, some blue from a sister's graduation, and khaki, too, snatched from the uniform he'd been proud of killing in in Korea a hundred lives ago. The day students had stitched a liberation flag in one corner. The night students had restuffed it and made a new border. She and Miz Mama Mae had stitched it and aired it. And Virginia had brought it back to him, wrapped in it. She had rolled herself all in it, to hide from him in her new earrings, childish. But he never teased that she was too big for games, and she liked that. He found her in it, his tongue finding the earrings first. Careful, girl, she'd warned herself. This could be a trap, she murmured under him.

"Be my woman," he whispered into her throat.

You don't have time for me, she didn't say, lifting his tikis and medallions up over his head. And there'd never be enough time here with so many people, so much land to work, so much to do, and the wells not even dug, she thought, draping the chains around his bedpost.

"Be my woman, Gin," he said again. And she buried her fingers in his hair and he buried his hair inside her clothes and she pulled the quilt close and closed him in, crying.

She was leaking. The earrings tinkling against her neck. The medallions clinking against the bedpost in her mind. Gray splotches stiffened in her new pink blouse, rubbing her nipples raw. But other than a dribble that oozed momentarily down her back, there was no sign of the baby aroused and hungry. If the baby slept on, she'd keep on. She wanted to reach Revun Michaels before the white men came. Came this time brazenly with the surveyors and the diggers, greedy for the granite under the earth. Wanted to catch Revun Michaels before he showed them his teeth and wouldn't hear her, couldn't, too much smiling. Wanted to hear him say it—the land's been sold. The largest passel of land in the district, the church holdings where the co-op school stood, where two storage sheds of the co-op stood, where the graphics workshop stood, where four families had lived for generations working the land. The church had sold the land. He'd say it, she'd hear it, and it'd be over with. She and Graham could go.

She was turning the bend now, forgetting to not look, and the mural the co-op had painted in eye-stinging colors stopped her. FACE UP TO WHAT'S KILLING YOU, it demanded. Below the statement a huge triangle that from a distance was just a triangle, but on approaching, as one muttered 'how deadly can a triangle be?' turned into bodies on bodies. At the top, fat, fanged beasts in smart clothes, like the ones beneath it laughing, drinking, eating, bombing, raping, shooting, lounging on the backs of, feeding off the backs of, the folks at the base, crushed almost flat but struggling to get up and getting up, topple the structure. She passed it quickly. All she wanted to think about was getting to Revun Michaels quick to hear it. Sold the land. Then she'd be free to string together the bits

and scraps of things for so long bobbing about in her head.
Things that had to be pieced together well, with strong thread
so she'd have a whole thing to shove through the mesh at
Graham that afternoon.

And would have to shove hard or he'd want to stay,
convinced that folks would battle for his release, would battle
for themselves, the children, the future, would keep on no
matter how powerful the thief, no matter how little the rain,
how exhausted the soil, 'cause this was home. Not a plot of
earth for digging in or weeping over or crawling into, but
home. Near the Ethiopic where the ancestral bones spoke
their speak on certain nights if folks stamped hard enough,
sang long enough, shouted. Home. Where "America" was
sung but meant something altogether else than it had at the
old school. Home in the future. The future here now developing. Home liberated soon. And the earth would recover. The
rain would come. The ancient wisdoms would be revived.
The energy released. Home a human place once more. The
bones spoke it. The spirit spoke, too, through flesh when the
women gathered at the altar, the ancient orishas still vibrant
beneath the ghostly patinas some thought right to pray to,
but connected in spite of themselves to the spirits under the
plaster.

WE CANNOT LOSE, the wall outside the church said. She
paused at the bulletin board, the call-for-meetings flyers limp
in the heat. She bent to spit but couldn't raise it. She saw
Revun Michaels in the schoolhouse window watching her.
He'd say it. Sold the land.

Virginia wondered what the men in her ruined garden were
telling themselves now about land as power and land and man
tied to the future, not the past. And what would they tell the
women when the bulldozers came to claim the earth, to maim
it, rape it, plunder it all with that bone-deep hatred for all
things natural? And what would the women tell the children
dangling in the tires waiting for Jake to ring the bell? Shouting from the clubhouses built in the trees? The slashed trees
oozing out money into the white man's pails, squeezing hard
to prolong a tree life, forestalling the brutal cut down to

stump. Then stump wasting, no more money to give, blown up out of the earth, the iron claw digging deep and merciless to rip out the taproots, leaving for the children their legacy, an open grave, gouged out by a gene-deep hatred for all things natural, for all things natural that couldn't turn a quick penny quick enough to dollar. She spit.

Revun Michaels, small and balding, was visible in the schoolhouse window. His expression carried clear out the window to her, watching her coming fast, kicking himself for getting caught in there and only one door, now that the shed was nailed on fast in back.

"Did you sell the land as well?" she heard herself saying, rushing in the doorway much too fast. "You might have waited like folks asked you. You didn't have to. Enough granite under this schoolhouse alone"—she stamped, frightening him—"to carry both the districts for years and years, if we developed it ourselves." She heard the "we ourselves" explode against her teeth and she fell back.

"Wasn't me," he stammered. "The church board saw fit to—"

"Fit!" She was advancing now, propelled by something she had not time to understand. "Wasn't nuthin fitten about it." She had snatched the ruler from its hook. The first slam hard against the chair he swerved around, fleeing. The next cracked hard against his teeth. His legs buckled under and he slid down, his face frozen in disbelief. But nothing like the disbelief that swept through her the moment "we ourselves" pushed past clenched teeth and nailed her to the place, a woman unknown. She saw the scene detached, poster figures animated: a hefty woman pursuing a scrambling man in and out among the tables and chairs in frantic games before Jake rang the bell for lessons to commence.

"And what did the white folks pay you to turn Graham in and clear the way? Disturber of the peace. What peace? Racist trying to incite a riot. Ain't that how they said it? Outside agitator, as you said. And his roots put down here long before you ever came. When you were just a twinkle in Darwin's eye." Virginia heard herself laughing. It was a

good, throaty laugh and big. The man was turning round now
on the floor, staring at her in amazement.

"Thirty pieces of silver, maybe? That's what you preach,
tradition. Thirty pieces 'bout as traditional as—"

"Just hold on. It wasn't me that— The board of trustees
advised me that this property could not be used for—"

The ruler came down on the stiff of his arm and broke.
Michaels dropped between two rickety chairs that came apart
on top of him. The baby cried, the woman shushed, as much
to quiet the woman that was her. Calm now, she watched the
man try to get up, groping the chairs the folks had put
together from cast-offs for the school. Her shoe caught him at
the side of his head and he went under.

The station wagon was pulling up as she was coming out,
flinging the piece of ruler into the bushes. She realized then
that the men had come in it, that the station wagon had been
sitting all morning in her garden. That they had come to take
her to see Graham. She bit her lip. She never gave folk a
chance, just like Miz Mama Mae always fussed. Never gave
them or herself a chance to speak the speak.

"We'll take you to him," Jake was saying, holding the
door open and easing the baby off her back.

The young one shoved over. "Mother Lee who's secretary-
ing for the board has held up the papers for the sale. We
came to tell you that." He waited till she smiled to laugh.
"We're the delegation that's going to confront the board this
evening. Us and Frankie Lee Taylor and—"

"Don't talk the woman to death," said Boone, turning in
his seat and noting her daze. He was going to say more, but
the motor drowned him out. Virginia hugged the baby close
and unbuttoned her blouse.

"That's one sorry piece of man," drawled Boone as they
pulled out. All heads swung to the right to see the short, fat,
balding preacher darting in and out among the gravestones for
the sanctuary of the church. To the phone, Virginia figured.
And would they jail her too, she and the baby?

Then everyone was silent before the naked breast and the

sucking. Silence was what she needed. And time, to draw together tight what she'd say to Graham. How blood had spurted from Revun Michaels's ear, for one thing. Graham might not want to hear it, but there was no one else to tell it to, to explain how it was when all she thought she wanted was to hear it said flat out—land's been sold, school's no more. Not that a school's a building, she argued with herself, watching the baby, playing with the image of herself speaking her speak finally in the classroom, then realizing that she already had. By tomorrow the women would have burrowed beneath the tale of some swinging door or however Revun Michaels would choose to tell it. But would the women be able to probe and sift and explain it to her? Who could explain her to her?

And how to explain to Graham so many things. About this new growth she was experiencing, was thinking on at night wrapped in his quilt. Not like the dread growing up out of her clothes as though she'd never stop 'fore she be freak, 'cause she had stopped. And not like the new growth that was the baby, for she'd expected that, had been prepared. More like the toenail smashed the day the work brigade had stacked the stones to keep the road from splitting apart. The way the new nail pushed up against the old turning blue, against the gauze and the tape, stubborn to establish itself. A chick pecking through the shell, hard-headed and hasty and wobbly. She might talk of it this time. She was convinced she could get hold of it this time.

She recalled that last visiting time trying to speak on what was happening to her coming through the shell. But had trouble stringing her feelings about so many things together, words to drape around him, to smother all those other things, things she had said, hurled unstrung, flung out with tantrum heat at a time when she thought there would always be time enough to coolly take them back, be woman warm in some elsewhere place and make those hurtful words forgettable. But then they had come for him in the afternoon, came and got him, took him from the schoolhouse in handcuffs. And when she had visited him in the jail, leaning into the mesh, trying to push past the barrier, she could tell the way the guards hovered around her and baby that clearly they thought she could do, would do, what they had obviously tried over and over to do, till Graham was ashy and slow, his grin lax. That she could break him open so they could break him down. She almost had, not knowing it, leaking from the breast as she always did not keeping track of the time. Stuttering, whining, babbling, hanging on to the mesh with one hand, the other stuffed in her mouth, her fingers ensnarled in the skein of words coming out all tangled, knotted.

"I don't mind this so much," he'd cut in. "Time to think."

And when she pulled her fingers from her mouth, the thread broke and all her words came bouncing out in a hopeless scatter of tears and wails until something—her impatience with her own childishness, or maybe it was the obvious pleasure of the guards—made her grab herself up. She grabbed herself up abrupt, feeling in that moment what it was she wanted to say about her nights wrapped up in the quilt smelling him in it, hugging herself, grabbing herself up and trying to get to that place that was beginning to seem more of a when than a where. And the when seemed to be inside her if she could only connect.

"I kinda like the quiet," he had said. "Been a while since I've had so much time to think." And then he grinned and was ugly. Was that supposed to make her hate him? To hate and let go? That had occurred to her on the bus home. But roaming around the house, tripping on the edges of the quilt, she had rejected it. That was not the meaning of his words or that smile that had torn his face. She'd slumped in the rocking chair feeding the baby, examining her toenail for such a time.

"They never intended to dig the wells, that's clear," Old Man Boone was saying. "That was just to get into the district, get into our business, check out our strength. I was a fool," he muttered, banging his pipe against his leg remembering his hopefulness, his hospitality even. "A fool."

"Well, gaddamn, Boone," the tall gent sputtered. "Can't you read? That's what our flyers been saying all along. Don't you read the stuff we put out? Gaddamnit, Boone."

"If you don't read the flyers, you leastways knows history," the young one was saying. "When we ever invited the beast to dinner he didn't come in and swipe the napkins and start taking notes on the tablecloth 'bout how to take over the whole house?"

"Now that's the truth," Jake said, laughing. His laughter pulled Virginia forward, and she touched his arm, moved. That he could laugh. His farm stolen and he could laugh. But that was one of the three most moving things about Jake, she was thinking. The way he laughed. The way he sweated. The way he made his body comfy for the children to lean against.

"Yeh, they sat right down to table and stole the chicken," said Jake.

"And took the table. And the deed." The tall gent smacked Jake on his cap.

"Yeh," Old Man Boone muttered, thinking of Graham.

"We ain't nowhere's licked yet though, huhn?"

The men looked quickly at Virginia, Jake turning clear around, so that Boone leaned over to catch the steering wheel.

"Watch it, watch it now, young feller."

"There's still Mama Mae's farm," Virginia continued, patting the baby. "Enough granite under there even if the church do— "

"But they ain't," said the young one. "Listen, we got it all figured out. We're going to bypass the robbers and deal directly with the tenant councils in the cities, and we're—"

"Don't talk the woman to death," soothed Boone. "You just tell Graham his landlady up there in the North won't have to eat dog food no more. No more in life. New day coming."

"And you tell him . . ."—Jake was turning around again— "just tell him to take his care."

By the time the bolt had lifted and she was standing by the chair, the baby fed and alert now in her arms, she had done with all the threads and bits and shards of the morning. She knew exactly what to tell him, coming through the steel door now, reaching for the baby he had not held yet, could not hold now, screened off from his father. All she wished to tell him was the bail'd been paid, her strength was back, and she sure as hell was going to keep up the garden. How else to feed the people?

Travelling

MARY PETERSON

In April when she drove away he looked at his hands. They were oily from the boat's engine, from the garage. But what a thing to notice. He turned and saw the children, who were watching from the steps, and wondered what she had given him now.

The day before she left they discovered something wrong with the Volkswagen. He swore it was running on only three cylinders, but she refused to take it to the shop. "It runs," she said. "That's all."

"But it won't get you there."

"It will."

Yet when she started it, the engine coughed and died. Warmed up, it raced too fast and he could hear her coming home a half mile down the road, sounding crazy, like a car without a muffler, a car with a problem. He didn't want her to leave that way. He wanted to trust the machine. That was the reason he did the premature tune-up and the oil change himself. And, too, it was the reason he urged a sleeping bag on her, in the trunk, although nights were warm. He wanted her to be safe.

When she had first brought up a trip alone he sensed she'd been thinking about it a long time and waited for the right moment. The time when she would tell, and not ask. In the last year he'd learned to expect statements from her rather than questions. Now she usually asserted what she would do. It was left for him to complain or to let it be.

And usually he said nothing.

In the thirteen years of their marriage they had hardly argued. When they did it was startling and important, reminding him of the time in Rockport when they were first engaged. He was captain and she was crew in the interclub races. She knew what the boat was for him. Respected it, too. It put an edge on him to prepare for a race. The night before one, he never slept. Yet, even knowing, she had risen up in the boat like a witch or an apparition when he ordered her to tack. Had risen up and said, "You won't use that voice with me! Sail the damned thing yourself!"

They were heading out and surrounded with sailboats, and the whole harbor heard. The whole harbor watched.

"What do you mean?" he shouted. "Ready about!"

"The hell!" she screamed.

They had fallen upon each other in the cockpit right there, in the middle of the race, rolling and grappling like scrappy dogs while the boats sailed on past them. He was a mild man. He couldn't believe this had happened. She was all fire but he couldn't believe it happened.

Afterward he told her what she already knew: the town of Rockport wondered what he was doing with this girl.

But she loved him and she would marry him on the condition that they leave Rockport. It wasn't the race. Only that as long as he was bound by his family and the town, he could be no husband to her. Did he care that much?

When they married and left, people said he was making a great mistake.

If loving her was a mistake it was one he wanted to make. They moved to Maine where he worked as a county psychologist. The first years were hard and slow, and she was restless. But the children transformed her. She had an instinct for being a mother, responding to the world as half a child herself. He watched her feeling he was attending a great mystery.

And they didn't stop being lovers. She was small and alert; he was reed-tall and gentle. He made love to her carefully in the beginning, teaching her as he himself had been taught by a woman while he was still young. She was as ardent as he had been.

So they had grown together, but apart too. He sensed in her, always had, an urgency that the marriage did not address. Or a need. He told himself her childhood did it. She was her father's daughter, and the man had raised her to be wild and intense and loving and desperate. Her nature was like a continual accident. She seemed as surprised by herself as he was. But she told him she couldn't be other than she was.

When she first said she was going to Nova Scotia alone, he didn't know how to answer. Rushing ahead of him, she said how at nineteen she'd planned to go to Alaska with some college kids. Alaska seemed a great adventure. To go so far, she said, was like running out to the end of something and teetering, balancing, looking dead-on into mystery. Her mother had opposed the trip, but the arguments did no good. Finally she told her daughter she thought the group leaders were lesbians and it wouldn't be safe, travelling with them.

She had not gone.

But the idea rankled in her, oppressed her, all these years afterward. She said her instincts were to go; said that to argue it her mother had craftily run instinct backwards into fear. And it worked. But left her feeling fundamentally failed. Something, she said, was stolen from her then. She couldn't name it. She wanted it back.

"It's because I have to do it," she said, turning that familiar look on him, her eyes so utterly blue they reminded him of the hearts of glaciers.

"Yes," he said. Just the word.

Leaning over the fireplace she talked until he better understood, or thought he did. When she went down the long driveway, the Volkswagen engine racing and exploding, one arm out the window waving goodbye, he understood less.

"I'm getting to know the kids better," he said when she phoned on the third night.

"Daddy plays ball with us," Paul said. "And he's good, Mom."

"He makes hamburgers better than McDonald's," Elisabeth said, pride in her voice.

"We miss you," he said, taking the phone again. He held it balanced against his ear, looked at the kitchen mess, cat food smeared on the floor.

"I miss you too, darling."

She said she was staying at a wonderful hotel directly on the ocean, and she would probably spend the whole remaining time there. Said she was fighting the impulse to go antiquing. That she had found a painter who did wonderful risky things with color and shape, and if his smaller pieces weren't too costly she'd bring one home. "Imagine a royal blue sky!" she told him. "The color of Elisabeth's jumper! Can you see it?"

During the day he went to work and the clinic felt the same as it had. His patients—but he preferred to call them clients—were unchanged by the change in his immediate life, and he listened to them closely, sorted their confessions and fears as if he were studying a very precious object. But what he wanted to read in them was the form of his own life.

At night when he came home the children were there and waiting. He announced the meals would be community business and they would all take a hand at cooking. Elisabeth made a banana cake with food-color blue frosting. Paul made hot dogs, carried them proudly into the dining room. Some nights they all cleaned up together. Other times, dishes from two days stood in the sink. It was not that unusual—she didn't do dishes faithfully either. When she cleaned, it was always with a violent activity that left nothing motionless: chairs, books, lamps, his mother's bone china. Elisabeth and Paul instructed him in their mother's routines and he tried to follow them, or adapt them for himself.

And he saw how generous his children were. Wondered what part of it was his own doing, what part hers. In their conversations over dinner he asked them questions which they answered more honestly than he would have thought possible. They were original, these children. At nine and ten they had an essential goodness about them. And they were fair. Old enough that perhaps they would carry these qualities into adulthood. He felt a pride that was embarrassing, even uncomfortable.

She sent post cards in the mail: "Dear Everybody. I love you and miss you all. The weather is perfect. When I eat alone I think of you hard. That's the worst time."

He never doubted, even for a single moment, that he wanted her to return to him.

When she was back, she did not seem much changed. For a few days she talked eagerly about things she'd seen, the thrill and fear of being alone in a strange place. But matters of the children, of the house, pressed them both into familiar patterns. Before long he expected dinner at night again, drinks before it. Paul and Elisabeth stopped asking him to play softball with them.

He felt a warmth with the children that wasn't there before, as if they shared a secret. But he reminded himself the secret was only their privacy and the small things they'd learned while she was gone.

They discovered they were lovers still, as if they had doubted it. He learned again the good security of being in bed with her. The third night she was home, when they lay in the dark looking at the window, he searched for a way to tell her. She was warm against him.

"There was a man in Nova Scotia," her voice came from the silence.

He waited, listening.

"He bought me dinner, and a drink. Took out all the pictures of his wife and kids. Even one of the family Doberman, for Christ's sake." She sat up and turned to face him in the dark, intent, like a Buddha. He couldn't see her face.

"I thought, why is he paying attention to me?" Then she laughed girlishly. "Then I knew why it was."

His question was in his silence.

"I told him I was tired." She leaned forward in the dark and he imagined her face, what it had. What did a face hold? Only more information, to help along a conclusion. Still the reality was that when they were apart, they were separate beings.

"He tried to convince me for another drink," she said. "I was flattered. He wanted me to stay with him."

He cleared his throat, thick from so much silence. "You're an attractive woman . . ."

"Middle-aged," she said. "They don't treat you that way anymore, at my age."

He realized he hadn't expected this, or feared it either. "I'll never know what happened to you, really," he said, as much to himself as to her.

"But nothing," she said too soon. "Really, just nothing."

It seemed to him they didn't spend enough time together. When he came home from work and they sat with gin and tonics, their conversation was good, encouraging, but not . . . he wasn't sure. Only that when she described her talks with Barbara, with Amy, they sounded more interesting. There was an energy that he seemed to miss, keep missing. As though she had things for these women she didn't have for him.

It came down to the boat, finally. Last summer they had bought a twenty-six-foot sloop with savings—it was that or work on the house. Now, their second summer, he was eager for them to be a family on the boat. The children were no problem. Elisabeth was a good sailor, a natural. Paul, though he was often sick on board, refused to leave even during the worst times.

It was different with her. She loved the boat, she said, but not as he did. Said she would cruise with the family but not just go out and sail in the harbor as he liked to do. That was dull. She had other things. He didn't need her company always. Couldn't he understand?

No, he could not understand. Beyond that, she should know. She'd seen him fool with the engine all winter. Seen him drive to the marina when the boat was in dry dock, just to look at it.

She said she understood he needed to unwind. He needed these weekends. But she needed her time too, and when he took the children to the boat she had her chance for privacy, for quiet . . . They were good enough words, and he thought he believed them. Their force carried him all the way to the harbor. Yet when he rowed out and climbed on board, prepared to get underway, he felt only that she belonged there with him.

So he argued. First he said he missed her. Then, when she wouldn't hear this, he said the other men with boats wondered about them. Other wives sailed. "People will think something's off in our marriage," he said. He was unable to keep the accusation from his voice.

"People will think!" she exploded. "Damn them, let them think what they want!"

"What do you have that's so important," he asked her.

The look on her face was like the one before she'd announced her trip alone. As though if he didn't understand, he should not ask. As if asking was the worst insult.

But he wanted to know.

If they were a family, if she was his partner, he reasoned, then they should be together on the boat. She had her days alone.

But those were for children and housework. It was the other time, private time, that she needed. She reminded him that the boat made her seasick.

He reminded her that she behaved like a perfect fool on board, eating sardines and corn chips and drinking beer; taking Dramamine that only made her dizzy. "It's in your head," he said. "Psychosomatic."

The arguments silenced her to a point where she went grudgingly to the boat sometimes, whole-heartedly others. Still she accused him of an internal logic that tangled himself with the boat, her love of him with sailing. It wasn't so. She could separate these things, and God knew she wanted to.

Couldn't he see she needed time for herself, after the pressures of family, of the town?

He caught himself wondering if there was another man. Stopped himself from wondering it.

In August they had planned a whole weekend on board, but she refused to go.

"This can't be," she said, pacing the length of the front windows. She stopped and looked out at the pine woods. "I'm lying to myself. To you. Sometimes I like sailing, but not so often as you. You can't force me to."

He looked at her standing there, her arms folded.

"The boat's become an issue," she said.

"Anything would be."

"But this is the one for us."

"I don't understand," he said.

She said she didn't expect understanding, but only tolerance. She wouldn't be pressured any more—"bullied," she called it. She accused him of failure of imagination. How could he want her on board, when she hated it?

"You won't give it a chance," he said.

"Damn it, what have I been doing all summer?"

When she left he sat in his brown leather chair and the house, his own house, felt like a stranger's. He was as uncomfortable there as an intruder. He reasoned with himself that their problem was an inability to live with differences. She was right, he couldn't understand her distaste for sailing. But he was right, too, in wanting to share what he loved most, with her.

He found her in bed, lying face down. It hurt him to see her bent, tense shoulders. He felt the loneliness and distance coiled in himself around the hollow it was making, had made. He didn't like feeling this way. "I'm going to the boat," he said.

She murmured something into the pillow.

He crossed the room and got his jacket, came back and sat on the edge of the bed to change his shoes. "I'll spend the night there."

"All right," came her voice from the pillow.

"It's not an argument," he said.

"I know."

"Just . . . something."

She didn't sit up. He stood, and with the jacket over his arm, bent and kissed her hair. He wanted to say more, but he was afraid of the words. They might become something he didn't mean.

It was a clear night, and the air was soft. He drove with the window rolled all the way down, feeling the air on his face. The moon was almost full and there were thin clouds around it. On the River Bridge he could see the harbor lights, and the stars as well. There was smoke coming from the factory.

What do I feel? he wondered, checking himself for feeling.

Down Kittery Point Road toward the harbor, he drove slowly looking at the houses with their lights and their dark lawns.

There were no other cars in the rental lot. As he walked along the dock with the oars on his shoulder, he listened to the bell buoy ringing out in the harbor. Water slapped on the dinghies and bumped them against one another. Their boat was moored quite far out, but he could see its beamy shape from where he stood.

The water was calm, and in the quiet, feeling the tug of the oars against the tide, he felt himself almost to be a trespasser. Still the secret feeling was a good one. Even in the dark, this was a world he knew.

Their boat rocked in the night like a seed pod, moonlight on her decks. When he crawled on board and tied up the dinghy, he felt something hard and tense let go inside him. The boat was an island and he was safe on it. He knew everything, here. If anyone came, he would hear the creak and groan of their oars in the locks. Even she would have to come that way.

As he unlocked the cabin, pulling the boards from its opening, he thought how privacy was what he'd wanted. He wondered if she understood that. Not to get away from her, or from the children either. Just to go to what he knew. The

boat was the best place. All the work of painting and repairing, he had done himself. The damned winches had had to be
ordered from England since the boat was English in design—
made for the Channel—and he'd done that too. He smiled.
He had done all that.

He sat and lit a cigarette, wondering what she thought
now. Imagining her, he found in himself a smugness that was
surprising. He had been thinking: now you will understand
how it felt, to stand on the lawn and watch you drive off to
Nova Scotia. To leave us. He had been thinking it all the way
to the harbor, his arm out the window. That she was getting
hers, now.

That was detestable. It said things he didn't want. Said
how much he was hurt by her travelling without him. More
than that, how resentful. But the worst thing it said, was that
he wanted to punish her. He hadn't known that, didn't want
to know it now.

He felt the boat rocking. Usually the harbor sounds relaxed
him. All the noises of water, metal, and wood. And over his
shoulder, the rotating beam of the Coast Guard Lighthouse.
He liked all of it. But like wasn't enough. Loved it, by God.
It was home to him. And she didn't love it.

The resentment was gone, not because he'd wished it but
only because it was worn away. That was a small part
anyhow, not substantially true of his feeling for her.

He wondered what was true, then. The emptiness he had
felt when he looked at her lying on the bed? Yes. The
hollowness? That too. Not only true, but growing in the last
year. She was changing. More of her was secret to him than
had ever been. Her fire had always been a mystery, but a
wonderful one. And now there was this . . .

So a man had to wonder what to do. He thought of the
children. In the last year he'd loved them not less, but more.

He tossed the cigarette into the water. It made a curve of
red light, then it was gone.

Do I want a woman? he asked himself. But he knew the
answer. They were different, she and he, but he loved her.
Perhaps even more for the way she pointed up their differences.

He thought that maybe for him it was this night alone on the boat, just as for her it was that time in Nova Scotia. Well, if that was so, she had courage then. He had to admire her courage. What else could it be, to risk him and the children, to drive off alone such as no woman her age ever did, certainly nobody in town? The risks of middle age were less dramatic, but then the stakes were higher. He was alone, now. Still, he thought, in going to what we love, we don't deny anything. When he looked, the boat had shifted in the tide so that the main mast seemed about to pierce the moon.

Something That Happened

JAYNE ANNE PHILLIPS

I am in the basement sorting clothes, whites with whites, colors with colors, delicates with delicates—it's a segregated world—when my youngest child yells down the steps. She yells when I'm in the basement, always, angrily, as if I've slipped below the surface and though she's twenty-one years old she can't believe it.

"Do you know what day it is? I mean do you KNOW what day it is, Kay?" It's this new thing of calling me by my first name. She stands groggy eyed, surveying her mother.

I say, "No, Angela, so what does that make me?" Now my daughter shifts into second, narrows those baby blues I once surveyed in such wonder and prayed *Lord, lord, This is the last*.

"Well never mind," she says. "I've made you breakfast." And she had, eggs and toast and juice and flowers on the porch. Then she sat and watched me eat it, twirling her fine gold hair.

Halfway through the eggs it dawns on me, my ex–wedding anniversary. Angela, under the eye-liner and blue jeans you're a haunted and ancient presence. When most children can't remember an anniversary, Angela can't forget it. Every year for five years she has pushed me to the brink of remembrance.

"The trouble with you," she finally speaks, "is that you

don't care enough about yourself to remember what's been important in your life.''

"Angela," I say, "in the first place I haven't been married for five years, so I no longer have a wedding anniversary to remember."

"That doesn't matter" [twirling her hair, not scowling]. "It's still something that happened."

Two years ago I had part of an ulcerated stomach removed and I said to the kids, "Look, I can't worry for you anymore. If you get into trouble, don't call me. If you want someone to take care of you, take care of each other." So the three older girls packed Angela off to college and her brother drove her there. Since then I've gradually reassumed my duties. Except that I was inconspicuously absent from my daughters' weddings. I say inconspicuously because, thank God, all of them are hippies who got married in fields without benefit of aunts and uncles. Or mothers. But Angela reads *Glamour*, and she'll ask me to her wedding. Though Mr. Charm has yet to appear in any permanent guise, she's already gearing up to it. Pleadings. Remonstrations. Perhaps a few tears near the end. But I shall hold firm, I hate sacrificial offerings of my own flesh. "I can't help it," I'll joke, "I have a weak stomach, only half of it is there."

Angela sighs, perhaps foreseeing it all. The phone is ringing. And slowly, there she goes. By the time she picks it up, cradles the receiver to her brown neck, her voice is normal. Penny bright, and she spends it fast. I look out the screened porch on the alley and the clean garbage cans. It seems to me that I remembered everything before the kids were born. I say kids as though they appeared collectively in a giant egg, my stomach. When actually there were two years, then one year, then two, then three between them. The Child Bearing Years, as though you stand there like a blossomed pear tree and the fruit plops off. Eaten or rotted to seed to start the whole thing all over again.

Angela has fixed too much food for me. She often does. I don't digest large amounts so I eat small portions six times a day. The dog drags his basset ears to my feet, waits for the plate. And I give it to him, urging him on so he'll gobble it fast and silent before Angela comes back.

Dear children, I always confused my stomach with my womb. Lulled into confusion by nearly four pregnant years I heard them say, "Oh, you're eating for two," as if the two organs were directly connected by a small tube. In the hospital I was convinced they had removed my uterus along with half of my stomach. The doctors, at an end of patience, labeled my decision an anxiety reaction. And I reacted anxiously by demanding an X-ray so I could see that my womb was still there.

Angela returns, looks at the plate which I have forgotten to pick up, looks at the dog, puts her hand on my shoulder.

"I'm sorry," she says.

"Well," I say.

Angela twists her long fingers, her fine thin fingers with their smooth knuckles, twists the diamond ring her father gave her when she was sixteen.

"Richard," I'd said to my husband, "she's your daughter, not your fiancée."

"Kay," intoned the husband, the insurance agent, the successful adjuster of claims, "she's only sixteen once. This ring is a gift, our love for Angela. She's beautiful, she's blossoming."

"Richard," I said, shuffling Maalox bottles and planning my bland lunch, "Diamonds are not for blossoms. They're for those who need a piece of the rock." At which Richard laughed heartily, always amused at my cynicism regarding the business which principally buttered my bread. Buttered his bread, because by then I couldn't eat butter.

"What is it you're afraid to face?" asked Richard. "What is it in your life you can't control; you're eating yourself alive. You're dissolving your own stomach."

"Richard," I said, "it's a tired old story. I have this husband who wants to marry his daughter."

"I want you to see a psychiatrist," said Richard, tightening his expertly knotted tie. "That's what you need, Kay, a chance to talk it over with someone who's objective."

"I'm not interested in objectives," I said. "I'm interested in shrimp and butter sauce, Tabasco, hot chiles and an end of pain."

"Pain never ends," said Richard.

"Oh, Richard," I said, "no wonder you're the King of the Southeast Division."

"Look," he said, "I'm trying to put four kids through college and one wife through graduate school. I'm starting five investment plans now so when our kids get married no one has to wait twenty-five years to finish a dissertation on George Eliot like you did. Really, am I such a bad guy? I don't remember forcing you into any of this. And your goddamn stomach has to quit digesting itself. I want you to see a psychiatrist."

"Richard," I said, "if our daughters have five children in eight years [which most of them won't, being members of Zero Population Growth who quote the foreword of *Diet for a Small Planet* every Thanksgiving] they may still be slow with Ph.D.'s despite your investment plans."

Richard untied his tie and tied it again. "Listen," he said. "Plenty of women with five children have Ph.D.'s."

"Really," I said. "I'd like to see those statistics."

"I suppose you resent your children's births," he said, straightening his collar. "Well, just remember, the last one was your miscalculation."

"And the first one was yours," I said.

It's true. We got pregnant, as Richard affectionately referred to it, in a borrowed bunk bed at Myrtle Beach. It was the eighth time we'd slept together. Richard gasped that of course he'd take care of things, had he ever failed me? But I had my first orgasm and no one remembered anything.

After the fourth pregnancy and first son, Richard was satisfied. Angela, you were born in a bad year. You were expensive, your father was starting in insurance after five years as a high school principal. He wanted the rock, all of it.

I had a rock in my belly we thought three times was dead. So he swore his love to you, with that ring he thee guiltily wed. Sweet Sixteen, does she remember? She never forgets.

Angela pasted sugar cubes to pink ribbons for a week, Sweet Sixteen party favors she read about in *Seventeen*, while the older girls shook their sad heads. Home from colleges in Ann Arbor, Boston, Berkeley, they stared aghast at their golden-haired baby sister, her Villager suits, the ladybug stickpin in her blouses. Angela owned no blue jeans; her boyfriend opened the car door for her and carried her books home. They weren't heavy, he was a halfback. Older sister no. 3: "Don't you have arms?" Older sister no. 2: "He'll take it out of your hide, wait and see." Older sister no. 1: "The nuclear family lives in women's guts. Your mother has ulcers, Angela, she can't eat gravy with your daddy."

At which point Richard slapped oldest sister, his miscalculation, and she flew back to Berkeley, having cried in my hands and begged me to come with her. She missed the Sweet Sixteen party. She missed Thanksgiving and Christmas for the next two years.

Angela's jaw set hard. I saw her reject politics, feminism, and everyone's miscalculations. I hung sugar cubes from the ceiling for her party until the room looked like the picture in the magazine. I ironed sixteen pink satin ribbons she twisted in her hair. I applauded with everyone else, including the smiling halfback, when her father slipped the diamond on her finger. Then I filed for divorce.

The day Richard moved out of the house, my son switched his major to premed at the state university. He said it was the only way to get out of selling insurance. The last sound of the marriage was Richard being nervously sick in the kitchen sink. Angela gave him a cold wash cloth and took me out to dinner at Senor Miguel's while he stacked up his boxes and drove them away. I ate chiles rellenos, guacamole chips in sour cream, cheese enchiladas, Mexican fried bread and three green chile burritos. Then I ate tranquilizers and bouillon for two weeks.

Angela was frightened.

"Mother," she said, "I wish you could be happy."

"Angela," I answered, "I'm glad you married your father, I couldn't do it any more."

Angela finished high school that year and twelve copies each of *Ingenue, Cosmopolitan, Mademoiselle*. She also read the Bible alone at night in her room.

"Because I'm nervous," she said, "and it helps me sleep. All the trees and fruit, the figs, begat and begat going down like the multiplication tables."

"Angela," I said, "are you thinking of making love to someone?"

"No Mother," she said, "I think I'll wait. I think I'll wait a long time."

Angela quit eating meat and blinked her mascaraed eyes at the glistening fried liver I slid onto her plate.

"It's so brown," she said. "It's just something's guts."

"You've always loved it," I said, and she tried to eat it, glancing at my midriff, glancing at my milk and cottage cheese.

When her father took over the Midwest and married a widow, Angela declined to go with him. When I went to the hospital to have my stomach reduced by half, Angela declined my invitations to visit and went on a fast. She grew wan and romantic, said she wished I taught at her college instead of City, she'd read about Sylvia Plath in *Mademoiselle*. We talked on the telephone while I watched the hospital grounds go dark in my square window. It was summer and the trees were so heavy.

I thought about Angela, I thought about my miscalculations. I thought about milk products and white mucous coatings. About Richard's face the night of the first baby, skinny in his turned-up coat. About his mother sending roses every birth, American Beauties. And babies slipping in the wash basin, tiny wriggling arms, the blue veins in their translucent heads. And starting oranges for ten years, piercing thick skins with a fingernail so the kids could peel them. After a while, I didn't want to watch the skin give way to the white ragged coat beneath.

Angela comes home in the summers, halfway through business, elementary education or home ec. She doesn't want to climb the Rockies or go to India. She wants to show houses to wives, real estate, and feed me mashed potatoes, cherry pie, avocados and artichokes. Today she not only fixes breakfast for my ex-anniversary, she fixes lunch and dinner. She wants to pile up my plate and see me eat everything. If I eat, surely something good will happen. She won't remember what's been important enough in my life to make me forget everything. She is spooning breaded clams, french fries, nuts and anchovy salad onto my plate.

"Angela, it's too much."

"That's OK, we'll save what you don't want."

"Angela, save it for who?"

She puts down her fork. "For anyone," she says. "For any time they want it."

In a moment, she slides my plate onto her empty one and begins to eat.

Plastic Edge
To Plastic Edge

MARY HEDIN

On this burnished Sunday morning in May, Dan and Valerie are driving north from San Rafael to the Sonoma wine country where their old friend Murray is marrying a woman approximately half his age. The day is particularly bright, the highway shimmers like a polished stove top, and the surrounding hills are rich enameled greens.

Valerie, leaning her arm on the doorframe and her dark head on her fist, is merely dryly resigned. Marriages, divorces. Marriages, divorces. It all used to mean something. Years back when someone she was fond of married, she felt true delight, celebrated with extravagant gifts. And those first divorces. How she had shared grief, frustration. Now weddings seem to be only first motions toward certain separations. For every friend's wedding promises, there is news of someone else unraveling the marriage vows.

Dan, however, is obviously happy—to be out in the glorious weather, to be going to the celebration. Always a participator, whatever the occasion, he moves in close to the event, does not get caught, as Valerie does, in the distances of irony. But it seems to Valerie that sometimes he shows little discrimination, and she feels now an old irritation at his failure to judge. He seems more flexible than she, but perhaps he is simply indifferent to Murray's choices, to the sadness of the ravaging break in his long marriage.

How different Dan was when he was young. Then he saw in black and white, judged quickly and positively. Valerie sometimes thinks that it is being a doctor that has changed him; caring for patients, witnessing their foibles and their tragedies, has made him see every human event with equable acceptance. She looks at him now, driving competently, the creases of pleasure in his face not hiding the fine lines showing wear, showing weariness.

"I keeping thinking of Lila, don't you?" she asks, and studies his expression for signs. Is she watching for betrayal? Does she want, really, out of oblique resentment, to shadow his lightheartedness, to punish him for his blithe acceptance of Murray's inconstancy?

Dan frowns. "Lila's a strong woman," he says, "and still very attractive. She'll be all right."

Yes, that's probably true. Lila is self-reliant, resilient. She'll be all right. Valerie saw her, just the past week, in Franchini's market, among the broccoli and cauliflower. Tall and vivid, very composed. Lila commented on the coming marriage. She and Murray had grown too far apart; they were no longer interested in the same things. Valerie believes that despite the perfect equanimity Lila affected, a note of compensatory bravery sounded in her words. It was Murray, after all, who had decided upon the divorce.

Rounding a curve in the rolling land, they come to a wooden road sign inscribed: Murray Warren. They turn left, bump down a length of unpaved roadway and arrive at a cattle gate, stop in a small flume of dust. A young boy stands near the open gate, waving his thin arms in broad dramatic gestures. He shouts in a high authoritative voice, "Park there!" and pumps his arm wildly. He is so pompous and so small that he is comic. As Dan eases the car onto the grassy field, the boy leaps in front of them and officiously guides them. Possessed as he is by excitement, the boy is catalyst, augury.

Valerie glances at Dan, catches the delighted gleam in his amber eyes. Yes, he is in tune, as usual. Married so long, Valerie thinks, like Siamese twins they infect each other's feelings, know each other's thoughts. Without words, as if traveling on connected bloodstreams, these cycles of emotion occur, the linked changes of mood. Sometimes that seems marvelous, and sometimes very comfortable, and sometimes . . . Well, marriage! Two human beings give up their differences to become one, overcome their separateness, diminish their loneliness, but also lose their individuality. How often she feels like Dan's shadow. How often her identity seems to be only mother of *his* children, partner in *his* various projects, *his* social secretary, *his* wife. Does anyone know her just as herself—Valerie, separate person?

Dan is reaching into the back seat for his blue jacket. Valerie reaches for her wide-brimmed straw hat. They step from the car into the clear light.

They have heard reports about Murray's vineyard, the antique barn, the Victorian house. But the reports have not prepared them for what they see. "Good lord," Dan exclaims. "Look at that."

Some distance away, the house—narrow-windowed, two-storied, square, porched and pillared—stands on a plateau of level ground. It looks over a rush-rimmed, man-made lake that shimmers darkly under the high sun, and beyond that to the orderly, patterned fields, the rows of vines, newly greened, acres and acres of them, stopping only at the tree-hidden river.

"Grant Wood," Valerie murmurs, at once perversely sardonic. "Andrew Wyeth . . . !" Yes, Murray must have such images in his head. He has shaped this place to fit a dream, has created a mythic setting, an Eden, for his new woman, his new life, himself. While Dan admires, appreciates, Valerie is stiffly indignant. "It's pretentious, it's not real," she asserts. "The place needs actors, film scripts, cameras!"

But of course the actors are present, at least a hundred of them, Dan and herself included. South of the house is an ancient white oak. Under its immense branches a table is set up, covered with trays of plastic glasses and crates of red apples. On sawhorses behind the table a large oak barrel rests. From it a young man in overalls is decanting wine into carafes. A young woman in calico blouse and skirt is pouring from the carafes into the waiting plastic glasses. Around the table, in the dapple of lemon sun and blue shade, is gathered a crowd of summery people. Middle-aged women wearing long, lacy dresses; middle-aged men in pastel slacks and bouclé shirts or dark trousers and linen jackets; young women wearing bare-backed prints; young men in jeans and casual shirts.

Some guests are lounging in the grass beside the lake. Others stroll about, their hats and jackets swinging in dreamy arms.

No, Valerie corrects, walking with Dan into the oak tree's shade, not Andrew Wyeth. Vuillard! The unburdened, drifting pastel look of the people, the patterned blue and brown and green landscape, the wine shimmering in carafes, in glasses. Yes, Murray's arrangement is perfect, his romantic fantasy achieved.

Dan moves toward the table. Valerie stops where Emmy Callam greets her. Emmy passes a plump hand through the benevolent air, queries on a lift of brow, "How do you like the spread, Val?"

Valerie slips her arm around Emmy's waist, gives a quick companionable hug. "I'm positively covetous," she replies. The edge of mockery in her words serves to hide, even from herself, the element of true confession.

Dan brings wine in two squat glasses, gives one to Valerie, lifts his own to Emmy's. "Zinfandel, Murray's first crush," he informs them. He sniffs the wine's bouquet, sips thoughtfully, pronounces it quite good, though green.

At that moment some woman sings out, "Look, there they come!" A carriage is moving slowly along the macadam road. Two chestnut horses with tossing heads and prancing steps draw an antique black surrey. The driver on the high box seat holds the reins at ceremonial height. Behind him Murray and his bride ride in charming splendor. Following the carriage, walking in pairs, in matched strides, are eight black-gowned, white-collared hatless men. Each holds his clasped holy hands against his sternum.

"Eight priests?" Valerie disbelievingly questions.

"Brothers," Emmy informs. "From the retreat." She watches, frowning icily. "Isn't that terribly romantic?" She folds her arms high up under her bosom, sniffs imperiously.

"Say, you two biddies," Dan rebukes them, grinning for lightness. "It's a wedding remember?"

Valerie and Emmy feel sheepish, offended. They slide quick defensive looks toward each other and watch, after that, in silence. The guests, startled into gaiety by the coming parade, gather along the earthen roadway, laughing, cheering, for all the world as if they were flung back into childhood and a circus was coming.

The gleaming horses, bridled with bells, garlanded with flowers and blue ribbons, draw up smartly to the house. They throw their heads in conscious disdain. Dust lifts from the stopped wheels, rises in a thin cloud that spins golden in the sun, and from that shimmering aura Murray beams out. His grin is wide as a pumpkin's, his gloved wave as regal as Henry the Eighth's. He is wearing kilts, and the brass-buttoned jacket is taut over his proud chest.

The bride, however, neither smiles nor waves. She holds her head high for inspection. In her auburn hair, white flowers are woven, and a blue ribbon adorns the curls massed thickly at the crown. On the steps of the house, a bagpiper has taken his place. He lifts from his pompous instrument loud, wheedling, arrogant tunes.

Oh, they are a royal pair, this bride and groom, the laird of the manor and his maid. Valerie sips her tart wine and watches the crowd cooperate in illusion, taking up their supportive, admiring roles.

Murray is standing in the surrey. His smile persists like a toothache. He puts his hand out to his bride. She rises to his command, and the close-fitting Victorian gown emphasizes her willowiness. Murray leaps from the high step. The kilt flashes over bulging thighs, gray knee socks curve over muscular calves. His bride gathers her skirts and lightly leaps to his side.

Ah, the city people, Valerie observes, Murray's old friends, middle-aged, office-bound doctors and lawyers and brokers, invited to witness Murray's successes, aren't they pale and deprived beside him? Envy shows on their faces. If they could choose, surely they would choose a life like this. Murray knows they would. He beams on them all, beneficent.

Valerie notes how Murray's blooming energy sparks the men's eyes, draws reluctant smiles. Yes, if Murray is cause for envy, he is also reason for hope. *So this is fifty,* their eyes are saying.

Well, fifty is quite young, after all. Fifty looks good, full of possibility, full of romance. Dan, too, Valerie judges, seeing how he stands, his red head thrown back, brown eyes merry, mouth sweet with wine, is perhaps taking some new perspective on his own life from viewing Murray's. "But he must love her," a woman Valerie does not know whispers to her sagging-throated friend, as if some debate were going on.

The women eye the bride with doubt, as if learning the configurations of threat. They have to believe in love, assert the dominance of the heart, for their own sakes. Only love that endures past corrupted middle-aged bodies, middle-aged losses, can safeguard their precarious peace.

In proof of love and its sanctity, one of the black-garbed men, the one who is the priest, approaches the immaculate shining-windowed house. He climbs the steps and stops where a wide blue ribbon bars entry to the plant-lush porch. He opens his book of prayers and sets his palm against the air for quiet. At his nod, Murray and his bride mount the steps and stand at the priest's left, facing, as royalty must, the attending crowd. The priest intones a blessing of the house, reading the prayers in a sustained tenor tone. His consonants are plucked perfectly from tongue, palate, teeth. The wind lifts the silver strands of hair crossing his bald dome, stirs the folds of black cassock. Murray's kilts move in red ripples, the bride's gown in white waves. The priest's hands turn, light-boned and eloquent, beneath his chanted words. Valerie half expects doves to rise up, signals from heaven.

Emmy fails to murmur along in the Lord's Prayer, though she is truly devout. Instead she studies the statement of vines over the earth, the inscriptions of a hawk on far air.

After the firm *Amen*, the bride is handed a large scissors. She leans toward the satin barrier. She snips, the groom scoops her up in muscular arms, hoists her over the threshold into the virgin holy house.

In the reception line Emmy turns back to whisper, "Good God, Val, she hasn't got a wrinkle!" and goes on to offer Murray a chastened, ambiguous kiss, as does Valerie in her turn. Valerie must kiss the bride too; her pride demands such generosity. The bride's hands, when Valerie grasps them, are hard with calluses.

Afterwards, gathered on the broad porch overlooking the fertile fields, Dan explains. "They say she drives a tractor like a man. She's a real goer, Murray's woman. Quite a gal." His jovial admiration puts him clearly in the enemy's camp. He too, Valerie imagines, would like such a mate. Certainly a young wife demonstrates to the world a man's virility, his worth. Naturally Dan would wonder whether he, too, though the least bit over the hill but still vigorous, obviously successful and certainly attractive to women, could be loved by a spirited handsome young woman like the bride. Aren't all the middle-aged husbands wondering that?

Cross with her own cool perceptions, conscious of her years, Valerie slips away to where Emmy chats with Liz Burnett. Liz is recounting how she ran into Agnes Carson in Long's Drug Store. Liz hadn't seen her in months, and when she said, "How are you, Agnes?" Agnes had burst into tears. Ray, her husband, had fallen in love with a twenty-two-year old law clerk and wanted to marry her; he hoped to father a male child and was demanding a divorce. Agnes, at sixty, loved only him and wanted him back. "She's pathetic," Liz asserts, her mouth wry with distaste. Valerie remembers how Agnes used to look like Queen Wilhelmina, full-bodied and stately. Now the skin under her chin is creped, her upper arms are looped with scallops of puckered flesh, and age does not protect from heartache, from wounded pride, from loss. No, not all.

And just last Monday Valerie had phoned Carol Wilson, whom she has known almost forever. Carol announced that she and Jake were separating. Carol is deeply in love with a professor of political science, a man committed to social change, alive to new ideas, not hung up on business, money, work. So Carol is writing poems to her new love, but Jake, when Valerie called him, was shocked, angry, crushed.

Valerie feels anger toward Carol. Jake Wilson is a fine, generous man. He loves his wife, his children. Is it right to purchase one's happiness at someone else's unwilling expense? And was the exchange worthwhile, in the end? Gained: a sensual, energizing, ego-rewarding new love. Lost: loyalty, faith, the years' investment of shared experience, family.

When Liz strides off, Emmy sighs. "We're the last of the one-marriage breed, Val."

Valerie responds on hard, glittering notes. "We're ridiculous, Emmy, hanging on to outworn convention. One man, one marriage. We're out of fashion."

Emmy gives a brief laugh. "But it's too late, now, Val. Who'd *want* me, except Ed?" and wanders off resignedly to find him.

Valerie stands solitary in the open space, watching the caterers in starched white carry trays to famished guests. Small tender rolls filled with pink beef, rosy ham, creamy turkey; mushroom caps puffed up with melting cheese; rounds of bread heaped with bright shrimp. Valerie refuses all, denies appetite, condescends to a glass from the waiter's tray.

Alone she walks over the dry grass toward the border of the vineyards, feeling her solitariness, her differences. She passes at some distance Al Sparrow lounging on the grass, slim and dandyish in a white nip-waisted suit and ruffled blue shirt. He leans close to a small brunette, babbles away with a pleased rosy expression. What has become of Lorraine, his first wife? Where is Jan, his second? What has happened to all the halves of married pairs she no longer sees?

On the lake the light opens and closes on wind-stirred ripples. The leaves of the far oak shiver, turn bronze. The sky sweeps back to impermeable glazed blue. Valerie holds on to her wobbling hat.

The day Carol told her she was leaving Jake, Valerie stood by the phone making out a grocery list and suddenly began to make a list of broken marriages. In no time at all, she had dashed off twenty-eight names of friends, acquaintances. The end of family. Migrating fathers, rotating mothers. The demise of lasting love.

Full of darkness in the glittering day, Valerie turns and slowly walks back. She sees Dan on the porch, talking in absorbed intimacy with Liz, his auburn hair like copper, his face shining and warm. He attends Liz as if nothing in the world could distract him. They seem closer, Val thinks, more private together than any husband and wife.

Often before she has seen women in such intimate conversation with Dan. It has to do, perhaps with his being a doctor. Women drawn to doctors turn to them with confessions of their most personal concerns—at parties, at ordinary social dinners. But those dialogues between Dan and some other woman exclude Valerie, make her seem alien, an unwelcome intruder. Sometimes she feels not especially necessary to him; that closeness that ordinarily belongs only to husband and wife Dan seems to share with many other women. She is, Valerie thinks, only more steadily his companion than they, more commonly his company, that's all.

Refusing claim, refusing to impose conjugal restrictions, Valerie now angles away from him. Be a millstone? Play the heavy? Not she, never! In the grassy field to her left Emmy is talking with Nora Barton, who is six feet tall and implacably good-willed. They call to her, and Valerie joins them. She listens as they admire the restored house—its authentic if rather ugly antiques; the sleigh bed with its hand-crocheted antique spread; the bathroom with its huge claw-footed tub and brass fixtures set before a low window viewing lake and vineyards; the kitchen with enormous new ranch stove, two ovens, huge grill. It all suggests a bigger-than-life domestic bliss. The women recall their own beginnings in married life: the shabby apartments, making do with scrounged furniture, dime-store dishes, Goodwill pots. They laugh, remembering babies, diapers, croup, chicken pox, no household help, rare baby-sitters.

Valerie does not laugh. "What's going to become of us all?" she blurts. "What is going to happen?"

Nora gives her hearty hoot of laughter, shrugs, turns the talk to summer at Tahoe. Valerie understands. No one knows what it will come to. Hell in a handbasket. End of an age.

On the porch Dan is now listening to the quick chatter of a gold-haired, green-frocked woman Valerie does not know. Their shared gaiety deepens Valerie's gloom. Bleakly, she tips her glass to her lips, toasting Dan's enduring charm. Of course such women amuse him, intrigue him. Why should he be different from Murray Warren or Al Sparrow or Ray Carson? Monogamy is not a natural state, she concedes.

And yes, she has to concede, twenty-four years of marriage is absurd. It reveals lack of imagination, lack of adventure-someness. How dull, really, to know exactly how the other brushes his teeth, the rhythms of his nighttime breathing. How ridiculous those matched turnings in the routine marriage bed!

Suddenly, Valerie believes she loves no one. She is, abruptly, utterly bored. She would, perhaps, like a lover—someone young, temperamental, fierce. That one there—his hard thighs; his tumbled, curly, glossy hair. But, ah, how silly. She is forty-four.

A stir of changed motion claims Valerie's attention. The bride and groom are making their way to the lake's edge. Murray's two grown daughters and several other young people pull a rowboat from its mooring, draw it up onto the bank. Murray climbs into the boat, stands wide-legged for balance. He holds out a gallant hand, the bride lifts high her delicate skirts, takes his hand and jumps aboard. Murray settles her on the broad seat in the prow, takes up the oars. The photographer goes to his knees, recording for history the journey to the other shore.

The boat is shoved off, the guests cheer and fling rice in bright arches over the bridal pair. Murray's dipping oars draw the boat through blue concentric rings. In the dazzing light they seem to be moving beyond tarnish, beyond the touch of time.

Valerie feels her breath quicken with desire and remorse. To start again, to gather priests to ring one's life with magic and luck. To have no burden of error, no knowledge of compromise, to have only hope circling your new mornings. What profound pleasure in that. What renewal.

She does not hear Dan come up behind her. When his arm circles her waist, she is startled, remote, and almost draws away. Smiling but intent, Dan studies her face and perceives what she is feeling.

"Val," he says, "wish them luck. They'll need it."

She looks long into Dan's calm face. How foolishly she resists change, battles where issues are already decided. An old fault, springing from a childish insistence on permanence. And as she looks at him, she knows she does not need to question. She knows she can trust him. His steadfastness has never failed in the long years of childbearing, child raising. Surely it will hold, despite the time's pressures for variation, despite the vivid and unreliable yearnings of these middle years.

Valerie lifts her glass, Dan lifts his. They touch plastic edge to plastic edge, smile for what they do not need to say. In companionable sympathy, they watch the boat's rocking journey over the small lake, sipping the wine in honor of idyllic, eternal love.

The Abortion

ALICE WALKER

They had discussed it, but not deeply, whether they wanted the baby she was now carrying. "I don't *know* if I want it," she said, eyes filling with tears. She cried at anything now and was often nauseous. That pregnant women cried easily and were nauseous seemed banal to her, and she resented banality.

"Well, think about it," he said, with his smooth reassuring voice (but with an edge of impatience she now felt) that used to soothe her.

It was all she *did* think about, all she, apparently, *could*; that he could dream otherwise enraged her. But she always lost when they argued. Her temper would flare up, he would become instantly reasonable, mature, responsible if not responsive, precisely, to her mood, and she would swallow down her tears and hate herself. It was because she believed him "good." The best human being she had ever met.

"It isn't as if we don't already have a child," she said in a calmer tone, carelessly wiping at the tear that slid from one eye.

"We have a perfect child," he said with relish. "Thank the good Lord!"

Had she ever dreamed she'd marry someone humble enough to go around thanking the good Lord? She had not.

Now they left the bedroom, where she had been lying down on their massive king-size bed with the forbidding ridge in the middle, and went down the hall—hung with bright prints—to the cheerful, clean kitchen. He put water on for tea in a bright yellow pot.

She wanted him to want the baby so much he would try to save its life. On the other hand, she did not permit such presumptuousness. As he praised the child they already had, a daughter of sunny disposition and winning smile, Imani sensed subterfuge and hardened her heart.

"What am I talking about?" she said, as if she'd been talking about it. "Another child would kill me. I can't imagine life with two children. Having a child is a good experience to have had, like graduate school. But if you've had one, you've had the experience and that's enough."

He placed the tea before her and rested a heavy hand on her hair. She felt the heat and pressure of his hand as she touched the cup and felt the odor and steam rise up from it. Her throat contracted.

"I can't drink that," she said through gritted teeth. "Take it away."

There were days of this.

Clarice, their daughter, was barely two years old. A miscarriage brought on by grief (Imani had lost her fervidly environmentalist mother to lung cancer shortly after Clarice's birth; the asbestos ceiling in the classroom where she taught first-graders had leaked for 40 years) separated Clarice's birth from the new pregnancy. Imani felt her body had been assaulted by these events and was, in fact, considerably weakened and was also, in any case, chronically anemic and run-down. Still, if she had wanted the baby more than she did not want it, she would not have planned to abort it.

They lived in a small town in the South. Her husband, Clarence, was—among other things—legal advisor and defender of the new black mayor of the town. The mayor was much in their lives because of the difficulties being the first black mayor of a small town assured, and because, next to the major leaders of black struggles in the South, Clarence respected and admired him most.

Imani reserved absolute judgment, but she did point out that Mayor Carswell would never look at her directly when she made a comment or posed a question, even sitting at her own dinner table, and would instead talk to Clarence as if she were not there. He assumed that as a woman she would not be interested in or even understand politics. (He would comment occasionally on her cooking or her clothes. He noticed when she cut her hair.) But Imani understood, for example, why she fed the mouth that did not speak to her; because for the present she must believe in Mayor Carswell, even as he could not believe in her. Even understanding this, however, she found dinners with Carswell hard to swallow.

But Clarence was dedicated to the mayor and believed his success would ultimately mean security and advancement for them all.

On the morning she left to have the abortion, the mayor and Clarence were to have a working lunch, and they drove to the airport deep in conversation about municipal funds, racist cops and the facilities for teaching at the chaotic, newly integrated schools. Clarence had time for the briefest kiss and hug at the airport ramp.

"Take care of yourself," he whispered lovingly, as she walked away. He was needed, while she was gone, to draft the city's new charter. She had agreed this was important; the mayor was already being called incompetent by local businessmen and the chamber of commerce, and one inferred from television that no black person alive knew what a city charter was.

"Take care of myself." *Yes*, she thought. *I see that is what I have to do.* But she thought this self-pityingly, which invalidated it. She had expected *him* to take care of her, and she blamed him for not doing so now.

Well, she was a fraud, anyway. She had known after a year of marriage that it bored her. "The Experience of Having a Child" was to distract her from this fact. Still, she expected him to "take care of her." She was lucky he didn't pack up and leave. But he seemed to know, as she did, that if anyone packed and left, it would be her. Precisely *because* she was a fraud and because in the end he would settle for fraud and she could not.

On the plane to New York her teeth ached and she vomited bile—bitter, yellowish stuff she hadn't even been aware her body produced. She resented and appreciated the crisp help of the stewardess who asked if she needed anything, then stood chatting with the cigarette-smoking white man next to her, whose fat hairy wrist, like a large worm, was all Imani could bear to see out of the corner of her eye.

Her first abortion, when she was still in college, she frequently remembered as wonderful, bearing as it had all the marks of a supreme coming of age and a seizing of the direction of her own life, as well as a comprehension of existence that never left her: that life—what one saw about one and called Life—was not a facade. There was nothing behind it which used "Life" as its manifestation. Life was itself. Period. At the time, and afterward, and even now, this seemed a marvelous thing to know.

The abortionist had been a delightful Italian doctor on the Upper East Side in New York, and before he put her under he told her about his own daughter, who was just her age and a junior at Vassar. He babbled on and on until she was out, but not before Imani had thought how her thousand dollars, for which she would be in debt for years, would go to keep his daughter there.

When she woke up it was all over. She lay on a brown Naugahyde sofa in the doctor's outer office. And she heard, over her somewhere in the air, the sound of a woman's voice. It was a Saturday, no nurses in attendance, and she presumed it was the doctor's wife. She was pulled gently to her feet by this voice and encouraged to walk.

"And when you leave, be sure to walk as if nothing is wrong," the voice said.

Imani did not feel any pain. This surprised her. *Perhaps he didn't do anything,* she thought. *Perhaps he took my thousand dollars and put me to sleep with two dollars' worth of ether. Perhaps this is a racket.*

But he was so kind, and he was smiling benignly, almost fatherly, at her (and Imani realized how desperately she needed this "fatherly" look, this "fatherly" smile). "Thank you," she murmured sincerely: she was thanking him for her life.

Some of Italy was still in his voice. "It's nothing, nothing," he said. "A nice, pretty girl like you, in school like my own daughter, you didn't need this trouble."

"He's nice," she said to herself, walking to the subway on her way back to school. She lay down gingerly across a vacant seat and passed out.

She hemorrhaged steadily for six weeks and was not well again for a year.

But this was seven years later. An abortion law now made it possible to make an appointment at a clinic, and for $75 a safe, quick, painless abortion was yours.

Imani had once lived in New York, in the Village, not five blocks from where the abortion clinic was. It was also near the Margaret Sanger clinic, where she had received her very first diaphragm, with utter gratitude and amazement that someone apparently understood and actually cared about young women as alone and ignorant as she. In fact, as she walked up the block with its modern office buildings side by side with older, more elegant brownstones, she felt how close she was still to that earlier self. Still not in control of her sensuality, and only through violence and with money (for the flight and for the operation itself) in control of her body.

She found that abortion had entered the age of the assembly line. Grateful for the lack of distinction between herself and the other women—all colors, ages, states of misery or nervousness—she was less happy to notice, once the doctor started to insert the catheter, that the anesthesia she had been given was insufficient. But assembly lines don't stop because the product on them has a complaint. Her doctor whistled and assured her she was all right and carried the procedure through to the horrific end. Imani fainted some seconds before that.

They laid her out in a peaceful room full of cheerful colors. Primary colors: yellow, red, blue. When she revived she had the feeling of being in a nursery. She had a pressing need to urinate.

A nurse—kindly, white-haired and with firm hands—helped her to the john. Imani saw herself in the mirror over the sink and was alarmed. She was literally gray, as if all her blood had leaked out.

"Don't worry about how you look," said the nurse. "Rest a bit here and take it easy when you get back home. You'll be fine in a week or so."

She could not imagine being fine again. Somewhere her child—she never dodged into the language of "fetuses" and "amorphous growths"—was being flushed down a sewer. Gone all her or his chances to see the sunlight, savor a fig.

"Well," she said to this child, "it was you or me, Kiddo, and I chose me."

There were people who thought she had no right to choose herself, but Imani knew better than to think of those people now.

It was a bright, hot Saturday when she returned.

Clarence and Clarice picked her up at the airport. They had brought flowers from Imani's garden, and Clarice presented them with a stouthearted hug. Once in her mother's lap she rested content all the way home, sucking her thumb, stroking her nose with the forefinger of the same hand and kneading a corner of her blanket with the three fingers that were left.

"How did it go?" asked Clarence.

"It went," said Imani.

There was no way to explain abortion to a man. She thought castration might be an apt analogy, but most men, perhaps all, would insist this could not possibly be true.

"The anesthesia failed," she said. "I thought I would never faint in time to keep from screaming and leaping right off the table."

*   *   *

Clarence paled. He hated the thought of pain, any kind of violence. He could not endure it; it made him physically ill. This was one of the reasons he was a pacifist, another reason she admired him.

She knew he wanted her to stop talking. But she continued in a flat, deliberate voice.

"All the blood seemed to run out of me. The tendons in my legs felt cut. I was gray."

He reached for her hand. Held it. Squeezed.

"But," she said, "at least I know what I don't want. And I intend never to go through any of this again."

They were in the living room of their peaceful, quiet and colorful house. Imani was in her rocker, Clarice dozing on her lap. Clarence sank to the floor and held both of them in his arms. She felt he was asking for nurturance when she needed it herself. She felt the two of them, Clarence and Clarice, clinging to her, using her. And that the only way she could claim herself, feel herself distinct from them, was by doing something painful, self-defining but self-destructive.

She suffered his arms and his head against her knees as long as she could.

"Have a vasectomy," she said, "or stay in the guest room. Nothing is going to touch me anymore that isn't harmless."

He smoothed her thick hair with his hand. "We'll talk about it," he said, as if that was not what they were doing. "We'll see. Don't worry. We'll take care of things."

She had forgotten that the third Sunday in June, the following day, was the fifth memorial observance for Holly Monroe, who had been shot down on her way home from her high school graduation ceremony five years before. Imani *always* went to these memorials. She liked the reassurance that her people had long memories and that those people who fell in struggle or innocence were not forgotten. She was, of course, too weak to go. She was dizzy and still losing blood. The white lawgivers attempted to get around assassination—which

Imani considered extreme abortion—by saying the victim provoked it (there had been some difficulty saying this about Holly Monroe, but they had tried), but they were antiabortionist to a man. Imani thought of all this as she resolutely showered and washed her hair.

Clarence had installed central air conditioning their second year in the house. Imani had at first objected. "I want to smell the trees, the flowers, the natural air!" she had cried. But the first summer of 110-degree heat had cured her of giving a damn about any of that. Now she wanted to be cool. As much as she loved trees, on a hot day she would have sawed through a forest to get to an air conditioner.

In fairness to him, he asked her if she thought she was well enough to go. But even to be asked annoyed her. She was not one to let her own troubles prevent her from showing proper respect and remembrance toward the dead, although she understood perfectly well that once dead, the dead do not exist. So respect, remembrance, was for herself, and today herself needed rest. There was something mad about her refusal to rest, and she felt it as she tottered about getting Clarice dressed. But she did not stop. She ran a bath, plopped the child in it, scrubbed her plump body while on her knees, arms straining over the tub awkwardly in a way that made her stomach hurt—but not yet her uterus—dried her hair, lifted her out and dried the rest of her on the kitchen table.

"You are going to remember as long as you live what kind of people they are," she said to the child, who, gurgling and cooing, looked into her mother's stern face with lighthearted fixation.

"You are going to hear the music," Imani said. "The music they've tried to kill. The music they try to steal." She felt feverish and was aware she was muttering. She didn't care.

"They think they can kill a continent—people, trees, buffalo—and then fly off to the moon and just forget about it. But you and me, we're going to remember the people, the trees and the fucking buffalo. Goddammit."

"Buffwoe," said the child, hitting at her mother's face with a spoon.

She placed the baby on a blanket in the living room and turned to see her husband's eyes, full of pity, on her. She wore pert green velvet slippers and a lovely sea green robe. Her body was bent within it. A reluctant tear formed beneath his gaze.

"Sometimes I look at you and I wonder, *What is this man doing in my house*?"

This had started as a joke between them. Her aim had been never to marry, but to take in lovers who could be sent home at dawn, freeing her to work and ramble.

"I'm here because you love me," was the traditional answer. But Clarence faltered, meeting her eyes, and Imani turned away.

It was a hundred degrees by ten o'clock. By eleven, when the memorial service began, it would be ten degrees hotter. Imani staggered from the heat. When she sat in the car she had to clench her teeth against the dizziness until the motor prodded the air conditioning to envelop them in coolness. A dull ache started in her uterus.

The church was not, of course, air conditioned. It was authentic Primitive Baptist in every sense.

Like the four previous memorials, this one was designed by Holly Monroe's classmates. All twenty-five of whom—fat and thin—managed to look like the dead girl. Imani had never seen Holly Monroe, though there were always photographs of her dominating the pulpit of this church where she had been baptized and where she had sung in the choir—and to Imani, every black girl of a certain vulnerable age *was* Holly Monroe. And an even deeper truth was that Holly Monroe was herself. Herself shot down, aborted on the eve of becoming herself.

She was prepared to cry and to do so with abandon. But she did not. She clenched her teeth against the steadily increasing pain and her tears were instantly blotted by the heat.

* * *

Mayor Carswell had been waiting for Clarence in the vestibule of the church, mopping his plumply jowled face with a voluminous handkerchief and holding court among half a dozen young men and women who listened to him with awe. Imani exchanged greetings with the mayor, he ritualistically kissed her on the cheek, and kissed Clarice on the cheek, but his rather heat-glazed eye was already fastened on her husband. The two men huddled in a corner away from the awed young group. Away from Imani and Clarice, who passed hesitantly, waiting to be joined or to be called back, into the church.

There was a quarter hour's worth of music.

"Holly Monroe was five feet, three inches tall and weighed one hundred and eleven pounds," her best friend said, not reading from notes but talking to each person in the audience. "She was a stubborn, loyal Aries, and best kind of friend to have. She had black kinky hair that she experimented with a lot. She was exactly the color of this oak church pew in the summer; in the winter she was the color [pointing up] of this heart-pine ceiling. She loved green. She did not like lavender because she said she also didn't like pink. She had brown eyes and wore glasses, except when she was meeting someone for the first time. She had a sort of rounded nose. She had beautiful large teeth, but her lips were always chapped, so she didn't smile as much as she might have if she'd ever gotten used to carrying chapstick. She had elegant feet.

"Her favorite church song was 'Leaning on the Everlasting Arms.' Her favorite other kind of song was 'I Can't Help Myself—I Love You and Nobody Else.' She was often late for choir rehearsal though she loved to sing. She made the dress she wore to her graduation in Home Ec. She *hated* Home Ec . . ."

Imani was aware that the sound of low, murmurous voices had been the background for this statement all along. Everything was quiet around her; even Clarice sat up straight, absorbed by the simple friendliness of the young woman's voice. All of Holly Monroe's classmates and friends in the

choir wore vivid green. Imani imagined Clarice entranced by
the brilliant, swaying color as by a field of swaying corn.

Lifting the child, her uterus burning and perspiration already a stream down her back, Imani tiptoed to the door.
Clarence and the mayor were still deep in conversation. She
heard "Board meeting . . . aldermen . . . city council . . ."
She beckoned to Clarence.

"Your voices are carrying!" she hissed.

She meant: *How dare you not come inside?*

They did not. Clarence raised his head, looked at her and
shrugged his shoulders helplessly. Then, turning, with the
abstracted air of priests, the two men moved slowly toward
the outer door and into the churchyard, coming to stand some
distance from the church beneath a large oak tree. There they
remained throughout the service.

Two years later, Clarence was furious with her: What is the
matter with you, he asked. You never want me to touch you.
You told me to sleep in the guest room and I did. You told
me to have a vasectomy I didn't want and *I did*. (Here, there
was a sob of hatred for her somewhere in the anger, the
humiliation: he thought of himself as a eunuch and blamed
her.)

She was not merely frigid, she was remote.

She had been amazed after they left the church that the
anger she had felt watching Clarence and the mayor turn
away from the Holly Monroe memorial did not prevent her
accepting a ride home with him. A month later it did not
prevent her smiling on him fondly. Did not prevent a trip to
Bermuda, a few blissful days of very good sex on a deserted
beach screened by trees. Did not prevent her listening to his
mother's stories of Clarence's youth as though she would
treasure them forever.

And yet. From that moment in the heat at the church door,
she had uncoupled herself from him, in a separation that
made him, except occasionally, little more than a stranger.

And he had not felt it, had not known.

"What have I done?" he asked, all the tenderness in his

voice breaking over her. She smiled a nervous smile at him, which he interpreted as derision—so far apart had they drifted.

They had discussed the episode at the church many times. Mayor Carswell—whom they never saw anymore—was now a model mayor, with wide biracial support in his campaign for the legislature. Neither could easily recall him, though television frequently brought him into the house.

"It was so important that I help the mayor!" said Clarence. "He was our *first!*"

Imani understood this perfectly well, but it sounded humorous to her. When she smiled, he was offended.

She had known the moment she left the marriage, the exact second. But apparently that moment had left no perceptible mark.

They argued, she smiled, they scowled, blamed and cried—as she packed.

Each of them almost recalled out loud that about this time of this year their aborted child would have been a troublesome, "terrible" two-year-old, a great burden on its mother, whose health was by now excellent; each wanted to think aloud that the marriage would have deteriorated anyway, because of that.

The Women Who Walk

NANCY HUDDLESTON PACKER

In the days right after Malcolm left her, Marian began to notice the women who walked the deserted streets near the university campus. They were a flash of color in the brilliant June sunlight at a distant intersection, a single shape thrusting through the shadows of the giant sycamores along the sidewalk. She did not at first differentiate one from another. She was too absorbed in her own suffering. Images of Malcolm that last day spun through her mind. The thin ankle over the thin knee as he sat on his luggage in the front hall. The silver lighter touched to the black cigarette. Well, Marian, he said. She pulled the car over to the curb and gave herself up to the blurring tears, the sudden thunder in her chest.

Soon, quieter, she looked around the empty streets. Had anyone seen her? She saw in the distance a lonely figure, walking, walking.

Two weeks had passed and she had not yet told the children. She had said, "He's out of town, he's at a conference, he's giving a lecture, he'll be back." One evening as they sat in the dying sun in the patio, Joseph, who was eleven, said, "When? When will he be back?"

A bluebird squawked in the high branches of the silver maple. "Your father . . ." she began. She felt suffocated by the heat in her throat. Molly began to cry and buried her face in Marian's lap. Joseph grew red and he ran into the house. Later that night, Marian called Malcolm at the backstreet hotel where he had taken a room. "I can't tell them," she managed to say, and quickly hung up.

Next day, Malcolm carried the children away for lunch. After that, each evening he spoke to them on the telephone. On the following Saturday, he took Joseph to a Giants game. On Sunday, he and Molly visited a horse farm in the hills. Marian longed to know what he had said, whether he had spoken of her. But they did not tell her.

Finally she asked. Molly grew somber, hooded, afraid. Joseph became moody and glared at the floor. Molly said, "Daddy says we're not to carry tales back and forth."

"You're my children," she said.

"His too," said Joseph, "just as much as yours."

She felt an explosion and a wind and a fire, but she sat silent and staring.

The first few weeks, women she had counted as friends called her on the phone, invited her to lunch, came by to visit. From behind the living room curtain, she saw them walk up the drive, often in tennis whites, practicing an overhead slam or a low backhand as they waited for her to answer their knock. When she opened the door, their faces were grave. They sat on the sofa and put their sneakers on the coffee table and frowned and shook their heads in sympathy.

She could not speak of him. She tried to talk of other things, but all paths through her mind led back to the injustice she had suffered, of which she could not speak. The silence soon weighed too heavily on them, and their faces grew round and flat as moons, and pale. They knew they could not help her. They must leave now, they said, but they would return. They wished her well. They were her friends. She heard their tires sighing as they escaped down the street.

They were not her friends. They were the wives of his friends, the mothers of his children's friends, the neighbors who were no more than friends of his house. She had no friends. She would never be able to speak of herself, to share herself with friends. He had exiled her to an island of silence. She stood up and began to move around the room, shifting ashtrays, picking lint from the floor. She felt a restless, angry energy gathering in her.

During the summer, Marian frequently saw the woman in the large black coat walking rapidly on the outskirts of the university or the residential streets bordering the business area of the town. She thought the woman was an older faculty wife who apparently spent her leisure doing good works, carrying petitions door-to-door or collecting for the Cancer Society or the Red Cross.

The woman wore sandals and heavy dark socks, a floppy straw hat, and the black coat. The coat was shaped like a wigwam, with sloping shoulders and a wide skirt that struck her just above the ankles. Marian thought the woman wore it like a burnoose, a protection against the dog-day heat of late August and September. The woman was obviously a character, a throwback to the days when faculty and faculty wives were rather expected to be eccentric. Marian liked her, liked her independence and freedom from vanity. Often Marian waved as she drove by, but the woman never seemed to see her. She kept her eyes down, as if she were afraid she might stumble as she rushed along in her waddling, slue-footed gait.

One hot day in late September as Marian waited for a stoplight, the woman in the black coat started across the street in front of the car. Marian had never seen her so close before. She was much younger than she looked from a distance, about thirty-five or so, Marian's age. And still quite pretty, with a high-bridged, delicate nose and delicate fine lips and a soft-looking pale skin. When she came even with the front of the car, she abruptly twisted her head and glanced at Marian through the windshield. As their gazes met, Marian knew that she had seen the woman before—how long ago, under what circumstances she could not recall, perhaps at a university party, a meeting, at the sandbox or the swings of the city park. She would never forget those startled pale gray eyes.

Marian waved but the woman ducked her head again and

hurried on to the sidewalk. Watching her—the hunched tension of her neck and shoulders, the awkward, powerful, rushing gait—Marian felt that when they had met, they had been drawn together in one of those rare moments of intense though inexplicable intimacy. And now Marian longed to recapture the strange, treasured feeling.

She drove around the block and pulled into a driveway in the woman's path. She got out and stood leaning on the fender, waiting, smiling. The woman walked straight at her, heedless, but at the last moment, without lifting her gaze from the ground, veered clumsily aside. Marian reached out and touched her shoulder. "Wait," she said. "Don't I know you?"

The woman stopped and after a long moment lifted her head. Her gaze whipped from Marian to the sky to the trees. She pulled her coat collar up around her face. Marian said, "What is it? Can I help you?"

The woman threw back her head, like a colt shying, and opened her mouth. Marian heard the sound—distant, muted—of a strangled voice and she thought the voice said, "I'm so very cold." For an instant the woman stared at Marian, and then she lowered her head and rushed down the street.

Malcolm came late one evening to settle details. He sat in the red leather chair he had always sat in. He looked handsome, tanned, his graying hair tousled and longer than he had ever worn it. When he asked how everything was, he was charming and attentive, his smile warm and pleasing, as if she were his dinner partner. She sat on the edge of the wing chair, her knees close, her hands kneading each other, and told him the lie he wanted to hear. Yes, everything was fine. He nodded at her approvingly, no longer angry and irritated with her.

"Well, now," he began, and leaned forward. She did not want to hear it all just then, and she stood up.

"I'll get some coffee," she said. "Turkish coffee," she pleaded. He sighed and nodded.

She went into the kitchen and turned on the faucet. She

waited for her heartbeat to slow. When she heard his foot-steps, she busied herself with cups and saucers. He stood in the doorway and gazed around him, smiling at the wall decorated with dinner plates from different countries.

"I always liked that one," he said, pointing at a Mexican plate he had brought to her from Mexico City where he had gone for a conference. But, he hastened to assure her, she needn't worry, all he wanted were a few mementos, keep-sakes that had been in his family for a long time. The tintype of his great-grandmother and of course its antique frame and the silver ladle his great-aunt had saved from the Yankees. He smiled. Everything else was hers, absolutely, he didn't want anything else. Nothing.

Nothing? she wanted to ask. Nothing? No memento, no keepsake of our fifteen years together?

"Nothing besides coffee?" she asked. "Some fruit?" She picked up an immense pineapple from the straw basket on the counter. It was just ripe, soft and yellow. He had always loved pineapples. "It's just ripe," she said. "I'll cut it for you." When he shook his head, she held it close to his face. "Smell it," she pleaded.

"I do not want to smell it, for God's sake," he said. For an instant his composure dropped away and she saw what she had remembered all these months: the rigid shoulders, the pinched mouth, the hard, irritated eyes. She could easily drag the sharp points of the pineapple across his face. She watched little specks of blood ooze from his skin, swell into a long thick ruby streamer that marked his cheek like a savage decoration. She put the pineapple down and handed him a cup of coffee. Back in the living room, he sat again in the red chair and put his feet up on the matching ottoman.

Molly and Joseph were already in bed, but when they heard his voice they ran into the living room. Joseph stood in the doorway, smiling quizzically. Molly climbed over Mal-colm's legs and onto his lap. He set the coffee down and Molly burrowed under his arm, into his armpit. He stroked her hair. Marian felt an uneasiness, a tension, and then she was suddenly shaken by a yearning—to be held, to be stroked—and she felt dizzy, as if she might faint.

"Run along now," said Malcolm to the children, "and I'll see you Sunday." As the children left the room, he explained. "They're coming to my new place for lunch on Sunday. If that's all right with you?" She nodded. "Did you know I had a place? It's not exactly elegant, but I like it much better than the hotel. I like having a place of my own."

"This is yours." She slid off her chair and dropped to her knees beside him. She pressed her face against his thigh. He did not move beneath her caresses. When she looked up, she saw the prim set of his lips. She stood up.

"Now about the arrangements," he said. "Here's what I thought, but I want you to be thoroughly satisfied."

He pulled a folded-up piece of paper from his wallet. It was covered with words and figures in his neat small handwriting. She saw the words "Insurance" and "Automobile."

"You really should get a lawyer," he said. She seized upon the kindness in his voice.

"Who should I get?"

He drew one of the black cigarettes from the box. He tamped it against the back of his hand and lighted it with his silver lighter. After a moment, he said, "You've got to start making that kind of decision for yourself, you know."

"Don't you see that it's too late?" she whispered.

He stood up, tapped ashes into the ashtray, drank off the last of the coffee, gathered together his cigarettes and lighter and wallet. "You're a perfectly competent woman," he said, "as no one knows better than I. After all," he went on, smiling at her, his voice remote, jocular, false, "you managed to get me through graduate school. I don't forget that. I'll always be grateful for that."

She went to the window and stared out at the darkness. "Then how can you desert me like this?" Her voice was hoarse, choked.

"There's no point going over this again," he said in an exasperated voice. "I know it's right for both of us."

She heard his sigh, the sound of the ottoman scraping over

the floor as he pushed it aside, his footsteps brushing across
the rug. The sky was cloudless, moonless, starless. The
leaves of the eucalyptus shivered. Dark spaces opened within
her. She spoke softly to the windowpane.

"Can't you stay just tonight?"

"Now, Marian," he said, moving into the hallway.

"Just to hold me," she whispered, "in the dark, a last
time."

"Good night," he called from the front door. Soon the
lights of his car vanished into the dark. She stood at the
window a moment longer. She felt the agitation rising, the
fury, the rush of movement through her body. She felt the
hardness gather in the center of her chest and she could make
no sound.

The rains came early, and by the middle of November the
ground was soggy. For days the sky was close in and gray.
Through the autumn Marian had become aware of the woman
in white, seen as a flash of light out of the corner of her eye
as she drove along. The woman was probably a nurse, cutting
through the campus on her way to the university hospital. She
was about five nine or five ten and very very thin, like a
wraith. She was swaybacked and as she walked she lifted her
knees high, her feet far out in front of her, like a drum
majorette on parade. The knobby joints between her long thin
bones made her look even more awkward and absurd. Yet she
walked without self-consciousness, head high, as if she had
better thoughts to ponder than the amusement of people driving by in their big cars. This lack of vanity was one of the
characteristics shared by the women who walked. That, and
the vigorous, almost heedless, way they moved.

Marian had only seen the wraith—as she came to think of
her—in the vicinity of the university until a drizzly Sunday
afternoon in early December when she saw her on a downtown
street. The children had eaten lunch with Malcolm and she
had contrived to pick them up. Malcolm lived in a cottage
behind a large Spanish house close by the freeway. Often she
had driven past and stared down the overgrown path that ran

alongside the house. Baskets of ferns and Wandering Jew hung from the roof of the little dilapidated porch, and there were bright flowered curtains behind the windows. Though appealing in the way that dark, shabby little cottages sometimes are, the charm of this one seemed utterly foreign to everything she believed she knew of Malcolm's taste. He had always insisted that their house be neat, clean, sparse. Something had changed in him, and she thought that if only she could see inside the place, she might at last understand what had gone wrong between them. And so she had told him that she was going on an errand and since she didn't want the children to return to an empty house, she would pick them up.

But even before she had turned off the ignition, she saw Molly running down the path toward her, and Joseph sauntering behind. Malcolm, in a bright green sweatshirt and jeans, stood on the porch and waved to her as if she were only the mother of children visiting at his house. She was filled with shame at her scheme, and with disappointment at its failure, and then with relief.

Joseph got in the front seat. He looked sullen, moody, as he often did after the Sundays with his father. Molly climbed in back and grasped Marian's ears and said, "Giddap." Marian patted Molly's hands. And she said, "I'll bet anything you had—let's see—bologna on store-bought bread and Coke. And of course Oreos." The thought of Malcolm's providing such a dreary lunch gave her pleasure, and revving the motor she laughed aloud.

"No," said Joseph. He crossed his arms and dropped his head.

"We had chicken with some kind of orange stuff all over it," said Molly. "I didn't like it but that lady said I had to eat it since she made it special."

Joseph turned to the back seat. "You're stupid," he said. "Nobody can trust you, you're a baby."

Marian thrust her foot against the accelerator and the car jumped from the curb, bucked, almost died, caught, sped away. That lady. A woman. No one had told her there was a woman. But who would? Who did she have to tell her anything? Yet she should have known. She was the stupid one. The secrecy. The children's silence. The shabby place with its shabby charm. The ferns. The bright curtains. And behind the curtains, a woman peering out at her, perhaps laughing at her. The rejected wife. The discard. Garbage.

"I didn't mean to tell," said Molly. She patted Marian's shoulder. "I'm, sorry."

Marian drove in silence, beneath the immense white oaks, past the fine old mansions, past the run-down rooming houses and flats. No life stirred. Even the downtown streets were empty. The car moved through empty gray streets. The day was cold, damp, dark. She saw a flash of shimmering white. Without thinking, she said,

"One of the walkers."

The woman strutted toward them on her long heron legs. She had on a pale pink jacket over her white dress. As the car drew near Marian saw that the jacket was short-sleeved, that it barely covered the woman's breasts, that it was loose-fitting, flimsy, crocheted. That it was a bed jacket. As Marian stared, the woman turned toward her. Her eyes were narrowed, glittering, defiant. She grinned fiercely.

"What walker?" asked Joseph. He dropped his feet from the dashboard and sat up to see. Marian pressed the accelerator and the car jerked forward and threw Joseph against the seat.

"Never mind. We've passed her." Marian flushed with embarrassment. She felt she had somehow humiliated the woman in front of Joseph and Molly.

"I saw her," said Molly. "She had on pink and white. Joseph just doesn't look."

Joseph spun toward her. "You shut up, you shut up," he said. His voice trembled. Marian touched his shoulder.

"Please don't quarrel," she said.

He pulled away from her hand. "I hate you and Daddy," he shouted. "You don't care about us, you don't care what you do to us."

"Mommy didn't do it, did you?" said Molly. "It was Daddy and that lady."

"He wouldn't have just left," said Joseph. "It was her fault, too."

Hot moisture bubbled into her eyes, and shrill sounds rose into her ears. She pulled the car over to the curb. Now she would tell them. Her fault? Her fault too? Now she would unleash her suffering, she would engulf them in her anguish. She would tell them, she would tell them. She turned to Joseph. His eyelids were slightly lowered and his nose and mouth were stretched down and pinched. She twisted to see Molly.

"Don't," said Molly. "Please don't look like that. Don't cry, please don't cry. You're so ugly when you cry. Please don't."

Marian pressed her fingers into her skull. She held her neck muscles taut. She pushed out her chest and belly to make room for the expanding pressure. They were her children. They were all she now had. She must protect them from misery and pain. From herself. In the rearview mirror, she could make out in the gray distance the comic cakewalk of the woman in white, alone, in the cold.

Over the next weeks, she longed to tell Malcolm that she knew about the lady. She longed to taunt him. How typical, how trite, how sordid. He had deserted his family for the sleaziest of reasons, another woman, a younger woman, probably a graduate student. Malcolm with his dignity and pride. How comical it was. She saw herself pick up the telephone and dial his number. She heard her contemptuous yet amused voice ringing through the wires. Sleazy and comical, she heard herself say.

But she did not call him. She was afraid. His voice would be hard and irritable, and he would say hateful things to her that she could not bear to hear. She imagined his saying, I never loved you, not even at the beginning. She heard him say, I married you only so I could finish my degree. He would infect her memories with doubt and ruin the past for her. He would leave her with nothing. While he had his lady.

Through the winter months, she spent hours at a time daydreaming about Malcolm and his woman. Often, she sat at her bedroom window and watched the rain break against the pane. She believed that if she concentrated hard enough, she would be able to conjure up an image of his woman. But always as the face began to form on the film of the glass, the wind swept the image away.

One day as the outline of the eyes appeared, she leaned close to fasten the face to the windowpane. She saw her own reflection, and she saw that her eyes were more haggard than she remembered, her lips thin, her nose taut. She had grown suddenly old and ugly. She drew back from the windowpane, and as she did, her reflection began to move away from her, as if the image were running to a distant point in the street. She saw her reflection grow smaller and smaller, and then vanish.

She jumped from the chair and rushed into the living room. She must come out of her misery. She had lost touch with the world, gone stale and sour inside herself. Her life had lost its shape. She had no purpose. She had been only marking time, waiting for relief that would never come. She had to build her life again, become a person again.

She sat down in the red chair, Malcolm's chair. No, she thought, it's my chair. She pulled the *New York Times Magazine* from the mahogany rack by the chair. The magazine was six months old. She dumped all the magazines on the floor, the *New Republic, Harper's,* the *New York Review.* They were all stiff and yellow with age. Malcolm's magazines. He had taken the subscriptions with him, and she had not even missed them. She had read nothing in months.

The blood rose to her head and pounded behind her eyes. She had once been an attractive, interesting woman who kept up, who could talk of anything. Yes, talk so that men listened to her and admired her and desired her. Malcolm had taken all that from her. That, too. Slowly, slowly. Over the years he had frequently said hurtful things to her—that she chattered, that she told everything in boring detail. Hurtful things that made her feel inadequate or silly and that broke her confidence. She had given up, content to let him do the talking, content with the warmth of his brilliance. To please him, she had become a cipher. And when he thought he had completed her destruction, he had deserted her.

But he was wrong: she was not destroyed. Free of him, she was ready to become the attractive woman she had once been. Everything was still there, ready to emerge from the half-life she had lived all these years. She felt that her powers were flooding back to her, washing away her fear of him, her timidity.

Exultant, triumphant, she rushed to the telephone and dialed his number at the university. But when a soft young female voice answered, she could not speak. She heard Malcolm ask, "Who is it, Teddy?" and then "Hello" into the phone. She could not remember what she had intended to say to him. A pressure began, swelled larger and larger until she feared it would explode in her chest, crash through her eardrums, shatter the delicate membrane of her nostrils and eyes. She opened her mouth to let the sounds out, but no sounds came.

Marian had often noticed the woman in the red plastic coat who walked with one hand palm up at her shoulder and the other on her hip. Her white hair was burnished to a metallic sheen and it stood high above her face like a chef's cap. She wore multicolored platform shoes with six-inch heels that threw her forward, and she took quick little mincing steps as if hurrying to catch up with her top before it fell. She was, Marian decided, probably a prostitute.

But prostitute or not, she was a human being and a woman, and a woman obviously mistreated by men. And so seeing her on a drizzly March afternoon walking with the red coat held straight-armed above the elaborate hair-do, Marian decided to give the woman a lift. She drew the car alongside the curb and leaned across the passenger seat to lower the window.

And then she noticed the sores on the woman's bare legs. Some of the sores were black holes with diameters the size of a pencil and some were raw looking with moist crusts and some were fresh, suppurating, leaving faint trails down her calves.

The woman turned. Her face was mottled and skull-like and Marian thought the flesh had already begun to rot back from the bones. Marian felt a hard spasm in her lower belly, as if a steel hand had fastened around her groin. The woman grinned then, a terrible grin of complicity, as if she had anticipated, had desired, now shared the sudden hatred Marian felt surging through her. As Marian reared back from the window and twisted the steering wheel toward the street, she heard a muffled, constricted whimpering, and she knew it was her own.

One Sunday afternoon in June, Malcolm came into the house with the children. It had been nearly a year since he had left; the divorce was final. He stood in the hallway and leaned casually against the wall. He was deeply tanned and his gray sideburns were long and bushy and somehow boyish. He seemed cheerful and lighthearted, qualities she thought he had long ago given up to his seriousness, his image of himself as a scholar. He wore his new happiness like an advertisement and he apparently expected her to rejoice with him.

He said, "I've got a plan I know you're going to like."

Her resentment was like a coagulant. As he spoke her blood and her energy ceased to flow, and she felt sullen, dull, thick.

He told her that he would take the children for July to one of the San Juan Islands off Seattle. No electricity, he exulted. No cars. No telephone. Just man against nature, with the necessities flown in, he said, laughing archly. He had never been there, of course, but—he paused no more than a heartbeat—he knew someone who had. He began to describe the island, as if he were enticing her to come along, the cliffs, the immense trees, the wild berries, the birds.

"This will be one of the best experiences of their lives," he said, "and you'll be free for a whole month."

"Free to do what?" she asked. Her tongue was thick and heavy, and her voice hardly rose to her mouth.

"See you next Sunday," he called to the children, and waving, waving, he backed out the front door.

"I'm going to have a shell collection," Molly said.

"There's a lot of driftwood," said Joseph, "so you can carve things and all."

"Teddy says the shells are beautiful and I'm going to make you a beautiful shell necklace."

"Be quiet," said Joseph.

"I've never been to an island," said Molly. "I wish you could come too."

"Yeah," said Joseph.

After her hot bath, she lay in bed in the dark, staring at the odd shapes the moon cast against the draperies. The moon on the water and the sandy beaches and the shadows of trees. The wind blew in her open window and the draperies billowed. She saw people in the moving folds. Heads. Bodies. Lovers moving against each other in the dark shadows. Malcolm and his lady. She drew her hands along her hips, squeezed her breasts between her fingers. No one would ever hold her, whisper to her in the night. For a moment she feared that she would scream out in her anguish, and she threw back the covers and sat up on the side of the bed.

If only she had someone to talk to, to whom she could tell her suffering. She thought of her parents, both dead, and of the brother she had not seen in years. The faces of girls she had been close to came to her, and one in particular who had blond hair in a Dutch boy cut and who had moved away when they were both eleven. She thought of a boy whose name she could not recall who had given her chocolates in a heart-shaped box and had kissed her clumsily on the ear. And of the boy who had loved her in high school and whom she had loved until she had met Malcolm. All these, and others she might have talked to, were gone.

She got up to close the window against the wind and she saw a light beneath Joseph's door. Molly had already deserted her, had said "Teddy" in an affectionate, accepting way. But Joseph, her first-born, suffered, too.

She went to his room. He lay prone on his bed, propped on his elbows, a book open in front of him. She said, "I want to talk to you."

He folded the book over his finger and turned over. He lay back against the headboard. The light from the bullet lamp fell across the side of his face. He looked frail and sad.

She sat down in the desk chair and dragged it closer to the bed. "You're going away," she said, "with them." She held his gaze.

"Mom, please don't," he said. His shadowed face turned away from her. "We're not supposed to talk about the other one. He never talks about you."

"Never? Has he never said anything?"

"All he ever said was he had a right to try to be happy," Joseph said in a soft, fretful, placating voice. He drew his knees up and folded his arms across them and buried his head in his arms. "Please don't talk to me, please," he said.

As he lifted his face to her, his head seemed to rise above the knees, disembodied. As she stared at him, his face grew larger and larger and whiter and whiter. It swelled toward her, a pale disc, like the moon. She got to her feet.

"Sleep well," she said.

She went to the kitchen to make sure she had turned off the oven and the burners. She checked the locks on outside doors. She listened for the sound of a forgotten sprinkler. The house was still and dark and hot. She felt dull and sluggish, and yet excited, too restless to stay inside.

She went into her bathroom and took her old flannel robe off the hook on the back of the door. She got in the car and drove over to the university lake. In the springtime, the students boated and swam and sunned at the lake, and often she and Malcolm had brought the children there to search for tadpoles and frogs. Now, in June, the lake was slowly drying into a swamp.

She sat on the dark bank and breathed in the cool night air. The moon shimmered in the puddles on the lake bottom. It was the end of Spring term and she heard the murmur of student lovers and the rustle of dry leaves. She imagined bodies touching, and the soft delicious look of desire on their mouths and in their eyes. She had known that ecstasy. She remembered the first night she and Malcolm had been together. They had been on Cape Cod. She saw them lying in a little pocket of leafy brush, protected from the wind by an overhanging cliff. She had felt nothing existed but the two of them, and nothing mattered but the act of love they performed.

And in the moonlight, sitting on the damp bank of the swampy lake, she began to cry. Her crying was a moan that returned to her as the sound of soft thunder. And then she saw movement in the shadows of the trees. The students, the lovers, were moving away from her along the shores of the lake. She had driven them away. In her groin was the pain that was like lust, like fear, like hatred. She didn't care what the lovers or anyone thought of her. Her chest swelled with sobs. They seemed to be exploding through her ribs, bursting from her armpits, ripping through her ears and eye-sockets.

She stood up. The streets were empty. She clutched her bathrobe tighter against the suddenly chilly night, and she began to walk quickly, recklessly, in the direction of the moon. As she walked, she felt the power of her thrusting stride, the rising flood of her energy, the release of her torment.

Infidelities

FLORENCE TREFETHEN

This young woman with whom I am lunching at a French restaurant in Boston has been living for thirteen months with my only son, Giles. They are graduate students at Berkeley. Theirs is, as they say, a relationship. "Is it serious?" I demand of Giles in my stuffier moments. "Yes, serious," he tells me, "but not necessarily permanent." Serious, not permanent; I think we did not have that type of relationship back in West Lafayette.

This tall slim young woman with thick auburn hair controlled by tortoise-shell barrettes, who knows four real languages plus three computer languages, who is always dressed in a pale gray-green like a celadon vase, who cooks vegetables in a wok and plays lacrosse, may become my daughter-in-law; but, then again, may not. It's hard to predict. Like many girls in her generation, she is called Jennifer. There are no Jennifers in my age group, and, so far as I can tell, no Virginias in hers. That's why I insist on being called Gina, a little more youthful and continental, a little less like middle America in the Depression.

Our lunch is turning into a semi-annual event. When Jennifer comes east to Maine to visit her mother, who was widowed at an early age, she phones me and we arrange to meet in a chic, neutral place. We dance around each other carefully, unsure of our ground. Her man, my son, is at Berkeley getting ready for his qualifying exams. My man for thirty years, Christopher Frost, is somewhere between San Diego and Tucson, probably in bed with Faith Briscoe. Jennifer, I ask her silently, how would a woman like you react to that fact? You who have lived intimately with someone since your sophomore year at Radcliffe and are now on your third relationship? How would you react if you had been married more than half your life to the same person, then found him drifting toward Faith Briscoe?

He always drifts back. In fact, he'd been sidling off for three years before I realized it. A researcher in photographic chemicals is often on the road, and who's to know at home what's happening in San Jose, Chicago, or Rochester? The affair was revealed accidentally, unnecessarily. Chris was reading some of the poems I was preparing to send to yet another quarterly. One was called "Ex-Lover Comes to Dinner," a persona poem spoken by a woman whose former lover has animal table manners that now disgust her. Chris assumed that the "I" speaking the poem was I his wife, and went one step further, casting an old family friend who slurps his soup in the role of former lover. "I'm glad to know this," he announced to me. "I've found somebody too."

I guess he was looking for an excuse to tell me. He has a Yankee conscience—not sharp enough to keep him from deceit, just enough to make him need to confess eventually. I was surprised, and angry. We'd been seeing a psychiatrist together, to help us through a mid-marriage crisis. One of Chris's complaints was that I had not updated my sex life as much as he had, that I was rejecting some of the ideas presented in *The Joy of Sex*. "This Alex Comfort," I asked him, "why do you regard him as an authority?" Chris would not discuss it. If I wouldn't assent to Comfort, I must be frigid. "Chris," I said, "I may not know much about sex, but I know a lot about publishing. Although this book is an intentional bestseller, it is not the Old and New Testament combined, so stop giving it so much reverence."

Our psychiatrist, Ferdinand Maurer, seemed intent on helping me loosen up, become more open, more agile, more involved, more ready for change. It disillusioned me to discover he'd known about Faith Briscoe all the time. Why was he telling me to be open (including playing tapes of my voice in arguments with Chris) while he and Chris were concealing this secret: I stopped seeing Ferdinand Maurer. I'm not sure if he committed psychiatric malpractice, but he certainly made a fool of me. You've got a big reputation in Boston, Ferdinand Maurer, and I'm merely a freelance editor who also writes poetry, so what can I do? But if ever I have a chance to get even with you, I'll take it.

I hate the way that sounds. The worst part of my situation is that it triggers in me emotions I thought belonged to Elizabethan tragedy. There are days when I keep alive only by composing scenes of revenge.

Such as this scene. Chris and I are summoned to Dr. Jason Sears, our internist and good friend. Jason says, "I have something serious to tell you; I hope you'll be brave. You, Chris, have leukemia, or cirrhosis of the liver, or a brain tumor (choose one). I'm sorry this turned up in your last annual check-up, but, after numerous rechecks, I must tell you your days are numbered. You people have some decisions to make. Chris, you can go to Mass General and be well looked after. Or, if you like, you can stay home, provided Gina is willing to nurse you through your final months." Chris wants to stay home. But am I willing to nurse? Not bloody likely! "How about in sickness and health till death us do part?" he begs, trying to make me feel guilty. "That counted while you were still observing your vows," I say forcefully. "It's canceled now. But if you'd like me to invite Faith Briscoe to come for the nursing, I'll oblige." We both know Faith won't sign on.

Or this scene. Chris comes home looking defeated. "Gina," he says, "we're wiped out. Our savings are worthless because of inflation, and the stocks I've bought have all plummeted. We'll have to retrench, sell everything we still own, and take a small house somewhere in, say Arkansas, where the living is easy and the cost is low." "Chris," I respond, "give my regards to Arkansas. As for me, I've been investing my extra money in Krugerrands, and the price of gold is soaring. See you around."

Or this scene. Chris is in Toronto, or Seattle, or Atlanta at a conference. He phones me at midnight. Instead of grabbing the receiver on the first ring because I'm so eager to hear his voice, I deliberately do not answer. He phones again at one A.M. I keep reading *The Spoils of Poynton*, declining to pick up the phone. He calls again at seven A.M. while I'm showering. I let him ring. The hell with it. If he asks, I'll say, "Oh, I guess that was the night I was up at Rockport," or "Sorry I wasn't home; there was a party at Professor Commeau's apartment."

Professor Commeau is one of my fantasy lovers. I have four. They are not exactly fantasies, since each is a real man I'm acquainted with and each has registered some interest in me. I think I would like to go to bed with one of them, or all of them, but I'm nervous. Having been only with Chris these many years and with my sex life rather dated, I lack confidence.

My best prospect for dalliance is Manfred Reutlinger, a dashing character once married to Chris's sister Elsie. Manfred and I have been waltzing together at parties whenever we meet for many years; also flirting and pretending we have a secret attachment. His third wife (a wife one wouldn't mind hurting) is sarcastic, and Manfred often gets fed up with her. I tell myself that if Manfred were to whistle I'd come running. That may be self-delusion. Two years ago he phoned to say he'd be in Boston on October 11th and could we spend the day together? I fell apart. That was the very date I'd organized a picnic at Plymouth for Giles, three of his Yale classmates, and their families. I couldn't disappoint them. I told this later to a feminist therapist. She said this shows I'm not ready for an affair—I devise family-centered excuses.

I also fantasize about Bruce Loring, Giles's godfather. We've known him and his wife Claire (whom I'd never want to hurt) since we were first married. Bruce has become thin, bald, and faded, and very conservative politically. But that old magic I remember from earlier days still tingles me.

When last we dined at the Lorings, he pulled me into the cloak room for a passionate kiss. This seems promising, except that he's been doing that periodically since before Giles was born, which probably proves that he's nervous too, just fooling around. He's not ready for a Faith Briscoe kind of relationship.

Even if I had the courage, would I want to make love with a new person? There would be advantages. I'd feel less like a victimized and injured wife, more Chris's equal. But that's a mean motive for going to bed with a nice man like Manfred or Bruce. If I had such an adventure, should I tell Chris? Part of the point is proving I can do it too, so I suppose I should let him discover my affair. On the other hand, it would be delicious to have something that's mine alone, that he didn't know about. There are many difficulties. Jennifer, I wish I could ask your advice. If I posed this problem, would you stare at me as though I had just arrived from a different planet?

It *is* a different planet. I grew up not knowing much about infidelities. In my orbit in West Lafayette, everybody who was married stayed faithful, or at least seemed to. Only my Uncle Conrad strayed—to Indianapolis. He was our family's outcast because of deserting his wife and children to share an apartment with a woman he'd known before his marriage. Nowadays, lots of our friends get divorced, but those who keep together don't seem to be having affairs. Ferdinand Maurer asked me when I was screaming like a banshee (all taped, of course) after discovering Chris's unfaithfulness, "What have other women you've known done in similar circumstances?" "I don't know anybody in similar circumstances," I told him. He gave me a pitying look, as though I wasn't observant. I have lots of women friends to talk to, but if their husbands are wandering they don't mention it to me, perhaps out of shame, out of loyalty, out of injured pride. I can understand that. I don't mention Faith Briscoe to them. These days one confides only in therapists.

Frankly, I'm surprised at Chris's taste in mistresses. To introduce such confusion into a marriage after so many years, the motivation should be more potent than Faith Briscoe. Someone like Lily Tomlin or Elizabeth Drew or Joanne Woodward I could understand. But why would they be interested in Chris? He's handsome, he's intelligent, but not distinctive enough to catch the eye of a celebrity. Besides, he's still having his mid-life crisis in which he questions whether he should ever have gone into photographic chemicals. He thinks he ought to have been a surgeon. Or an architect.

One reason I like Professor Commeau is that he knows exactly what he wants to do and does it thoroughly. He's a historian, Western Europe, especially France in the twelfth century. I was a history major at Smith, which is probably why Professor Commeau keeps hiring me to edit his books. He's like a medieval cleric, dark and brooding, and wears exquisite neckties. We lunch together at the Faculty Club from time to time to discuss a manuscript. His manners are courtly, precise. He holds my coat at just the right height. And he always mentions me enthusiastically in his "Acknowledgments." Twice I've caught him staring at me in a sad and pensive way; his eyes seemed to be trying to transmit an important message. Perhaps he was thinking, "Gina, why do we keep this pretense of author and editor when we want to be lovers?" Is he waiting for me to make a move? What kind of signal should I send? Help, Jennifer! What do I do next?

In the case of my fourth lover, Joe, the obstacles are age and geography. He's only thirty-four, an archaeologist, usually digging in Turkey. He's a murky writer, so I ghostwrite his grant requests, research reports, and papers. His face is suntanned, and he has beautiful crinkles near his eyes and very long lashes. Whenever he comes to Boston, we meet for dinner with much wine. He holds my hand and kisses me hello and goodbye. But he's loaded with worries. His wife is divorcing him and asking for exclusive custody of their three-year-old twins on the argument that Joe is never around. She has a point. "But I can't abandon Justin and Psyche," he lamented when we were together last month. I wanted to say, "Joe, let's check in at the Ritz. Just for tonight, let's be loving friends.'' Would that have sounded corny, like ''Come with me to the Casbah?'' What would Joe have answered?

Though psychologically unprepared for an affair, I'm ready otherwise. Over the past two years, I've been buying up lingerie of various types. I now have six new pairs of spandex and lace pants, three new bras, two camisoles, two halfslips, and the most expensive pajamas I've ever owned. I've kept my old housecoat. It's Chinese brocade. Chris bought it for me in San Francisco, whether out of love or guilt I don't know. But it's beautiful. I've chucked out my old makeup case and bought a new one. Have makeup case, will travel—to the Ritz, to the Hyatt-Regency, to the Copley Plaza, just name it, one of you guys, and I'll appear discreetly at your door with the best collection of lingerie you've ever seen.

How do you relate to lingerie, Jennifer? I know one of your nightgowns. I helped Giles buy it. That shows how strange life has become—my son asks his mother to help him buy a nightgown for his girl, who is a serious but not necessarily permanent attachment. I took him to Filene's. It was a new experience for Giles, leafing through those racks of nightgowns, floor-length, knee-length, mini-length, in white, ecru, pink, peach, mint, aqua, powder, buttercup. He looked bemused. Finally we settled on a long white gown with lace around a plunging neckline. My feminist therapist claims Giles was trying to signal me that he now has a woman of his own, that he's no longer my little boy. O.K., Giles, I get the message; got it long ago.

In this family, it is not I with the empty-nest syndrome but Chris. Being a father appealed to him, and he did the job well. When Giles first left for Yale, Chris began to get restless. That's when he started doing all those push-ups in the morning and playing so much tennis. Another wedge between us. My right shoulder hurts when I hit a ball overhand, so I don't play tennis. No problem; there are lots of partners for Chris where we live. But he seems to think this is a flaw in me. ''You should keep in shape,'' he says. God knows, I try. I swim and go for long walks and do stretch exercises. I am size 10. I am eight pounds heavier than when we got married.

I have another flaw. I hate to drive in traffic and will do almost anything to avoid it. When I'm on the road with cars on both sides, in front and in back, I sweat. I feel that a collision is inevitable, as though we were all in bump cars at an amusement park. It's a serious fear, and Chris resents it. "But I'm not afraid of other things," I protest. "I'm not afraid of flying. And I'm not afraid of snakes." Chris is afraid of snakes, but he blames that on racial memory so he doesn't feel responsible. "I'm not afraid of publishing things," I twist the knife once more. Chris has a block against sending papers out to journals and hardly ever does it. But he thinks that's more natural than not liking to drive because his family has always been keen on cars and gets a lot of its kicks and status that way. He has a brother with two Cadillacs, a nephew with a Cadillac and a Jaguar. Chris himself favors a white Mercedes.

Because of my faults and hang-ups, there are times when I think I'd better hang on to Chris because nobody else will ever care for me. Those are the days the black clouds roll in. Why, I ask myself, should Manfred Reutlinger, Bruce Loring, Professor Commeau, or Joe want me? They're attractive men. They can pick and choose, and they'll choose someone younger. Several men we know have divorced their wives and married younger women. One of our neighbors married his daughter's Wellesley roommate. "How can I fight this?" his wife, Myra, asked me. "How can I compete with a twenty-one-year-old kid in a bikini who is also captain of the debating team? If twenty-five years together and three children and a comfortable home won't hold him, I'm sunk, kaput." I wonder whether Myra's husband used to nag her about tennis and *The Joy of Sex*. I also wonder about that Wellesley roommate. Why would she want to marry a man of fifty? Isn't there something peculiar about a young girl like that? I know one such in the History Department at B.U. She's a new assistant professor, and she told our consciousness-raising group that the only way to get tenure these days is to attach yourself firmly and sexually to a source of power. She's chosen her person, and he's almost retirement age. I'm glad Jennifer and Giles are contemporaries. It's more honest, more natural.

It's to Chris's credit that he didn't fall for a juvenile. Faith Briscoe is our age. I assume she's updated her sex, and I know she loves to drive. I think they drive around expansively when Chris is on his business trips. Faith has no job so is free to fly to wherever Chris is. I keep in mind a map of the continental United States with a red pin everywhere they've been together. I know about Sacramento, Carmel, San Diego, Las Vegas, Santa Fe, Tampa, Montauk, and maybe Phoenix. Some of these I know because I pried the information out of Chris. Some I've intuited, like Montauk. Chris didn't phone for four days; I didn't know where he was. Finally he called from Montauk and said he'd had trouble finding a phone. I thought it must be a primitive place, but my friend Betsy, a New Yorker, told me Montauk is up-to-date.

Chris declares his affair is over, but I don't count on it. He said that before, but returned to Faith last summer. We were in California visiting Giles. I had to fly back to Boston to meet a publisher's deadline. Having more time, Chris said he'd drive down the coast and enjoy some scenery, maybe play a little tennis. I found out later he'd arranged to meet Faith in Carmel. Perhaps he'll always be like that.

I guess Faith has the advantage of primogeniture, since Chris knew her first. "Why the hell didn't you marry Faith?" I shouted at him when the affair first came to light. "I was working happily in Washington, marriage nowhere in my mind. Did I ask you to come barging into my life, to make me fall in love with you and move to Boston? Faith was available. Why me?" I think I know why. In those days, Chris had a precise notion of the person he wanted to marry. She had to be bright and well educated, interested in something more than the domestic round, with a sense of humor and lots of energy. I had all that, plus good health and good looks. Faith was also healthy, handsome. But she'd never had much education, and her only jobs have been typing and shorthand drags. She was glad to get married and give up working altogether.

I don't know whether her husband knows about Faith and Chris. Unless he's retarded, he must think something's fishy whenever she disappears to be with Chris. Perhaps she tells him she's visiting her mother or having a facelift. In my revenge fantasies, I sometimes write that husband a letter.

Dear Mr. Briscoe:

We are not acquainted, but I'm told you are a decent person. That is why you should know that you are being hoodwinked by your wife and her paramour, Christopher Frost. Don't take my word for it. The next time she goes off on a trip, have her followed. You'll discover the truth whereof I speak.

A wellwisher

Sometimes I devise a different letter.

Dear Emmett Briscoe:

You and I have one hell of a lot in common. Are you aware that our spouses are seeing each other regularly? This has been droning on like a tired old soap opera for many years, and I'm getting sick of it. Would you care to meet and plan a joint strategy for coping with our mutual difficulty?

Gina Frost
known in pre-Liberation days as
Mrs. Christopher Frost

Naturally I send neither letter. If there's one thing I fear more than being ill-used it's making waves. I was raised in times when we were taught to smooth things over for the general benefit. Perhaps that too should be updated.

Fortunately, I still have my sense of humor and see the funny elements in my situation. For example, Chris always asks me to choose his ties when he's going on a trip. That's worse than buying a nightgown for Giles's girl! I'm tempted

to make awful choices. Chris is colorblind and wouldn't
know if I gave him a bright green tie to wear with a lavender
shirt. Would being poorly matched reduce him in the eyes of
Faith Briscoe? Who knows? Once when I was helping by
unpacking his suitcase on return, I found a copy of *Hustler*
under his shorts. It was very updated sexually, also nauseat-
ing. Does Faith read *Hustler?* Who knows? Anyway, she has
more courage than I about getting in touch with men. I asked
Chris how he happened to encounter her again after more
than twenty years. He said she'd dropped in at his office and
said she just happened to be in town. Tacky, yet it worked. I
never drop into offices; not my style. But maybe that's why
I'm not this very minute at the Ritz with Manfred or Bruce or
Professor Commeau or Joe.

Humor carries you only so far. Some things cut too near
the bone for laughter. When my father died suddenly in West
Lafayette three years ago, Chris was away and I couldn't find
him. Giles and I tried phoning several places around Santa Fe
where we thought he was. No luck. Fortunately, he phoned
home and got to the funeral and to the university memorial
service for Dad. Just afterward, though, he picked a fight
with me, said I wasn't turning to him in my hour of grief and
need. Maybe I wasn't. I felt so numb I couldn't communicate
with anybody. Chris packed up and went back to Santa Fe, I
thought to continue his business. Later it came out that Faith
was waiting there in a motel for him to get the last rites over
with and get back to her. The infidelity I might forgive, the
callousness, even the deceit; but making it all seem like my
fault is beyond forgiveness. We may spend the rest of our
lives together, Chris, and this bitterness may wear away.
Perhaps I'll be able to put on my wedding ring again without
having my finger swell up and turn blue. But some things are
indelible and will not fade.

The waiter is here with the dessert menu. I have not eaten
dessert for many years. Jennifer debates between pastry and
chocolate mousse. There is no extra flesh in her future for as
far ahead as she can see. Oh, Jennifer, I do not love you yet,
though I will, eventually, if you and Giles stay together. But

I feel close, remembering how it was to be your age, even on a different planet. I wish we could change places now. I would bask in the freedoms you take for granted, hoping they would erase my uptightness. All loyalties seem uptight these days, but I was programmed for loyalty. Serious but not permanent may now be the only way to go. I want to learn how to have courage for that much uncertainty. I would love it, Jennifer. And I would order the chocolate mousse.

Bunny Says It's
the Death Watch

STEPHANIE C. GUNN

My younger brother Pete is as tall as a horse. He calls everybody Fred. No matter what his name is, or who he is, or what he does. He calls even our father Fred. Father doesn't know. Mother does and thinks it's funny. She'd been looking for a name for him ever since he moved away into a new house painted white, in the beach town next to ours. He moved into a new sky-blue sailboat that leaks when it heels to starboard, and a new wife, exactly half his age, who sleeps in mascara, who ties her pig and pony tails up in red wrapping bows. Mother's been looking all over for a name for Father ever since he moved away into that new house with the new silver slide in the front yard. The slide squeaks when his two new children go down it. Their midget shorts and skirts ride up their infantile bare legs. Their elastic-loose underpants ride up their white bottoms that become pink bottoms when they squeak down the slide.

His two new children land on Father's new grass that has some of Father's new woodchips lying in it. Amongst the woodchips there is a fleet of Father's old iron toy soldiers that were once made, by little hands, to do great battle. Now the toy soldiers lie forgotten except when a foot of one of Father's new children finds one and, only for a second, feels it before running on, before sinking it into the grass, sinking some toy soldiers that no longer have painted faces, and others that have lost their heads, and still others that have lost their shoes that had their feet in them.

Mother has been looking everywhere for a name for Father ever since he moved to that woodchip driveway lined with old skinny pine trees that, in the summer sun, bleed their sticky sap all down their barks. Mother has been looking. But it was Pete who found it. Pete found: Fred.

The sun melts the trees, melts their insides out. The sun sets the crickets to doing whatever they do with their legs to make that ZZZZZ, that ZZZZZ that means that they're hot and have to tell each other, or else one of Father's happy, hand-clapping children, or else both of Father's happy children clapping. The crickets ZZZZZ and give away where they are, and then they are chased and cornered and caught and suffocated in two hands or all four little hands. They ZZZZZ and they become members of the cricket corpse collection in the garage in Father's sail box.

Don't tell Father.

Father ties ropes with rings onto the pines lining the woodchip driveway and snaps the clues of wet spinnakers onto these rings. The sails dry in the wind, in the sticky needles and cones. They swell bright red and bright blue and bright yellow, they are as big as airplanes. You have to put your aerial down coming up the drive. You have to turn off the radio and get out of the car and put the aerial down. Father considers the sails to be the flags of his estate, his own country. He flies them at all times except in small craft warning winds. He flies them and, in foul weather gear and rubber boots, stands under them and hoses their bellies salt-less. The new woodchips get all salty.

Father tells his small children of mahogany eyes and lips like raspberries that the trees come by colored parachutes. That's how they were born. They were dropped out of the sky in twins in a long row down the driveway. The trees like to have spinnakers tied to them, he says. The tugging sails comfort them, remind them of a past. He actually TELLS his children this. He fuels their little minds, pliant, with myths and magic before they grow up, before they're fed to the wolves. That's how he puts it. The world, the wolves, what's the difference? He teaches them fun so they'll always have had at least THAT with him. When they are in their adolescence and he is an old man they will remember his stories. Trees by parachute. What about babies? Them by parachute, too? I ask Father who shrugs and smiles and knows that by the time they'll be interested in that kind of thing, they will likely hear all about it from some place else. He says, They're only six and four. I know, I say. And the one who's four looks up at me and says, Six and four, that's ten—right? That's how many fingers—right? And how many toes? I ask her. And she sits down on Father's new woodchips, takes off her summer sandals, and counts.

Mother has not talked to Fred in many years. She does not want to. She SAYS that she doesn't want to. She forbids him to call our house. But sometimes he calls. If there is an emergency, say, if the wind comes cruel, if the spinnakers rip, if the trees work at flying, if the new woodchips rise and swirl, making a bonfire out of themselves, Father calls our house.

If, when he calls, Mother answers, he hangs up. Then Mother finds one of us on the patio watching through German submarine binoculars. We watch the strong off-shore breeze and all that goes with it to the horizon: a lady in a tire, boys in a stalled motor boat emptying cans of beer into themselves, and an all-colored beach ball. One of us watches the all-colored beach ball being grieved over by a child on the end of a jetty with her fists in her eyes, or does she grieve the loss of the lady in the tire? Not the boys in the boat with the beer? Mother finds one of us and says, "You-know-who just called. Why don't you call him back. I'll go into my room."

They lived together for twenty-nine years. She can tell the difference between him and a person who, having the wrong number, hangs up without a word.

After Mother delivers this message of hers, she disappears into her end of the house. On the half-hour you can hear her yell from behind her door, "Is it safe to come out yet?"

Today, it is summertime and we are in Dennisport. Waves are shush-shushing outside the house, up onto the beach, up onto the foot of the seawall. Pete and I are in the kitchen in bare feet. The radio is on behind the basket of seedless sea-green grapes and plums as purple as fresh bad bruises. Reggae is all over the kitchen. Last night's popcorn dish is in the sink soaking. There is the toaster going up and down, and a pair of wooden toast tweezers are stuck onto it by magnets. Pete is using a knife to unlodge an English muffin from the toaster's inner combings.

"What do you think these are for, Pete-baby?" I point to the toast tweezers. "The decor? Your imagination? Your bicycle?"

"Yep," Pete says. He is not yet fully awake. Sleep is caked on his eyelashes like oatmeal, and he has sliced the muffin in the toaster into quarters and still can't get it out.

Frankie, our oldest brother, walks into the kitchen holding between his index finger and his thumb, as far away from himself as he can, a pair of white boxer underpants. They are as big as a pillow case.

"Did you put these in my room?" Frankie's voice is much louder than the reggae. There is disturbance in his eyes.

Mother steps in through the back door screen in her bathing suit that looks like a sundress. It is blue with bunches of seedless sea-green grapes on it. She has been lying outdoors in the sun and there is a piece of aluminum foil folded over her nose. There is sun-prevention lipstick on her chin and cheeks and lips. Frankie is staring at Pete in his inside-out red elephant pajamas. Frankie is staring at me wrapped in an over-sized crimson towel, my hair dripping like a faucet. Frankie is staring at Mother in her bathing suit that goes down to her knees.

"Well?" he asks.

There is a draft of air coming in from the back door. It is

surprisingly cool for a sunny day like today, not a cloud in the sky. Frankie fixes his eyes on Pete who, leaning over his blue and white breakfast plate, jams a whole buttered blueberry muffin into his mouth. Pete is tapping his foot that is hard and thick from walking on our rock road and Fred's new woodchips, he is tapping his foot to AM reggae.

"Well?" Frankie asks again. "Did you?"

Pete swallows before he says, "Nope."

"Who put them in my room, then?" Frankie's black eyebrows are down over his eyes. "Whose are they?"

Mother stops pouring cranberry juice into a glass crowded with ice. She looks over at Frankie from under her visor hat. There is the moment of everyone thinking. You can see that Mother is thinking. I am thinking. Even Pete is thinking. Pete is looking at the underpants in their reflection in the toaster. Whose ARE they? As big as a pillow case. Whose else.

"Throw them in the garbage!" Mother says through her sun-prevention lipstick. "I mean it. In the garbage right now!"

"Gee, I'm sorry, Mum," Pete says licking blueberry off his thumbs. "They must have gotten into my backpack or something. I wonder how THAT happened." Pete goes off into himself wondering.

"In the garbage!" Mother says in a loud voice, a very loud voice, not like Mother at all.

"You mean, just because you're divorced, you're not going to do Fred's laundry any more?" I ask her, but just then, Frankie lurches to the back door and in a strong underhand, throws them outside. Through the kitchen window Mother and Pete and I see their white blob flash across the patio and hook themselves onto the arm of a three-and-a-half-legged deck chair.

"They look very nice there, Frankie. Very nice. Don't they improve breakfast," I say.

"Frankie! What are you doing? What are they doing there?" Mother wants to know. She is quite serious but then she is about to laugh. Now she is laughing, not a lot, not from the stomach, but she is laughing, which is something.

"I threw them there!" Frankie replies, making kisses at her in the air. His navy blue eyes are smiling. A hero, he is thinking. Then, right off his mouth, right out of his eyes, his smile fades. He bends his head down to look at the floor. A morning couple of black locks falls over his face like gloved fingers. He leaves them there.

"Well, where else?"

"In the compost heap?" I ask.

"They cannot stay THERE!" Mother says and she walks away into her room.

And they don't, of course. They don't stay there at all.

Pete stuffs them into his backpack on his way to the end of the road to meet Fred. They are going sailing together. They are going to try to figure out a way to fix the leak under the railing by the starboard side-stay. Eventually, around noon, Pete will probably beach the boat and scrape barnacles off of the bottom. He will take a little paint off, too. He will make the bottom of the boat as smooth as the bottoms of Father's new little ones. That's how Father puts it. That's how Father puts what he wants done.

Wearing cutoffs, Pete is walking up the hill in our road. Fred will be along any minute in his red-interior convertible. Its front seat is very low, and when Fred drives it he has to sit forward to see over the dashboard. Mother has seen Father in this car. He looks like a child in it, she has said. She does not see him often. They live in neighboring towns and it is not surprising that they should stand together in the same check-out line at the grocery stores, or the same teller line at the bank. It is not surprising that they should sit in seats that share the same arm in a movie theater. But of course they never do.

But that doesn't mean to say that they don't spy on each other. Mother drives by Father's white house on her way to play tennis or on her way to visit her sister, Bunny. This is how she knows that one of Father's children is a foot taller than the other. That wearing orange life preservers going down the slide is one of their favorite things to do. What she does not know is that they yell, Man Overboard! as they go down, that they are pretending to be part of a 747 emergency landing. She does not know that they love airplanes, and the sky. That they love the thought of trees arriving by parachute. That their eyes are ever up in the air watching for more births. If their eyes were down the driveway, they would see Mother slowing in her car, they would see her watching them slide.

And Fred, the same goes for Fred. He, pretending impatience, will drive up the hill in our road and wait at its top. He will honk his horn. He will sit there and die to know what is going on in our house, his old one. He will spy on the baby carrots in the garden, the seawall crumbling under the tides, and of course, Mother, always Mother. He will want to see her.

Freckles on Pete's shoulders and their sharp blades have run into each other. He is at the top of the hill when he hears an upstairs window fly open. He turns his head to look back at our house.

"Don't get stuck wheelbarrowing!" Frankie yells at him through the screen of his bedroom window. Frankie laughs to himself all the way over to a set of golf clubs in the corner. He picks out a putter, drops two Titalists onto the wooden floor, and aims for a bed leg. He begins an imitation of the very low excited voice of a sport's announcer. And now here we are on the eighteenth green. Fred is attempting a nine-foot putt. If he sinks this one he will total out at ten under, certainly a winning score here at the Fred Open. If he sinks it.

Pete sits in the deep, clean beach sand that has found its way to the road's end, or was there before the road was. He puts on his beaten running shoes, and waits. His shoes have holes in their toes, and their laces are broken and not long enough to go all their way around. He takes apart an oak leaf at its veins. He aims a rock at a dog's water dish across the street. Aims a couple of more rocks there. The dog's not around. He gets one right in the bowl, a tiny spurt of water jumps out of it and lies in the sand, a dead crooked snake. The sun is out and hot, the snake is disappearing. Fred's not around either. Pete throws one more rock as far as he can into the woods on the other side of the road, far beyond the dog dish. He doesn't hear where it ends up. So he just lies down in tree shadow, his head on his backpack, and dozes off. The pine trees melt all around him. Crickets start their ZZZZZ sound and just when he's getting used to them, just when he doesn't hear them any more, they stop. Their stopping, as sudden as their starting, nearly wakes up Pete.

An hour later, Mother wants to drive to the store. She says, "Do you think it's safe?" She waits half an hour more and just as she is walking out the back door, the phone rings. It might be her tennis partner or her sister, Bunny, and she answers it. "Hello?" she asks. There is dial tone.

"It was you-know-who," she says to me. I am at the kitchen sink cleaning out the gold fish bowl. Two gold fish and one red and white one are squirming for space in a drinking glass that is too small for the three of them to be in. The red and white one lies on the bottom of the glass and fights with itself to keep belly-down. Not a good sign, I think as I rinse the fake coral piece that the fish adore swimming in and out of. But the red and white one must be at least a year old. I try to count the months but I cannot remember the time I first saw the fish. Why not throw ALL of them into seawater at a low tide, I think. What a good idea. At low tide so that they can get used to sea motion before the tide gets deep and carries them away.

The gold ones are bumping into each other soundlessly. They wave their see-through fins at each other and their mouths are startled, their mouths are saying O. Their eyes are skidding their way along the inside of the glass. The fish are gulping air out of the water, feed out of the water, water out of itself. Through the glass you can see the threads of their bowels as dark as pencil lines. You can see the threads come right out of the fish and swim behind them like spouses. The threads are all over the bottom of the bowl. At full speed boiling water runs into the bowl and up to the bowl's lip and over. I let it run by itself. Through the glass the fish watch their bowl come clean.

Just as a hand of Mother's is on the back door pushing to get out, the phone rings. THIS time it might be her tennis partner or her sister, Bunny. She answers it.

"No, I'm sorry, he's not. WHAT?"

I hear her slam down the phone.

"Lord, what I go through!"

I wipe my hands on the hem of my oversized crimson towel and peek around the corner at Mother, who sits in the rocker beside the phone, rocking. Rocking, rocking, with her hands in a white-knuckled grip of the chair's arms.

"What is it?"

"That man, that man," she is saying.

"Fred?"

"Do you know what that was? Do you?" she asks me.

"No. WHO?" She does not answer. "Who was it, Mother?"

"I said, Hello, and this little voice asked to speak to Pete." Mother breathes in, then out. The piece of aluminum foil falls off her nose into her lap. With the care of a blind woman learning a jigsaw piece so that she can fit it, Mother fingers the foil. "I said that Pete wasn't here, then SHE said, the little voice said, Oh, well, just tell him to call up Daddy."

"Oh, dear," I say.

"I just can't get over that man sometimes." Mother's head is shaking slowly from side to side, she is slowly rocking herself back and forth.

"I know."

"You can tell that Father of yours not to do that ever again. He just can't do that to me." Mother is not crying. She will not either. Her cheeks are as soft and worried as pillows after night, her eyes are true blue, her hair is a bright white, and has been since the day Frankie was born. Tomorrow she will make jokes about talking on the phone to one of Father's new little ones. But it is not tomorrow yet.

At the end of the road, right beside the sleeping Pete, Mother honks her horn. Pete sits up abruptly.

"Oh, hi, Mum!"

"Hi, darling. You having fun? Fred just called. Probably looking for his underwear. And you'll never guess who ELSE

I talked to. He must be desperate for them. BYE!'' Mother says and off she drives. She has one eye out for Fred in his red-interior convertible. Off she drives and Pete hears her voice, when she stops the car a block away, yelling back at him.

"Pete, please don't sleep in the road!''

Nearly evening, the bowl is clean, the fish are back in it and they are swimming through their fake coral reef. Outside the house clouds have been rolling in. Wind has picked up. The seas have begun to turn. Thunder from the sky shakes the silver candlesticks on the warped dining room table. They move closer together, scared children. The cooking pots on nails on the kitchen wall shake, their tops hung over them clatter. The fish in the water in the bowl quiver. Hanging tea cups in a closed kitchen cabinet tink each other in delicate toasts. Thunder loosens the magnets holding the wooden toast tweezers and they, the tweezers, fall off the toaster and lie in burnt crumbs in the toaster tray.

Deck chairs from the front of the house slide past side windows to the back of the house. They screech on the patio like copulating cats. Some lift off and bang against the side of the house in flight. They are trying to get into the house through the walls. One deck chair gets stuck in a bush thats arms are open wide as if it's been waiting for this moment all its life, to hold something, anything, the deck chair. The three-and-a-half-legged deck chair flies off onto the driveway. Mother is going to run it over when she drives home from shopping.

Ocean waves are up all over the picture windows. Waves and rain both come hard. There is a window upstairs that is open too much or too little. It has caught the wind, and is a fog horn.

Through the storm I rush outside to the clothesline. In the darkness white pajama legs are slapping at each other. As I near them they slap at me. Like coats of plaster, wet towels stick to me. The hooks of Mother's bras are sharp at my face but I make them stop. I take the linen into my arms into the house. I drape them over the arms and across the shoulders of the living room chairs and couches, and they are people who have been in a boating accident. They drip and make the rug black.

Lightning comes in fast from the outside. I run with pots from the kitchen to places I know in the house, to places where the rain is leaking. I make Frankie run, too.

Staring out the picture windows, I wait three lightning flashes before I say, "Hey, Frankie. There's a boat out there."

Frankie and I look out at the sailboat shooting under and then up over the ocean's blackness and whiteness and waves.

"I can't believe ANYBODY'd be crazy enough to be out in this weather," Frankie says.

I grab the German submarine binoculars from the sill of the picture windows.

"Frankie, that boat looks sky-blue to me."

"I don't believe it," Frankie says flatly and goes up the stairs.

All the pots are off their nails in the kitchen. There are many more leaks than pots. I begin with pot tops but soon there are none left of them either. I put the fish bowl on the floor in the upstairs bathroom under the slowest leak. When the drops fall into the bowl, the fish open their mouths, then shut them quickly and open them again. They do not bump into each other, or that fake coral piece. They are not THAT confused. But they do dart this way and that. Is it eating time? Is it time to clean the bowl? Didn't we do that this morning?

The wind blows, blows the house down. The house creaks, an old ship keeling over. There is the wind moving through the blankets on the beds. I go up the stairs four at a time and shut the window that is making the fog horn noise. Now there is the sound of the pots overflowing, the splashing of the water on the rugs. I can hear from upstairs the splashing downstairs. I run down and call for Frankie to help. But there is thunder and he cannot hear. Or else he does hear but he does not come.

I hear the roll of golf balls on the floor above. I hear one in five hit a bed leg. I hear one escape the course altogether and run down the hall to where the stairs come down. But the ball doesn't. It stays at the top.

Every light goes out.

"Power's off!" Frankie yells. "Hey, the power's off!" He is beside me in a second.

Mother blows in through the back door with groceries in wet paper bags and her sister, Bunny.

"There's a boat out there," I tell Mother and Bunny.

"In this storm?" Mother says wiping the side of her face with the back of her hand.

"Yah," I say. "And I think," I catch Mother's blue eyes in mine. "I think it's Fred."

Mother goes to the picture windows. Her breath fogs the glass as she speaks. "Who else would it be?"

In her boy's haircut, Bunny stands beside Mother. Glaring through the German submarine binoculars she says, "Sure, it's him. Fred and all the little bastards in their foul weather coats and orange life preservers."

"How can you see in the dark?" Mother asks.

"Oh, I can FEEL it when he's around. I wonder if he'll hit a jetty or run aground and sink," Bunny says.

I think of the white bottoms that become pink bottoms when they squeak down the new silver slide. In their orange life preservers. In their pretend emergency landings. If the sky-blue sailboat sinks today, Father's new little ones will know exactly how to behave.

"I suppose Pete's out there with him," Mother says staring out into the electric air, out to where her son sails.

"I mean, one would like to think of their Father as a sensible man?" This is a question I ask Mother. She turns from me to light the fireplace fire and, for a while, we all sit in front of it.

Upstairs, by the light of one candle, I dump water from the full pots into the sink. As suddenly as a cat, Frankie stands beside me. "You might as well know the facts," he says. He is combing his black hair back. He is wearing a golf glove, three T shirts one on top of the other, ankle socks that don't match or have heels, and a pair of pink golf pants.

"Why do you think Fred orders us around all the time, has us do all the work? So SHE won't have to do it. He wants her to be ready for him in bed." The roof is low, a hat over our heads. The rain spits and splatters on it. Frankie's eyes are shyly at the mirror as if he were seeing in it himself as a child. Frankie parts his hair cleanly on the left. "He wants her to be ready for him. Not tired like Mum. That's one of the reasons Dad left, you know. He told me. Mum was too out to lunch in bed at night. I'm too tired, she would say. That's why he had to look elsewhere. And now he has us doing the wheelbarrowing. Oh, yah, Dad's pretty cagey. He has us doing HER work. But I'm not going to do it any more. No, sir. Not me. Oh, no wonder my golf's lousy!" Frankie flips his comb into the sink. "I can't even go over there without him telling me to wheelbarrow a ton of woodchips from the back of the house and spread them evenly all over the dumb driveway, and SHE's always standing there watching, stamping her foot saying, Not over THERE, over HERE!"

"Stop arguing!" Mother yells up the stairs at us.

"We're not!" Frankie yells back in a very excited voice. He stomps into his room and comes out with a driver in his hand. He extends the club down the stairwell to see its silver shaft glimmer in the downstairs fire light.

"Frankie! Are you playing golf in this weather?" Mother's voice is laughing until it is cut off by a bonehard clap of thunder. Frankie runs back into his room.

"Frankie?" I stand in his doorway. The chimney that runs up the center of the house is heating the upstairs now, it is heating Frankie and me. I can hear Frankie tapping balls. I can hear them rolling. He is putting in the dark. "Hey, Frankie? I wouldn't take it so hard. Listen, I do the wheelbarrowing, too, when I'm—"

"Oh, shut up!" Frankie says.

With my hands feeling the way of the hall, I take myself back into the bathroom. The fish bowl has overflowed and the red and white one is on the floor. I pick it up by the tail and lay it on my palm. Its eyes are dry. I flip it back into the bowl. And it is not dead. It is slithering through the water. Be thankful for the little things in life, I think. The little things that happen one after the next. Cupping my hands over the bowl's lip, I pour half of its water out, and sit it under the slow leak that had quickened. The red and white one trembles around the gold ones and the fake coral piece. It is asking them if they saw it through the glass, on the outside of the bowl, on the wooden bathroom floor.

Now it is evening. We are all in front of the fire. Even Pete is here. He has emptied his plate of swordfish and is warming his toes as wrinkled as sponges. He is calling each toe Fred. This Fred went to market, this Fred stayed home.

It is Frankie's night to do the dishes and he is going at it crash bang in the candlelit kitchen. He is yelling about the popcorn pot. It was from LAST night and last night was Pete's night to do the dishes, so why doesn't HE do it? Pete is poking at the fire with a stick. Now he is setting up a game of checkers beside him on the floor. He positions the checkers as big as bracelets on the black and red checkered rug that is the size of a card table. Pete is setting up the game and waiting for his partner, Frankie The Dishwasher, to be through.

While Mother and Bunny are in the kitchen drying and putting away, Pete is telling me that Fred had not taken the spinnakers down before their sail, before the storm, and when the sailors returned they found the spinnakers ruined. Fred had gone into his sail box in the garage to count how many he had left. Pulling out three, they had filled up the garage, and then they had deflated onto the floor. With their little hands on their cheeks, Father's new little ones had watched their carefully piled cricket corpses fly into the air like bird seed. They had watched as each cricket corpse became, upon landing, ash. Father had yelled, Now, WHAT'S THIS? The sails outside are soaked and stretched beyond any light of hope, and these sails inside are full of bugs! Father's new little ones had mourned ever so silently the loss of their cricket corpse collection. And when Father had seen the sorrow in their mahogany eyes, he had patted them on their heads and ruffled up their hair. He had said, Oh, don't worry, girls. Now we can leave the sails up over the driveway forever. Now we no longer have to worry about the winds that blow bigger than the small craft warning winds.

"Now," added Pete to me, "we don't have to put the aerial down when we drive up the drive. We can leave the radio on, and the aerial where it is, and we can slice the spinnakers into streamers."

"Did you tell this to Fred?" I ask him.

"No. He'll find out," Pete replies.

"Who will find what out?" Bunny asks.

She and Mother come to sit beside the fire and Peter stops his talking about Fred. He removes some of the giant checkers off the rug-board and works at setting up an impossible checker situation. Crawling on hands and knees from the black side to the red, he plays at both.

"Who will find what out?" Bunny asks again.

"Pete was just telling me that Frankie will find out that doing the popcorn pot is good for his golf swing," I say. There is laughter from all except Frankie, who does not hear our talk. Or else he is pretending not to. Now, in the fire light, we are all quiet, and out of this quiet Mother begins to speak.

"Well, all right," she says. Now Mother has had a bit of scotch. To warm herself up. Not too much. A bit. She sits on the floor with her legs stretched out in front of her and while she talks, she works at touching her toes. "So, your Father's not home, aye?" Bunny has taken her turn with the stick and is brightening up the fire. She is throwing on another log and then brushing her hands together. Under her plucked eyebrows, she has dark eyes. They are being hypnotized by the fire, by Mother's voice, the rain on the roof, the rain on the rug. Mother has a soft sweater on, her eyes are sapphire. She is touching the tips of her fingers to her ankles and saying, "So, your Father's not even in the country." She is turning to me. "I'm pregnant with you. I don't know whether to have you or not. Frankie doesn't walk. He doesn't talk. He won't eat. I take him to a psychiatric clinic at Yale. Bunny comes with me. I don't know WHAT I would have done without Bunny.'' Pete has got two red kings into a corner with a black one. Not one can make a move. He has his hand under his chin and is frowning thoughtfully.

"The Yale doctor talked to me for four full hours. I told him everything. I thought I might as well. Things I've never told anyone. Things I never told your Father. Well, at the end of our session, the doctor didn't even want to see Frankie. He watched him for a minute, and then he said to me, There's nothing wrong with that child. That boy is fine. YOU need someone to talk to. Someone, your husband. That's what he said. That's all he said.''

When the clock bongs twelve times, the storm lessens outside. Bunny looks out the picture windows and then drives her car over the three-and-a-half-legged deck chair and up the hill in our road and down the other side. Rain stops coming into our house. Frankie is finished with the washing of the popcorn pot. Thunder and lightning have gone far enough, have stopped. Have now gone away. There is no wind in the blankets on the beds. Only Pete is in his bed, and Mother is in hers. They are sleeping warm and dry, dreaming dreams. The air outside is cool like fall time. The sea is smoothing itself like a lady does her skirt. A little at a time. The waves have thrown up onto the shore seaweed the size of human bodies, horse-shoe crabs that have lost their tails, and conks. We will see these things on the beach tomorrow. Logs, that turned into a million radiant fingernails, are now turning black. The fire dies. The light on Frankie's and my faces stops.

Frankie has heard every word Mother has said about him. Him at the age of three. Him at the psychiatric clinic.

Frankie is the last to go up to bed. Before I go to sleep, I move the fish bowl from the bathroom floor onto a dresser in the hall. Bunny is driving through our town and into the next. She is driving by Father's new white house. There are the drowned spinnakers hanging from the pines. In the proper beds Father's two new little ones, and Father's new wife half his age, sleep on their backs and on their fronts like the toy soldiers that lie under the grass beside the slide.

There is one light on in Father's new house.

Beside it, Fred is wide awake.

A Mythological Subject

LAURIE COLWIN

It is often to the wary that the events in life are unexpected. Looser types—people who are not busy weighing and measuring every little thing—are used to accidents, coincidences, chance, things getting out of hand, things sneaking up on them. They are the happy children of life, to whom life happens for better or worse.

Those who believe in will, in meaning, in intentionality, who brood, reflect, and contemplate, who believe there are no accidents, who are born with clear vision or an introspective temperament or a relentless consciousness are quite another matter.

I am of the former category, a cheerful woman. The first man who asked me to marry him turned out to be the perfect mate. It may be that I happily settled for what came my way, but in fact my early marriage endured and prospered. As a couple we are even-tempered, easy to please, curious, fond of food and gossip. My husband Edward runs his family's import business. We have three children, all away at school. We are great socializers, and it is our chief entertainment to bring our interesting friends together.

Of our set, the dearest was my cousin Nellie Felix. I had known her as a child and was delighted when she came to New York to live and study. After all, few things are more pleasing than an attractive family member. She was full of high spirits and emotional idealism. What would become of her was one of our favorite topics of conversation.

In her twenties she had two dramatic love affairs. These love affairs surprised her: she did not think of herself as a romantic, but as someone seeking honor and communion in love. Her idealism in these matters was sweet and rather innocent. That a love affair could lead to nothing stumped her. When she was not seriously attached she was something of a loner, although she had a nice set of friends.

At the age of thirty Nellie fell in love with a lawyer named Joseph Porter. He was lovable, intelligent, and temperamental enough to make life interesting. With him Nellie found what she had been looking for, and they were married. Nellie believed in order, in tranquility, in her household as a safe haven, and she worked harder than even she knew to make sure she had these things. She taught three days a week at a women's college an hour outside New York. Her students adored her. She and Joseph expanded their circle, and eventually they had a child, an enchanting daughter named Jane. They lived in a town house and their life was attractive, well organized, comfortable, and looked rather effortless.

But Nellie did not feel that it was effortless. She had so ardently wanted the life she had, but she felt that she had come close to not having it; that her twenties had not been a quest for love but a romantic shambles; that there was some part of her that was not for order and organization but for chaos. She believed that the neat and tidy surfaces of things warded off misery and despair, that she had to constantly be vigilant with everything, especially herself. She once described to me a fountain she had seen on her honeymoon in the close of the Barcelona Cathedral. It was an ornamental fountain that shot up a constant jet of water. On top of this jet bobbled an egg. This seemed to Nellie a perfect metaphor to express the way she felt about her life. Without constant vigilance, self-scrutiny, accurate self-assessment, and a strong will, whatever kept the egg of her life aloft would disappear and the egg would shatter. She knew the unexamined life was not worth living. She never wanted to do things for the wrong reason, or for no reason or for reasons she did not understand. She wanted to be clear and unsentimental, to believe things that were true and not things that it consoled her to believe. When her colleague Dan Hamilton said to her: "You're very rough on me," she said: "I'm rougher on myself, I promise you."

My husband and I introduced Nellie to Dan Hamilton. We had been planning to get the Porters and the Hamiltons together for some time, but the Hamiltons were hard to pin down. Miranda Hamilton was a designer whose work frequently took her abroad. Dan was an historian. Once every three or four years he would produce a popular and successful book on some figure in colonial history. Over the years these books had made him rich, and he had become a sort of traveling scholar. Now that their three sons were grown-up and married they had more or less settled down in New York. Dan had taken a sabbatical from writing and was the star appointment at Nellie's college—all the more reason to bring the two couples together.

They got along famously. My husband and I looked down from our opposite ends of the table flushed with the vision of a successful dinner party. How attractive they all looked in the candlelight! Joseph, who was large, ruddy, and beautifully dressed, sat next to Miranda. They were talking about Paris. Miranda wore her reddish hair in a stylish knot. She was wiry and chic and smoked cigarettes in a little black holder. Nellie sat next to Dan. Her clothes, as always, were sober and she looked wonderful. She had straight ashy hair that she pulled back off her face and hazel eyes full of motion and expression. Dan, who sat next to her, was her opposite. As Nellie was immaculate and precise, Dan looked antic and boyish. He had a mop of curly brown, copper, and grey hair, and he always looked a little awry. His tie was never quite properly tied, and the pockets of his jackets sagged from carrying pipes and books and change in them. He and Nellie and my husband were being silly about some subject or other at their end of the table, and Nellie was laughing.

Over coffee it was discovered that Nellie and Dan shared the same schedule. Dan said: "In that case I ought to drive you up to school. I hate to drive alone and the trains are probably horrible." At this Miranda gave Dan a look which Nellie registered against her will. She imagined that Dan was famous for loving to drive alone and that he was teasing Miranda by flirting.

But the idea of being driven to school was quite heavenly. The trains *were* awful. The first week of Dan and Nellie's mobile colleagueship was a great success. They talked shop, compared notes on faculty and classes and family. Dan knew some of the people who had taught Nellie at college. The time, on these trips, flew by.

After two weeks Nellie became uneasy about the cost of gas and tolls and insisted on either paying for them or splitting them. Dan would not hear of this so Nellie suggested that she give him breakfast on school days to even up the score. Dan thought this was a fine idea. Nellie was a good plain cook. She gave Dan scones, toasted cheese, sour cream muffins, and coffee with hot milk. On Thursdays when they did not have to be at school until the afternoon they got into the habit of having lunch at Nellie's. They sat in the kitchen dining off the remains of last night's dinner party.

A million things slipped by them. Neither admitted how much they looked forward to their rides to school, or their breakfasts or their unnecessary Thursday lunches. Nellie told herself that this arrangement was primarily a convenience, albeit a friendly one.

One stormy autumn night, full of purple clouds and shaking branches, Nellie and Dan sat for longer than usual in front of Nellie's house. They were both restless, and Nellie's reluctance to get out of the car and go home disturbed her. Every time she got set to leave, Dan would say something to pull her back. Finally she knew she had to go, and on an unchecked impulse she reached for Dan's hand. On a similarly unchecked impulse, Dan took her hand and kissed it.

* * *

What happened was quite simple. Nellie came down with the flu—no wonder she had felt so restless. She canceled her classes and called Dan to tell him. He sounded rather cross, and it was clear he did not like to have his routines interrupted.

On Thursday she was all recovered, but Dan turned up in a terrible mood. He bolted his breakfast and was anxious to get on the road. Once they hit the highway he calmed down. They discovered that both Miranda and Joseph were away on business and that Jane was on an overnight school trip. They decided to stop for dinner at the inn they always passed to see if it was any good.

That day Nellie felt light and clear and full of frantic energy. She taught two of the best classes she had ever taught, but she was addled. She who never lost anything left her handbag in her office and her class notes in the dining commons. Although she and Dan usually met in the parking lot, they had arranged to meet in front of the science building, but both kept forgetting what the plan was, necessitating several rounds of telephone calls.

Finally they drove through the twilight to the inn. The windows were made of bull's-eye glass, and there were flowers on the sideboard. Nellie and Dan sat by the fireplace. Neither had much in the way of appetite. They talked a blue streak and split a bottle of wine.

Outside it was brilliantly clear. The sky was full of stars, and the frosty, crisp air smelled of apples and woodsmoke. Dan started the car. Then he turned it off. With his hands on the steering wheel he said: "I think I've fallen in love with you and if I'm not mistaken, you've fallen in love with me."

It is true that there is something—there is everything—undeniable about the truth. Even the worst true thing fills the consciousness with the light of its correctness. What Dan said was just plain true, and it filled Nellie with a wild surge of joy.

It explained everything: their giddiness, their unwillingness to part, those unnecessary lunches and elaborate breakfasts.

"My God," she said. "I didn't mean for this to happen."

She knew in an instant how much care she had been taking all along—to fill her conversation with references to Joseph and Jane, to say "us" and not "me," not to say any flirtatious or provocative thing. How could she have not seen this coming? Falling in love is very often not flirtatious. It is often rather grave, and if the people falling in love are married the mention of a family is not so much a banner as it is a bulletproof vest.

They sat in the cold darkness. Someone looking in the window might have thought they were discussing a terminal illness. Nellie stared at the floor. Dan was fixated on the dashboard. Neither said a word. They were terrified to look at one another—frightened of what might be visible on the other's face. But these things are irresistible, and they were drawn into each other's arms.

They drove home the long way through little towns and villages. Nellie sat close to Dan, who kept his arm around her and drove with one hand, like a teenage boy. At every stop sign and red light they kissed each other. Both of them were giddy and high. They talked and talked—like all lovers worth their salt they compared notes. They had dreamed and daydreamed about each other. They recited the history of their affections: how Dan had once come close to driving the car off the road because he was staring at Nellie one afternoon; how the sight of Dan with his shirttail out had brought Nellie near to tears she did not understand, and so on.

With their families away they had the freedom to do anything they liked but all they did was to stand in Nellie's kitchen and talk. They never sat down. When they were not talking they were in each other's arms, kissing in that way that is like drinking out of terrible thirst. Twice Nellie burst into tears—of confusion, desire, and the terrible excess of happiness that love and the knowledge that one is loved in return often brings. Nellie knew what she was feeling. That she was feeling it as a married woman upset her terribly, but the feeling was undeniable and she did not have the will to suppress it. They stood on opposite sides of the kitchen—this was Nellie's stage direction—and discussed whether or not they should go to bed. They were both quite sick with desire but what they were feeling was so powerful and seemed so dangerous that the idea of physical expression scared them to death.

Very late at night Nellie sent Dan home. In two separate beds in two separate places, in Nellie's house and Dan's apartment, separated by a number of streets and avenues, these two lovers tossed and ached and attempted to sleep away what little of the night remained to them.

The next morning Nellie woke up exhausted and keen in her empty house. When she splashed water on her face to wake herself up she found that she was laughing and crying at the same time. She felt flooded by emotions, one of which was gratitude. She felt that her life was being handed back to her, but by whom? And from where?

Alone in her kitchen she boiled water for tea and thought about Dan. For a moment he would evaporate and she could not remember what had passed between them. She drank her tea and watched a late autumn fly buzz around the kitchen. When it landed on the table, she observed it. The miraculous nature of this tiny beast, the fact that it could actually fly, the complexities and originality of things, the richness of the world, the amazing beauty of being alive struck Nellie full force. She was filled up, high as a kite. Love, even if it was doomed, gave you a renewed sense of things: it did hand life back to you.

But after a certain age, no joy is unmitigated. She knew that if she did not succeed in denying her feelings for Dan her happiness in his presence would always mix with sadness. ‌e had never been in love with anyone unavailable, and she never been unavailable herself.

er heart, she felt, was not beating properly. She did not ..nk that she would take a normal breath until she heard from Dan. When the telephone rang, she knew it was him.

"May I come and have breakfast with you?" he said. "Or do you think it's all wrong?"

Nellie said: "It's certainly all wrong but come anyway."

This was their first furtive meeting. Friday was not a

school day: they were meeting out of pure volition. If Joseph asked her what she had been up to she could not say casually: "Dan Hamilton stopped by." It might sound as innocent as milk, but they were no longer innocent.

The sunlight through the kitchen windows suddenly looked threatening. The safe, tidy surfaces suddenly looked precarious and unstable. Her life, the life of a secure and faithful wife, had been done away in an instant, and even if she never saw Dan Hamilton again it was clear that something unalterable had happened to her. She could never again say that she had not been tempted. She felt alone in the middle of the universe, without husband or child, with only herself. Surely at the sight of Dan everything would fall into place and everything would be as it had been a day ago. She would see that Dan was her colleague and her friend, and that a declaration of love would not necessarily have to change everything.

But as soon as she saw him from the window she realized that a declaration does in fact change everything and that Dan was no longer just her colleague and friend. They could not keep out of each other's arms.

"I haven't felt this way since I was a teenager," said Dan. Nellie didn't say anything. She *had* felt this way since she was a teenager.

"It feels sort of heavenly," Dan said.

"It will get a little hellish," Nellie said.

"Really?" said Dan. "It's hard to believe."

"I've felt this way a couple of times," said Nellie. "Back in the world of childhood when everyone was single and nothing got in the way of a love affair. You could spend your every minute with the one you loved. You could have the luxury of getting *tired* of the one you loved. You had endless time. This is the grown-up world of the furtive, adulterous love match. No time, no luxury. I've never met anyone on the sly."

"We don't have to meet on the sly," said Dan. "We're commuters."

"I don't think you realize how quickly these things get out of hand," Nellie said.

"I'd certainly like to find out," said Dan, smiling. "Can't we just enjoy our feelings for a few minutes before all this furtive misery comes crashing down on us?"

"I give it an hour," said Nellie.

"Well, all right then. Let's go read the paper. Let's go into the living room and cozy up on the couch like single people. I can't believe you actually went out this morning and got the paper. You must have it delivered."

"We do," said Nellie.

"We do, too," said Dan.

Miranda was due back the next day, and Joseph in the early evening. Dan and Nellie stretched out on the couch in the sunlight and attempted to browse through the paper. Physical nearness caused their hearts to race. Adulterous lovers, without the errands and goals and plans that make marriage so easy, are left horribly to themselves. They have nothing to do but be—poor things.

"Here we are," said Nellie. "Representatives of two households, both of which get the *Times* delivered, curled up on a couch like a pair of teenagers."

They did not kiss each other. They did not even hold hands. The couch was big enough for both of them, with a tiny space between. They kept that space between them. Everything seemed very clear and serious. This was their last chance to deny that they were anything more than friends. Two gestures could be made: they would become lovers or they would not. It seemed to Nellie a very grave moment in her life. She was no longer a girl with strong opinions and ideals, but a mortal woman caught in the complexities of life. Both Nellie and Dan were silent. Once they were in each other's arms it was all over, they knew, but since falling in love outside of marriage is the ultimate and every other gesture is its shadow, when they could bear it no longer they went upstairs to Nellie's guest room and there became lovers in the real sense of the word.

Of all the terrible things in life, living with a divided heart is the most terrible for an honorable person. There were times when Nellie could scarcely believe that she was the person she knew. Her love for Dan seemed pure to her, but its context certainly did not. There was not one moment when she felt right or justified: she simply had her feelings and she learned that some true feelings make one wretched; that they interfere with life; that they cause great emotional and moral pain; and that there was nothing much she could do about them. Her love for Dan opened the world up in a terrible and serious way and caused her, with perfect and appropriate justification, to question everything: her marriage, her ethics, her sense of the world, herself.

Dan said: "Can't you leave yourself alone for five seconds? Can't you just go with life a little?"

Nellie said: "Don't you want this to have anything to do with your life? Do you think we fell in love for no reason whatsoever? Don't you want to know what this means?"

"I can't think that way about these things," Dan said. "I want to enjoy them."

Nellie said: "I have to know everything. I think it's immoral not to."

That was when Dan had said: "You're very rough on me."

Any city is full of adulterers. They hide out in corners of restaurants. They know the location of all necessary pay telephones. They go to places their friends never go to. From time to time they become emboldened and are spotted by a sympathetic acquaintance who has troubles of his or her own and never says a word to anyone.

There are plain philanderers, adventurers, and people seeking revenge on a spouse. There are those who have absolutely no idea what they are doing or why, who believe that events have simply carried them away. And there are those to whom love comes, unexpected and not very welcome, a sort of terrible fact of life like fire or flood. Neither Nellie nor Dan had expected to fall in love. They were innocents at it.

There were things they were not prepared for. The first time Nellie called Dan from a pay 'phone made her feel quite awful—Joseph was home with a cold and Nellie wanted to call Dan before he called her. That call made her think of all the second-rate and nasty elements that love outside marriage entails.

The sight of Nellie on the street with Jane upset Dan. He saw them from afar and was glad he was too far off to be seen. That little replica of Nellie stunned him. He realized that he had never seen Jane before: that was how distant he and Nellie were from the true centers of each other's lives. He was jealous of Jane, he realized. Jealous of a small daughter because of such exclusive intimacy.

When Nellie ran into Dan with his middle son Ewan at the liquor store one Saturday afternoon, it had the same effect on her. Both she and Dan were buying wine for dinner parties. Both knew exactly what the other was serving and to whom. This made Nellie think of the thousands of things they did not know and would never know: that family glaze of common references, jokes, events, calamities—that sense of a family being like a kitchen midden: layer upon layer of the things daily life is made of. The edifice that lovers build is by comparison delicate and one-dimensional. The sight of the beloved's child is only a living demonstration that the one you love has a long and complicated history that has nothing to do with you.

They suffered everything. When they were together they suffered from guilt and when apart from longing. The joys that lovers experience are extreme joys, paid for by the sacrifice of everything comfortable. Moments of unfettered happiness are few, and they mostly come when one or the other is too exhausted to think. One morning Nellie fell asleep in the car. She woke up with a weak winter light warming her. For an instant she was simply happy—happy to be herself, to be with Dan, to be alive. It was a very brief moment, pure and sweet as cream. As soon as she woke up it vanished. Nothing was simple at all. Her heart felt heavy as a weight. Nothing was clear or reasonable or unencumbered. There was no straight explanation for anything.

Since I saw remarkably little of Nellie, I suspected something was up with her: she was one of those people who hide out when they are in trouble. I knew that if she needed to talk she would come to see me and eventually she did just that.

It is part of the nature of the secret that it needs to be shared. Without confession it is incomplete. When what she was feeling was too much for her, Nellie chose me as her confidante. I was the logical choice: I was family, I had known Nellie all her life, and I had known Dan for a long time, too.

She appeared early one Friday in the middle of a winter storm. She was expected anyway—she and I were going to pick up Jane later in the afternoon and then my husband and I, Nellie, Joseph, and Jane were going out for dinner.

She came in looking flushed and fine, with diamonds of sleet in her hair. She was wearing a grey skirt, and a sweater which in some lights was lilac and in some the color of a pigeon's wing. She shook out her hair, and when we were finally settled in the living room with our cups of tea I could see that she was very upset.

"You look very stirred up," I said.

"I am stirred up," said Nellie. "I need to talk to you." She stared down into her tea and it was clear that she was composing herself to keep from crying.

Finally she said: "I'm in love with Dan Hamilton."

I said:" Is he in love with you?"

"Yes," said Nellie.

I was not surprised at all, and that I was not surprised upset her. She began to cry, which made her look all the more charming. She was one of those lucky people who are not ruined by tears.

"I'm so distressed," she said. "I almost feel embarrassed to be as upset as I am."

"You're not exempt from distress," I said. "You're also not exempt from falling in love."

"I wanted to be," she said fiercely. "I thought that if I put my will behind it, if I was straight with myself I wouldn't make these mistakes."

"Falling in love is not a mistake."

She then poured forth. There were no accidents, she knew. That she had fallen in love meant something. What did it say about herself and Joseph? All the familiar emotional props of girlhood—will, resolve, a belief in a straight path—were gone from her. She did not see why love had come to her unless she had secretly—a secret from herself, she meant— been looking for it. And on and on. That she was someone who drew love—some people do, and they need not be especially lovable or physically beautiful, as Nellie believed— was not enough of an explanation for her. That something had simply happened was not an idea she could entertain. She did not believe that things simply happened.

She talked until her voice grew strained. She had not spared herself a thing. She said, finally: "I wanted to be like you—steady and faithful. I thought my romantic days were over. I thought I was grown up. I wanted for me and Joseph to have what you and Edward have—a good and uncomplicated marriage."

It is never easy to give up the pleasant and flattering image other people have of one's own life. Had Nellie's distress not been so intense, I would not have felt compelled to make a confession of my own. But I felt rather more brave in the face of my fierce cousin: I was glad she was suffering, in fact. I knew she divided the world into the cheerful slobs like me and the emotional moralists like herself. A serious love affair, I thought, might take some of those sharp edges off.

I began by telling her how the rigorousness with which she went after what she called the moral universe did not allow anyone very much latitude, but none the less, I was about to tell her something that might put her suffering into some context.

"I have been in love several times during my marriage," I said. "And I have had several love affairs,"

The look on her face, I was happy to see, was one of pure relief.

"But I thought you and Edward were so happy," she said.

"We are," I said, "But I'm only human and I am not looking for perfection. Romance makes me cheerful. There have been times in my life when I simply needed to be loved by someone else and I was lucky enough to find someone who loved me. And look at me! I'm not beautiful and I'm not so lovable, but I'm interested in love and so it comes to find me. There are times when Edward simply hasn't been there for me—it happens in every marriage. They say it takes two and sometimes three to make a marriage work and they're right. But this had nothing to do with you because I picked my partners in crime for their discretion and their very clear sense that nothing would get out of hand. I can see that an affair that doesn't threaten your marriage is not your idea of an affair, but there you are."

This made Nellie silent for a long time. She looked exhausted and tearstained.

"One of the good things about this love affair," she said, "is that it's shot my high horse right out from under me. It's a real kindness for you to tell me what you've just told me."

"We're all serious in our own ways," I said. "Now I think you need a nap. You look absolutely wiped out. I'll go call Eddie and tell him to meet Joseph and then when you wake up we can plot where we're going to take Jane for dinner."

I gave her two needlepoint pillows for her head, covered her with a quilt, then went to call my husband. When I got back I sat and watched my cousin sleeping. The sleety, yellowish light played over her brow and cheekbones.

She was lying on her side with her hand slightly arched and bent. Her hair had been gathered at her neck but a few strands had escaped. She looked like the slain nymph Procris in the Piero di Cosimo painting *A Mythological Subject* which depicts poor Procris who has been accidentally killed by her husband Cephalus. Cephalus is a hunter who has a spear that never misses its mark. One day he hears a noise in the forest, and thinking that it is a wild beast, he takes aim. But it is not a beast. It is Procris. In the painting a tiny jet of blood sprays from her throat. At her feet is her mournful dog, Lelaps, and at her head is a satyr, wearing the look of a heartbroken boy. That picture is full of the misery and loneliness romantic people suffer in love.

The lovely thing about marriage is that life ambles on—as if life were some meandering path lined with sturdy plane trees. A love affair is like a shot arrow. It gives life an intense direction, if only for an instant. The laws of love affairs would operate for Nellie and Dan: they would either run off together, or they would part, or they would find some way to salvage a friendship out of their love affair. If you live long enough and if you are placid and easygoing, people tell you everything. Almost everyone I know has confessed a love affair of some sort or another to me.

But I had never discussed my amours with anyone. Would Nellie think that my affairs had been inconsequential? Certainly I had never let myself get into such a swivet over a man, but I had made very sure to pick only those with very secure marriages and a sense of fun. Each union had been the result of one of the inevitable low moments that marriages contain, and each parting, when the right time came to part, had been relatively painless. The fact was, I was not interested in love in the way Nellie was. She was interested in ultimates. I remembered her fifteen years ago, at twenty-three, rejecting all the nice, suitable young men who wanted to take her out for dinner and in whom she had no interest. She felt this sort of socializing was all wrong. When my husband and I chided her, she said with great passion: "I don't want a social life. I want love, or nothing."

Well, she had gotten what she wanted. There she lay, wiped out, fast asleep, looking wild, peaceful, and troubled all at the same time. She had no dog to guard her, no satyr to mourn her, and no bed of wild flowers beneath her like the nymph in the painting.

What a pleasant circumstance to sit in a warm, comfortable room on an icy winter's day and contemplate someone you love whose life has always been of the greatest interest to you. Procris in the painting is half naked, but Nellie looked just as vulnerable.

It would be exceedingly interesting to see what happened to her, but then she had always been a pleasure to watch.

A Wonderful Woman

ALICE ADAMS

Feeling sixteen, although in fact just a few months short of sixty, Felicia Lord checks into the San Francisco hotel at which her lover is to meet her the following day. Felicia is tall and thin, with the intense, somewhat startled look of a survivor—a recent widow, mother of five, a ceramicist who prefers to call herself a potter. A stylish gray-blonde. Mr. Voort, she is told, will be given the room next to hers when he arrives. Smiling to herself, she then follows the ancient wizened bellboy into an antique elevator cage; once inside, as they creakingly ascend, he turns and smiles up at her, as though he knows what she is about. She herself is less sure.

The room to which he leads her is a suite, really: big, shabby-cozy living room, discreetly adjoining bedroom, large old-fashioned bath, on the top floor of this old San Francisco hotel, itself a survivor of the earthquake and fire, in an outlying neighborhood. All in all, she instantly decides, it is the perfect place for meeting Martin, for being with him, in the bright blue dazzling weather, this sudden May.

San Francisco itself, connected as it is with Felicia's own history, has seemed a possibly dangerous choice: the scene of her early, unlikely premarital "romance" with Charles, her now dead husband; then the scene of holiday visits from Connecticut with the children, treat zoo visits and cable-car

349

rides, Chinese restaurants; scene of a passionate ill-advised love affair, and a subsequent abortion—all that also took place in San Francisco, but years ago, in other hotels, other neighborhoods.

Why then, having tipped the grinning bellboy and begun to unpack, silk shirts on hangers, silk tissue-papered nightgowns and underthings in drawers, does she feel such a dizzying lurch of apprehension? It is too intense in its impact to be just a traveler's nerves, jet lag. Felicia is suddenly quite weak; she sits down in an easy chair next to the window to absorb the view, to think sensibly about her situation, or try to. She sees a crazy variety of rooftops: mansard, Victorian curls, old weathered shingles and bright new slate. Blue water, paler sky, green hills. No help.

It is being in love with Martin, she thinks, being "in love," and the newness of Martin Voort. I've never known a farming sailor before, and she smiles, because the words don't describe Martin, really, although he owns some cranberry bogs, near Cape Cod, and he builds boats. Charles was a painter, but he was rich (Martin is not rich) and most of his friends were business people. Martin is entirely new to her.

And at my age, thinks Felicia, and she smiles again, a smile which feels tremulous on her mouth.

"Wonderful" is the word that people generally have used about Felicia. She was wonderful with Charles, whose painting never came to much, although he owned a couple of galleries, who drank a lot. Wonderful to all those kids, who were a little wild, always breaking arms or heads.

Her lover—a Mexican Communist, and like Charles a painter, but a much better painter than Charles—Felipe thought she looked wonderful, with her high-boned face, strong hands and her long, strong voluptuous body. She was wonderful about the abortion, and wonderful too when he went back to his wife.

Felicia was wonderful when Charles died, perfectly controlled and kind to everyone.

Wonderful is not how Felicia sees herself at all; she feels

that she has always acted out of simple—or sometimes less simple—necessity.

Once married to Charles, and having seen the lonely, hollow space behind his thin but brilliant surface of good looks, graceful manners, skill at games—it was then impossible to leave him; and he couldn't have stood it. And when the children had terrible coughs, or possible concussions, she took good care of them, sometimes staying up all night, simply because she wanted them well, and soon.

During the unanesthetized abortion, she figured out that you don't scream, because that would surely make the pain much worse, when it is already so bad that it must be happening to someone else, and also because the doctor, a Brazilian chiropractor in the Mission District, is hissing, "Don't make noise." And when your lover defects, saying that he is going back, after all, to his wife in Guadalajara, you don't scream about that either; what good would it do? You go back to your husband, and to the clay pots that you truly love, round and fat or delicately slender.

When your husband dies, as gracefully as he lived, after a too strenuous game of tennis, you take care of everything and everyone, and you behave well, for your own sake as well as for everyone else's.

Then you go to visit an old friend, in Duxbury, and you meet a large wild red-haired, blue-eyed man, a "sailor-farmer," and you fall madly in love, and you agree to meet him for a holiday, in May, in San Francisco, because he has some boats to see there.

She is scared. Sitting there, in the wide sunny window, Felicia trembles, thinking of Martin, the lovely city, themselves, for a long first time. But supposing she isn't "wonderful" anymore? Suppose it all fails, flesh fails, hearts fail, and everything comes crashing down upon their heads, like an avalanche, or an earthquake?

She thinks, I will have to go out for a walk.

Returned from a short tour of the neighborhood, which affords quick beautiful views of the shining bay, and an amazing variety of architecture, Felicia feels herself restored;

she is almost her own person again, except for a curious
weakness in her legs, and the faintest throb of blood behind
one temple, both of which she ascribes to fatigue. She stands
there for a moment on the sidewalk, in the sunlight, and then
she re-enters the hotel. She is about to walk past the desk
when the bellboy, still stationed there, waves something in
her direction. A yellow envelope—a telegram.

She thanks him and takes it with her into the elevator,
waiting to open it until she is back in her room. It will be
from Martin, to welcome her there. Already she knows the
character of his gestures: he hates the phone; in fact, so far
they have never talked on the telephone, but she has received
at least a dozen telegrams from Martin, whose instructions
must always include: "Deliver, do not phone." After the
party at which they met he wired, from Boston to Duxbury:
HAVE DINNER WITH ME WILL PICK YOU UP AT SEVEN MARTIN VOORT.
Later ones were either jokes or messages of love—or both:
from the start they had laughed a lot.

This telegram says: DARLING CRAZY DELAY FEW DAYS LATE
ALL LOVE.

The weakness that earlier Felicia had felt in her legs makes
them now suddenly buckle; she falls across the bed, and all
the blood in both temples pounds as she thinks: I can't stand
it, I really can't. This is the one thing that is too much for
me.

But what do you do if you can't stand something, and you
don't scream, after all?

Maybe you just go to bed, as though you were sick?

She undresses, puts on a pretty nightgown and gets into
bed, where, like a person with a dangerously high fever, she
begins to shake. Her arms crossed over her breast, she clutches
both elbows; she presses her ankles together. The tremors
gradually subside, and finally, mercifully, she falls asleep,
and into dreams. But her sleep is fitful, thin, and from time to
time she half wakes from it, never at first sure where she is,
nor what year of her life this is.

A long time ago, in the early Forties, during Lieutenant
(USN) Charles Lord's first leave, he and Felicia Thacher,

whom he had invited out to see him, literally danced all night, at all the best hotels in town—as Felicia wondered: Why me? How come Charles picked me for this leave? She had known him since childhood; he was one of her brother's best friends. Had someone else turned him down? She had somewhat the same reactions when he asked her to marry him, over a breakfast glass of champagne, in the Garden Court of the Palace Hotel. Why me? she wondered, and she wondered too at why she was saying yes. She said yes, dreamily, to his urgent eyes, his debonair smile, light voice, in that room full of wartime glamor, uniforms and flowers, partings and poignant brief reunions. Yes, Charles, yes, let's do get married, all right, soon.

A dream of a courtship, and then a dream groom, handsome Charles. And tall, strong-boned, strong-willed Felicia Thacher Lord.

Ironically, since she had so many, Felicia was not especially fond of babies; a highly verbal person, she was nervous with human creatures who couldn't talk, who screamed out their ambiguous demands, who seemed to have no sense and who often smelled terrible. She did not see herself as at all a good mother, knowing how cross and frightened she felt with little children. Good luck (Charles's money) had provided her with helpful nurses all along to relieve her of the children, and the children of her, as she saw it. Further luck made them all turn out all right, on the whole. But thank God she was done with all that. Now she liked all the children very much; she regarded them with great fondness, and some distance.

Her husband, Charles, loved Felicia's pregnancies (well, obviously he did), and all those births, his progeny. He spoke admiringly of how Felicia accomplished all that, her quick deliveries, perfect babies. She began to suspect that Charles had known, in the way that one's unconscious mind knows everything, that this would be the case; he had married her to be the mother of his children.

"I have the perfect situation for a painter, absolutely perfect," Charles once somewhat drunkenly declared. "Big house, perfect studio, money for travel, money to keep the kids

away at school. A wonderful kind strong wife. Christ, I even
own two galleries. *Perfect.* I begin to see that the only thing
lacking is talent,'' and he gave a terrible laugh.

How could you leave a man in such despair?

Waking slowly, her head still swollen with sleep, from the
tone of the light Felicia guesses that it must be about midaf-
ternoon. Eventually she will have to order something to eat,
tea or boiled eggs, something sustaining.

Then, with a flash of pain, Martin comes into her mind,
and she begins to think.

She simply doesn't know him, that's half the problem,
''know'' in this instance meaning able to predict the behavior
of, really, to trust. Maybe he went to another party and met
another available lady, maybe someone rather young, young-
fleshed and never sick or tired? (She knows that this could be
true, but still it doesn't sound quite right, as little as she
knows him.)

But what does FEW DAYS mean to Martin? To some people
a week would be a few days. CRAZY DELAY is deliberately
ambiguous. Either of those phrases could mean anything at
all.

Sinkingly, despairingly, she tells herself that it is sick to
have fantasies about the rest of your life that revolve around a
man you have only known for a couple of months.

Perfectly possibly he won't come to San Francisco at all,
she thinks, and then: I hate this city.

When the bellboy comes in with her supper tray, Felicia
realizes for the first time that he is a dwarf; odd that she
didn't see that before. His grin now looks malign, contemptuous, even, as though he recognizes her for what she now is:
an abandoned woman, of more than a certain age.

As he leaves she shivers, wishing she had brought along a
''sensible'' robe, practical clothes, instead of all this mocking
silk and lace. Looking quickly into the mirror, and then
away, she thinks, I look like an old circus monkey.

She sleeps through the night. One day gone, out of whatever ''few days'' are.

When she calls to order breakfast the next morning, the

manager (manageress: a woman with a strong, harsh Midwestern accent) suggests firmly that a doctor should be called. She knows of one.

Refusing that suggestion, as firmly, politely as she can, Felicia knows that she reacted to hostility rather than to concern. The manageress is afraid that Felicia will get really sick and die; what a mess to have on their hands, an unknown dead old woman.

But Felicia too is a little afraid.

Come to think of it, Felicia says to herself, half-waking at what must be the middle of the afternoon, I once spent some time in another San Francisco hotel, waiting for Felipe, in another part of town. After the abortion.

She and Felipe met when he had a show at one of Charles's galleries; they had, at first tipsily, fallen into bed, in Felipe's motel (Charles had "gone to sleep") after the reception; then soberly, both passionately serious, they fell in love. Felipe's paintings were touring the country, Felipe with them, and from time to time, in various cities, Felicia followed him. Her excuse to Charles was a survey of possible markets for her pots, and visits to other potters, which, conscientiously, she also accomplished.

Felipe was as macho as he was radical, and he loved her in his own macho way, violently, with all his dangerous strength. She must leave Charles, Charles must never touch her again, he said. (Well, Charles drank so much that that was hardly an issue.) She must come with him to Paris, to a new life. All her children were by then either grown or off in schools— why not?

When they learned that she was pregnant he desperately wanted their child, he said, but agreed that a child was not possible for them. And he remembered the Brazilian chiropractor that he had heard about, from relatives in San Francisco.

The doctor seemingly did a good job, for Felicia suffered no later ill effects. Felipe was kind and tender with her; he said that her courage had moved him terribly. Felicia felt that her courage, if you wanted to call it that, had somewhat unnerved him; he was a little afraid of her now.

However, they celebrated being together in San Francisco, where Felipe had not been before. He loved the beautiful city, and they toasted each other, and their mutual passion, with Mexican beer or red wine, in their Lombard Street motel. Then one afternoon Felipe went off alone to visit a family of his relatives, in San Jose, and Felicia waited for him. He returned to her very late, and in tears: a grown man, broad-backed, terrifically strong, with springing thick black hair and powerful arms, crying out to her, "I cannot—I cannot go on with you, with our life. They have told me of my wife, all day she cries, and at night she screams and wakes the children. I must go to her."

Well, of course you must, said Felicia, in effect. If she's screaming that's where you belong. And she thought, Well, so much for my Latin love affair.

And she went home.

And now she thinks, Martin at least will not come to me in tears.

Martin Voort. At the end of her week in Duxbury, her visit to the old school friend, Martin, whom in one way or another she had seen every day, asked her to marry him, as soon as possible. "Oh, I know we're both over the hill," he said, and then exploded in a laugh, as she did too. "But suppose we're freaks who live to be a hundred? We might as well have a little fun on the way. I like you a lot. I want to be with you."

Felicia laughed again. She was secretly pleased that he hadn't said she was wonderful, but she thought he was a little crazy.

He followed her home with telegrams: WHEN OH WHEN WILL YOU MARRY ME and ARRIVING IN YOUR TOWN THIS FRIDAY PREPARE.

And now, suppose she never sees him again? For the first time in many months (actually, since Charles died) Felicia begins to cry, at the possible loss of such a rare, eccentric and infinitely valuable man.

But in the midst of her sorrow at that terrible possibility, the permanent lack of Martin—who could be very sick, could have had a stroke: at his age, their age, that is entirely

possible—though grieving, Felicia realizes that she can stand
it, after all, as she has stood other losses, other sorrows in her
life. She can live without Martin.

She realizes too that she herself has just been genuinely ill,
somewhat frighteningly so; what she had was a real fever,
from whatever cause. Perhaps she should have seen a doctor.

However, the very thought of a doctor, a doctor's office, is
enough to make her well, she dislikes them so; all those years
of children, children's illnesses and accidents, made her terribly tired of medical treatment. Instead she will get dressed
and go out for dinner, by herself.

And that is what she does. In her best clothes she takes a
cab to what has always been her favorite San Francisco
restaurant, Sam's. It is quite early, the place uncrowded.
Felicia is given a pleasant side table, and the venerable
waiters are kind to her. The seafood is marvelous. Felicia
drinks a half-bottle of wine with her dinner and she thinks:
Oh, so this is what it will be like. Well, it's really not so bad.

Returned to the hotel, however, once inside her room she
experiences an acute pang of disappointment, and she understands that she had half consciously expected Martin to be
there; Martin was to be her reward for realizing that she could
live without him, for being "sensible," for bravely going out
to dinner by herself.

She goes quickly to bed, feeling weak and childish, and
approving neither her weakness nor her childishness, not at
all.

Sometime in the middle of the night she awakes from a
sound sleep, and from a vivid dream; someone, a man, has
knocked on the door of her room, this room. She answers,
and he comes in and they embrace, and she is wildly glad to
see him. But who is he? She can't tell: is it her husband,
Charles, or one of her sons? Felipe? Is it Martin? It could
even be a man she doesn't know. But, fully awake, as she
considers the dream she is saddened by it, and it is quite a
while before she sleeps again.

The next morning, though, she is all right: refreshed,
herself again. Even, in the mirror, her face is all right. I look

like what I am, she thinks: a strong healthy older woman. She dresses and goes downstairs to breakfast, beginning to plan her day. Both the bellboy and the manager smile in a relieved way as she passes the desk, and she smiles back, amiably.

She will see as much of San Francisco as possible today, and arrange to leave tomorrow. Why wait around? This morning she will take a cab to Union Square, and walk from there along Grant Avenue, Chinatown, to North Beach, where she will have lunch. Then back to the hotel for a nap, then a walk, and dinner out—maybe Sam's again.

She follows that plan, or most of it. On Union Square, she goes into a couple of stores, where she looks at some crazily overpriced clothes, and buys one beautiful gauzy Indian scarf, for a daughter's coming birthday. Then down to Grant Avenue, to walk among the smells of Chinese food, the incense, on to North Beach, to a small Italian counter restaurant, where she has linguine with clam sauce, and a glass of red wine.

In the cab, going back to the hotel, she knows that she is too tired, has "overdone," but it was worth it. She has enjoyed the city, after all.

An hour or so later, from a deep, deep sleep she is awakened by a knocking on her door, just as in her dream, the night before.

Groggily she calls out, "Who is it?" She is not even sure that the sound has been real; so easily this could be another dream.

A man's impatient, irritated voice answers, "It's *me*, of course."

Me? She is still half asleep; she doesn't know who he is. However, his tone has made her obedient, and she gets out of bed, pulling her pale robe about her, and goes to the door. And there is a tall, red-haired man, with bright blue eyes, whom of course she knows, was expecting—who embraces her violently. "Ah, Martin," she breathes, when she can.

It is Martin, and she is awake.

The only unfamiliar thing about his face, she notes, when she can see him, is that a tooth is missing from his smile;

there is a small gap that he covers with his hand as soon as she has noticed. And he says, "It broke right off! Right off a bridge. And my dentist said I'd have to wait a week. How could I send you a telegram about a goddam dentist? Anyway, I couldn't wait a week to see you."

They laugh (although there are tears somewhere near Felicia's eyes), and then they embrace again.

And at last they are sitting down on the easy chairs near the window, next to the view, and they are quietly talking together, making plans for the rest of that day and night.

All the Days of Our Lives

LEE SMITH

It's been a real bad week for Helen. She drives her big Riviera home from work quickly, carelessly, flipping it around the corners and curves of the town that she has lived in all her life. Almost. Except for the time when she ran away with Joe, a time that seems so long now, all stretched out in a big arch over years and years like a giant rainbow only of course it wasn't long at all, only two months actually, or one month and three weeks to be exact.

Helen recalls the Seascape Inn at Daytona Beach, recalls the day they checked in. She was writing a fake name on the register and the fat man behind the desk started up explaining about the name. He said he owned this place. He said that after careful thought he had named this place the Seascape Inn, which had two meanings. He didn't know if they had noticed that or not. The two meanings were *seascape*, like a painted picture of the ocean, and then *sea-plus-escape*, an escape to the sea, get it? Helen said she got it. She walked up the stairs.

Joe never said they would come to Florida, she didn't even have a bathing suit in her bag. In fact she didn't have a bag. She opened the door of their room, 217, and he was in there, pulling the drapes. He turned around in the shadows and held out his arms. Later she woke up and left him still sleeping in the double bed while she went over and opened the drapes and pushed the sliding door open and went out on the balcony and looked at the beach good for the first time. It was so wide, a mile wide it looked like, all the white sand with dots of bodies on it and then the dark blue ocean, far out beyond the sand. Helen sat out on the balcony in her slip while Joe slept in the room behind her and the night came down like a big slow rain across the beach. When it was completely dark, they turned the underwater lights on in the pool of the Seascape, a bright green rectangle right straight below their balcony. She hadn't noticed it before. It glowed out in the night like a big emerald, green and precious and strange. Helen sat out there looking down at the pool for a long time, letting the wind from the sea lift her hair.

Now she smokes three Salems on the twenty-five-minute drive home from work, pushing them out in the overflowing ash tray in her car. Her lungs are the last thing she's worried about, she's got too much on her mind as it is. If she turned left at this light, she would be only five minutes away from Howard, the man she was married to for thirteen years. Tears well up in her eyes. Right now he is over at his neat little office in the Wright Building adding up columns of numbers, moistening his pencil with the tip of his tongue. Howard is a CPA, a sweet steady man. But Howard has left her now. He has married another woman.

Of course *she* was the one who ran off, *she* was the one who went to Daytona Beach with an insurance claims adjustor, as Howard pointed out in court. Once the children are gone, though, Helen will grow old alone. She will have to cut all the packages of frozen food in two with a carving knife, cooking for one. Helen floats all alone through the world. Suddenly she wishes she was a nurse. She wishes she had a white uniform and a pin with her name on it and some of those creepy white shoes.

Instead she wears a floral polyester pants suit and a lime green blouse which is sticking to her back in this heat and lime green high-heeled sandals with straps. Helen is a big woman with long bleached-blond hair, dark brown eyes, and a hard, strong body. She used to think she was made for love, but she doesn't think that anymore.

Helen pulls into her driveway, gets out, and slams the door. The sun comes down like something solid on her head. The only good thing about Helen's present job, which otherwise is beneath her, is that she gets home around four in the afternoon. Will A. Okun, the pest control man who lives in the other side of the duplex that Helen lives in, pops out of his screen door like a man in a clock.

"*Hi* there," he says. Will A. Okun is a bachelor because he took care of his sick mother for twenty years before she finally died, and all his girlfriends married other people. Now he, like Helen, is loose in the world. Sometimes he makes casseroles and gives her half of them, so her kids will get all the vitamins they need to grow on. He worries abut her kids.

"*Hot day*," Will A. Okun remarks, shifting from foot to foot. He has curly red hair that springs in puffs like a clown's hair behind his ears, and Helen won't give him the time of day.

"What?" she asks now.

"*Hot day!*" Will A. Okun says again. He shuffles his feet.

Helen just looks at him and goes in her side of the duplex, banging the screen door shut. She sits down in front of the air conditioner in the kitchen and lets the cold air flow up over her like water.

"Mama, Denise wouldn't let us go down to Rexall," Billy starts in right away. "I wanted to go spend my allowance and Denise wouldn't let us."

"You said I was the boss," Denise says. Denise is fifteen. "Either I'm the boss or I'm not," she says.

"I don't see why I get an allowance if I can't ever spend it!" Billy hollers. He goes in his room and slams the door. Billy is going on nine.

Helen picks Davey up from the floor and takes the pacifier out of his mouth. "Hi Mama," Davey says. He's so old to have a pacifier that sometimes women grab it out of his mouth in Food Town and then he screams bloody murder, which serves them right in Helen's opinion. He can have that pacifier as long as he wants, in her opinion. In fact sometimes she wouldn't mind having one herself.

"Who's this?" she asks. She points at the little pink dog in Davey's fist.

"That's Baby Pink," he says around the pacifier. He always has something to hold.

"I hate you!" Billy hollers from his room.

"Can I go swimming now?" Denise asks. She is too young to babysit as much as she has to this summer, but in some funny way she is not young at all. She has light blue eyes that go straight through you, and curly light brown hair.

"OK, hon," Helen says. "Have a ball."

"*Mama.*" Denise says. Denise will never have a ball in her life, and both of them know it.

Denise puts on her bathing suit and leaves. Helen, still carrying Davey on her hip, goes to the refrigerator and gets a Coke and pops the top off, all with one hand, and sits down on the couch with Davey. She lights a Salem and flicks on the TV. This is Helen's favorite time of the day. She likes the Coke fizz in the roof of her mouth, the drone of the air conditioner, the dim blue flicker of the TV, the way Davey smells musty and sweet like a steamy bathroom after somebody has taken a bubble bath in it. Helen switches to Channel 11.

This part of Helen's show is about Nick, Mike, and Felicity. Felicity is in the labor room having a baby. Pale blue overhead lights glare down on her pale, tired face. Nurses and doctors in face masks cluster around. But is this Nick's baby or Mike's baby? Felicity isn't telling. Felicity is an heiress whose parents died in an airplane crash when she was only three. Felicity tosses her long curly hair back and forth on the pillow—no-o-o! Only her old Spanish nursemaid, Mrs. Belido, knows whose baby it is, but Mrs. Belido is illiterate and has been unable to speak since birth. She makes a strangling noise "Yi-yi-yi!" way back in her throat whenever anybody asks her about Felicity's baby. One thing we all know for sure is that Felicity really loved Nick last year, before he went off to Hollywood to write a screenplay for his novel *The*

Young Doctors. This is the famous best-selling novel he wrote while he was in medical school, which he has now quit. Oddly enough one of the main characters in the novel is a lot like Mike, the intern right here in Fernville who has become so fond of Felicity in Nick's absence.

There is Mike now in a face mask, fooling around with some medical tools. Over the top of the face mask, his eyes are filled with concern and love. "Bear down!" instructs the kindly white-haired senior resident, Dr. Godfrey. Felicity screams. "Darling!" Mike says. All this pain and emotion is almost too much for him, you can tell, even though he has seen plenty during his internship. "Forceps!" Dr. Godfrey calls out in a tone of command. Mike wipes Felicity's forehead with a little damp cloth. Felicity moans. "Now!" says Dr. Godfrey. Then the *baby* cries, a thin long wail that fills the emergency room and the tiny living room of Helen's duplex. "Darling," Mike says. "Darling, it's a boy!" He rushes out to the waiting room to give Mrs. Belido the news. Mrs. Belido, wearing a funny back lace handkerchief on her head, is right on the edge of her seat. "It's a boy!" Mike cries tearing off his face mask and embracing Mrs. Belido. Mike's face is young and sweet. Nick, of course, is somewhere out in California and doesn't know anything about any of this. "Yi-yi-yi!" cries Mrs. Belido.

Helen gets Davey some Hawaiian Punch during the commercial. She can hear Billy in his room, kicking the wall. She sighs. She settles down again with Davey as the scene switches elsewhere in Fernville to Michelle, a real bitch who is trying to break up Sandra and Bland's marriage just for her own amusement. Right now Michelle has tricked Bland into coming over to her penthouse apartment by telling him she has a problem to discuss. Bland has always been a sucker for other people's problems, just a big Boy Scout.

"Hello!" Michelle says in her throaty voice as she opens the door. Helen never gets tired of Michelle's apartment, or of Felicity's house, or of any of the places where any of the people on this show live. They have glass coffee tables, thick wall-to-wall carpeting, ferns on fancy little stands, discreet housekeepers in uniforms back in the kitchen, and everyone is so well dressed. Like Michelle, who does not, however, look like she is dressed to discuss a problem. Helen knows, even if Bland doesn't, exactly why Michelle has gotten him over there. Now Michelle is bringing in two frosty drinks on a little tray, and urging Bland to get comfortable.

"What seems to be the problem?" Bland asks. Michelle is busy removing his tie. Bland looks uncomfortable and puzzled. He is so dumb. Michelle pushes him down on the couch and sits down beside him, too close, showing a lot of leg. A light dawns in Bland's face. He jumps up and goes to look out at the city lights from the high picture window. While his back is turned, Michelle quickly hides his tie pin under the couch. Then she gets up and goes over to him and puts her arm around him from behind. Bland hops away. "I have to be going!" he says. He grabs up his tie and leaves. Michelle is left alone in her penthouse apartment with two full frosty glasses and a terrific view of the city lights. She picks up one glass and drinks it down. She lifts up a sofa cushion and gets the tie pin and stands before the picture window with it, turning it around and around in her hands and smiling a bitchy little smile to herself, while the theme music rises and falls.

Helen stretches and goes in the kitchen to see what she's got for supper. Helen's sister, Judy, comes in like a tornado, hugs Davey, and pours herself some Coke. It seems to Helen that Judy likes her a lot more since Howard left her, but she can't be sure. Judy has always kept secrets, not like Helen who tells everything she knows. Helen remembers when they were little girls and Judy spent all of her allowance on a red imitation leather diary with a little lock and key. Every night after supper Judy used to go to their room and close the door and write in her little diary with a fountain pen. If Helen made up an excuse and went in there, Judy closed the diary and just sat until Helen left, and then she wrote some more. What in the world was she writing about? What words did she think of to put on page after page, when nothing ever happened in their lives except the same old stuff?

"He's really too old for that now," Judy says, drinking her Coke and pointing to Davey, who is building a tower of pans on the floor, his pacifier stuck square in his mouth.

"Well," Helen says.

Judy snorts, her way of laughing.

"No, Judy, really. I swear I can't do a thing with the kids anymore. It's been awful ever since school let out, they haven't got anything to do all day except get after each other. And I get so tired. Sometimes I just don't know. Sometimes I wish I had Howard back, believe me."

This really cracks Judy up. "Listen here," she says. "I can't believe my ears. Don't you remember how you used to complain about Howard? How Howard had to have the sheets changed three times a week? And the kids used to drive him crazy, remember? He used to go in the bathroom and sit for hours with the door locked. You came over to my house to take a bath. Don't you remember that?"

Helen stares at her sister. "I just loved Howard," she says.

"What about when Howard didn't want to go on the honeymoon?" Judy keeps on, wrinkling up her face behind her glasses. "He said let's just stay here and give the house a real good cleaning before we move in. Don't you remember that? You cried and cried."

"We cleaned it too," Helen says, dreamy. "It was just spotless." This was the house on Robinson Street, not where she is now. "Howard could clean all night." Howard stands tall in her mind, pale and serious in his shirtsleeves, wearing a dark narrow tie. His glasses gleam. Howard stands so tall that his head's in the sky.

"Well, I think Howard has some problems," Judy says flatly. "I always thought so, and so did Lawrence." Lawrence is Judy's husband, a dark, heavy electrician, and Judy has been married to him for twenty years. One time on New Year's Eve, Lawrence came in a bathroom where Helen was and tried to kiss her, but Helen never told Judy. It's the only secret she has ever kept from Judy, all her life, but it's not that important anyway. Lawrence *didn't* kiss her, nothing happened at all except he broke the soap dish.

"Good riddance is what Lawrence said," Judy reports. "Haven't you got anything around here except Coke?" she asks, and Helen puts some rum in it and fixes one for herself. In the Seascape Inn at Daytona Beach, she and Joe got drunk on Piña Coladas.

Billy comes out of his room whistling. "Hi, Judy," he says. "Mom, I'll be out riding my bike."

"Hello, cutie," Judy says. Billy is really her favorite. "How's Jill?" She loves to hear about Billy's girlfriend.

Billy makes a face. "Oh, I gave her to John," he says. "See you."

"Speaking of Howard," Judy says when he's gone and she finally quits laughing, "what about his *mother*?"

"Oh God!" Even tragic Helen has to laugh. "His *mother*!" she says.

"Lord God!" Judy pours herself another drink.

"Here honey, hush now," Helen says to Davey. She puts him up in his high chair, opens a can of fruit cocktail, and pours it out on his tray.

"Do you remember that time I cut her that piece of cake and she wouldn't eat it because it was too *thick*?" Judy shrieks. "Then I cut her that thin piece and she wouldn't eat it either."

"That was nothing," Helen says, "nothing at all. Listen. That was minor. In the first place she won't eat anything that's not light-colored. Everything has to be white. If you've got any colored food, like meat or green beans or anything, forget it. Then everything has to be mashed up, but none of the food can be touching any of the other food. I mean it can't even be close."

Judy, who has heard all of this before, loves to hear it again and again. She whoops with laughter. "Real problems," she says. "See what I mean?"

Just in time, Helen remembers her daughter. "Oh, I've got to pick up Denise," she says, fishing around under the kitchen table for her shoes. "She's over at the Y pool. I won't let her walk home by herself in the dark."

"I'll stay here with Davey," Judy says. "Won't I, honey?" She pinches Davey's cheek.

It's not far and Helen drives with all the windows push-buttoned down. The wind on her cheeks is hot and dry, making wrinkles no doubt but who cares now? Thank God for Judy anyway, ditto Lawrence, who have stood by her through thick and thin. Helen shakes her head when she thinks how she almost kissed Lawrence back. Judy and Lawrence will have been married twenty-one years come June, no children. Judy has an inverted ovary. Every night Judy and Lawrence watch TV together from seven P.M. on, and on holidays they drive off in their camper, to a new place every time. So far they have been to thirty-one states. They have stickers all over the back of the van. Helen can't figure out how they've stayed married so long, what they *do*, anyway. *What is the secret of a happy marriage?* One time she asked Judy, but Judy wouldn't tell her. "Just luck," Judy said. Helen didn't believe it.

When they were kids, Judy never even wanted to get married, that's the crazy part. Never even had boyfriends. While all Helen ever wanted to do, for the entire length of their childhood, was grow up. All she ever wanted to be was married. Helen knew how marriage would be, herself all dressed up in a frilly little net apron with appliqués on it, cozy little dinners with burning candles and flowers in cut-glass vases, moments of tenderness, walks in the woods. It didn't much matter who you married, you just had to marry somebody to have all that. Never mind that their own parents fought a lot, never mind that their mother died slowly of uterine cancer before their very eyes and their father married a woman named Lyde who never opened her mouth to talk or smile or anything else. Never mind any of that. Helen had known all about marriage anyway, that it was like a beautiful pastel country out there, waiting for her to walk into.

She pulls into the parking lot and there's Denise all wrapped up in her striped towel, huddled against a phone pole. Some teenage boys stand nearby, pushing and jostling each other and calling out into the night. Denise ignores them. Good for her! Helen thinks. She hopes Denise will grow up to be a nurse and an old maid, an old maid nurse.

"I thought you'd *never* get here!" Denise says. "What took you so long?"

"Judy came by. I just don't know what I'd do without her and Lawrence." Helen begins to cry.

"Mama, come on, what's the matter now?" Denise has a dry, knowing, grownup kind of a voice.

As she pulls back out into the traffic, Helen notices the lighted YMCA pool in her rearview mirror, watches a young boy dive off the high board. His body is caught and held still in the air for a second, and then he flashes down into the water like a knife. This pool reminds her a lot of the pool at the Seascape Inn, only that one was smaller, of course.

"Your father is a wonderful man," Helen sobs.

"My father is a turkey," says Denise.

When they get back, Judy is putting on her lipstick, brushing her bangs down, getting ready to leave. "Oh, honey, now now," she says when she sees Helen's face.

"She'll be OK," says Denise. "Don't worry."

But Helen grabs Judy's sleeve. "Listen," she says. "Don't you remember when you used to write in that red diary all the time?"

Judy stares at her. "What red diary?"

"You know," Helen says. "That red one you got with your allowance."

"Oh, that one," Judy says. She pulls Helen's hand off her sleeve. "Well, to tell you the truth, I don't remember."

"What's for supper?" Billy comes in just as Judy is leaving.

Helen stares around her little kitchen, her eyes catching on the stack of pots and pans that Davey has left on the floor.

"Oh no. Not again," says Denise.

But Helen is saved by a knock at the door. It's Will A. Okun wearing orange potholder mitts on both hands. He carries a steaming casserole.

"Hi, there!" He beams. "Just thought this might come in handy for you." He puts it down on a dish towel on the table and pretends to wrestle with Billy. Both boys like him because

of the way he looks in the mornings when he puts on all his pest control gear to go to work, like a man from Mars.

"I thought you might want the recipe," he says, and hands it to her on an index card.

"Thank you," Helen whispers.

"Anything you need," he says again, backing out the door, "anything at all—"

Helen looked at it while Denise sets the table.

Will A. Okun's Sausage-Corn combo

1 lb. sausage
1 can creamed corn
½ c. bread crumbs
4 eggs
1 teas. salt
¼ teas. pepper

Mix up. Bake for 1 hr. at 350.

Helen changes Davey, makes a salad, and when they finally sit down to eat, the casserole is delicious.

At work the next day, Helen proofreads brochures for a civic House Tour. These brochures have been ordered by Wells Murdock, a silver-haired businessman with a million-dollar smile who comes in the office sometimes. He and his wife are big in community affairs, and his picture is in the paper all the time. Helen sees that his own house, Blackberry Hill, will be a featured attraction on the House Tour, and she knows without even seeing it that it will be full of Oriental rugs and big jars full of dried stuff on the floor. The brochure is OK. She sends it back to the pressroom, then starts typing letters for Mr. Malone. After that, she files all the new work orders in the outer office where she works, and then she files the completed work orders in Mr. Malone's office.

He's in there behind his desk, smoking and working his calculator. "Oh, Mrs. Long," he says. His voice is old and raspy from smoking.

"Yes sir," Helen says.

"I was just wondering," he says. He looks over his glasses at her. "Whether or not you would be interested in learning a little bit more about the printing business."

"Well, I don't know, sir," Helen says. "I mean, I hadn't really thought about it. What do you mean exactly?"

"I mean becoming a salesman," he says, "like myself, or Bill, or Bob Foxwood, or John Jr. Calling on customers, making estimates on jobs, checking to see that it's done right back there in the pressroom, following through. That kind of thing. We could use a woman on our sales staff, and I can tell you right now that your salary would substantially improve."

It couldn't get any worse, Helen thinks. She stares at Mr. Malone. "I appreciate this a lot," Helen says. "I'll think about it and let you know right away. *Tomorrow*," she adds, as Mr. Malone draws his brows together in a frown. He's old and grouchy. He can't understand why Helen isn't jumping up and down with joy and squealing about her new job. He wants her to. Helen can't understand why she's not, either.

"I sure do appreciate the offer," she adds in a bright voice. "It's really a chance, isn't it?"

"All right, Helen," Mr. Malone says. "You think about it and let me know tomorrow."

Helen backs out the door. Millie and Joyce, at their desks in the outer office where they have sat for ten years, stare up at her with some suspicion in their eyes as she goes back to her desk. They know something is up. Millie is a secretary/bookkeeper. Joyce is a secretary/file clerk. Helen is a secretary/proofreader. Of all of them, why has Mr. Malone singled her out in this way? Why isn't she happy about it? She's been bitching about this job ever since she got it, $3.35 per hour and no sick pay. In high school, all the teachers thought she was so smart. In fact Mr. Hall almost cried when she told him she was going to marry Harold Long and not go on to school. So? So does she want to grow old in one lousy job, like Millie and Joyce have, get all ingrown and petty so she can't see the forest for the trees? Although their desks are side by side, Millie and Joyce have not spoken directly to each other since an argument they had three years ago over the price of a chair, and whether Joyce had agreed to fix the right front leg before Millie bought it or not. Helen knows she doesn't want her life to be taken up by chair legs. But still.

She thinks about Mr. Malone's offer for the rest of the day, while she files orders, waits on the walk-in customers, punches out for lunch at McDonald's and then back in, proofreads copy for a School of Nursing student manual and an advertising flyer, and answers the phone. "Aesthetic Printers," she says when she answers. Sometimes she just says "Aesthetic."

"Aesthetic *what*?" It's a man's voice, silvery and deep and amused.

"Aesthetic Printers," Helen says. She knows right away who it is: Wells Murdock.

"Who is this?" he asks. "Is this the blonde by the front door?"

"Helen Long," Helen says. "Yes sir."

Wells Murdock chuckles again. He is not in any hurry to get down to business. Helen thinks he probably has a sunken tub and mirror tiles on the wall in his bathroom, in his house on the House Tour. Helen tells him that all his brochures will be ready by ten A.M.

"I'll see you tomorrow," Wells Murdock says. He manages to sound both important and intimate at the same time. But maybe Helen is making this up. Maybe it's all in her mind. When Joe made a pass at her that first time, she wasn't sure of it either. Sometimes it's hard to tell. Helen wonders where Joe is now, where he went when he left the Seascape Inn, and settles on Texas for no real reason. He probably has another woman in Texas by now.

Helen goes to the ladies' room and cries for Howard. Then she goes out to pick roses, which is another one of her jobs. Mr. Malone grows them in a little garden at the side of the building, and every two days during the summer Helen goes out and cuts some and arranges them in bud vases, one for everybody's desk. Then she proofreads some graduation certificates, finds a mistake, and takes them back to the linotype operator for correction. One of the pressmen, Johnston Rhodes, sits drinking a Coke while the big Heidelburg Press that he runs prints calendars behind him. He squints up at Helen. The press makes a loud, regular, thumping noise.

"You ever go bowling?" Johnston Rhodes asks. Helen chokes back a sob.

Helen pretends like she doesn't hear him over the noise of the press, and the rest of the day she works in a fog, thinking about tomorrow and what she'll say to Mr. Malone, and trying to picture herself as a salesman. For instance, what would she *wear*?

Helen's half of the duplex is too quiet when she gets there and her heart jumps right up in her mouth when nobody answers her yell. Then she remembers that it's Howard's afternoon off and that he and his new wife, Louise, have taken the kids over there for a visit. Actually, Howard won custody of the kids in the first place, but that didn't last long. Louise, a real housekeeper after Howard's own heart, couldn't stand the mess. Even though she keeps all the furniture wrapped up in plastic sheets, according to Denise. It sure is quiet with them gone.

On Helen's show, Felicity continues to keep the baby's father a secret. She names him Everett, for her own father, deceased. But Everett develops jaundice and has to be placed in an incubator. Mike keeps watch over him night and day. Shadows show up under Mike's eyes, above the white mask. Along with flowers and a bunch of cards from well-wishers, Felicity receives a one-line note, written in a familiar hand. "Coming back—see you soon. Nick." *Nick!* Felicity puts the note quickly under her pillow, so Mrs. Belido and Mike won't know. Yet. She has to think.

Now it's early morning in Fernville. Michelle gets all dressed up in a forest green dress with a matching jacket and goes to visit Sandra. Sandra and Bland's house is one of Helen's favorites, a two-story traditional house with dormer windows and shutters and a graceful, winding staircase in the front hall. Bland has just left for work, and Sandra is still wearing a long striped robe that might as well be an evening dress. Michelle rings the doorbell. Sandra yawns as she goes to answer the door, expecting maybe the milkman, or anybody except Michelle in her forest green suit.

"Why, Michelle, what a surprise!" Sandra says. Her eyes narrow, but her good manners win out in the end. "Won't you come in for a cup of coffee?" she asks. Sandra is all heart, a really devoted wife who seems to have overcome the leukemia she had last year.

"Oh, how kind of you," Michelle says in her airy way. "But actually I have to run. I just came by to leave this for Bland." She hands Sandra a plain white envelope, sealed. Then she's gone—her high heels click away down the walk. After only a moment's hesitation, Sandra rips it open. *Bland's tie pin! the one she gave him on their first Christmas together!* She knows there's only one way Michelle could have gotten this. Sandra sobs. She slumps down onto the graceful winding stairway in the front hall of her house.

Elsewhere in Fernville, Lydia stands before the gold-leaf mirror in the front hall of her Tudor home, brushing and brushing her hair. Lydia, like Michelle, is sort of a bitch. But unlike Michelle, she doesn't seem to mean to be bitchy. She acts like she can't help it, like she is driven by a lot of desires that she doesn't have any control over. Like right now, for instance. She is brushing her hair so much because she is getting ready to go back to art school to fulfill herself. That's what she told John and all the kids. They were real nice about it, too. Of course! John said. I understand. By all means. Take all the courses you want! Lydia looks at herself once more in the mirror before she leaves. She wears beige slacks and her short mink coat. Her blond page-boy hair swings down below her ears. Lydia goes out and gets in her car and leaves.

The scene changes to an art studio of some kind, full of hippie-looking young people in blue jeans and dirty shirts, all working away at their easels. A black-haired man prowls like a panther among them, giving suggestions now and then. Sometimes he grabs a student's brush and shows how to do it. He is fiery and intense, with a black beard.

The studio door opens and there is Lydia, already late for her first class at art school, looking out of place to say the least in that mink coat.

"Oh, I—I—" she stutters.

The artist walks toward her.

"I—I'm—" she stutters.

He comes even closer. She falls silent, her mouth in a big O.

"I know who you are," he says.

Helen gets up and stretches. It's hot in here. She goes over and fools with the air conditioner but it's quit running and she can't get it to come back on. One more bill to pay. Helen feels like she's asleep this afternoon, or maybe it's only the heat. When Judy comes by, she tells her what Mr. Malone said and Judy says, "Well, you'd be a fool not to take it."

A fool. Helen is so sleepy and so hot. After Judy leaves, she goes in the bedroom and puts on a yellow terrycloth playsuit she bought in Florida. She hasn't worn it since she left there, but in the mirror she doesn't look half bad. The kids come bursting in the door then but before Helen can get to the window for a look at Howard he's gone, gunning it off down the street faster than she ever knew him to drive. The kids are as frisky and shaggy as puppies, with wet hair all in their eyes. Howard and his new wife have taken them swimming. Davey has a new little doll named Baby Red. "What happened to the air conditioning?" Billy asks. "Louise gave me this," says Denise. She hands Helen an index card that reads:

From the kitchen of Louise Long:

Beer Bread

2 c. self-rising flour
3 tbsp. sugar
1 can beer

Mix until blended. Turn into loaf pan. Bake at 375 for 20 to 25 min. or until pick inserted in center comes out clean. Brush with melted butter.

"Did you all eat some of this bread for lunch?" Helen asks.

"I guess so," says Denise. Denise is eating potato chips now.

"Well, was it *good*?" Helen asks. "I mean, how was it?"

"It was all right," Denise says with her mouth full. "I guess I've had better before."

"I'm going out to ride my bike," Billy says.

"How's your father?" Helen asks.

"He's a turkey," says Denise. "Can't we do anything about this heat?"

"Take Davey out in the back and turn on the sprinkler," Helen says. "I'll be out there myself in a minute."

Denise goes out and Helen mixes herself a rum and Coke and lights a Salem off the stove since she's run out of matches. While she waits for the burner to heat up, she thinks about Mr. Malone and his rose food and the job, which she knows by now that she won't even tell Denise about, although so far she isn't sure why. She picks up a piece of paper that the kids have left on the kitchen table where they were coloring, last night. It's a list, in Billy's third-grade writing:

Cool Club Rules
1. Bee cool how you walk
2. Ride your bike ruff
3. Get Donny
4. Fix up your
   room cool
5. Yell loud!
6. Jump from high places!

Helen laughs. She gets everything she needs and goes out the back door and positions herself in the lounge chair to face the last of the sun. Denise has turned on the sprinkler and put

Davey down at the edge of it so that every time it comes around, he hollers and giggles out loud. Denise sits in the other chair reading a library book, shielding her eyes from the sun. Helen's backyard is closed in by a chain-link fence. Helen lights another cigarette off her first one.

Will A. Okun jumps out of his house like a jack-in-a-box. His hair springs out from his head like cotton, like fluff, like bright angel hair in the sun. He points at the sun, in fact. *"A real scorcher,"* he says.

Helen nods agreeably. "And I just don't know what to do. Of all days, my air conditioner just broke down!" she cries.

Denise looks hard at her mother and then back down at her book.

"Why, I'll take a look at that for you!" Will A. Okun beams. "Just a minute." He pops back into his house and then reappears with an olive green toolbox, which he carries by a handle on the top. He opens the chain-link gate and goes in their back door by himself, whistling a little tune.

Helen puts her cigarette out in the grass and leans further back in her chair. Maybe Howard is a turkey, after all. But there are other fish in the sea. Helen can't figure out what has gotten into her, these recent months. She can't figure out why she's been mooning around like she has. The future rises up before her in a flash. She knows she won't take that job. She knows she will have a cup of coffee with Wells Murdock in the morning, she will go on the House Tour, she will change her attitude toward Will A. Okun, she might even go bowling, and who knows what she might do after that? Somebody in the neighborhood is mowing grass. Helen hears the mower and also she smells the grass. She loves how it smells. Somebody else is cooking out, hamburgers or something, and that smells good too across the yards. Suddenly Helen sits straight up. A little breeze comes out of nowhere, lifting her hair. The last rays of sun, shining through the sprinkler, made a shimmering pastel rainbow across her whole backyard. It's so beautiful that Helen catches her breath. When she leans this way or that, the rainbow moves too. It moves with her. It arcs up over the duplex, over the neighborhood, over the town and all the towns beyond this one, promising everything: another chance, another love, another world.

Shiloh

BOBBIE ANN MASON

Leroy Moffitt's wife, Norma Jean, is working on her pectorals. She lifts three-pound dumbbells to warm up, then progresses to a twenty-pound barbell. Standing with her legs apart, she reminds Leroy of Wonder Woman.

"I'd give anything if I could just get these muscles to where they're real hard," says Norma Jean. "Feel this arm. It's not as hard as the other one."

"That's 'cause you're right-handed," says Leroy, dodging as she swings the barbell in an arc.

"Do you think so?"

"Sure."

Leroy is a truckdriver. He injured his leg in a highway accident four months ago, and his physical therapy, which involves weights and a pulley, prompted Norma Jean to try building herself up. Now she is attending a body-building class. Leroy has been collecting temporary disability since his tractor-trailer jackknifed in Missouri, badly twisting his left leg in its socket. He has a steel pin in his hip. He will probably not be able to drive his rig again. It sits in the backyard, like a gigantic bird that has flown home to roost. Leroy has been home in Kentucky for three months, and his leg is almost healed, but the accident frightened him and he does not want to drive any more long hauls. He is not sure what to do next. In the meantime, he makes things from craft kits. He started by building a miniature log cabin from notched Popsicle sticks. He varnished it and placed it on the TV set, where it remains. It reminds him of a rustic Nativity scene. Then he tried string art (sailing ships on black velvet), a macramé owl kit, a snap-together B-17 Flying Fortress, and a lamp made out of a model truck, with a light fixture screwed in the top of the cab. At first the kits were diversions, something to kill time, but now he is thinking about building a full-scale log house from a kit. It would be considerably cheaper than building a regular house, and besides, Leroy has grown to appreciate how things are put together. He has begun to realize that in all the years he was on the road he never took time to examine anything. He was always flying past scenery.

"They won't let you build a log cabin in any of the new subdivisions," Norma Jean tells him.

"They will if I tell them it's for you," he says, teasing her. Ever since they were married, he has promised Norma Jean he would build her a new home one day. They have always rented, and the house they live in is small and nondescript. It does not even feel like a home, Leroy realizes now.

Norma Jean works at the Rexall drugstore, and she has acquired an amazing amount of information about cosmetics. When she explains to Leroy the three stages of complexion care, involving creams, toners, and moisturizers, he thinks happily of other petroleum products—axle grease, diesel fuel. This is a connection between him and Norma Jean. Since he has been home, he has felt unusually tender about his wife and guilty over his long absences. But he can't tell what she feels about him. Norma Jean has never complained about his traveling; she has never made hurt remarks, like calling his truck a "widow-maker." He is reasonably certain she has been faithful to him, but he wishes she would celebrate his permanent homecoming more happily. Norma Jean is often startled to find Leroy at home, and he thinks she seems a little disappointed about it. Perhaps he reminds her too much of the early days of their marriage, before he went on the road.

They had a child who died as an infant, years ago. They never speak about their memories of Randy, which have almost faded, but now that Leroy is home all the time, they sometimes feel awkward around each other, and Leroy wonders if one of them should mention the child. He has the feeling that they are waking up out of a dream together—that they must create a new marriage, start afresh. They are lucky they are still married. Leroy has read that for most people losing a child destroys the marriage—or else he heard this on *Donahue*. He can't always remember where he learns things anymore.

At Christmas, Leroy bought an electric organ for Norma Jean. She used to play the piano when she was in high school. "It don't leave you," she told him once. "It's like riding a bicycle."

The new instrument had so many keys and buttons that she was bewildered by it at first. She touched the keys tentatively, pushed some buttons, then pecked out "Chopsticks." It came out in an amplified fox-trot rhythm, with marimba sounds.

"It's an orchestra!" she cried.

The organ had a pecan-look finish and eighteen preset chords, with optional flute, violin, trumpet, clarinet, and banjo accompaniments. Norma Jean mastered the organ almost immediately. At first she played Christmas songs. Then she bought *The Sixties Songbook* and learned every tune in it, adding variations to each with the rows of brightly colored buttons.

"I didn't like these old songs back then," she said. "But I have this crazy feeling I missed something."

"You didn't miss a thing," said Leroy.

Leroy likes to lie on the couch and smoke a joint and listen to Norma Jean play "Can't Take My Eyes Off You" and "I'll Be Back." He is back again. After fifteen years on the road, he is finally settling down with the woman he loves. She is still pretty. Her skin is flawless. Her frosted curls resemble pencil trimmings.

*   *   *

Now that Leroy has come home to stay, he notices how much the town has changed. Subdivisions are spreading across western Kentucky like an oil slick. The sign at the edge of town says "Pop: 11,500"—only seven hundred more than it said twenty years before. Leroy can't figure out who is living in all the new houses. The farmers who used to gather around the courthouse on Saturday afternoons to play checkers and spit tobacco juice have gone. It has been years since Leroy has thought about the farmers, and they have disappeared without his noticing.

Leroy meets a kid named Stevie Hamilton in the parking lot at the new shopping center. While they pretend to be strangers meeting over a stalled car, Stevie tosses an ounce of marijuana under the front seat of Leroy's car. Stevie is wearing orange jogging shoes and a T-shirt that says CHATTA-HOOCHEE SUPER-RAT. His father is a prominent doctor who lives in one of the expensive subdivisions in a new white-columned brick house that looks like a funeral parlor. In the phone book under his name there is a separate number, with the listing "Teenagers."

"Where do you get this stuff?" asks Leroy. "From your pappy?"

"That's for me to know and you to find out," Stevie says. He is slit-eyed and skinny.

"What else you got?"

"What you interested in?"

"Nothing special. Just wondered."

Leroy used to take speed on the road. Now he has to go slowly. He needs to be mellow. He leans back against the car and says, "I'm aiming to build me a log house, soon as I get time. My wife, though, I don't think she likes the idea."

"Well, let me know when you want me again," Stevie says. He has a cigarette in his cupped palm, as though sheltering it from the wind. He takes a long drag, then stomps it on the asphalt and slouches away.

Stevie's father was two years ahead of Leroy in high school. Leroy is thirty-four. He married Norma Jean when they were both eighteen, and their child Randy was born a few months later, but he died at the age of four months and three days. He would be about Stevie's age now. Norma Jean and Leroy were at the drive-in, watching a double feature (*Dr. Strangelove* and *Lover Come Back*), and the baby was sleeping in the back seat. When the first movie ended, the baby was dead. It was the sudden infant death syndrome. Leroy remembers handing Randy to a nurse at the emergency room, as though he were offering her a large doll as a present. A dead baby feels like a sack of flour. "It just happens sometimes," said the doctor, in what Leroy always recalls as a nonchalant tone. Leroy can hardly remember the child anymore, but he still sees vividly a scene from *Dr. Strangelove* in which the President of the United States was talking in a folksy voice on the hot line to the Soviet premier about the bomber accidentally headed toward Russia. He was in the War Room, and the world map was lit up. Leroy remembers Norma Jean standing catatonically beside him in the hospital and himself thinking: Who is this strange girl? He had forgotten who she was. Now scientists are saying that crib death is caused by a virus. Nobody knows anything, Leroy thinks. The answers are always changing.

When Leroy gets home from the shopping center, Norma Jean's mother, Mabel Beasley, is there. Until this year, Leroy has not realized how much time she spends with Norma Jean. When she visits, she inspects the closets and then the plants, informing Norma Jean when a plant is droopy or yellow. Mabel calls the plants "flowers," although there are never any blooms. She always notices if Norma Jean's laundry is piling up. Mabel is a short, overweight woman whose tight, brown-dyed curls look more like a wig than the actual wig she sometimes wears. Today she has brought Norma Jean an off-white dust ruffle she made for the bed; Mabel works in a custom-upholstery shop.

"This is the tenth one I made this year," Mabel says. "I got started and couldn't stop."

"It's real pretty," says Norma Jean.

"Now we can hide things under the bed," says Leroy, who gets along with his mother-in-law primarily by joking with her. Mabel has never really forgiven him for disgracing her by getting Norma Jean pregnant. When the baby died, she said that fate was mocking her.

"What's that thing?" Mabel says to Leroy in a loud voice, pointing to a tangle of yarn on a piece of canvas.

Leroy holds it up for Mabel to see. "It's my needlepoint," he explains. "This is a *Star Trek* pillow cover."

"That's what a woman would do," says Mabel. "Great day in the morning!"

"All the big football players on TV do it," he says.

"Why, Leroy, you're always trying to fool me. I don't believe you for one minute. You don't know what to do with yourself—that's the whole trouble. Sewing!"

"I'm aiming to build us a log house," says Leroy. "Soon as my plans come."

"Like *heck* you are," says Norma Jean. She takes Leroy's needlepoint and shoves it into a drawer. "You have to find a job first. Nobody can afford to build now anyway."

Mabel straightens her girdle and says, "I still think before you get tied down y'all ought to take a little run to Shiloh."

"One of these days, Mama," Norma Jean says impatiently.

Mabel is talking about Shiloh, Tennessee. For the past few years, she has been urging Leroy and Norma Jean to visit the Civil War battleground there. Mabel went there on her honeymoon—the only real trip she ever took. Her husband died of a perforated ulcer when Norma Jean was ten, but Mabel, who was accepted into the United Daughters of the Confederacy in 1975, is still preoccupied with going back to Shiloh.

"I've been to kingdom come and back in that truck out yonder," Leroy says to Mabel, "but we never yet set foot in that battleground. Ain't that something? How did I miss it?"

"It's not even that far," Mabel says.

After Mabel leaves, Norma Jean reads to Leroy from a list she has made. "Things you could do," she announces. "You could get a job as a guard at Union Carbide, where they'd let you set on a stool. You could get on at the lumberyard. You could do a little carpenter work, if you want to build so bad. You could—''

''I can't do something where I'd have to stand up all day.''

''You ought to try standing up all day behind a cosmetics counter. It's amazing that I have strong feet, coming from two parents that never had strong feet at all.'' At the moment Norma Jean is holding on to the kitchen counter, raising her knees one at a time as she talks. She is wearing two-pound ankle weights.

''Don't worry,'' says Leroy. ''I'll do something.''

''You could truck calves to slaughter for somebody. You wouldn't have to drive any big old truck for that.''

''I'm going to build you this house,'' says Leroy. ''I want to make you a real home.''

''I don't want to live in any log cabin.''

''It's not a cabin. It's a house.''

''I don't care. It looks like a cabin.''

''You and me together could lift those logs. It's just like lifting weights.''

Norma Jean doesn't answer. Under her breath, she is counting. Now she is marching through the kitchen. She is doing goose steps.

Before his accident, when Leroy came home he used to stay in the house with Norma Jean, watching TV in bed and playing cards. She would cook fried chicken, picnic ham, chocolate pie—all his favorites. Now he is home alone much of the time. In the mornings, Norma Jean disappears, leaving a cooling place in the bed. She eats a cereal called Body Buddies, and she leaves the bowl on the table, with the soggy tan balls floating in a milk puddle. He sees things about Norma Jean that he never realized before. When she chops onions, she stares off into a corner, as if she can't bear to look. She puts on her house slippers almost precisely at nine o'clock every evening and nudges her jogging shoes under the couch. She saves bread heels for the birds. Leroy watches the birds at the feeder. He notices the peculiar way goldfinches fly past the window. They close their wings, then fall, then spread their wings to catch and lift themselves. He wonders if they close their eyes when they fall. Norma Jeans closes her eyes when they are in bed. She wants the lights turned out. Even then, he is sure she closes her eyes.

He goes for long drives around town. He tends to drive a car rather carelessly. Power steering and an automatic shift make a car feel so small and inconsequential that his body is hardly involved in the driving process. His injured leg stretches out comfortably. Once or twice he has almost hit something, but even the prospect of an accident seems minor in a car. He cruises the new subdivisions, feeling like a criminal rehearsing for a robbery. Norma Jean is probably right about a log house being inappropriate here in the new subdivisions. All the houses look grand and complicated. They depress him.

One day when Leroy comes home from a drive he finds Norma Jean in tears. She is in the kitchen making a potato and mushroom-soup casserole, with grated-cheese topping. She is crying because her mother caught her smoking.

"I didn't hear her coming. I was standing here puffing away pretty as you please," Norma Jean says, wiping her eyes.

"I knew it would happen sooner or later," says Leroy, putting his arm around her.

"She don't know the meaning of the word 'knock,' " says Norma Jean. "It's a wonder she hadn't caught me years ago."

"Think of it this way," Leroy says. "What if she caught me with a joint?"

"You better not let her!" Norma Jean shrieks. "I'm warning you, Leroy Moffitt!"

"I'm just kidding. Here, play me a tune. That'll help you relax."

Norma Jean puts the casserole in the oven and sets the timer. Then she plays a ragtime tune, with horns and banjo, as Leroy lights up a joint and lies on the couch, laughing to himself about Mabel's catching him at it. He thinks of Stevie Hamilton—a doctor's son pushing grass. Everything is funny. The whole town seems crazy and small. He is reminded of

Virgil Mathis, a boastful policeman Leroy used to shoot pool with. Virgil recently led a drug bust in a back room at a bowling alley, where he seized ten thousand dollars' worth of marijuana. The newspaper had a picture of him holding up the bags of grass and grinning widely. Right now, Leroy can imagine Virgil breaking down the door and arresting him with a lungful of smoke. Virgil would probably have been alerted to the scene because of all the racket Norma Jean is making. Now she sounds like a hard-rock band. Norma Jean is terrific. When she switches to a Latin-rhythm version of "Sunshine Superman," Leroy hums along. Norma Jean's foot goes up and down, up and down.

"Well, what do you think?" Leroy says, when Norma Jean pauses to search through her music.

"What do I think about what?"

His mind has gone blank. Then he says, "I'll sell my rig and build us a house." That wasn't what he wanted to say. He wanted to know what she thought—what she *really* thought—about them.

"Don't start in on that again," says Norma Jean. She begins playing "Who'll Be the Next in Line?"

Leroy used to tell hitchhikers his whole life story—about his travels, his hometown, the baby. He would end with a question: "Well, what do you think?" It was just a rhetorical question. In time, he had the feeling that he'd been telling the same story over and over to the same hitchhikers. He quit talking to hitchhikers when he realized how his voice sounded— whining and self-pitying, like some teenage-tragedy song. Now Leroy has the sudden impulse to tell Norma Jean about himself, as if he had just met her. They have known each other so long they have forgotten a lot about each other. They could become reacquainted. But when the oven timer goes off and she runs to the kitchen, he forgets why he wants to do this.

The next day, Mabel drops by. It is Saturday and Norma Jean is cleaning. Leroy is studying the plans of his log house, which have finally come in the mail. He has them spread out on the table—big sheets of stiff blue paper, with diagrams and numbers printed in white. While Norma Jean runs the vacuum, Mabel drinks coffee. She sets her coffee cup on a blueprint.

"I'm just waiting for time to pass," she says to Leroy, drumming her fingers on the table.

As soon as Norma Jean switches off the vacuum, Mabel says in a loud voice, "Did you hear about the datsun dog that killed the baby?"

Norma Jean says, "The word is 'dachshund.' "

"They put the dog on trial. It chewed the baby's legs off. The mother was in the next room all the time." She raises her voice. "They thought it was neglect."

Norma Jean is holding her ears. Leroy manages to open the refrigerator and get some Diet Pepsi to offer Mabel. Mabel still has some coffee and she waves away the Pepsi.

"Datsuns are like that," Mabel says. "They're jealous dogs. They'll tear a place to pieces if you don't keep an eye on them."

"You better watch out what you're saying, Mabel," says Leroy.

"Well, facts is facts."

Leroy looks out the window at his rig. It is like a huge piece of furniture gathering dust in the backyard. Pretty soon it will be an antique. He hears the vacuum cleaner. Norma Jean seems to be cleaning the living room rug again.

Later, she says to Leroy, "She just said that about the baby because she caught me smoking. She's trying to pay me back."

"What are you talking about?" Leroy says, nervously shuffling blueprints.

"You know good and well," Norma Jean says. She is sitting in a kitchen chair with her feet up and her arms wrapped around her knees. She looks small and helpless. She says, "The very idea, her bringing up a subject like that! Saying it was neglect."

"She didn't mean that," Leroy says.

"She might not have *thought* she meant it. She always says things like that. You don't know how she goes on."

"But she didn't really mean it. She was just talking."

Leroy opens a king-sized bottle of beer and pours it into two glasses, dividing it carefully. He hands a glass to Norma Jean and she takes it from him mechanically. For a long time, they sit by the kitchen window watching the birds at the feeder.

Something is happening. Norma Jean is going to night school. She has graduated from her six-week body-building course and now she is taking an adult-education course in composition at Paducah Community College. She spends her evenings outlining paragraphs.

"First you have a topic sentence," she explains to Leroy. "Then you divide it up. Your secondary topic has to be connected to your primary topic."

To Leroy, this sounds intimidating. "I never was any good in English," he says.

"It makes a lot of sense."

"What are you doing this for, anyhow?"

She shrugs. "It's something to do." She stands up and lifts her dumbbells a few times.

"Driving a rig, nobody cared about my English."

"I'm not criticizing your English."

Norma Jean used to say, "If I lose ten minutes' sleep, I just drag all day." Now she stays up late, writing compositions. She got a B on her first paper—a how-to theme on soup-based casseroles. Recently Norma Jean has been cooking unusual foods—tacos, lasagna, Bombay chicken. She doesn't play the organ anymore, though her second paper was called "Why Music Is Important to Me." She sits at the kitchen table, concentrating on her outlines, while Leroy plays with his log house plans, practicing with a set of Lincoln Logs. The thought of getting a truckload of notched, numbered logs scares him, and he wants to be prepared. As he and Norma Jean work together at the kitchen table, Leroy has the hopeful thought that they are sharing something, but he knows he is a fool to think this. Norma Jean is miles away. He knows he is going to lose her. Like Mabel, he is just waiting for time to pass.

One day, Mabel is there before Norma Jean gets home from work, and Leroy finds himself confiding in her. Mabel, he realizes, must know Norma Jean better than he does.

"I don't know what's got into that girl," Mabel says. "She used to go to bed with the chickens. Now you say she's up all hours. Plus her a-smoking. I like to died."

"I want to make her this beautiful home," Leroy says, indicating the Lincoln Logs. "I don't think she even wants it. Maybe she was happier with me gone."

"She don't know what to make of you, coming home like this."

"Is that it?"

Mabel takes the roof off his Lincoln Log cabin. "You couldn't get *me* in a log cabin," she says. "I was raised in one. It's no picnic, let me tell you."

"They're different now," says Leroy.

"I tell you what," Mabel says, smiling oddly at Leroy.

"What?"

"Take her on down to Shiloh. Y'all need to get out together, stir a little. Her brain's all balled up over them books."

Leroy can see traces of Norma Jean's features in her mother's face. Mabel's worn face has the texture of crinkled cotton, but suddenly she looks pretty. It occurs to Leroy that Mabel has been hinting all along that she wants them to take her with them to Shiloh.

"Let's all go to Shiloh," he says. "You and me and her. Come Sunday."

Mabel throws up her hands in protest. "Oh, no, not me. Young folks want to be by theirselves."

When Norma Jean comes in with groceries, Leroy says excitedly, "Your mama here's been dying to go to Shiloh for thirty-five years. It's about time we went, don't you think?"

"I'm not going to butt in on anybody's second honeymoon," Mabel says.

"Who's going on a honeymoon, for Christ's sake?" Norma Jean says loudly.

"I never raised no daughter of mine to talk that-a-way," Mabel says.

"You ain't seen nothing yet," says Norma Jean. She starts putting away boxes and cans, slamming cabinet doors.

"There's a log cabin at Shiloh," Mabel says. "It was there during the battle. There's bullet holes in it."

"When are you going to *shut up* about Shiloh, Mama?" asks Norma Jean.

"I always thought Shiloh was the prettiest place, so full of history," Mabel goes on. "I just hoped y'all could see it once before I die, so you could tell me about it." Later, she whispers to Leroy, "You do what I said. A little change is what she needs."

"Your name means 'the king,'" Norma Jean says to Leroy that evening. He is trying to get her to go to Shiloh, and she is reading a book about another century.

"Well, I reckon I ought to be right proud."

"I guess so."

"Am I still king around here?"

Norma Jean flexes her biceps and feels them for hardness. "I'm not fooling around with anybody, if that's what you mean," she says.

"Would you tell me if you were?"

"I don't know."

"What does *your* name mean?"

"It was Marilyn Monroe's real name."

"No kidding!"

"Norma comes from the Normans. They were invaders," she says. She closes her book and looks hard at Leroy. "I'll go to Shiloh with you if you'll stop staring at me."

On Sunday, Norma Jean packs a picnic and they go to Shiloh. To Leroy's relief, Mabel says she does not want to come with them. Norma Jean drives, and Leroy, sitting beside her, feels like some boring hitchhiker she has picked up.

He tries some conversation, but she answers him in monosyllables. At Shiloh, she drives aimlessly through the park, past bluffs and trails and steep ravines. Shiloh is an immense place, and Leroy cannot see it as a battleground. It is not what he expected. He thought it would look like a golf course. Monuments are everywhere, showing through the thick cluster of trees. Norma Jean passes the log cabin Mabel mentioned. It is surrounded by tourists looking for bullet holes.

"That's not the kind of log house I've got in mind," says Leroy apologetically.

"I know *that*."

"This is a pretty place. Your mama was right."

"It's O.K.," says Norma Jean. "Well, we've seen it. I hope she's satisfied."

They burst out laughing together.

At the park museum, a movie on Shiloh is shown every half hour, but they decide that they don't want to see it. They buy a souvenir Confederate flag for Mabel, and then they find a picnic spot near the cemetery. Norma Jean has brought a picnic cooler, with pimiento sandwiches, soft drinks, and Yodels. Leroy eats a sandwich and then smokes a joint, hiding it behind the picnic cooler. Norma Jean has quit smoking altogether. She is picking cake crumbs from the cellophane wrapper, like a fussy bird.

Leroy says, "So the boys in gray ended up in Corinth. The Union soldiers zapped 'em finally. April 7, 1862."

They both know that he doesn't know any history. He is just talking about some of the historical plaques they have read. He feels awkward, like a boy on a date with an older girl. They are still just making conversation.

"Corinth is where Mama eloped to," says Norma Jean.

They sit in silence and stare at the cemetery for the Union dead and, beyond, at a tall cluster of trees. Campers are parked nearby, bumper to bumper, and small children in bright clothing are cavorting and squealing. Norma Jean wads up the cake wrapper and squeezes it tightly in her hand. Without looking at Leroy, she says, "I want to leave you."

Leroy takes a bottle of Coke out of the cooler and flips off the cap. He holds the bottle poised near his mouth but cannot remember to take a drink. Finally he says, "No, you don't."

"Yes, I do."

"I won't let you."

"You can't stop me."

"Don't do me that way."

Leroy knows Norma Jean will have her own way. "Didn't I promise to be home from now on?" he says.

"In some ways, a woman prefers a man who wanders," says Norma Jean. "That sounds crazy, I know."

"You're not crazy."

Leroy remembers to drink from his Coke. Then he says, "Yes, you *are* crazy. You and me could start all over again. Right back at the beginning."

"We *have* started all over again," says Norma Jean. "And this is how it turned out."

"What did I do wrong?"

"Nothing."

"Is this one of those women's lib things?" Leroy asks.

"Don't be funny."

The cemetery, a green slope dotted with white markers, looks like a subdivision site. Leroy is trying to comprehend that his marriage is breaking up, but for some reason he is wondering about white slabs in a graveyard.

"Everything was fine till Mama caught me smoking," says Norma Jean, standing up. "That set something off."

"What are you talking about?"

"She won't leave me alone—*you* won't leave me alone." Norma Jean seems to be crying, but she is looking away from him. "I feel eighteen again. I can't face that all over again." She starts walking away. "No, it *wasn't* fine. I don't know what I'm saying. Forget it."

Leroy takes a lungful of smoke and closes his eyes as Norma Jean's words sink in. He tries to focus on the fact that thirty-five hundred soldiers died on the grounds around him. He can only think of that war as a board game with plastic soldiers. Leroy almost smiles, as he compares the Confederates' daring attack on the Union camps and Virgil Mathis's raid on the bowling alley. General Grant, drunk and furious, shoved the Southerners back to Corinth, where Mabel and Jet Beasley were married years later, when Mabel was still thin and good-looking. The next day, Mabel and Jet visited the battleground, and then Norma Jean was born, and then she married Leroy and they had a baby which they lost, and now Leroy and Norma Jean are here at the same battleground. Leroy knows he is leaving out a lot. He is leaving out the insides of history. History was always just names and dates to him. It occurs to him that building a house out of logs is similarly empty—too simple. And the real inner workings of a marriage, like most of history, have escaped him. Now he sees that building a log house is the dumbest idea he could have had. It was clumsy of him to think Norma Jean would want a log house. It was a crazy idea. He'll have to think of something else, quickly. He will wad the blueprints into tight balls and fling them into the lake. Then he'll get moving again. He opens his eyes. Norma Jean has moved away and is walking through the cemetery, following a serpentine brick path.

Leroy gets up to follow his wife, but his good leg is asleep and his bad leg still hurts him. Norma Jean is far away, walking rapidly toward the bluff by the river, and he tries to hobble toward her. Some children run past him, screaming noisily. Norma Jean has reached the bluff, and she is looking out over the Tennessee River. Now she turns toward Leroy and waves her arms. Is she beckoning to him? She seems to be doing an exercise for her chest muscles. The sky is unusually pale—the color of the dust ruffle Mabel made for their bed.

About the Authors

Alice Adams (b. 1926)

A long-time resident of San Francisco, Alice Adams was born in Fredericksburg, Virginia, and educated at Radcliffe College. She has received grants from the Guggenheim Foundation and the National Foundation of the Arts. Her fiction has appeared in *Atlantic Monthly*, *The New Yorker*, and *Paris Review*, and ten of her stories were selected for the annual series of anthologies of O. Henry award-winning fiction. Her books include four collections of stories—*Beautiful Girl* (1979), *You Can't Keep a Good Woman Down* (1981), *To See You Again* (1982), and *Return Trips* (1985)—as well as the novels *Careless Love* (1966), *Families and Survivors* (1974), *Listening to Billie* (1978), *Rich Rewards* (1980), and *Superior Women* (1984).

Louisa May Alcott (1832–1888)

Raised in Concord, Massachusetts, Louisa May Alcott was the daughter of Bronson Alcott, a social reformer, poet, experimental educator, and Transcendentalist who was often unable to support his wife and four daughters. Obliged at an early age to do physical labor to help earn money for her family, she soon turned to a career as a writer. At the age of sixteen she wrote *Flower Fables*, but her first widely read work was *Hospital Sketches* (1863), which was based on her experiences as a volunteer nurse in a Civil War army hospital. With the publication in 1869 of *Little Women*, a novel which was dramatized for the stage and later filmed twice, she achieved a considerable degree of fame and success. Among her other works are two adult novels, *Moods* (1864) and *Work* (1873), as well as *An Old-Fashioned Girl* (1870), *Little Men* (1871), *Eight Cousins* (1875), *Rose in Bloom* (1876), *Under the Lilacs (1878), and Jo's Boys* (1886).

Toni Cade Bambara (b. 1939)

An alumna of Queens College and the City University of New York, Toni Cade Bambara published her early work under the name Toni Cade. She added "Bambara," a maternal family name, as a tribute to the Bambara people of the Sudan. A native New Yorker, she has worked as a social investigator for the New York State Department of Welfare, a community organizer, and a youth counselor. She has taught at Rutgers, Duke, and Atlanta Universities as well as at Spellman College in Atlanta. In addition to editing two anthologies, *The Black Woman* (1970), and *Tales and Stories for Black Folks* (1971), she is the author of two collections of short stories, *Gorilla, My Love* (1972) and *The Seabirds Are Still Alive* (1977), as well as the novel *The Salt Eaters* (1980).

Ann Beattie (b. 1947)

Born in Washington, D.C., Ann Beattie earned a B.A. at American University in Washington and an M.A. at the University of Connecticut. A recipient of a Guggenheim Fellowship and a grant from the American Academy of Arts and Letters, she has taught creative writing at the University of Virginia and Harvard. Among her books are three collections of stories, *Distortions* (1976), *Secrets and Surprises* (1978), and *The Burning House* (1982), and the novels *Chilly Scenes of Winter* (1976), which was made into the film *Head Over Heels, Falling in Place* (1980), and *Love Always* (1985).

Sallie Bingham (b. 1937)

Born in Louisville, Kentucky, Sallie Bingham received a B.A. at Radcliffe College. Her stories have appeared in *The Atlantic, Transatlantic Review, Ms., Redbook, Ladies' Home Journal,* and *Mademoiselle.* Two of her stories have won O. Henry Awards. She has published a novel, *After Such Knowledge* (1960), and two collections of stories, *The Touching Hand* (1967) and *The Way It Is Now* (1972).

Kate Chopin (1851–1904)

As a widow with six children, Kate Chopin began a literary career at the age of thirty-eight. She had returned to her native St. Louis after a dozen years devoted exclusively to married life in New Orleans and a small town in Louisiana, Cloutierville. Her first novel, *At Fault,* was published in 1890, and within a short period of time she had gained national prominence as a short story writer. Most of her stories, which dramatized Creole and Cajun life, were collected in two volumes, *Bayou Folk* (1894) and *A Night in Acadie* (1897). Amid a storm of outrage from reviewers, her masterpiece, the novel *The Awakening*, was published in 1899. In recent years, this novel has finally attained the critical stature of an American classic.

Laurie Colwin (b.1944)

Brought up in Chicago and Philadelphia, Laurie Colwin now lives in New York City. Her stories have appeared in *The New Yorker, Redbook, McCall's, Cosmopolitan,* and

Mademoiselle and have been selected for volumes of the O. Henry Award collection and *Best American Short Stories* series. She has written three novels, *Shine On, Bright and Dangerous Object* (1975), *Happy All the Time* (1978), and *Family Happiness* (1982), as well as three collections of stories, *Passion and Affect* (1974, published in England the following year as *Dangerous French Mistress and Other Stories), The Lone Pilgrim* (1981), and *Another Marvelous Thing* (1986).

Mary Wilkins Freeman (1852–1930)

At the age of thirty, Mary Wilkins Freeman succeeded in selling two adult stories to magazines after almost a decade of failing to publish her work, which included numerous children's poems and stories. During the next two decades, she wrote, prolifically and successfully, drawing on small New England towns as the background for her depiction of the lives of varied women characters. Among the almost forty volumes of her published work are the novels *Jane Field* (1893), *Pembroke* (1894), and *The Shoulders of Atlas* (1908), as well as collections of her short stories: *A Humble Romance and Other Stories* (1887), *A New England Nun and Other Stories* (1891), and *Six Trees* (1903). In 1908, she participated in an unusual joint fiction-writing project with authors such as William Dean Howells and Henry James which resulted in the publication of *The Whole Family: A Novel by Twelve Authors*.

Charlotte Perkins Gilman (1860–1935)

Divorced from her first husband, Charles Stetson, at the age of thirty, Charlotte Perkins Gilman moved to California, where she supported herself by lecturing on the status of women and on socialism, teaching school, running a boarding house, editing newspapers, and writing. Among her works on social and feminist issues are *Women and Economics* (1898),

Concerning Children (1900), *Human Work* (1904), and *The Man-made World; or Our Androcentric Culture* (1911). Among her novels are *The Crux* (1911) and *What Diantha Did* (1912), as well as three feminist, Utopian works—*Moving the Mountain* (1911), *Herland* (1915), and *With Her in Ourland* (1916). *The Living of Charlotte Perkins Gilman*, her autobiography, was published in 1935. Terminally and painfully ill with cancer, she chose to end her life.

Joanne Greenberg (b. 1932)

A resident of Colorado, where she is a member of a paramedic emergency team, Joanne Greenberg published an early novel, *I Never Promised You a Rose Garden* (1964), under the pseudonym "Hannah Green." The novel, which dramatizes the return to sanity of a sixteen-year-old girl who had created her own mad world to escape the painful real one, was made into a film in 1977. A graduate of American University in Washington, D.C., and the University of London, Greenberg is a registered "Interpreter of the Deaf" who has taught sign language. Among her works are three collections of short stories—*Summering* (1966), *Rites of Passage* (1972), and *High Crimes and Misdemeanors* (1980)—as well as the novels *The King's Persons* (1963), *The Monday Voices* (1965), *In This Sign* (1970), *Founder's Praise* (1976), *A Season of Delight* (1981), and *The Far Side of Victory* (1983).

Stephanie C. Gunn (b. 1954)

Born in Toronto, Stephanie C. Gunn received a B.A. from Mount Holyoke College and an M.F.A. from Columbia University. Her stories have appeared in *Fiction, Columbia: A Magazine of Poetry and Prose, The Penny Dreadful, The Random Review,* and *Mss. Magazine.* A recipient of a National Endowment for the Arts Grant and a Creative Arts

Public Service Grant, she recently spent time at the MacDowell Colony in Peterborough, New Hampshire, working on a novel about a modern family.

Mary Hedin (b. 1929)

Educated at the University of Minnesota and the University of California at San Francisco, where she received a Master's degree, Mary Hedin has taught at the College of Marin in California for almost two decades. A recipient of the Iowa School of Letters Award for Short Fiction and the Great Lakes College Association Award for New Fiction, she has been Writer in Residence at the Robinson Jeffers Tor House Foundation. She has contributed short stories to *Redbook, McCall's, Southwest Review,* and *South Dakota Review,* and several of her stories have been included in the annual anthologies *Best American Short Stories* and *O. Henry Prize Stories. Fly Away Home* (1980) is a collection of her stories, and *Direction* (1983) is a collection of her poems.

Zora Neale Hurston (c 1901–1960)

Raised in Eatonville, Florida, the first self-governing all-black town in the United States, Zora Neale Hurston was educated at Morgan Academy in Baltimore, Howard University, and at Barnard College where she was the only black student on campus. Combining her talents as an anthropologist and creative writer, she published a collection of southern folklore, *Mules and Men* (1935), followed by a volume utilizing her research in Haiti and the West Indies titled *Tell My Horse* (1938). The author of four novels—*Jonah's Gourd Vine* (1934), *Their Eyes Were Watching God* (1937), *Moses: Man of the Mountain* (1939) and *Seraph on the Suwanee* (1948)—she also published a play titled *Singing Steel* (1934) and her autobiography, *Dust Tracks on a Road* (1942).

Marilyn Krysl (b. 1942)

Born in Anthony, Kansas, Marilyn Krysl was educated at the University of Oregon, where she received a B.A. and M.F.A. "A Woman's Story," which originally appeared in the *Seneca Review*, is reprinted in her collection *Honey, You've Been Dealt a Winning Hand* (1980). Presently an associate professor of English at the University of Colorado, where she teaches creative writing and literature, she has published two collections of poetry—*More Palomino, Please, More Fushia* (1980) and *Diana Lucifera* (1985)—as well as another volume of stories, *Mozart, Westmoreland and Me* (1985).

Paule Marshall (b. 1929)

Born in Brooklyn, New York, Paule Marshall was graduated Phi Beta Kappa from Brooklyn College. She has received a Guggenheim Fellowship, a Rosenthal Award from the National Institute of Arts and Letters, a Ford Foundation Theater Award, and a grant from the National Endowment for the Arts. Among her works are the novels *Brown Girl, Brownstones (1959), The Chosen Place, The Timeless People* (1969), and *Praisesong for the Widow* (1983), as well as the collections of stories *Soul Clap Hands and Sing* (1961) and *Reena and Other Stories* (1983).

Bobbie Ann Mason (b. 1940)

Raised on a farm near Mayfield, Kentucky, Bobbie Ann Mason received a B.A. from the University of Kentucky, an M.A. from the State University of New York at Binghamton, and a doctorate from the University of Connecticut. A recipient of a Guggenheim Fellowship and grants from the National Endowment for the Arts and American Academy and Institute for Arts and Letters, she has taught English and journalism at Mansfield State College. Her stories, which have appeared in such magazines as *Atlantic Monthly, Ascent, The New Yorker, Redbook,* and *Vanity Fair,* have been selected for inclusion in the *Pushcart Prize* and *Best American Short Stories* series. *Shiloh and Other Stories* (1982) received the Ernest Hemingway Foundation Award for the Best Short Fiction in 1982.

Rebecca Morris (b. 1935)

Born in Dayton, Ohio, and educated at Case/Western Reserve and Columbia Universities, Rebecca Morris has worked as a newspaper feature writer and corporate speech writer. She has published fiction in *The New Yorker, The Saturday Evening Post, Virginia Quarterly,* and *Southwest Review.* Currently a resident of New York, she is completing a novel about the 1968 hoof and mouth epidemic in North Wales. In 1972, "The Good Humor Man" was made into a film by MGM titled *One Is a Lonely Number.*

Joyce Carol Oates (b. 1938)

Born in Lockport, New York, and educated at Syracuse University and the University of Wisconsin, Joyce Carol Oates now teaches at Princeton University. Among her novels, which often depict female characters against a background of a violent and grotesque American society, are *With Shuddering Fall* (1964), *Expensive People* (1968), *them* (1969), *Do with Me What You Will* (1973), *Bellefleur* (1980), *A Bloodsmoor Romance* (1982), and *Marya: A Life* (1986). Her story "Where Are You Going, Where Have You Been?" was made into a film titled *Smooth Talk* in 1986. She has published numerous collections of stories, such as *By the North Gate* (1963), *The Wheel of Love* (1970), *Where Are You Going, Where Have You Been?* (1974), *The Poisoned Kiss* (1975), and *Night-Side* (1977), in addition to volumes of poetry and criticism.

Nancy Huddleston Packer (b. 1925)

Born in Washington, D.C., Nancy Huddleston Packer was educated at Birmingham-Southern College, the University of Chicago, and Stanford University, where she is a professor of English. Her stories have appeared in the *Sewanee Review, Southwest Review, Greensboro Review,* and *Crosscurrents* as well as in *O. Henry Prize Stories* and *The Best American Short Stories*. A collection of her stories titled *Small Moments* appeared in 1976, and she has co-edited two anthologies of stories, *Twenty Years of Stanford Stories* (1966 with Wallace Stegner and Richard Scowcroft) and *The Short Story: An Introduction* (1983 with Wilford Stone and Robert Hoopes).

Mary Peterson (b. 1944)

Born in Minneapolis, Mary Peterson was educated at the University of Minnesota, the University of New Hampshire, and the University of Iowa. A contributing editor to *North American Review* and the Pushcart Prize series, she is currently an editor at the University of New Hampshire's Communications Office. Her stories have been published in *Ms., Ploughshares, North American Review, Fiction International, Missouri Review,* and *Story Quarterly*. With the help of a grant from the National Endowment for the Arts, she wrote and compiled a collection of stories, *Mercy Flights* (1985).

Elizabeth Stuart Phelps (1815–1852)

Born in Andover, Massachusetts, Elizabeth Stuart Phelps, the daughter of a scholarly clergyman, was educated at the Abbott Academy in Andover and the Mount Vernon School in Boston. Suffering from insomnia as a child, she was oppressed by the children's Sunday-school literature which she was given to read because it invariably connected the idea of early piety with that of early death. Later, her own children's books, such as *Little Kitty Brown and Her Bible Verses* (1851) and *Kitty Brown and Her Little School* (1852), though highly didactic, would contain numerous realistic details. In addition to children's fiction she published newspaper and magazine articles, two novels anonymously—*The Sunny Side; or, The Country Minister's Wife* (1851) and *A Peep at "Number Five"; or, A Chapter in the Life of a City Pastor* (1852)—and the posthumous collection of stories and sketches, *The Tell-Tale; or Home Secrets Told by Old Travellers* (1853).

Jayne Anne Phillips (b. 1952)

Born in West Virginia, Jayne Anne Phillips received a B.A. at West Virginia University and an M.F.A. at the University of Iowa. She has taught at Williams College, Boston University, and Humboldt State University. She is the recipient of a Fels award, a National Endowment for the Arts Fellowship, and the 1979 St. Lawrence Award for Fiction. Her stories have appeared in *Pushcart Prize: Best of the Small Presses* (1977 and 1979), *Best American Short Stories (1979)*, and *Prize Stories 1980: The O. Henry Awards*. *Black Tickets* (1979), a collection of stories, won the Kaufman Prize of the American Academy and Institute of Arts and Letters, and *Machine Dreams* (1984) was nominated for the National Book Critics Circle Award. Both volumes have been translated into eight languages.

Sylvia Plath (1932–1963)

Educated at Smith College and Cambridge University, Sylvia Plath was recognized as a talented young writer of poetry and fiction while still at college. Married to Ted Hughes (now Poet Laureate), the mother of a young child and expecting a second, she received a Eugene F. Saxton Fellowship in 1961, enabling her to complete her only novel, *The Bell Jar*. It was published in January 1963, one month before her suicide. Separated from her husband and anxious about her future and her children's, she suffered a recurrence of the breakdown which had precipitated a suicide attempt in 1953. *The Collected Poems* (1981), which was awarded a Pulitzer Prize, includes *The Colossus* (1962), *Ariel* (1966), *Crossing the Water* (1971), and *Winter Trees* (1972). Her stories and articles are collected in *Johnny Panic and the Bible of Dreams and Other Prose Writings* (1978), and in 1975 a selection of her letters was published in *Letters Home: Correspondence 1950–63*.

Katherine Anne Porter (1890–1980)

Born in Indian Creek, Texas, Katherine Anne Porter supported herself as a ghost writer, newspaper reporter, and magazine writer. In 1930, a collection titled *Flowering Judas and Other Stories* appeared, but only five years later, after the addition of four other tales, did it achieve its final form. In 1931 she received a Guggenheim Fellowship, making possible her trips to Mexico and Germany. Best known as a writer of short stories, she received both a National Book Award and a Pulitzer Prize in 1966 for her work in this genre. Among the collections of her stories are *Pale Horse, Pale Rider* (1939), *The Leaning Tower and Other Stories* (1944), and *Collected Stories* (1965). *The Days Before* (1952), a collection of essays and book reviews, was revised and enlarged to be republished as *The Collected Essays and Occasional Writings of Katherine Anne Porter* in 1965, while *The Never-Ending Wrong* (1977) is a brief memoir of her protest during the Sacco-Vanzetti case. Her only novel, *Ship of Fools* (1962), was made into a film in 1965.

Marjorie Kinnan Rawlings (1896–1953)

Marjorie Kinnan Rawlings made her literary debut at the age of eleven when she won a two-dollar prize for a story which the *Washington Post* published. A graduate of the University of Wisconsin, she supported herself as a newspaper writer and, later, as a farmer with an orange grove in Cross Creek, Florida. Among her works are the novels *South Moon Under* (1933), *Golden Apples* (1935), *The Yearling* (1938)—which won a Pulitzer Prize and was made into a successful motion picture in 1946—and *The Sojourner* (1953), as well as a collection of short stories titled *When the Whippoorwill——* (1940). In 1942, she published a series of autobiographical essays, *Cross Creek*, as well as *Cross Creek Cookery*, a cookbook of local recipes described in an engaging personal style.

Lee Smith (b. 1944)

Educated at Hollins College, Lee Smith is presently an associate professor of English at North Carolina State University. Her stories have appeared in *Redbook, McCall's, Carolina Quarterly,* and *Southern Exposure*. She has won two O. Henry awards, a College English Association—Book-of-the-Month Club fellowship, The Sir Walter Raleigh Award for Fiction (1984), and The North Carolina Award for Literature (1985). Her novels include *The Last Day the Dogbushes Bloomed* (1968), *Something in the Wind* (1971), *Fancy Strut* (1973), *Black Mountain Breakdown* (1981), *Oral History* (1983), and *Family Linen* (1985), and some of her stories have been collected in *Cakewalk* (1981).

Elizabeth Spencer (b. 1921)

Born in Carrollton, Mississippi, Elizabeth Spencer has been writing fiction since early childhood. After graduation from Bellhaven College in 1942, she received an M.A. in English at Vanderbilt University the following year. She has been a reporter for the *Nashville Tennessean* and taught creative writing at the University of Mississippi. She is a recipient of two O. Henry awards, the Rosenthal Award of the National

Institute of Arts and Letters, and a Guggenheim Fellowship. Among her novels are *Fire in the Morning* (1948), *This Crooked Way* (1952), *The Voice at the Back Door* (1956), *The Light in the Piazza* (1960), *Knights and Dragons* (1965), *No Place for an Angel* (1967), *The Snare* (1972), and *The Salt Line* (1984). Her stories have been collected in *Ship Island and Other Stories* (1968), *Marilee* (1981), and *The Stories of Elizabeth Spencer* (1981). For more than two decades she has made her home in Montreal.

Florence Trefethen (b. 1921)

Born in Philadelphia, Florence Trefethen was educated at Bryn Mawr College and Cambridge University. During World War II she served as an officer in the WAVES before turning to a career as writer, teacher, and editor. Presently Executive Editor for the Council on East Asian Studies at Harvard, she has taught at Tufts University, Northeastern University, and the Radcliffe Institute (now The Mary Bunting Institute at Radcliffe). A collection of studies she edited with Joseph McCloskey, *Operations Research for Management* (1954), has been widely translated for use in other countries. Her poems, articles, and short fiction have appeared in *Harper's*, *Virginia Quarterly Review*, *Christian Science Monitor*, *The New York Times*, *Boston Globe*, and *Poetry*. In 1970 she published *Writing a Poem*, and since 1966 she regularly has contributed a column titled ''The Poet's Workshop'' to *The Writer*.

Alice Walker (b. 1944)

Born in Eatonton, Georgia, Alice Walker was educated at Spelman College and Sarah Lawrence College. She has served as a voter registration worker in Georgia as well as working in a Head Start program in Mississippi. More recently, she has taught at the University of California at Berkeley and at Brandeis University. Among her works are three volumes of poetry—*Once* (1968), *Revolutionary Petunias and Other Poems* (1973), and *Good Night, Willie Lee, I'll See You in the Morning* (1979)—as well as the novels *The Third Life of Grange Copeland* (1970), *Meridian* (1976), and *The Color Purple* (1982), which won the Pulitzer Prize and American Book Award in 1983 and was made into a highly successful film in 1985. *In Search of Our Mothers' Gardens: Womanish Prose* (1983) is a collection of her essays, and *In Love and Trouble* (1973) and *You Can't Keep a Good Woman Down* (1981) are collections of her stories.

Patricia Zelver (b. 1923)

A native Californian who has spent most of her life on the San Francisco Peninsula, Patricia Zelver was educated at the University of Oregon and at Stanford where she received a Master's degree. Her fiction has appeared in such magazines as *The Virginia Quarterly, Atlantic Monthly, Esquire, The Ohio Review,* and *Shenandoah.* Six of her stories were chosen for O. Henry short story awards. She has published two novels, *The Honey Bunch* (1969) and *The Happy Family* (1972), as well as a novella and short story collection titled *A Man of Middle Age and Twelve Stories* (1980).

AMERICAN SHORT STORY COLLECTIONS

☐ **THE SIGNET CLASSIC BOOK OF AMERICAN SHORT STORIES, edited and with an Introduction by Burton Raffel.** From the early nineteenth century to the outbreak of World War II, here are thirty three of the finest stories written by American authors. Includes works by Hawthorne, Poe, Twain, Thurber, James, Saroyan, and many others. (520327—$4.50)*

☐ **BILLY BUDD AND OTHER TALES by Herman Melville.** Herman Melville's short stories, somewhat neglected during his lifetime, today are considered to be among the small masterpieces of American fiction. This outstanding collection includes "The Piazza," "Bartleby," "Benito Cereno," "The Lightning-Rod Man," "The Encantadas," "The Bell-Tower," and "The Town-Ho's Story." (517148—$1.95)

☐ **SHORT FICTION OF SARAH ORNE JEWETT AND MARY WILKINS FREEMAN, edited and with an Introduction by Barbara H. Solomon.** These stories by two important American writers explore the intimate world of women fighting for dignity and independence in a society that seeks to fit them into crippling molds. (520106—$4.95)*

☐ **THE CELESTIAL RAILROAD and Other Stories by Nathaniel Hawthorne.** By means of weird yet inescapably convincing fables Hawthorne explores the corroding desires of superior men and women, whose pursuit of perfection causes them to lust for the ideal and unwittingly commit evils in the name of pride. (517849—$2.95)

*Prices slightly higher in Canada

Buy them at your local bookstore or use this convenient coupon for ordering.

NEW AMERICAN LIBRARY,
P.O. Box 999, Bergenfield, New Jersey 07621

Please send me the books I have checked above. I am enclosing $_____
(please add $1.00 to this order to cover postage and handling). Send check
or money order—no cash or C.O.D.'s. Prices and numbers are subject to change
without notice.

Name _____

Address _____

City_____State_____Zip Code_____

Allow 4-6 weeks for delivery.
This offer is subject to withdrawal without notice.

By the year 2000, 2 out of 3 Americans could be illiterate.

It's true.

Today, 75 million adults...about one American in three, can't read adequately. And by the year 2000, U.S. News & World Report envisions an America with a literacy rate of only 30%.

Before that America comes to be, you can stop it...by joining the fight against illiteracy today.

Call the Coalition for Literacy at toll-free **1-800-228-8813** and volunteer.

Volunteer Against Illiteracy. The only degree you need is a degree of caring.